MIDNIGHT
WORLD
VOLUME TWO

MIDNIGHT WORLD VOLUME TWO

WRAPPED IN DARKNESS

DALIVIA PLAUT

DARK PLOT
PUBLISHING

• • •

First Edition, March 2019
Story by Dalivia Plaut
Written by Dalivia Plaut
Edited by Ireland Lelisio

ISBN: 978-09976453-8-5
Plaut, Dalivia, 1983—
Wrapped In Darkness
I. Title. Fiction. Dark Fantasy/Horror

ISBN: 978-09976453-8-5 pbk.

Cover Design by Low Key
Book Design by Dalivia Plaut
Cover Photograph by Krzysztof Czernecki/vladko13
(istockphoto.com)

This is a work of fiction.
Names, characters, places, and incidents
are the products of the author's imagination.
Any resemblance to actual persons, living
or dead, is entirely coincidental.

Printed in the United States of America

PUBLISHER'S NOTE
This is a work of fiction. Names, characters, places, and incidents either are the product of the author's imagination or are used fictitiously. Any resemblance to actual persons, living or dead, business establishments, events, or locales is entirely coincidental.

• • •

TABLE OF CONTENTS

Author's Note

The world presented beyond this page is a fictitious one, as are its characters. Any resemblance to actual persons, living or dead, is entirely coincidental.

MIDNIGHT WORLD VOLUME TWO:
WRAPPED IN DARKNESS

BLAINE held his breath as he snapped in the *last* piece of the jigsaw puzzle.

With utmost persistence, he then ran his callused hand over the bumpy surface of the puzzle, ironed out the remaining bulges, and secured any loose pieces.

He exhaled.

Everything about Blaine, his chest, both his shoulders, elbows and hands, loosened and uncoiled; and for the slightest moment, he felt as if the invisible fist of a giant had been released from his entire body.

More composed, he sat back and examined the finished product from a broader view.

"*Now*," Blaine whispered as if he was speaking to an unknown presence skulking inside the room, "it's your move, Buddy Boy."

To the immediate right of Blaine sat a bottle of Hennessy, along with a tumbler, a box of matches, and a blistering-white cigarette hand rolled with dried tobacco leaves, ready to be smoked down to a butt, perched in a seesaw-like tilt over the brim of a silver ashtray on top of his mama's side table, which had been handed down to her by her mama, Blaine's nana.

He walked over to the weathered but sturdy table and poured himself a glass, two-fingers worth. He took a sip of Hennessy, savored it as if it was his last; then, he pulled out a matchstick from the tiny drawer-like box and with his arthritic hand, flicked the red tip against the rough edge of his thumbnail, igniting a flame.

He lifted the cigarette to his mouth with his left hand. Two of his five fingers, his ring and pinkie finger, gone; and all that remained of the two fingers were the round nubs along his dry, almost powdery knuckles, the skin cracked like the surface of a hardpan desert, and the two ghosts of fingers unknowingly clinging onto the patterns of past lives.

Blaine lit the end of the cigarette and took a drag and, like the sip of Hennessy, savored it.

As smoke filled his lungs, Blaine embraced the smoke as if, for a moment and only a moment, he was basking in yet another unlikely victory.

As Blaine did every time he finished not just any new puzzle but "the" puzzle, he was fixing to frame it, encase it with glass, and then, finally, have it pinned and mounted like a trophy where he'd irrevocably claim it as his own.

With the rusty blade of an orange box cutter that he kept from his last job as a hardware "specialist," Blaine meticulously trimmed the cardboard underneath the puzzle until it fit perfectly around the perimeter of the puzzle.

After that, he used two sheets of aluminum foil to secure the puzzle—once he tried with cling wrap but jigsaw pieces stuck to it and it took hours to remove the cling wrap without disrupting the integrity of the puzzle.

Blaine transported the secured puzzle in his white beat-up van, which most of the neighbors, especially the kids who were raised by Hollywood tropes and clichés, called "creepy" and at times, "sketchy," due to the lack of windows; they thought the "creepy" and at times "sketchy" old man was lugging around a dead body in there or something that once had a name. Blaine did all he could do, which was laugh off their hushed murmurings whenever he drove by these highly-imaginative kids whenever they shot him still-eyed stares as they hung around the street corner on their bikes. Every now and then, he'd fuel their imaginations and give them a scare, like squirt a couple of ketchup packets along the door handle of the van and smear all of that movie-red ketchup along the sides of the door, making it look like the finger marks of a bloody hand.

After he was finished goofing off, he dropped off the puzzle at the frame shop, Frame of Mind. All the employees who worked at the framing shop knew Blaine by name; and as always, they knew exactly what he was bringing them and how he wanted it.

⊞

ON the way home from Frame of Mind, Blaine figured that he'd get some practice done before the next puzzle arrived. The place where he normally got his puzzles, The Puzzle Palace, was about a thirty-five minute drive and he didn't think he had enough gas to get there.

He took a minor detour and stopped by one of those big-chain bookstores in one of those new cut-and-paste shopping malls, which was only a couple of minutes away from home. The store was part video-part music store, part-café—and it had a "small" section for books too. Being an avid reader, Blaine loathed stepping foot inside these types of soft consumer-friendly establishments that not only attempted to put legitimate bookstores, like his local one, Bailey's, which specifically sold books, out of business, but also undermined the concept of a bookstore, the dusty, ragged homeyness of one, *not* the commercialized staleness, with each mysteriously-dim aisle being like a portal into a new uncharted world. He'd often go on these long-winded tirades with Jezebel, not about things that he didn't understand, but things he simply didn't want to understand. For instance, he didn't want to understand why a once profitable bookstore that started off small not only abandoned its base of loyal bookworms, but also everything that made them once successful in order to lean toward a tech-driven society, which was moving faster than the Industrial Revolution. He'd often compare—and repeat over and over—the drastic yet inevitable shift to the popular burger joint, Burgersaurus, overhauling and expanding their four-item menu in order to appeal to the *easily* offended, *easily* outraged, *easily* versatile, *easily*-everything, *self*-proclaimed, vegan by selling salads and healthier foods—basically, eroding the meat-terrific foundation that made the burger establishment truly one of a kind. Blaine knew once all the "suits" got involved, the show was over and that final act usually went out with a damp fizzle.

Or, like a small person from a small town who became a celebrity and all of a sudden, he or she turned to politics. Blaine called the contagious disease the "big head syndrome." And Blaine certainly knew a thing or two about the tragic sickness that plagued America. He was a *victim* to it.

Blaine kept his head down as if he was ashamed of himself and went straight to the puzzle aisle at the front of the store and quickly picked out a fifteen hundred-piece puzzle. Once he found what he was looking for, he couldn't get out of there quick enough.

THAT night, Blaine put the *Fairy Maker* puzzle aside to rest his aching hands and grabbed a cold bottle of Dealer's Choice from the fridge. He sat down in his raggedy recliner in a dark living room with his beer sweating in one hand and an old metal flashlight in the other. He sipped from his beer while he rested the flashlight against the arm of the chair and aimed the bulb directly at the backdoor that he kept unlocked throughout the night. He turned on the flashlight for a second—and *only* a second—the yellowish light briefly highlighting the screen door. Then turned off the flashlight. Except for the distant floodlight peppering the corner of living room, the blackness swallowed him whole. Blaine did this routine over and over, *clicking* the flashlight on and off, on and off, until, finally, the minute hand snuck past the hour hand, which was stuck on twelve, and inched its way toward two. His eyelids started to grow heavy from the consummation of alcohol and his religion of staring into an unlit horizon. But, as he did each go-around, he carried on. He thought maybe she'd show up tonight due to the accomplishment of the day and pay him one last visit for old time's sake and maybe—just maybe—she'd look exactly the same as he remembered her.

THE following morning, Blaine had a visitor at the front door.

Turns out it was someone whom he least expected.

His name was Wally Copel, Wally being "Wally" and not a nickname for what Blaine thought to be Walt. The man looked familiar as if Blaine might've known him in another life, as in the Celebrity World or even that hazy period before his rise to stardom. Even the way the man carried himself was slightly familiar, as if his identity was surrounded by fog and all Blaine could make out was the distant shape. He knew he *had* met the man before but didn't exactly know where. He was dressed nice in what Blaine fancied to be his Sunday best. He claimed that he was a filmmaker who had put out a couple of pictures—none of which Blaine would know but he told Blaine anyway—including one drama called *The Throwback*, but, as expected, Blaine had never heard of such a film.

Over the years, Blaine had run-ins with many filmmakers, directors, both amateur and seasoned, collaborative or auteur, and all of them wanted something from Blaine. Unlike Wally Copel, most of them were unprofessional, rude, pretentious, and dressed as if they had slept in their clothes. Blaine could spot the phonies, but most importantly, the opportunists before they could finish a sentence;

however, it was fair to say that the young man standing at the door was nothing like the ones from Blaine's past. Blaine thought he looked as if he came from money but not the kind earned from movies—maybe *his old man was in the biz*, Blaine thought, but then invested his money elsewhere. Unlike the others, the kid didn't appear as if he was trying to make any money off *my story* but, better yet, trying to make a name for himself, which, *I know*, was hard to do these days with everybody wanting to be famous—at least, that was what Blaine perceived.

Wally cut straight to business and told Blaine that he knew all about him, his life, his history, *his* "incredible" *story*, and with Blaine's permission, he wanted to sit down with Blaine for an interview about his life, as well as his legacy.

There they go again, Blaine thought, *using that word* wanted.

Wally said the interview would be recorded on both film and a tape recorder and then later, the footage, as well as at the tape recordings from the interview would be used in a documentary. Wally said he also "wanted" to document Blaine—if it was okay with him—as he went about his daily life to shed light on what he was up to these days and what life was like for Blaine out of the limelight, but he told Blaine that he was more interested and "creatively invested" in the interview. If Blaine didn't feel too uncomfortable about being followed around by a camera while he was cooking a meal or running errands or whatever, then that extra "behind-the-scenes" footage was like an added bonus, icing on the cake; but Wally made sure not to push his luck. Hollywood wanting to work on a "project" with Blaine or throw together a movie—or documentary—about his tumultuous career as a controversial NFL player who went on to become one of the most famous professional wrestlers ever since Hulk Hogan wasn't at all unfamiliar to Blaine; however, Blaine picked up a strange vibe from Wally—a "familiar" one, he'd say.

Once Blaine put aside the young man's intent, he questioned Wally as to how he found him but was given a smart aleck answer in return. If there was one thing that burned him up—really made his blood piping hot—it was when people, especially kids—*punks* was more like it—recited facts back to him. Blaine knew all about the "Internet" and how uncomplicated it was to find an address. He most definitely knew he was currently living in the "twenty-first century" and certainly didn't need some "boy," some little brat, reciting it back to him as if he was senile.

As Wally waited for Blaine to show him inside, Blaine slammed the front door in the fool's face.

He'd wait around for another "fool" to show. After all, it wasn't the first time he slammed the door on a "supposed" filmmaker's face.

"The fool will come back," Blaine said to himself. "They always do."

AROUND lunchtime, Blaine heard a knock on the door.

He's back.

Blaine put the puzzle aside and stormed to the front door.

"You wanna make a little movie, huh?" he seethed to himself. "I'll give you a goddamn movie."

Frustrated, Blaine swung open the front door and found Jezebel standing with his grandson at the doorway. Her eyes fell to her feet. She kneeled down, picked up a business card from the ground, and handed it to Blaine.

"Here," she said casually. "Must've fallen from the door."

Still frustrated, Blaine flipped over the business card.

He read the name: Wally Copel.

Who in the hell names their kid, Wally, anyway?

"Is everything okay?" asked Jezebel.

Blaine hesitated.

"Yeah," he said. "Sure. What you doing here?"

"Well, it's good to see you too, Dad."

Blaine waved off the comment and hugged Jezebel first, then little Damiere.

"I'm sorry," Blaine groaned. "I wish you'd call, that's all."

"I did."

"You did?" Blaine snapped, "When?"

"Yesterday," Jezebel said, as she and Damiere stepped inside the house. "You said you would watch Damiere while I go do my thing."

"What 'thing?'"

"You know, my 'thing.'"

Her eyes shot down at Damiere. Her lips tightened. Head twitched downward.

"Ah," Blaine said finally, as the thought of the holiday season was looming around the corner. Which meant everything "Christmas" was about to be shoved down his throat until he was shitting out red and green—all those damn *Christmas ads* and *Christmas songs*, Christmas *trees* and *lights*. *How'd I forget? Christmas cookies and cakes, a sugar-nightmare!* "*That* thing, huh?" Blaine finally said.

Damiere was only seven-going-on-eight and he still believed in Santa Claus, even though the *real* jolly-ole fatass was standing two feet away from him. Just as Blaine was about to uncover the truth about Santa Claus, he thought about his recent interaction with a strange man who went by the name, Wally. He glanced down the business card in his hand and a flash of his glory days came to him. "All right, well, I guess it's just you and me, Damiere," Blaine said, as he hunched over Damiere. "How about I read you a book?" he suggested.

"That's fine," Jezebel answered for her son. "It'd probably be best if you just let him play on his tablet."

"His tablet?"

Jezebel pulled the tablet from the Dinosaur-themed bulletproof bookbag. The sight alone of the "tablet" sent a ripple of disgust through Blaine. She placed the bag on the floor and handed the tablet to Blaine, but Blaine knew exactly what he was going to do with it.

Blaine asked Jezebel, "So, how long you think you'll be?"

"An hour or two maybe," she guessed. "I should be back around two o'clock."

Blaine looked down at his watch.

"Sounds good."

Jezebel kissed Damiere goodbye and before she left the house, she pointed her finger at Blaine and demanded in a motherly manner, "If he gets hungry, fix him a almond butter and banana sandwich."

"A what? You mean a PB and J?"

"No," she drawled. "*Almond* butter and *banana* sandwich. And whatever you do, please do *not* use your peanut butter. Make sure you use the organic almond butter in his backpack, but make sure to cut off the crusts because he doesn't like the crust. Make sure he gets only one juice box. Two, makes him a little cranky. Also, if he starts to get whinny, fix him a glass of milk. You don't have soy milk, do you?"

Blaine was still trying to understand what Jezebel meant by almond butter. He wasn't even aware that there was another type of "butter."

Then, she threw the word *soy* at him and he was left even more baffled.

"Soy milk?"

"Forget it," Jezebel waved it off. "Just plain milk will do. I left his sippy cup in the side pocket. Also, another thing, make sure to give him eye drops. He was scratching his eyes the other day and Damiere's doctor, Doctor Singh, said it wasn't pinkeye; but I went on the Internet and did tons of research on eye infections." She paused to catch her breath. "Medicine is in the front pocket. Just one drop in each eye, *not two*, just one. Also, Dad, do *not* let him out of your sight. Last week, I found Damiere messing around with an electrical outlet and he damn near got electrocuted. Marshall and I ended up having to childproof the entire house. We even had to duct tape pillows against the sharp corners of the fireplace—"

"—Jezebel, dear," Blaine said patiently and escorted his overly frazzled daughter from the house. "He's in good hands. Don't worry. You worry too much."

"Okay, okay," she said shortly.

As she was walking down the porch steps, she was hit by a sudden thought.

"I almost forget."

"Jezebel, we'll be just fine."

"No," she said. "There was this guy asking about you the other day. He sort of creeped me out."

Blaine thought about the guy, the stranger, the boy, that spoiled brat.

"What guy?" asked Blaine.

"I dunno," Jezebel said. "But he was asking me a lot of questions about you. I thought he might've been, you know," she leaned closer and whispered to Blaine without Damiere listening in, "one of your followers?"

"You mean, a fan?"

"I guess so."

"Did you get a name?"

"William, I think."

"Wally?"

"That's it," she said. "You know him?"

"No," Blaine hesitated. "Did he tell you what he wanted?"

"I was literally headed out the door when I bumped into him. I was running Damiere to a play date."

"Excuse me?" Blaine said shortly. "A what?"

"Play date," Jezebel emphasized. "He goes on a play date twice a week."

"You're telling me that you're taking my seven year old grandson on dates?"

"*Play* dates, Dad. What'd you think?" The top corner of her brow curled into a question mark. "He was going on an actual date, like a date-date?"

Blaine didn't respond, still baffled.

"No, Dad," Jezebel laughed. "To play with another child. You still remember what it was like to be one. Swinging from monkey bars. Sliding down the slides. Playing. It's all chaperoned, of course. Usually, we'll have two or three parents in rotation, one keeping a watch while another one documenting their activities."

Blaine turned to Damiere, who was ramming two toy dinosaurs together.

"You'd never know by the way you treat the poor kid," was what Blaine really wanted to say to her but kept it to himself in order to prevent another unnecessary blow-up.

"So," Jezebel broke through the awkward silence, "I best get going. And remember—"

"Yes," Blaine said abruptly. "Two drops in both eyes. Or, was it three?"

"No, Dad! I told you—"

"I know, I know," he said foolishly. "One drop. Can't you take a joke?"

"Funny, Dad."

Jezebel waved goodbye.

As she opened the door, she said from the driveway, "Oh yeah if you get bored, take Damiere to the park. He likes to ride the swings. If you do, just make sure to wipe down the seat with the Clorox wipes before he gets in the seat and use hand sanitizers in his backpack."

Blaine thought over the comment—*The Swings.*

"We'll see."

"Everybody knows 'we'll see' is code for 'no,' Dad."

"You need to get out more at your age. It's not healthy for you, staying inside, doing puzzles all day. You need to move around, get the blood flowing. You remember what the doctor said?"

"Bye!"

This time, it was Blaine who waved goodbye.

Jezebel shrugged off Blaine and got into the car.

Blaine watched her speed away. Then he turned to Damiere.

"Your mother's one Nervous Nelly, isn't she?"

Damiere didn't answer; in fact, he turned to Blaine with a blank expression on his face and then continued to ram the two dinosaurs together like cars.

"I don't know where your mother gets it," he said to Damiere. Then, he muttered to himself, "Certainly not from me. That's for sure."

"What's a *Nervous Nelly?*" asked Damiere.

"Someone who's nervous all the time," he said.

13

Blaine walked back into the house and guided Damiere into the living room.

"Don't tell her I said that," he said to Damiere. "Promise?"

Damiere looked up at Blaine and nodded.

⊞

BLAINE made Damiere an old-fashioned PB and J sandwich on white bread.

He threw away a Ziploc bag of gluten-free bread in the trash. He was curious to sample the almond butter. Unlike peanut butter, it was way more liquidy, almost syrupy. He opened the jar, stuck a knife down inside, and licked the almond butter from the edge of the knife like a cat. He ended up spitting it out in the sink.

Damiere giggled at Blaine's exaggerated disgust.

The sight alone of his grandson's amusement brought back yet another flash of his glory days.

Blaine snapped from his trance and told Damiere not to let the sandwich go to waste.

At first, he didn't eat the sandwich. Blaine made himself a PB and J and ate it in front of Damiere. Eventually, Damiere mimicked his poppa and ate the entire sandwich, even the crust.

⊞

JACKED up on peanut butter and artificial grape jelly, Damiere rushed into the living room where he rolled around on the carpet and played with his dinosaurs.

While Damiere was going to battle with T-Rex and stegosaurus, Blaine walked to his library located in the next room where he searched for a book to read to his grandson. Blaine knew all about Damiere's fascination with the animal kingdom, particularly fossil reptiles from the Jurassic and Cretaceous periods. Just the other day, it was birds, mainly cardinals, blue jays, and finches. Last week, it was cats, particularly a cat, Blaine's skittish cat, Suzie, who ran and hid under the bed every time she felt Damiere's presence. Last month, sharks, the TV kind.

With the furry creatures in mind, Blaine came across two books, the first one *The Call of the Wild* by Jack London and the second, *To Kill A Mockingbird* by Harper Lee. He decided to introduce Damiere to a husky named Buck.

Blaine brought *The Call of the Wild* into the living room and as he was about to sit down on the couch and read Damiere a story, he thought about another boy, *that boy*. The stranger. Blaine placed the book aside for the time being and told Damiere to play with his dinosaurs while he went upstairs for a minute.

Damiere whined. Blaine remembered what his daughter said about the tablet and how, the last time she visited, she stuck that device in front of her son's face and it was as if it seized all control over Damiere's mind. He temporarily handed Damiere the tablet in order to keep him quiet.

Once Damiere was plugged in, he was like a zombie. This gave Blaine enough time to step out of the room for a minute. Blaine crept upstairs and as quietly as he could without disrupting Damiere downstairs, he cracked open the attic in the ceiling by pulling down on the cord attached to the door.

Up there, in the dusty dark, he came across an attic full of old cardboard boxes. Hundreds of boxes. Inside each one were his "glory days," all boxed up and left to age like a worn memory covered in the dust of time, but still there, as if waiting in limbo.

The sight of the memorabilia caused his body to shake and stir, as if his insides were being wrung and the only extract came in the form of a teardrop dangling on the corner of his eye, not running, but sitting there as if afraid to fall.

He didn't waste anytime. He removed the special glove from his left hand and pulled out videos, VHS tapes, action figures, rolled up posters with the ends crinkled and yellowish brown with age. He dug out outfits, socks, various wrestling attire, mostly decorated in gaudy colors, feathered bandannas, a necklace with the baseball-sized pendant of a disco ball, mink scarves, white faux fur coats, the pink wrestling boots he used to wear which matched his pink wrestling getup, slightly dull in color, more of a pastel, but still as sleek and shiny as ever, then, last but not least, the patent pink vest he wore. He pulled out the vest and flipped it over. On the back of the vest read the words, *THE JAM*, the crooked letters stitched into the polyester.

Cautiously, Blaine lugged a torn box of VHS tapes down the ladder. He set the edge of the box along the wooden steps, which served as an extra limb lessening the burden of the awkward load. One hand, the left one with only three fingers—or what Damiere called his poppa's "claw"—curled underneath the corner of the box like the talons of a falcon, while the other gripped a wobbly handle alongside the narrow ladder.

With the box pressed against his chest, he—more or less—slid the box down the ladder as he made his way down. Blaine ended up losing his grip on the second to last step. The side of the box ripped and fell onto the floor, the VHS tapes spilling out like guts. He called out for Damiere to give him a hand, but Damiere didn't respond to his voice. He used all of the frustration, which, in what his doctors called his "advanced years," as a concealed form of energy, and stuffed each tape back into the box and lugged the ripped, wobbly box downstairs all by himself. A couple of VHS tapes slipped from their sleeves and skipped down the stairs; however, he managed to make it to the living room in one piece.

Out of breath, Blaine looked for his grandson.

Damiere was nowhere around.

Blaine called out to Damiere, thinking maybe that little squirt might've been hiding or something, possibly playing games on his ole poppa, preparing an ambush, doing kid stuff. He didn't hear a peep from Damiere.

Once more, he called out but received nothing in return.

He checked each room.

No Damiere.

As panic started to creep in, he found Damiere standing in front of his bedroom dresser. In his hand he was holding a black and white framed picture of an attractive woman.

"Why didn't you answer me, boy?" asked Blaine.

Damiere moved his eyes from the picture to Blaine.

"Is this grandma?" asked Damiere.

"That's your nana," Blaine said and stepped into the bedroom. "You know her name?"

Damiere shook his head.

"No."

"Havana," said Blaine. "Her name was Havana."

"Like the country?"

"Close."

Blaine waited for Damiere to correct himself.

"You mean, the capital of Cuba."

"That's what I said," he said. "*Que*-bah."

"Sure you did."

Blaine walked behind Damiere and lost himself in the picture.

"Your nana and I met during—I guess you can call—a rather peculiar time in our lives."

"Pocula?"

"*Pe*-culiar. *Strange*." Blaine paused. "She was a nurse, a mighty fine one too. One of the best. She helped me. Took care of me. Got me back up on my feet."

"Were you sick?" asked Damiere.

"Not sick," he said and looked down at his crippled hand. "Just hurt. But I'm much better now."

"She fixed the claw?"

"Sure," Blaine said and kneeled down toward Damiere's level. "She fixed my hand. She fixed me. If it weren't for Havana's relentlessness, I don't know what would've become of me. She showed me the man who I always wanted to be."

"Where'd she go?"

"She left me."

"Why?"

"She was sick. I thought your momma told you. She's no longer with us."

"Jezebel says she went to Heaven. Is that true?"

Once more, Blaine paused.

"*Your momma* is right," he lied. "She's in Heaven."

He grabbed the picture frame from Damiere's hand and placed the picture back on the dresser.

"I brought down some things I'd like you to see," Blaine said and motioned to the living room.

"Okay," Damiere said and hurried into the living room.

At times, Blaine wished he had Damiere's ability to forget and move on. An easy concept, to move on and not look back, to put all of that ugly behind you, and just keep trucking on, while, every now and then, stopping just for a moment to catch your breath to ask a couple of questions where the answers were more complicated than a one-sentence response and required a more in-depth discussion; yet they were only accepted at face value, verbal "said-so's," which acted like bright red stop signs.

▣

LITTLE Damiere remained enchanted by the bloody wrestling match between The Jam and his longtime heated rival, Too Smooth, when Jezebel took one step into the living room. She witnessed a much younger version of her father during his heyday—those "all-or-nothing" days as a professional wrestler rightfully defending "His" Heavyweight belt. Then, her eyes moved to her boy and his heinie planted in the carpet as he sat cross-legged inches away from the television; his face basking in the glow of TV radiation; eyes perfectly still and glaze-dipped as if he was stuck in a nasty trance of masculine savagery. Jezebel's eyes swelled. Her teeth barred like a dog. Her face changed colors.

Blaine didn't hear the door close behind Jezebel nor did he hear the floor *creak* below his daughter's foot; however, he could sense her presence and the heat that radiated off her. He glanced over his shoulder and witnessed her standing at the edge of the living room. Her arms were tightly folded across her chest. He turned back around and pretended she wasn't there. He actually "wished" her to disappear, to up and vanish from the living room, but only for a while. Or, better yet, like rewinding a VHS tape, Blaine yearned to rewind reality by aiming the VCR remote at

Jezebel and rewinding the precise moment when she stepped foot into his house and rewind her back in time: backpedaling through the kitchen, through the front door, down the porch, down the pathway, and back into her car. Only this would give him plenty of time to spring from the recliner, eject the VHS tape from the VCR player, toss it under a pillow, pick up *The Call of the Wild*, and act as if he was reading to Damiere. He'd do anything but watch his daughter beam with red from the sight of her son sitting in front of the TV and rooting on The Jam to bash his opponent's brains in with a pair of "fake" brass knuckles.

Even with his momma's presence humming over his shoulder, Damiere's eyes remained glued to the screen.

Jezebel finally lashed out: "Damiere Goodwin, what in the world do you think you're doing?"

Blaine sighed, hit the pause button on the remote, and sat up from the recliner.

Jezebel stormed into the living room and snatched Damiere by the arm.

"But Jezebel—"

"Not on my watch," retorted Jezebel.

She yanked Damiere from the floor and dragged him straight toward the door. Blaine followed close behind.

"Why don't you wrap him in goddamn bubblewrap while you're at it—"

She stopped in her tracks and chewed out Blaine, "How many times do I have to tell you, Dad? I don't want you exposing Damiere to that lifestyle, especially with all the violence in today's world. He's only seven years old!"

"For crying out loud, he's not a baby!"

"He's my son."

The comment alone caused the words to ball in the back of his throat. He did what he had been doing for the past couple of years. He bit his tongue.

"What were you thinking, Dad?" asked Jezebel.

"What was I thinking?" he repeated. "I'm thinking of that kid who got shot the other day. I'm thinking of all those innocent kids who get shot up—all for what? I'm thinking about how soft and hypersensitive this god*damn* country has gotten, how you can't say or do anything without offending somebody!"

Jezebel's eyes widened even more, her jawline formed and tightened in perfect geometrical shapes. She suddenly covered Damiere's ears with her hands.

"The world is filled with a bunch of cowards who hide behind computers and pick fights that they can't even finish," he went on to say. "Hell! Nowadays, you get shot if you look at someone the wrong way. Damiere needs to be tough, Jezebel—"

"—By what? Rehashing your glory days?

"If that's what it takes, then, yes."

"No," Jezebel said, shaking her head. "He doesn't need to know about *that*."

"Eventually, he'd find out."

"Yeah," she snapped. "*Eventually*. But his brain is still developing and he certainly doesn't need to be around that—"

"—That what? Say it."

"That garbage." Jezebel threw her hands down to her side. "There. I said it."

"Well, that 'garbage' is who I was, Jezebel."

"Exactly. *Was*, Dad. You're not that man anymore—"

"—But it's what made me into the man I am today. It's my legacy!"

Jezebel turned to a long-faced Damiere, who was cowering beside the kitchen counter.

"No, Dad. He's your legacy." She pointed at the TV in the living room as if she was pointing directly at the past, something miles away, distant and unobtainable. "Not *that*. Besides, I thought you were over all that stuff."

"It's not stuff. It's my life. Damiere has a right to know who his grandfather was. Plus, he looked as if he enjoyed watching me—"

"No, no," she said and then turned to Damiere. "Damiere, wait on the porch."   Damiere   didn't budge.

Jezebel shouted, "Now!"

Damiere budged; in fact, he scurried out the door.

Once Damiere was outside, Jezebel said to Blaine, "Do you really want to open *that* door, Dad? The pain it caused you and all of the damage it did to your name. And what happened to Elmira. . . "

"Don't you dare say her name," Blaine seethed. "You didn't know her. You weren't even born, Jezebel! You have no right!"

"Dad. I'm sorry. Really." Jezebel reached for Blaine's hand, but he pulled his hand away. She threw her hands in the air with child-like annoyance. "I can't do this right now," she said with frustration. "I gotta go."

"Then go," Blaine said.

Jezebel stormed out of the house and drove away.

NIGHT couldn't arrive soon enough.

As Blaine normally did each night, he sat in his recliner positioned at the backdoor. He craved a cold beer to wash away the frustration that had built inside him throughout the day. The anger was still raw and tight, though, and at any moment could morph. He was aware of how he got when he drank angry, how the emotion flipped on him, how it took hold, how it turned him into the one thing he feared worst. Liquid poison, as irresistible as the idea alone of it flooding through his veins and aiding his internal wounds, was sneaky and cruel like that. A seductive bitch who knew exactly how to wrap Blaine around her finger. The darkness had a particular way of making a smooth criminal look sloppy.

Blaine focused on the backdoor, his flashlight *clicking* on and off, on and off.

All of a sudden, he heard something clawing at the door. Maybe it was the raccoon that had been riffling through his trash in the middle of the night. Perhaps a possum.

More cautiously, Blaine leaned forward in his chair and switched the flashlight back on. He witnessed a dark silhouette of a tall man standing on the back porch.

"Hey," Blaine called out and stood up to his feet, "you there!"

Blaine kept the light on the strange man.

As he started to approach the backdoor, the strange man took off running.

Blaine swung open the screen door and chased after him, but he only made it down three steps before he stopped and scanned the night darkness. He remained as quiet as his breath would let him and listened to the night. He heard the distant traffic ambience rolling off the interstate. He thought maybe he heard footsteps racing down the sidewalk alongside his backyard. He shone the flashlight around the backyard but didn't see anything out of the ordinary.

Above, Blaine heard the wispy surge of electricity humming through an overhead floodlight.

For a moment, the amber-colored light flared like the sun and forced Blaine to shield his eyes.

He squinted from the brightness of the light. In his squint, he peered through the narrow doorways of his fingers.

As Blaine once did so many years ago, he embraced the light and the darkness that encompassed it. All of a sudden, the light above *popped* and crackled in a fit of strobe-light flickers before it finally burned out in cool dimmer-like fashion.

At that very moment, Blaine couldn't help but bring himself back to the final moment he shared with Elmira, his Mira, watching her take her last breath before life made its last exodus from her body; then, a year after his high-profiled murder trial, her ghost encouraging him to ward off the very demon which was starting to consume his soul.

⊞

SHE was the only one who brought me back.

From the Darkness.

If it wasn't for Mira, I never would've escaped Dark Hill. If it wasn't for her, I would've been stuck in that awful place. My soul lost forever. . .

I can remember seeing her face flickering in and out of the light. I thought I lost it. But there it was. Staring at me.

Blaine traveled back in time, to Dark Hill, to the Hell where he laid over a pile of rubble and debris. Hanging from a wiry beam in the concrete was the tiny, circular photograph of Elmira trapped inside a silver pendant that she gave him for his thirty-ninth birthday, three days before he left for the Canadian Tour. Her face was so close to him as if he could touch her, her still face reshaping, her lips curling upward into her cheeks, yet, the dark gaps between the flickers of light caused her face to appear so far away as if, the farther he reached, her face became fuzzier and more blurred to the point of becoming a faded memory trapped within all that gray. He remembered those last three days at the cabin before his final Tour, every detail, every moment, the days feeling dream-like, as if he was stuck in a movie that he never wanted to end. Yet, as he started to bleed out, his hand smashed and the bones sticking out like pieces of crushed glass, that sneaky darkness inside him was doing everything it possibly could to tarnish the one good image he had left of Elmira. But whatever it said to him, whatever it showed him, whatever it offered him, he had those three days at the cabin and they were his alone to hold until the end of time.

Comforting me.

My daddy told me something when I was a little boy and I guess, in a way, his words have stayed with me till this day. He told me: 'When a task has just begun, you never leave it until it's done. Whether the effort great or small, do it right or not at all.'

After RIN was destroyed, I felt as if I failed, in a way. I could still feel its presence there, as if the machine itself was only a vessel to contain the evil inside. But my Mira—even the thought of Mira—was my own shield, a protective barrier that couldn't be penetrated by evil. I held onto that one image of Mira as close as I could, thinking maybe, once the light went out, then, so, too, would my Mira, my angel, my world.

"Are the rumors true, Blaine?" asked Wally. "Was her death an accident?"

◫

BLAINE switched on the porch light before he went back inside his house.

He walked into his bedroom where he grabbed Wally's business card from the top drawer of his nightstand. He stared at the card, the name, *Wally Copel.*

He knew exactly what had to be done.

◫

WALLY arrived at Blaine's with a car full of film equipment, cases carrying three cameras, an old camcorder that Wally said was going to be used more for artistic purposes, Tupperware boxes of cords and adapters, tripods, lighting, light stands, umbrella reflectors, microphones and mixers. Over the phone, Blaine specifically told Wally—in fact, emphasized—he wanted to focus the story on what happened the months following the murder trial and the events that went down in Maven, particularly at Dark Hill. Throughout his wrestling/acting career, Blaine had done hundreds of interviews for magazines, radios, and talk shows. A majority of The Jam's fans knew all about his background, *his story*, a Creole boy who was raised by a single mother named Tamara Toussaint who migrated from Haiti to New Orleans, then, later moved to Baton Rogue where she gave birth to a ten-pound baby boy who was named after the famous bandit, Blaine Ramsey, who wreaked havoc across the entire Midwest. Even though Blaine shared no relation to the very man whom he was named after, Blaine spent most of adolescence in and out of prison, as well as juvenile correctional facilities, before a charming man, who went by the name Thomas Arkham, found the troubled Toussaint boy and placed a football in his two hands and told him a great future awaited him. After several attempts of convincing, eventually, the game of football became Blaine's escape from crime, an outlet, a detour from trouble and an inevitable life for him behind a jail cell. Blaine was a "scrawny" kid with a body made of rubber and other kids would often mistake him as "Stretch Armstrong" because he had a particular gift to slip and bounce off other tacklers; however, all of his coaches said he was too skinny, not strong enough to be a running back. Time and time again, he proved them *all* wrong with his extraordinary talents, which rightfully earned him a starting running back position on a predominantly all-white high school football team, The Thomasville Crawdads.

After Blaine graduated from high school, Tamara, who secretly suffered from schizophrenia for most of her adult life, was dragged from her bed after an outburst in public and locked up in a mental institution. Years later, she was eventually released; however, she wasn't the same woman. She was no longer his momma, but, more or less, a broken woman, a stranger—more or less—who was nowhere around during the height of Blaine's career. Tamara's sickness inspired Blaine to keep moving because he once said in an interview he did with the fashion magazine, *Fab*, that he "treated the earlier years like his days as a running back. Moving was living, and no matter where I went, I could never settle. I believe that's why I traveled all of the time and was with so many ladies. All of that changed when I met Elmira in 83." He held onto that mentality all the way through college and later, in his wrestling career.

After Blaine ventured out West to San Diego where he attended the University of Portman on an athletic scholarship, he was later drafted by the Marauders in 1969. He played for the NFL for five years; and after he led the Marauders to a Super Bowl championship in 1974 by setting an all-time record with over two hundred yards in rushing, he shocked the entire football world. Number Thirty-Seven retired. In the several years following his football career, Blaine traveled the world, did action movies, made guest appearances and cameos in TV shows, created his own clothing line. Then, déjà vu all over again. Instead of being handed a football, Blaine was approached with the *idea* of professional wrestling. From there, Blaine's career skyrocketed; *however*, nobody really knew exactly what happened to The Jam after his wrestling career came to an end.

Except for all the locals who lived in the town of Maven, all that was known to the public were the rumors.

⊞

"WHERE do you want me to start?" asked Blaine.

"Start with the town of Maven, the moment you arrived," Wally insisted, as he filmed Blaine sitting at the kitchen table. "Of all places, why North Carolina?"

"I visited once before. I did a match in Charlotte, North Carolina. It was home of many legendary wrestlers. So, I knew it was a gamble moving to a state where watching professional wrestling was as common as flossing your teeth. However, when I first arrived in Maven, I knew it was the right place."

"Why?"

"It seemed like a place that was trapped in its own bubble, like the world outside Maven and the people who came from that faraway world didn't exist. And me—being not only a black man but also a successful black man from that outside world, a mystical place well-beyond those distant mountains running like a jagged sawtooth across the faded horizon—surprisingly enough, I felt like I finally came home, even though I was the *Stranger* living in a strange land."

"Do you believe that moving to such a small remote town, like Maven, was your own way of escaping your past?"

"In a way, I suppose so. But I was tired of running. I've been running my entire life. On the field *and* off the field, literally and figuratively speaking," Blaine said despairingly, as he leaned back in his chair. "A part of me just wanted to be left the heck alone. And that's what Maven did—at least, for a while."

⊞

I didn't know anybody in Maven. Not a soul. Which, in hindsight, was good for me. The whole point was to get away from it all. The trial. The media circus. People in general. Start over from scratch. Which, I tell you this, I never would've been able to do in today's world, with social media and smartphones and the lack of privacy. But, somehow, I knew, if there was a will, there was a way. The moment I stepped foot in Maven, I knew it was the place where I could finally settle—especially after many years of traveling and being a celebrity and spending a lot of time surrounded by all walks of life. I didn't know why. I just had a feeling and if there was one thing that I've learned throughout life, you never go against it. Never. Maven only had a population of about two thousand or so folks. Your typical small town, Main Street America-vibe. On the downside, it was definitely one of those towns where people knew each other's business, you know? I knew that, within a week or two, I'd find out whether or not I was welcomed. Unless you're talking about a churchgoing town, most small towns don't want a man who was charged with murder walking around in their own quiet little community. I knew, based on a couple of trips into town, that eventually the word would travel fast. Weeks passed in Maven and nothing—a month. The people of Maven treated me as if I was one of them. After the first fall, I started to get more comfortable in Maven. Strangely enough—and I know this might sound silly to you, especially with everything that I've been through—but for the first time in a very long time, I started to feel as if I could live again. Be my old self. Without all the scrutiny. Without people always 'wanting' something from me. Without the shame. I bought this two-story house on the edge of town. A real piece of shit that needed serious renovation. Toilet didn't flush half the damn time. Floors popped and creaked in the middle of the night and half the time, I swear I was either losing my mind or the house was talking to me. The spicket water smelled as if it had gasoline in it. Walls were falling apart. I went from living in a mansion with a chandelier the size of a Cadillac to this piece of junk that was barely livable. The house reminded me of that one from the movie Money Pit with that one cat, Tom Hanks. Regardless of its many faults, the house kept me busy. Most importantly, it kept my mind off her.

WALLY waited outside the bathroom and gently tapped on the closed door.

"Are you okay in there, Blaine?" asked Wally. "Listen, I know how much this may upset you. . . " Wally paused and then pressed his ear against the side of the door ". . . Blaine, *you okay?*"

Blaine suddenly opened the door.

"Why shouldn't I be?" he asked, as he stepped into the hallway.

Wally stepped out of Blaine's way.

"We don't have to do this today," he said and followed Blaine into the living room. "I can come back tomorrow, if you like?"

"I'm curious, Mr. Copel—"

"—Please, Blaine. Call me, Wally."

"Okay, *Wally*," Blaine said and faced the young film-maker. "Who's going to be watching this? What's your target audience? What's the 'shtick,' as they used to call it? I mean, Wally, do folks really care about what an old has-been like myself has to say? Don't you think they've moved on with their lives?"

"If there's one thing I've learned in the business, Blaine, people love nostalgia. Think of it like an addictive drug but without the harmful side effects."

"That's a terrible analogy."

"Whatever the case," Wally said, "people can't get enough of nostalgia, especially when it's real and most importantly, done right. It's my job to capture you, Blaine, at your realest moments. We both know what it's like to be in a profession where you're trying to sell the illusion. But what if the illusion is real? *What if*, Blaine, we give the people something real? I know it may be hard at times, going back and talking about some of the worst moments in your life—"

"No, Wally," Blaine interrupted. "That's where you got it all wrong. Those days in Maven weren't the worst days in my life. It was there, in Maven, where I finally felt like a free man."

◫

LIFE in Maven was simple. You slept in. You ate good. You went to your trade. You ate again. Slept. And you did it all over again. It's routine and after the life I lived before Maven, I needed routine to grab me by the shoulders and tell me that this was the way things were and were going to be as long as my feet were above the ground. Most of the older folks who still hung around in Maven came from old money passed down by relatives who used to operate the mines. They mined mainly sapphire; and from what I was told, they made quite a killing until the mines were shut down due to an accident, which killed hundreds of miners. Some of the Native Americans who lived on the Reservation next to Maven would, at times, come into town for goods or whatnot, and tell stories about what happened. There was one story floating among the elders that what happened past Dark Hill, in the mountains, was no accident at all but a planned attack by a disgruntled miner who retaliated against his fellow miners. There was another story that the miner who blew up the mine didn't live in Maven. Yet, he was an outsider posing as a miner. Whatever the case may be, Maven wasn't the same. A lot of its residents left after the accident. The ones who stayed don't really talk much about it. Most of them were young when it happened. But despite its horrific past, Maven was the kind of place where you could sleep with your door unlocked. Crime didn't even exist. But, like they say, nothing is too good to be true. Underneath all that good was darkness and I didn't see it at the time. Maybe I was blind by the façade of Maven's innocence and unable to see right through it. But, in time, I soon realized that this darkness was controlling the entire town of Maven.

All of the money was starting to dry out from lawyer expenses and civil lawsuits against me by The Compton's. I couldn't work on my house forever without any bread to show. So, I abandoned everything my daddy had told me day in and day out and set aside work on the house. The fact is I was broke and barely had a dollar to my name. After days of searching, I finally found an opening

29

*at a nightshift position at the local press, Powell Printing Press—
or 'The PPP,' as I used to call the place. That's when it all started.
The strange stuff. A couple of weeks after I started working at the
Printing Press, the blinders were slowly pulled from my eyes and I
no longer saw an innocent-looking town but rather a place that
was holding a secret much darker than my very own.*

SINCE they had been filming for over four hours, Blaine and
Wally decided to take a break for lunch.

Wally insisted on treating Blaine to lunch. Blaine, who
habitually ate lunch at home, was hesitant about leaving
the house. Blaine hadn't gone out for lunch in years; in
fact, the last time Blaine went out in public for lunch was
the time he attended Damiere's third birthday party at The
Pizza Factory. Just a week before the hyped-up party,
Blaine got himself caught in a bind with a flat tire. The
temperature must've been at least in the teens outside—
subzero, if you factor in the wind chill—and after being
stuck on the road for hours with his balls shriveled up like
California raisins, Blaine had no other choice than to give
Jezebel a ring. She dropped everything she was doing and
came to her dad's rescue. A few days later when Jezebel
called her dad and demanded that he go to the party, she
had something that Blaine rarely had: leverage. She ended
up begging Blaine to go—nagging, really. He caved in and
went, as promised. At the party, Blaine overindulged by
eating three slices of pizza—normally, being a light eater
and all, he'd be fine with one slice but he was nervous; and
often times, he overate when he was nervous. That night,
Blaine ended up paying the price with a horrible case of
heartburn, which he had mistaken for a heart attack. The
incident took him at least two weeks to recover. His doctor
put him on a strict bland diet for two weeks, which was
more like two weeks of hell. Looking back, Blaine realized
it wasn't worth it. Damiere was whiny and hard to handle
and he mostly threw a fit that day. Whenever his son-in-
law's family was around or even in the vicinity of his

nephew—which, most of the time, was always the case (birthday parties, holidays, play days, weekend grill outs, backyard barbeques, monthly trips to the Zoo and amusement parks, or basically, anything involving mimosas or hand foods, mostly in tube-form)—Damiere hardly paid much attention to Blaine—at times, ignored him as if he wasn't even there. The Goodwin's were the types of people who unwittingly smothered their grandson with new "hot" toys, gadgets, electronics, money, candy, or clothes. And Blaine wasn't even about to attempt to win over Damiere's affection with *stuff*.

From the looks, Wally Copel wasn't trying to win over Blaine either. Wasn't his style. Instead, Wally mentioned he was in the mood for a good burger. Wally didn't care if Blaine went or not and frankly, he was going to grab a good burger with or without Blaine; and it was with his sort of carefree attitude in front of Blaine that allowed him to make an easy decision.

They ended up at a trendy-looking burger joint called THE CHOMP, which was located inside an old industrial-sized textile mill not too far from Blaine's house. Blaine had driven by the place many times—always drew a crowd—but never had the nerve to check it out.

While Blaine and Wally were seated at a table near the back of the restaurant and waiting for the waitress to take their orders, Blaine scanned the inside of the restaurant in a state of rushed-wonder.

"Something, huh?" said Wally.

"Just seems like a whole waste of space, if you ask me."

"I've read good reviews." Wally followed Blaine's cue and looked around as well. "I'm sure, though, most of the people come here for the atmosphere."

Blaine looked down at his seat, felt its material.

"Did this used to be a car seat?" asked Blaine.

"I believe so," Wally said as he looked down at his seat as well. "It's like one of those themed restaurants."

"Themed restaurant?" Blaine furrowed his brow in confusion. "So, what's the theme?"

Wally pointed out a stack of crushed cars stacked like pancakes along one side of the wall. Above the center of the restaurant hung a giant round magnet from a chain.

"As a matter of fact, I think it's supposed to look like the inside of a junkyard."

"Junkyard? Who in the hell would want to eat at a junkyard?"

"Beats me." Wally shrugged off the question and skimmed through the menu, which was a sheet of aluminum, the menu items inscribed like names on a trophy. "I could care less. As long as they make a good burger."

Blaine paused and studied Wally, whose main focus was on the menu. He followed suit and looked over the industrial-like menu as well. A waitress, who was dressed in greasy overalls, eventually came by and took both their orders and then an awkward minute later, returned with their drinks, which were both served inside a mug made of copper.

As they waited on their burgers, Wally pulled out his brown notepad from his coat pocket and skimmed through his notes.

"Working lunch?" Wally suggested.

"Well," Blaine said as he made slipknots with his straw, "the sooner I get rid of you, the better."

Wally grinned.

Then read from his notes: "You said that this employee, Dario Silvestri, who worked the night shift before you started at Powell Printing Press, was not from Maven, correct?"

"That's right. I thought I heard somewhere that he was from up North. I think it might've been Jersey. Maybe Pittsburg. I'm not sure. Besides, I don't think it would've made much of a difference. Once *The Almighty RIN* chose you," Blaine emphasized, "that was it."

"And you believe this RIN-*thing* chose Mr. Silvestri?"

"I know it did," Blaine said certainly. "This printing press, Wally, wasn't like your everyday press. Believe it or not, some of the Mavenites called the machine by another nickname."

"Which was?"

"God," Blaine said directly.

"God?"

"I heard somewhere that RIN earned its name after one of the employees at the PPP discovered that the three letters had remained from the word *Providence*; the other letters had been rubbed off from either age or wear and tear."

"Providence? So, you believe it had special power, a spiritual power?"

"It doesn't matter what I believe, Wally," Blaine said grimly. "Sure, it printed out basically anything you could name: puzzles, books, posters, even *newspaper*. Nothing special about that, right?" Blaine asked Wally but didn't expect any answer in return. "It wasn't whatever RIN printed out that was special; rather, it was what it *did* to people. The way it could manipulate anybody, regardless of *what* he or she believed."

Wally asked, "What did RIN look like?"

"I couldn't even describe if I tried," Blaine said bluntly.

Wally remained in silence, waiting for a more thorough answer, something to work with.

"It looked ancient," Blaine finally said, "like it had come from another time or world. Before they hired me, they made me get a tetanus shot because it was so damn rusty and no doubt, you could easily cut your arm on it if you rubbed up against it; and it had what looked like black roots growing underneath it."

"*Roots?*" Wally repeated. "You sure they weren't cables?"

"No," Blaine said, more seriously. "Roots, like a tree. Even the structure of it appeared as if it was throbbing; and often, whenever it was just me in the room with it, parts of it would light up in an orange light that looked identical to eyes."

Once more, Wally repeated Blaine, but this time with a pale shade of trepidation.

"Eyes?"

"That's what I said, didn't I?"

Wally leaned back in the seat, more color in his face.

"If you knew what was going on in Maven, with the townspeople and their secret with this special machine which possessed some sort of supernatural power to 'manipulate' people, then why'd you stay?"

"I had a suspicion that something was going on, something bad, but I guess, in a way, a part of me was still living in denial. I finally found a place where I felt at peace. A place where I belonged, where I didn't have to run anymore. I wasn't going to let go of that. So, I guess I ignored the red flags."

"Which were?"

"For starters, the fact that not a single person who worked there had an interview with me." Blaine held his crooked index finger in the air. "Red flag number one. I told them about a flyer I saw in the paper and how I was looking for work. They basically handed me the job."

"Who's *they?*"

"The people who were running the press," Blaine said. "One man, went by the name, Barlow, Chuck Barlow I think, he was the one who set me up with the job. Showed me the ropes and whatnot."

Wally wrote down the name with a question mark next to it: Barlow?

"I filled out a couple of forms," Blaine said. "They said they'd pay me in cash. Which, I guess, depending on how you looked at it, could've been yet another red flag. But I told myself 'I needed the money.'"

"What did the job entail?" asked Wally.

"Not like it was rocket science. Most of the job consisted of making sure the place was kept clean and the other machines were tuned and running right and if they weren't for some reason—which, in most cases, was rare—then, I was to call the head of operations immediately. My only involvement with RIN was to make sure it didn't run out of printing material. However, if there was one thing they couldn't clarify enough to me, no matter what happened, I was given specific instructions not to ever touch RIN." Blaine broke through the seriousness by letting out a rare laugh. "I swear, most of the time, though—if I wasn't getting lost in a good book—I'd be chasing away the rats. But other than that, like I said, it was money and I needed it."

"How sure are you that it was this machine, 'RIN'—as the townspeople called it—that was responsible for Mr. Silvestri's death?"

"According to the papers, he died of a heart attack on the job. Which, I guess, depending how you looked at it, could've been *yet* another red flag. He was only in his forties. Appeared to be in tiptop shape. From what I heard around town, he was a healthy man. Seemed like a decent man. I read in the paper he was having a visitation. It was open to the public. So, I paid him a visit; however, I was there for other reasons."

"Was this *before* or *after* you found the teeth underneath RIN?"

"After."

"Why were you so invested in finding out what happened to Mr. Silvestri?" Wally asked. "You didn't even know him."

"No," Blaine said. "You're right. I didn't know him. But I knew a lie. And they were lying about his death. During the visitation—when nobody was looking—I reached inside Dario's mouth. His jaw was wired shut, but I could see his teeth or shall I say, lack of teeth. He was also wearing gloves on his hands. Even the shape of his body seemed odd, not natural. I remember touching his chest and hearing bones crumble and it sounded like crushed glass. Dario's wife was there. I met her. She told me Dario was complaining of chest pains the day before but I wasn't buying it."

"How so?"

"She was acting."

"Acting?"

"I dealt with plenty of actors in my time and she stunk. Out of curiosity, I did a little investigation of my own. After the visitation was over, I followed her back to her home—her real home, that is—which was located a couple of towns away. Turns out Dario Silvestri didn't even have a wife. In fact, he was never even married. Apparently, this actor—or whoever was at the visitation—had been handsomely rewarded and was only there at the visitation to draw any suspicion away from what really happened to her 'supposed' husband. I didn't know who exactly was behind it all. But I had an idea."

"Who do you think it was?" asked Wally, as he took a sip of water.

"Clay Powell, the man who was in charge of the printing press."

"Why do you think it was him?"

"For one, he had enough money to buy elections," Blaine said. "And two, not to judge and all, but the man looked as crooked as scoliosis. I mean nobody's that *fucking* charming, especially for a man who was a recluse who hardly showed his face in town and used representatives to speak for him. Like during Thanksgiving time when he used to hand out turkeys to all the townspeople, he liked to remain anonymous even though everybody knew who it was. So, I knew someone like Dario, a man who dropped dead all of a sudden, knew something that he shouldn't have known about Powell and somebody wanted to shut him up—OR! One could also look at it and say Dario was killed out of retaliation."

"Let's put what you saw at the visitation aside," Wally said, skimming through his notes. "What makes you so convinced Mr. Silvestri death was premeditated?"

"One night, I came in extra early to work. I overheard a couple of employees talking in the break room about Dario. They were saying that he used to get really mad at RIN. One time, he even kicked it because it wasn't working the way he wanted it to."

"So, you're saying, not only was this machine alive, but according to what you said about Mr. Silvestri and what happened to him, the machine also had. . . feelings?"

"Whatever it was, Wally, it wasn't like anything I've ever seen and I think I've seen a lot in my days. This thing was connected to a power far greater than you and me. A force far behind our control." Blaine turned his shoulder and nodded at the people seated in the dining area. "And if these people ever find out about it, most of them wouldn't believe it. But there'd be some who would. And those are the ones who scare me the most."

"But, again, do you have any proof, Blaine?"

Blaine turned away as he sat in silence.

"I'm sorry," Wally said, putting aside the notepad. "It's just a bizarre story. A printing press that murders people. Imagine the person who has to write that kind of head-line. . ."

Wally almost laughed at the remark.

"Whether you like it or not, it's the truth," Blaine said, as he placed the stickman made of straws on the table.

"Okay, let's say it is the truth." Then Wally asked, "Why would a company go to such lengths to cover up a man's death? If you're saying that this machine has 'super-natural power,' then where is the evidence? You and I both know there's hardly anything left of Maven; in fact, when you look at it on a map, it doesn't even exist anymore. And except you, Blaine, most—if not all—of the residents who once lived in Maven are either dead and hard to reach and the ones whom I've reached out to talk to, act like they're afraid to utter a word about what went down in Maven."

"Your point?"

"My point. . ." Wally hesitated for a moment and then, finally, asked the million-dollar question, "My point: How in the hell can a town disappear off the face of the earth?"

Before Blaine could answer, the waitress arrived at the table with their burgers.

They decided to put the work aside.

For the time being.

⊞

IF I had to start somewhere, I guess the best place to start would be the day I first met Clay Powell, the owner of Powell Printing Press. I didn't care much for the man. During that time, I had only spent a couple of weeks at the Press and was contemplated finding another job, considering the blatant lie I had recently un-covered about Dario's make-believe wife. The very moment I met

Powell, I knew something was off about him. He had a certain way about him that rubbed me the wrong way. A hatred that he disguised with arrogance. I didn't know where his hatred had come from. But it was there. I could feel it radiating off his body. This ability to read people was like a gift I picked up during my days as a professional wrestler. You have to possess a certain intuition, an instinct, to have a feel for your opponent, mentally and physically, and what moves he's about to make. You can practice and choreograph all you want, but if you're not on the same page, then the match is doomed from the very start. Powell and Karl Rieber, the mayor of Maven, were most definitely not on the same page; in fact, the two had apparently got themselves into quite a nasty feud which wasn't kept secret around town. It all started when Rieber threatened Powell to sell his property. Rieber knew folks with deep pockets—the kind of folks who bought politicians. It was later known to the public that his whole 'future' plan for Maven was to tear down the Printing Press, buy the land from Powell, and build a new state-of-the-art shopping center in its place. His whole idea was to bring in new companies, new jobs, and basically, choke the town with outsiders and turn Maven into one giant melting pot. Which would inevitably drive out most of the small businesses; not to mention, the folks who were born and raised in Maven. Some folks were ready to vote Rieber's ass out of office. Some even ready to storm the mayor's house like they did in the olden days, with pitchforks and torches, once word surfaced about his plans. If things couldn't get any worse for the mayor, an interview he did with a local magazine was released to the public. The journalist who interviewed Rieber was young and when asked to clarify to the public, she couldn't recall what Rieber had originally said about the military. At first, I thought it might've been a typo. I mean, it had to be—considering a lot of the residents in Maven were either veterans or had a family member who was a veteran. By the time Rieber tried to set the record straight, it was already too late. The public had already made up their minds on Rieber. They wanted his head. Rieber vehemently denied using the word and claimed that the journalist didn't hear him right or maybe thought he misspoke. A word like 'commend' can easily be misspelled or even replaced with the word 'condemn,' despite having two completely different meanings. But then, once I realized that there was an unseen force behind the printing press, the more I started to pick out things that normally I'd ignore and just shrug off. Like signs or billboards. This force—this Dark Entity—was brainwashing the entire town. Maven had become a town of many layers and the more I started to peel away each layer, the more rot I uncovered, the more darkness, as if this strange entity was living in the soil right under everybody's feet. On the façade, it was a pleasant town where decent folks lived. But that's all it was, a façade. After Rieber was murdered, I realized RIN's influence was everywhere you turned.

⊞

WITH his head held downward in thought, Wally stepped away from the camera.

"What's a matter?" asked Blaine.

Wally paced around the kitchen and mumbled to himself, "It doesn't make any sense."

"What doesn't make sense?" asked Blaine.

"The whole story."

"You think I'm making all of this up, don't you?"

Wally turned to Blaine and said unsurely, "No. Of course not."

He grimaced and started to rub his stomach.

"Is something bothering you, Wally?" Blaine asked, more concerned.

"The burger," he said. "It's not sitting well."

Blaine pointed to the hallway.

"Bathroom's down the hallway, *first door* on the *right.*"

Wally excused himself for a moment while he tended to the restroom. Instead of stopping at the first door on the right—Blaine couldn't be more specific about these instructions—Wally kept walking down the hallway. At the very end of the hallway was a closed door. Except for the door at the end of the hallway, all the other doors were open along the hallway, including the bedroom door as well as the office door; however, that one particular door was pleading for Wally's attention. Wally crept to the door. He tried to open the door, but it was locked.

More intrigued than concerned, Wally peeked under the door and swore he saw a shadow moving underneath the doorway. As he was about to knock on the door, he heard a sudden *clank*ing-sound coming from the kitchen.

Back to Blaine, who decided to boil some water on the stove. As the water started to boil, he grabbed two mugs from the cabinet, as well as two tea bags, and set them on the countertop.

While he was preparing the tea, he couldn't help but overhear the toilet flush twice.

Eventually, Wally returned to the kitchen.

"Better?" Blaine asked.

Wally appeared as if his upset stomach was the least of his concerns.

"Yeah," Wally said shortly. "Good. So, let me get this straight. You're saying it was RIN who caused the accident?"

Blaine handed the steaming mug to Wally.

"Thanks," he said. "You read my mind."

"I have a cup of tea every afternoon. It's become part of my routine."

Blaine sat back down at the table with Wally.

"So, you were talking about the accident?" Wally said, as he waited for Blaine to shed more light on his original question before he strayed off topic.

"I saw it with my own eyes," Blaine said, as he started to steep his tea bag. "I happened to be driving to the pharmacy to pick up some cold medicine when he got creamed. He had a green light and as he was driving through the intersection, that green light suddenly turned red. Just like *that*." He snapped his fingers together. "No yellow. Yet, the light went straight from red to green."

"Could've been a glitch."

"No," Blaine said, shaking his head. "No glitch. Sure enough, there happened to be another car crossing the intersection as soon as Rieber was crossing. It, too, had a green light. Rieber ended up getting T-boned. The other driver was okay. Dazed. Bloody nose. But he lived. Can't say the same about the mayor. I went to check on Rieber, but he was already dead. Something else had caught my eye."

Blaine paused for a moment and reflected more on the accident.

▦

WHEN I found Rieber unresponsive behind the steering wheel, I couldn't help but notice the gun on the floor. It made absolutely no sense why the mayor of a small town was driving around with a loaded gun in his car.

▦

"DID you try to revive, Mayor Rieber?" asked Wally.

For a moment, Blaine looked away from the camera and put more thought into his next answer.

"No," he said finally. "I checked his pulse. But, like I said earlier, he was already dead."

▦

IT wasn't until the next day after the six o'clock news showed my face on TV when I found out that I had a fan club in Maven, one small enough to fill this kitchen. Apparently, one of the kids saw my face on TV while one of the reporters was asking me about the accident and immediately recognized me from all the posters he had of me hanging on the back of the closet door. A kid named Simon. When I first saw Simon snooping around my house, he told me the postman Mr. January pointed in a general direction of where I lived, but in plain sight, I saw him stalking me one day when I went into town for some groceries. He followed me on his bike back to my house. Turns out there was a group of them. Five, I remember, and every one of them watched my matches, apparently, behind their parents' back. They said their parents would kill them if they found them watching 'that barbaric nonsense.' Simon happened to be the outcast of the group. He once told me

41

that the kids he hung out with weren't really his friends. He was completely obsessed with me and what I used to do for a living. At first—I admit—he was a pest. He'd follow me around everywhere I went. After awhile, I figured, if he was going to be bugging the hell out of me all the time, then I might as well put him to good use. I told him that I could use an extra pair of hands while working on my house. He didn't miss a beat. Before I could even finish my sentence, he was already agreeing to whatever I was asking from him. Eventually, word got around that Simon was working with The Jam and the next thing I knew, I had all of his buddies—even kids pretending to be Simon's friends—showing up at my house, ready to lend a hand; and it looked as if I was running some kind of child labor camp. They helped me put in new hardwood floors. We repaired the damage to the roof with new shingles. Refurbished and revamped the entire place. I guess, after awhile, Simon and I ended up becoming good friends. You could say I looked at him as the son I never had; and Simon, he looked at me as a father who filled in for the father who was never there. His old man and mine would've made great pals. They shared a lot of similarities: they were both drinkers. Simon's father, Frank, call him the local drunk who spent his nights hanging around the bars, was the kind of man who worked hard and played hard; and at times, Simon would feel the repercussions the morning after. One time, Simon showed up at my house ready to help me fix a gutter. He was wearing a fresh bruise on the side of his face and he told me he got it from rough housing with his older brother. The kid wasn't much of a good liar. The truth was that Frank got drunk the night before and the next morning, he lashed out at Simon for no reason at all. Let's just say I made sure Frank never laid a hand on Simon ever again.

Despite the constant drama with Simon's father, I continued to look after those kids. We continued to work like ants on the house. Tearing down walls—which the kids loved the most. You hand an angry boy a sledgehammer and it's amazing the destruction he'll do. In a matter of weeks, the house looked as if it was brand new. But it wasn't like anybody was forcing them to work. I guess it was fair to say I enjoyed their company equally as much as they enjoyed mine. Every now and then, I'd give them pointers about life and surprisingly enough, they kept me up-to-date with the latest trends and slang. Even till this day, I still can't figure out why in the hell kids back in the day would refer to something cool as 'the bomb.' Simon and his friends—at least the ones closer to him—were also into backyard wrestling. I didn't know much about it, but I'd be lying if I said I wasn't interested. One time, they brought over a video that they had made in their backyard. They were using old mattresses as their ring. They had wooden tables positioned around the ring along with all sorts of junk that they stole from their parents. Aluminum cooking sheets. A toaster. Chairs. Trashcans. Fluorescent light bulbs. Pretty much anything they could get their hands on. At the start of my career, I dabbled in extreme wrestling—which, at the time, was like the minor leagues before you moved up to the Show. Once, I did a barbwire match with the great Molasses, who whooped my ass all across the ring and made me look like a fool. I remember I lost so much blood that night. Another time, I was in what they called a 'tables match' with Skinhead. First one through the table wins. I ended up coming up with my finishing move by accident—the move that would later be known as the infamous 'Slam Jam.' The whole plan was to pile drive Skinhead from the top rope through a table below. But Skinhead—being the avid sweat machine that he was—his body was slippery. It was like his sweat was made out of KY jelly. As I was about to finish off Skinhead, my hands slipped when I was in midair and Skinhead started to fall forward. If it wasn't for a beautiful thing called gravity, then the move would've ended up in disaster. Worst-case scenario: Skinhead breaking his neck. My body weight ended up falling forward and my face was just inches away from Skinhead's ass.

"BACK in the day, the ladies used to call it 'sixty-nine.' You still call it that?"

"Are you talking about the sexual position?"

"That's right," Blaine said.

"People still call it that."

"Well, imagine that position, only Skinhead turned the other way around."

□

WHEN we both landed, my body pancaked Skinhead through the table. My chin went straight up into his ass. Fans didn't know what the hell happened. I didn't either. And that's where the idea for the Slam Jam was born. I remember later that same night, after the match was over, Skinhead ended up going to the hospital with a broken collarbone. He was pissed off and throwing a hissy fit backstage as he tried to pick out splinters from his neck. Earlier that night, he had been pounding one beer after another. I could even smell it on his breath during the match. But most of the guys who had wrestled with Skinhead will tell you that the son of a bitch wrestled better when he was drunk. On the flip side, if things didn't go his way, he could be a real pain in the ass. I guess, in this case, the shoe was on the other foot. The last time Skinhead and I talked was the twenty-fifth reunion I went to some few years back and the guy still held a grudge against me. After the match with Skinhead, I guess you can say my extreme wrestling days were over. In a way, though, I don't regret any of it. I had nothing to lose and everything to gain. In a way, I was trying to prove that I was worthy to be a professional wrestler and if I failed, that was okay. But at least I gave it a try. Plus, it gave me the Slam Jam, although I did, however, make some minor modifications to the finishing move and tweaked it to a more of an inverted power slam. A year later after my extreme wrestling days, I'm fighting Captain Crusher at the fifth annual Wrestlepark in Atlanta, Georgia. It was there, at Wrestlepark V, that I finally made it. Forget all the rushing records that I broke in college or the Super Bowl title I won with The Marauders or all those times I was rejected either from being skinny or small or not strong enough to all the scrutiny I constantly received because of the dark complexion of my skin. Standing in that ring face-to-face with Captain Crusher in front of eighty thousand people wasn't just any milestone in your career. To me, it was 'everything.' Like my entire life was meant for this one moment and it didn't matter whether or not I won or lost. The fact is that I made it to this one moment where many others before me have failed. I no longer had to prove anything to anybody.

When I was a young man eager to enter the real world, I thought the planet Earth was like a giant disco ball and the stars twinkling above were only the tiny reflections and glares of the people who were living below. I was naive—a fool, some might say—another dumb kid who thought the world was his dance floor and the sky was a mirror highlighting the brightness people gave off. But I held onto that idea, that each and every person on Earth was special. All of that faded away after the murder trial and all I saw was the darkness in people. Simon reminded me of myself when I was young. He carried that same light in his eyes. No matter what he did or if he ever got in trouble, he didn't have to prove anything to me or to the world. He and his friends were good kids with good hearts. The evil that controlled Maven recognized that goodness in each and every one of those kids and that's why it took it away from them.

"AFTER a few months in Maven," Blaine told Wally, as they both stepped outside and walked onto the porch, "I started to notice things, the strange things, *not* just the signs and everything written in print, but the people and their behavior. After the house was finished, Simon would occasionally stop by on his bike just to see how I was doing. Every now and then, he'd tag along with me while I went fishing at the lake behind my house. Normally, he wouldn't shut up and at times, he was like he ran on batteries. But I enjoyed listening to Simon. For most of my life, I've done most of the talking whether it be from trash talking an opponent to smooth talking the ladies. For once in my life, it felt good to listen to somebody else talk. On that one particular day, when Simon stopped by my house right before I was about to go fishing, I knew that there was something bothering him and it was something that wasn't normally spoken to people like me."

Wally asked, "What do you mean by 'people like you?'"

As Blaine stopped against the railing of the porch, he turned to Wally and said seriously, "Outsiders."

SIMON *told me that every full moon puzzles of the 'Chosen One'
were printed out at Powell Printing Press but disguised under the
company name, Hard-Pressed. These particular puzzles were
then distributed to a local toy store in Maven called Play Ball!,
which was owned by a man named Avery Christenson. The puzzles depicted the final moments of the Chosen One's life before his
or her soul was welcomed into Heaven, a freeze frame capturing
the moment before he or she died; however, there was one catch:
He—or she—who was chosen into 'God's Kingdom,' had an opportunity to save his or herself from death by completing the puzzle
before two minutes after midnight. If these Chosen Ones didn't
finish the puzzle by that exact time, twelve o' two, then the Chosen
Ones' fate was already sealed and in a matter of weeks, days,
hours, minutes, or even seconds, the picture on the puzzle would
come to fruition. I heard stories about rituals that went on at
night—weird stuff. Animal sacrifices—satanic lore and whatnot,
spells from witches and demons. Mentally deranged kids offering
blood to the monster only known as RIN.*

*On that particular day when the moon was at its fullest,
Simon's father, Frank, was picked as one of these chosen ones or
sacrifices—if you will. I didn't believe Simon. A part of me
didn't want to believe the kid, especially the whole idea of a puzzle
showing you the last moments before you died. But another part of
me—my gut—knew Simon wasn't playing some kind of sick joke
on me. I think I—or at least thought I did—knew him well
enough to know that he wasn't joking. There was only one way to
find out for myself. Later that day, after I met with Simon, I
stopped by Play Ball! The shelves were completely empty, which
wasn't much of a surprise considering Christmas was right around
the corner. Mr. Christenson said he had sold out of all these 'Chosen' puzzles. Said they usually sell like hot cakes every full moon
and that he was holding one for a close friend. But, after a little
convincing, I talked the owner into selling me his last one. Having worked at Powell Printing Press for a while now, I knew it
wasn't my place to question what was printed out. However, I
remember seeing this one particular puzzle when I first started
working there. A thousand piece puzzle of a young boy walking*

his dog on the sidewalk. At the time, I didn't think much about the puzzle. Nothing special about it. The puzzle looked as if it was an oil painting taken from everyday life.

When I went back home and inspected Frank's 'Chosen' puzzle, I saw Frank in the puzzle. That's when I realized there was a chance that Simon might have been telling the truth. That night, I called out sick to work and ended up putting the puzzle together. I spent nearly the entire night working on it. The next morning, I finished the puzzle. I made sure to check the news, the papers, wondering when I'd find Frank's name in the obituary section. Two days passed and nothing. On the third day, I was tempting to pay a visit to Simon and tell him all about his joke and how, for a moment, he had almost 'got me' and how he almost had me thinking that there was a particular reason as to why I, of all places to live, chose a special place like Maven. Later that day, news broke of his father's death. His body—or what was left of it—was found underneath a pile of metal beams. I heard that a scaffold had collapsed on top of Frank. Immediately, I retraced the puzzle. Frank's 'final' moments. In the puzzle, Frank, a welder, was sitting on top of a metal scaffold suspended next to what looked like the hull of a massive boat while other welders were busy either cutting through metal or softening the metal with torches; however, of all the welders and cutters around Frank, he was the only one not working. In fact, of all the workers, his welding helmet hat was raised upward and rested over the top of his head. From the picture, he looked as if he was deep in thought. I know that a picture doesn't exactly tell the whole truth. But Frank had a tranquil look on his face. I couldn't help but wonder what he was thinking about at that particular moment in time.

When I spoke to Simon, he said his father didn't want to go to work anymore. On that third day, Frank's boss called and told Frank that if he didn't show up for work then Frank was going to be out of a job. I'd like to think that Frank had another choice. A Plan B. He could've quit his job and found another one where he would've skipped death and possibly passed it along to somebody else, like some criminal or two-faced politician or somebody who deserved to be put out of his or her misery. But the all-important question: Would death eventually find Frank? Was it his boss's threats that set his fate into motion? Were those people around

Frank, loved ones, like his wife and even Simon or Simon's older brother, persuaded by this evil into pushing Frank toward his ultimate destination?

Then, I started to think about the other puzzles, like the one with the boy and his dog. I wondered how these 'Chosen Ones' died. Or, if these so-called 'Chosen Ones' actually finished the puzzle before their time was up.

And why that particular time—twelve o' two?

As I started to think more about the puzzles, I remembered hearing a story on the news. About a boy being impaled by a metal pipe. He was walking down the street when, all of a sudden, a truck hauling construction supplies came speeding by. Somehow, a pipe had fallen from truck and struck the boy, killing him. In any other place, you'd call it a 'freak accident.' But, in a small town like Maven, such a word didn't exist. According to Mavenites, everything was preordained, pieces of a much greater puzzle.

If the boy was the same one from the puzzle, then the ultimate question: Why him? Did this strange entity, this evil—or God, as some Mavenites called it—choose those who were sinners, like Frank? Or, did it choose people who have atoned for their sins, according to Simon, like his father, Frank, had done after I found out the harm he was inflicting on his own son? But the boy—why him? Why that one innocent boy?

THEY decided to call it a day. Wally was eager to continue filming the documentary—even hinting at staying the night—but Blaine was exhausted and from what Wally could tell, the story about Frank's death had taken a lot out of Blaine.

That night, Blaine went about his routine. In the dark, while sitting in his recliner, he drank a beer. Normally, he'd just drink one. "One and done," he'd call it. But, on this particular night, he felt the need to drink more than just one. He was down to three when his mind started to drift to dark places.

All of a sudden, he flung the flashlight toward the door and ended up putting a hole in the wall.

He thought about her, his Mira, and why she had to leave him so soon. Then, his mind drifted farther back in time, months after the two had met. They were at an art gallery in New York City, supporting a spunky up and coming artist named Earl Lake, who was from Newbay, which happened to be the same hometown as Elmira. Elmira found out about Earl's work through a friend of a friend and was an admirer of his and based on all the wonderful things Elmira had said about Earl and his work—in fact, at times, whenever Earl's name came up in a conversation, it'd be nearly impossible to pull Elmira away or even get her to change the subject—Blaine decided to create this whole elaborate setup for Elmira's birthday by lying about visiting Times Square and seeing off-Broadway shows when the real reason as to why he flew her all the way out to New York was for her to meet the one and only, Earl Lake. *Of all things*, he seethed in the dark as if he was talking directly to Elmira, *you had to pick out that one sculpture.*

Why, Mira?

Why goddamn it?

Blaine could picture the sculpture in the art gallery, the sharp point of that hideous, worthless thing called art glimmering at him as if, for a moment, he could see the light of God beaming down on it, not warning Blaine but, better yet, showing Blaine his future. All this time, Blaine thought to himself, *He knew. Yet, He let it happen.* Blaine tried to think of the other signs. The more he put his mind on the days leading up to his wife's death, the more he realized that there were so many signs that he couldn't even count them all. For instance, the puddle of blood on the ring during his last cage match with Fantastico and how it closely resembled the very shape of the sculpture in their living room. At the time, Blaine didn't think anything of it and yet, as he did with a lot of things during that turbulent time of his life, Blaine simply ignored it.

▣

MORE Hard-Pressed puzzles were printed out. Some not on full moons. I think the whole 'every full moon' thing was a gimmick. Either way, the people of Maven still bought into it. Some people who were 'Chosen' did the puzzles. Others didn't. They just accepted everything that it was and nothing that it wasn't. I was still on the fence about RIN and I questioned whether or not it was, as the townspeople referred to it as, a direct channel to God and those who happened to be chosen were granted a free ticket into His kingdom. I started to wonder if It, as in this evil entity, specifically targeted those who were talkers, as if It could pick out the talkers, the blabbermouths who would jeopardize the future of the town, print them out a puzzle of their own—a really hard one, too, like a two-thousand piece puzzle which would take any normal person days or even weeks to finish. Like It was doing whatever was necessary by taking out those who would inform outsiders about their supposed 'God' theory and how He was living through a printing press in a small town that rhymed with Haven. Just saying the notion alone out loud sounds ridiculous. God communicating through puzzles. One night, I decided to put my faith to the test. I spoke to the machine and it spoke back.

▣

FROM the bedroom Blaine returned to the living room with a letter-sized piece of paper inside a black frame.

He handed the framed sketch to Wally.

"Is this what was printed out?" asked Wally.

In the sketch was a black and ink crosshatched picture of a German Shepard.

"Mira was what I like to call a dog person," Blaine said as he sat back down in his recliner. "Despite the character I played in the ring, Elmira and I were like opposites. She liked dogs—had almost a borderline obsession with them. Me, on the other hand, I enjoyed the company of cats. In a way, both of our personalities matched our favorite furry creature. Before we met, she used to have a German Shepard—Willow was her name. She was a sweet dog but could be a nuisance at times. I knew Mira wasn't going to give her up. So, when Mira moved in, so did Willow. Unfortunately, Mira had Willow put to sleep a couple of years after she moved in. She developed some kind of rare illness and Mira had no other choice than to put her down. After Willow passed away, that's when Mira started getting involved in painting. I guess it was like therapy for her. Her way of getting over Willow's death. Mira didn't have to tell me, but I knew she wanted another dog. I wouldn't allow it. I saw what Willow's death had done to her and I didn't want to see her like that ever again. So, she started painting more of them. She painted all kinds of dogs. She was exceptional too. She even sold one of her paintings to a billionaire in New York, one of those hotshot investor-types who had so much money he didn't know what to do with it. But he bought one of Mira's paintings. I remember I was so proud of her. On the night I spoke to RIN, it printed out this very image of Mira's dog, Willow."

"*That's insane*," were the only two words Wally could muster as he stared at the sketch of the German Shepard.

Blaine replied, "Insanity was just the beginning, Wally."

🔲

AFTER that night I confronted RIN, my feelings started to change about the printing press and I questioned myself, 'What if these townspeople are right?' I guess there was only one way to find out. As before, I started doing a little investigating of my own. I needed to find out what was going on here and I knew it was much bigger than me. I started snooping around, trying to get as much information about Maven as I could. I kept my head down, started with the one place that I could trust: the library. I dug up as much information on Maven as I could find. Back in the early 1920's, when the town was more populated, the mining business in Maven was booming. In 1928, there was a deadly explosion in the mine, which killed ninety-eight people, mostly miners. Months later, there was another explosion. Killed three times as many and was ruled one of the deadliest mining accidents in history. While I was scrolling through the microfiche, I came across one photo in a headline of a Native American tribe—the Chiayokee—on the day of the second explosion, which was ruled an 'accident' as well, waiting outside one of the mine's entrances. The members of the Chiayokee tribe were protesting and pleading the miners not to enter the mine, warning them it was not safe and that the mines were cursed by 'evil spirits.' Some of the locals believed it was one of the tribe members who caused the first explosion, like it was their own sick way of warning the miners. If there wasn't already a rift between Maven and the Chiayokee, the two accidents further divided the two communities. In 1958, Powell Printing Press was opened. I came across a staff photo with the owner, Clay Powell. I thought it might've been a misprint. Maybe Clay's father had started the company and handed it down after he passed or retired. Either that, or the man was a goddamn vampire. In the photo, Powell hadn't aged a day. He looked the same as the day I met him. Then, that's when the engines started running. I couldn't stop thinking about that photo and the more I thought about it, the more Mayor Rieber's story started to make sense. The apparent 'typo.' The signs. The posters. The billboards. The 'faulty' streetlight. If RIN could misprint a newspaper, then, surely, it could alter an old photograph. I didn't know how exactly it could've done it, but there was only one man who knew the answers to all my questions.

⊞

"YOU broke into his house?" asked Wally.

Blaine continued to steep the teabag into the cup of steamy water.

"I had no other choice," he said. "Fortunately for me, Powell wasn't home."

⊞

THE moment I stepped foot inside that house, it felt as if I was traveling back in time. Everything was old and outdated and most of the furniture looked as if it was over a hundred years old. Even the house smelled of dust. Yet, everything, even the top of the refrigerator was polished to a mirror shine. It was also hard to

*believe that a man, who had no wife, no children, lived in this
great big house all by himself. Rumors had it that he had several
illegitimate children through various women. But that's all they
were really, just rumors. I snooped around the entire house but
didn't see any photographs of children—or even family. I did,
however, find that very same photo back in the library. The
1958 staff photo of each employee who worked at Powell Printing
Press. In the middle was Clay Powell. However, he wasn't the
same man who was in the other photo. He appeared to be a few
years older, salt and pepper hair, in his sixties, maybe seventies.
But he wasn't the same man whom I met when I first got the job
at the PPP.*

▦

"AN impostor?"

"Who else could he have been?" Blaine returned.

"He wasn't his son?" asked Wally.

"No." Blaine paused. "The two men dressed alike. Expensive suits, tie. Even wore their hair the same. Slicked-back. Their facial features were different."

"He could've been adopted."

"No," Blaine said, determined. "The photo was from the same year. 1958."

"So, the photo could've been photoshopped?"

"Photoshopped?"

"Wait," Wally suddenly corrected, "Photoshop probably wasn't even invented back then."

"Whatever the case may be, Wally, the photo back at the library was altered. It got me thinking, 'What else was altered?'"

"If it was, then why would this man be posing as Clay Powell?"

Blaine sipped from his cup of tea, the steam rising up his face.

"Because, Wally, the man who was posing as Clay Powell was Clay Powell's murderer."

᎒

IN the original photo, I recognized a face in the back row. His name was Thomas Bach. He was the editor-in-chief of Maven's local newspaper. He was younger, early twenties. I held the photo under a microscope and realized this man, Thomas Bach, was Clay Powell—or at least, posing as Clay Powell. I didn't know why Bach would want to steal Powell's identity. Plus, if Bach really wanted to keep his identity a secret, then why would he risk exposure by keeping the original photo for others to possibly find. I pocketed the photo and paid a visit to Play Ball! I asked Mr. Christenson if he had any vintage puzzles, specifically ones from the late 50's or early 60's. Like Simon, he wasn't a good liar. Not to draw any suspicion, I told him that I was looking for an older puzzle for 'my nephew,' a puzzle by the company 'Hard-Pressed,' and that he didn't care much for their newer ones. After I left, I staked out the toy store. A few minutes after I left, I saw Mr. Christenson pulling his car around the back of the store. He was loading up boxes into his trunk. He went back into the store. When he finally closed shop, I tailed him to a storage unit at the edge of town where he stored the boxes. I knew whatever was in those boxes might've been a clue as to what was really going on in Maven. I went back home and grabbed my bolt cutters from the garage. The only security at the storage unit was a guard dog. But that was an easy fix. Good thing for me: dogs loved hamburgers. By the end of the night, I had myself a new best friend.

᎒

WALLY asked, "You think it was a coincidence that RIN chose each employee at Powell Printing Press?"

"Are you kidding me?" Blaine said. "What other reason would Avery want to hide these puzzles?"

"To keep you quiet?"

"That's right," Blaine said. "But, if there's one thing I've learned through all my years, that's 'Never underestimate a man who has nothing to lose.' I guess when they saw me and the state I was in when I first arrived in Maven, they saw a damaged man, a man who wanted to escape the world. What they failed to realize was that I've seen the world and despite all of the pain I had endured, I carried a piece of that world with me. And, *I knew*, deep down inside, that there was good in that world and that one day, when I finally left Maven, the world would forgive me."

Blaine got up from his seat and walked to the sink.

Wally asked Blaine, "So, do you believe this Avery Christenson guy was in on Powell's murder?"

"No," Blaine answered, his back turned to Wally. "But he didn't want me to find those puzzles. That's for damn sure. I did some more digging. I found out that one of the former employees was still alive. His name was Clarence Fogg."

CLARENCE Fogg figured out how to beat RIN. One day, he strolled into a grocery store and shot the butcher right between the eyes. Some young kid who was working there to pay off student loans. Then, Clarence stalked each aisle of the store, searching for anyone who had meat in their shopping carts and he shot them as well. He pleaded insanity and said the animals made him kill all those people. He said it was the animals' voices that had told him to target that one particular store. Instead of getting the death penalty, Clarence was transferred to a mental institution for the criminally insane. I paid Clarence a visit and it turns out the man wasn't insane. He was only pretending to be. A grade-A faker. He said he couldn't be touched by the evil as long as he was in there. He said it was the only way to keep the evil from getting in, being around so much evil, murderers, rapists, and child molesters, the bottom scum of the human race. When I came back to Maven, I guess people started to notice that I was up to something. The second time I went back to the library was when people started to act different around me. Even the way they talked to me had drastically changed. So, I guess, with me finding out about Maven's dark past, I was destined to be the next 'Chosen One.' The word spread around town. Flyers and all kinds of commercial ads about a new puzzle coming soon. I no longer went to work. I stayed inside mostly, hardly left the house. Frankly, I thought I'd turned out just like the guy who I replaced at Powell Printing Press. I started to wonder how I'd go out. They'd end up making something up, like a heart attack or stroke—but how would I really go out? Crushed by the printing press? Electrocuted? An on-the-job type of 'accident'? Or, would it find me in my house? While I was taking a bath? Or, washing the dishes? Or, reading a book in bed? There were so many possibilities, so many scenarios. So, I figured, if I'm going to beat death, then I might as well not put myself in a position where I'd make it easy for RIN. But maybe that was the whole point, for the machine to keep me scared, scared to leave my house, scared to do anything. When I heard there was a new puzzle out before the next full moon, in fact, only a few days after my return, I knew it was for me. It wasn't. Instead, RIN had targeted the one person whom I was close to in Maven. And RIN didn't just target Simon. Yet, it targeted all of them. Every single kid who helped work on my house.

"I tried to rescue them, but it was already too late," Blaine said. "It already found them."

"Curious," Wally said. "What was the puzzle?"

"It was a puzzle of two older folks standing in the middle of your typical den watching television," Blaine said to Wally. "The strange part about it: Simon and his friends weren't even in the puzzle—at least, *not* that the trained eye could see. As for the two standing in front of the television, both of their backs were facing the puzzler. I later determined that it was Oscar's parents. When I spoke to them, Oscar's mother said she recognized their living room. She figured it was her and her husband who were chosen. The two of them spent the entire day putting together the puzzle. Eventually, they both put it together before *twelve o' two*. But they weren't the ones who were chosen, they realized. Instead, if you looked real close with a magnifying glass, you'd see that it was the very same people who Oscar's parents were watching on TV. In the puzzle, Oscar's parents were watching a video of Simon and his friends wrestling in the backyard. They didn't know it was their own kid at the time because, like most people who had done the puzzle, they couldn't recognize him on TV. Apparently, they didn't approve of Oscar lying to them about where he spent his afternoons. A few days after the 'Chosen' puzzles were released to the public and things appeared to return back to normal, Oscar's parents found a video of one of Oscar's backyard wrestling matches. The kids had just filmed a match at Simon's house while Simon's mother was at work; and as they normally did after their match was over, they hung out on the roof of Simon's house. The roof suddenly caved in and the entire roof ended up collapsing on top of them. In the 'Chosen' puzzle all you could see were these tiny silhouettes standing on top of a house on the TV screen. The image was so tiny that it was all captured on one puzzle piece, making it virtually impossible to identify the kids in the puzzle. But that was the whole point, Wally," Blaine said, the anger rising in him. "RIN didn't want these innocent kids to put together the puzzle before the time was up. And it didn't want to kill them, either. RIN, God, Messiah, the Devil, Satan—whatever the hell you want to call it—*It* was sending me a message."

"What message?" asked Wally.

"'*Back off,*' it was saying," Blaine said.

Not missing a beat, Wally asked, "What happened to them—these kids?"

"Two of them ended up paraplegics," Blaine said, "one had a brain injury and wasn't able to walk or talk ever again and had to eat out of a feeding tube for the rest of his life—I remember his name was Banjo. Of all the kids, he was probably the closest one to Simon. Another one shattered his arms and legs. Simon's injuries were the most severe. He ruptured his diaphragm, had a collapsed lung, severed his spleen, internal bleeding. Simon ended up slipping into a coma." Blaine drifted into a trance as he thought about Simon. "Last time I spoke to Simon, he told me, '*Hey, Jam, you can't body slam evil, especially when evil doesn't have a body.*' I wish I would've known sooner it was him inside that puzzle. I would've done anything in my power to save him from death, even it meant sacrificing my own life. I have many regrets, but that's probably the one I still carry around with me: not acting *quick* enough."

"Did Simon ever wake from the coma?" asked Wally.

"No," Blaine said, as he hung his head in sorrow. "He never did. I later found out that his mother pulled the plug on him. I guess, she had eventually given up on hope. I think—in a way—we *all* did."

⊞

AFTER the visit with Clarence Fogg and then what happened to the kids, it was clear to me what I had to do. I realized RIN wasn't what the townspeople had made it out to be. They could call 'God' or their 'protector' all they wanted, but, at that moment, I knew exactly what it was. And I knew exactly what needed to be done.

I went to Powell Printing Press, ready to destroy RIN, send it back to whatever hell it came from.

When I arrived, I made yet another discovery. In a secret room, I found a team of puzzlers—the real homely type who looked as if they hadn't showered in days—putting together a puzzle with Thomas Bach. He looked like a deer in headlights. All I remember was a massive table in the center of a dimly lit room, that team of hyper puzzlers all gathered around the table, frantically sorting through puzzle pieces with Bach looming over, when, all of sudden, the blood rushed through my veins. My world started to spin before it went completely black. I woke up inside the basement of Powell's house with a group of roughnecks standing guard—Bach's own personal scumbags.

⊞

"STILL have the scar to show."

Wally stood up from the table, walked over to Blaine, and looked at the scar on the backside of his head.

"Got me with the butt of his gun," Blaine said. "Split my head wide open.

THOMAS *was standing in the corner of the basement. He walked from the shadows, surprising me, as if he was standing there the entire time, watching me. He told me everything that happened and why he murdered Clay Powell. He was just like any other man who was stuck on himself. It was there I found out that he had been obsessed with RIN and its magic. For years, Bach had worked under Clay Powell—the real one, that is. Call it jealously. Call it 'sinister' or evil. Call it whatever you like. The man wanted what Clay had. He told me he wanted to harness RIN's power and use it to manipulate the people of Maven when, in fact, the whole purpose of the printing press was for the 'balance' of order, an otherworldly entity that decided who died and who didn't and spared those who acted upon free will. For instance, if you knew a drunk driver was going to cross the line and cause your car to swerve off the road and then overcorrect into oncoming traffic and kill you while driving to the store, would you still get inside that car? For most, they'd say 'No.' You'd stay home. Wait a day or two before going out. Be more cautious on the road. Or, if you knew a mugger was going to stab you to death when you were out jogging in the park, would you still go on that jog? For most of these townspeople, they'd call it 'fate' or 'God's plan.' That's power like no other, Bach said. To be able to control people, their day-to-day lives, their so-called 'destiny.' I asked him about Frank, if he had him killed. Bach smiled and said back, 'You think that scaffold just magically came down on its own?' That's when I suddenly realized that Bach was involved in everything. He was fate's own little nudger. If a Chosen One did not complete the puzzle or failed to carry out the final moment that was chosen for them, then Bach was there to give them a little nudge. Despite Bach being the recluse that he was, he had other people working for him. Mr. Christenson from the toy store. Even the editor of the local newspaper. The town's coroner. Even one of the doctors. All of these actors were nothing but pawns, puppets, and peddlers; and Bach happened to be one of the greatest manipulators of his time. The king of all puppeteers. One may look at RIN as the thumb of God. Another, the Devil. Whatever it was, it wasn't from this world. Bach, being a narcissistic asshole he was, wanted*

59

what Clay Powell had, so he decided to take it from him. But strangely enough, a piece of Clay Powell still survived.

☐

WALLY furrowed his brow in confusion.

"What do you mean 'survived'?"

Blaine emphasized for Wally, "*Survived*, as in a piece of Powell was still alive inside the machine."

☐

EVERY so often, Bach would get chosen. Those people I walked in on in that secret room under Powell Printing Press were 'hired puzzlers' putting together Bach's 'Chosen' puzzle for him. Their whole job was to put together his puzzle before that deadline. Then, when the time was ready, he'd place the final piece in the puzzle, undoing his fate and saving himself from his ultimate death. He called it a real 'honor' to be chosen, Bach did, to have such a brilliant perfectionist like Clay Powell wanting him dead. He didn't know how Powell wound up in the machine—maybe there was a connection the two had that nobody else knew about, an unnatural bond—but somehow, he was still alive and kicking around in there, constantly battling with that strange entity inside, and every now and then, Powell would sneak away on top as the victor; and then, in return, out of his own indulgence, spit out a tricky puzzle for Bach as if it was his own warped way of seeking vengeance beyond the grave. Bach, on the other hand, felt as if it was the machine testing him, to see if he was worthy enough to manage the company without any outside interference. The sick son of a bitch even kept Powell's body around, as if it was some kind of trophy or something for kicks.

As for the town's mayor, Rieber, I asked Bach if he was the one responsible for his death. Bach said it was RIN who killed the mayor. He said Rieber was headed to Dark Hill before his car accident. Rieber even had a team on standby, waiting on orders to bulldoze the entire place down. But the machine couldn't let Rieber do it. Bach wouldn't let Rieber do it.

Somehow, I managed to find a window—a bulb hanging above Bach's head. I knew if I hit the bulb with the rock that I was secretly hiding under my leg, I'd have a chance to flee toward an underground passageway behind an armoire. Bach was going on a rant about immortality, power, and control, how he's so special, the one and only 'Chosen One' to lead the world into a new age of law—the cliché regurgitation every self-righteous movie villain spews in order to 'explain' to the audience the methods of his madness. I didn't care what Bach had to say. I just wanted to get the hell out of there.

As he turned his back to me for a moment, that was my window. I flung the rock at the bulb. I never had good aim. Once I tried throwing a football during a flea-flicker but ended up throwing an interception and costing the game for my team. But, somehow, I knew I was going to hit the bulb, cause it to shatter, then escape this hellhole. The rock struck the bulb, shattering it. The basement went pitch-black. I ran toward the narrow passageway, ducking and dodging as gunshots suddenly rang out behind me. I turned my shoulder for a moment and witnessed Bach's face in the flashes of gunfire. I remember Bach's face, the evil in it. I'll never forget such a look. He looked as if he was wearing the face of someone—or something—else. His eyes, like black marbles. His teeth, sharp, stained, and gnarly. His look, demonic. I managed to push aside the heavy armoire and slither my way into the passageway. Bach—or whatever he was—struggled to push the armoire aside. Which gave me enough time to gain distance from him. I ran. I didn't look back. I just ran through the darkness, not having a clue as to where I was going. I must've run three miles through that underground tunnel. Eventually, the tunnel led me directly underneath Powell Printing Press, to the power source of the machine. Never have I seen such a beautiful light. The light was a blue color, pale like the moon, and the light looked comforting in the way it basked against the surface of the shaft, as if it was luring me in, welcoming me to my final destination. I approached the light, which was humming like an electrical current. The closer I got to this energy source, the more I could feel its powerful grip and the horrors that consumed it. Once I reached the blinding light, thousands—millions—of voices cried out in great agony, as if they were coming from the souls that *were trapped inside. As soon as I realized where exactly the light was taking me, I tried to yank myself from its pull. In one last desperate attempt to escape, I reached out and mistakenly touched the light.*

◫

AND what did you see?

"Blaine?"

The words passed right through Blaine like specters.

Wally stood from his chair and walked over to Blaine.

Blaine suddenly snapped from his deep trance.

"I'm not feeling too well," he uttered. "Why don't we finish tomorrow?"

"Is there anything I can do?" asked Wally.

"No," Blaine said quietly. "I'd like to be left alone for now."

"I see."

"Well, what time do you want me to come back tomorrow?"

"Whenever you like," Blaine said to Wally.

◫

ONCE Wally gathered the rest of his things, he drove back to the hotel that he was currently staying in and went through the footage that he had recorded earlier that day on his laptop. He couldn't stop thinking about what Blaine said about Bach and how he was the one who murdered Clay Powell.

Wally placed the laptop aside for a moment and skimmed through some of his notes in his notepad. He flipped to the page about Powell's murderer and saw the name Blaine circled with many passings as if he was highlighting the name when, in fact, he specifically remembered circling the name *Bach* on his notepad.

"That can't be right," Wally said to himself and pulled the laptop back in front of him.

Wally scrolled directly to the moment when Blaine was talking about Powell's murderer and watched the video.

Blaine said directly into the camera: "*He was an old man desperately clinging onto life when I met him. I had no other choice. Powell had to die. So,*" he said, "*I did what was necessary. I slit his throat. I remember checking the time and it was exactly two minutes past midnight when he let out his final gasp of air. So, I guess, it started to make sense, with the whole deadline thing. If I had to guess, I bet it was Powell's idea. His way of giving the 'Chosen Ones' a chance to a second chance at life.*"

Wally rewound the video.

He watched it again.

Then, again.

"*I did what was necessary,*" Blaine said. "*I slit his throat.*"

Once more: "*I slit his throat.*"

However, in his mind, Wally remembered the interview turning out much differently. Blaine specifically said that it was Thomas Bach who had slit Powell's throat. Yet, there he was, on the video coldheartedly confessing to Powell's murder.

Wally scrolled through other footage and then listened to the other mediums that he used to document Blaine, such as a tape recorder.

While listening to Blaine speak in the background, he came across one particular video where he excused himself from the kitchen table to use the restroom after the two came back from eating lunch at the trendy burger joint, The Chomp.

In the video: Blaine was making two cups of tea; while Wally was off "using the restroom," Blaine grabbed a dark vile from the top cabinet to the right of the stovetop and poured a strange liquid into Wally's cup of tea.

The sight of the video caused Wally to back away from the laptop as if the laptop itself was corrupted. Wally knew Blaine wasn't the murderer. He was one of the main suspects in his wife's murder trial; however, on the surface, Blaine was far from a murderer. Yet, on the video, he said he was. Wally also knew that he wouldn't slip poison, or whatever the hell that was, in Wally's drink without him knowing—and most importantly, not in front of a camera, which Blaine knew was still recording. And yet, on the video, Blaine was doing exactly that. He remembered feeling awful that day they grabbed burgers at The Chomp. But he felt sick to his stomach long before they had tea. As a matter of fact, Wally remembered feeling like he was about to shit himself on the drive back to Blaine's house.

Or, *was it after I left Toussaint's, after we had tea?*

Wally watched the interview again.

Then, after he finished watching the interview, he watched it again.

🎞

BLAINE was in bed staring up at the ceiling when the thought suddenly smacked his mind. He removed the paperback, *The Invisible Man* by H.G. Wells, which was spread flat across his chest, and rolled out of bed. He tottered to the dresser, pulled out the business card from the top drawer, and held it under the lamp.

With his reading glasses, he read the name on the card: WALLY COPEL.

Below the name: FILMMAKER.

Suspicious of the name, Blaine grabbed the closest piece of paper that he could find which happened to be the back of an envelope. Then, searched the desk for a pen. He found one, but it was out of ink.

Fiendishly, he tossed the pen across the room and fished out another one. He wrote down the name on the back of the envelope and then started deconstructing the name, Wally Copel.

He'd write down a letter underneath the name. For starters, the letter C.

Then, he'd cross out the C from the name Copel.

One down.

Next, he'd think of the next letter that came to mind. Then, he'd search for it. There it was. He wrote down the letter L from the leftover name *opel*.

Then, A.

He'd slash away the A from the name Wally as if the pen was his sword.

Then, the letter Y.

Once more, like the A, he'd cross out a Y from the leftover name Wlly.

Only six letters remained on the envelope.

Blaine studied the remaining letters: *Wll ope.*

He didn't even have to finish the second name.

All he had written down was the name CLAY.

After a quick shuffle of letters, the next name jumped out at Blaine and nearly knocked the wind out of him.

A cold rush of air came over me as if I was stepping inside a giant freezer. Once I pushed past the light, I found myself back in the art gallery staring at one of Earl Lake's sculptures, as if RIN was showing me where everything changed for me, as if right then and there two avenues opened up on an invisible timeline and my next decision would either take me in one direction or another. A part of me knew exactly where one path would take me. The first thing that came to my mind was the jagged point of the corner of the sculpture and how dangerous it could've been. Mira fell in love with the sculpture. She wasn't thinking of different scenarios or the possibility that one of us could bump or rub against the sculpture and end up getting hurt—or worse.

"WHAT was the sculpture?" Wally asked, as he sat with Blaine at the kitchen table.

He took a moment to glance down at his notepad below him. He carefully followed the pen jotting down the word *sculpture*. His eye remained like the eye of an unblinking doll. With his eyes burning, he looked up at Blaine, then drew his eyes back down at the notepad, wondering if the word would somehow change or rewrite itself into something completely different. Nothing happened.

"The sculpture was called *The Host*, or something like that," Blaine went on to say. "Or was it *The Visitor*? I'm not sure. Anyway, the sculpture was this lanky alien-like figure with arms in the shape of tentacles standing in a rather provocative position. The corner of the sculpture—an elbow, I believe—was as sharp as a knife and had 'accident' written all over it. Figuratively, not literally."

MIRA thought the sculpture would look best underneath the chandelier inside the foyer. I thought Mira was out of her mind to want to stick that piece of junk in the middle of the foyer, with it being the first thing our guests would see when they stepped into our house. But that's what she wanted. I couldn't say no. After all, she was the boss. And I was madly in love with her. Yet, as the months went by, I failed to appreciate the sacrifices she made for me. I failed to appreciate her devotion to me, to have an understanding of my lifestyle, with me being on the road all the time. She made a sacrifice when she first met me. Maybe that's why she turned to her dogs and her art. Maybe it was those things that kept her company while I was away. Regardless, no matter how many times we fought or how many times she caught me with another woman, I still loved her. I adored her. Mira was my everything. My world. The night she was killed, we had a fight. Earlier that night, we went out to eat at one of my favorite restaurants, Leo's Table—the restaurant named after the famous Italian painter, Leonardo da Vinci. I wasn't in a good mood the entire night. The tension between me and Mira was evident; in fact, I think everybody in the restaurant could sense that we were headed for a blow up. Halfway through dinner, Mira suddenly snapped at me. I had been drinking and I said some things that I later regretted. For those witnesses who have never been married before, I know how it may have looked. So, it was obvious to me as to why I was suspected of murdering Mira. The argument continued when we got back home. Mira was threatening to leave me. She couldn't get inside the house quick enough and said she was going to pack her bags and stay with her sister who hated my guts from the first day we met. I knew how Mira acted whenever she visited her sister, and how, at times, Gale would talk about me as if I was a dog; and then, if necessary, she'd tell all kinds of lies about me, how I was a monster, even with her left hand on the Good Book. When I opened the door, Mira stormed into the house and headed straight for the stairs. I grabbed her by the arm and told her that she was overreacting, but she acted as if she wanted absolutely nothing to do with me anymore. She couldn't even stand the sight of me. She tried to jerk her arm away, but I wouldn't let go. A part of me had drifted away, left, had gone somewhere else. I found myself back at the art galley. The fork in the road. Two avenues. It all led here. At that moment. I don't know what happened. I just let go, my hand let go. She stumbled backwards and landed on the sharp-side of the sculpture. She suddenly cried out in pain. In all my years of wrestling, I've heard grown men cry out, either it pretend or for real. But this was a different kind of cry, like all that life inside her had been smothered with a pillow. I knew it was serious from the moment it happened, but I didn't want to believe it. So, I played off the injury, thought maybe she twisted an ankle or something. I'd fix her up, wrap it up, and then we'd laugh about it the next morning. It wasn't until I pulled Mira from the sculpture that I realized the extent of her injuries.

⊞

SHOCKED by the recent discovery, Wally switched off the camera.

"*No*," Blaine said to Wally. "You wanted the *whole* story. I'm giving you exactly what you wanted."

"The story is about Maven, *not* what happened to Elmira."

"Elmira is the story," he said. "If it wasn't for what happened to Elmira, then I would've never wound up in Maven in the first place."

"Okay," Wally said and turned the camera back on. "What happened next?"

⊞

IT all happened so fast, like a nightmare I so desperately wanted to wake up from.

By the time I reached the phone to call for an ambulance, my Mira was already dead. I didn't know what to do. I panicked. I called a close friend of mine, one of my bodyguards, Dante, who'd take a bullet for me. I knew he knew friends on the inside. He had served time behind bars. Dante was loyal, though. He said he'd handle it.

⊞

WALLY asked, "So, you're saying it was Dante Jackson who made Elmira's death look like a robbery gone wrong?"

Blaine finally said into the camera, "Yes."

⊞

DANTE told me to get in my car and drive around to make it look as if I was blowing off steam since there were witnesses at the restaurant who saw the two of us fighting. It was Dante's idea to smash in the door and make it look as if someone had broken into our house; however, it was my idea to take Mira's jewelry from her bedroom and plant it somewhere else. Dante knew a couple of cats who had just gotten out of prison but had no reason for being out. Type of cats who belonged behind bars. So, he informed me about one in particular. His name was Jeffery Mooney. A couple of days later after Mira's death, the cops were tipped off. They took Jeffery into the station for questioning. Mooney doesn't even make it through the first few hours of interrogation. They dangle some phony story in front of Mooney's face and all of a sudden, Mooney turns into a parrot. Till this day, I tell myself it was an accident. Not thinking of the jagged edge of the sculpture sticking out behind Mira, my hand slipped. Mira tripped and fell onto the sculpture. She died. Till this day, I think of her everyday and what life would've been like if she didn't die. Where would we be? How many kids would we have together? The fact is I was supposed to protect Mira from the man whom I had become. I failed her. I failed myself. . . but the other part of me had so many doubts about whether or not it was an accident. Maybe I was so frustrated with

her that I wanted to kill her at that moment in time. Maybe
something else had come over me, just like that very same 'some-
thing' I saw with Bach, the darkness inside him, that demon.
Whatever it was—this evil—I destroyed it after I escaped from
Dark Hill. At least that's what I first thought.

WITH last night's encounter fresh on his mind, Wally asked,
"Even though Powell Printing Press was destroyed in a
massive explosion, do you believe that the evil is still out
there, altering what we watch or manipulating what we
read?"

"You mean, like the name Wally Copel?" Blaine asked,
his eyes narrowing.

A tense silence formed over the interview.

Confused, Wally tilted his head.

"I'm sorry—"

"Don't play with me, Wally—if that's even your real
name. Or, is it Clay?"

Wally's face went pale, slack.

"I don't know what you're talking about."

"Clay Powell?"

Wally cleared his throat and readjusted himself in the
seat.

"You know you had me going for a while," Blaine said.
"Of all the folks who have come by here, wanting to know
what happened to me in Maven, you were the only one who
had me convinced that you were actually genuine. Boy!
Was I wrong? Turns out you're just like the rest of them,
just a man who wants something from me. So, Clay, what
you want from me? You want to know if I killed your
grandfather?"

Wally paused.

"Well, did you?" he asked.

"I told you," Blaine said with a stern expression gripping
his face, "it was Bach who killed your grandfather. You believe me, don't you?"

Once more, Wally paused.

"Yes," he said, eventually. "I do. *But*," Wally started as he stood up quickly, "I don't believe this." Wally removed the camera from the tripod and slammed it on the table. "I saw things *in here*," he said, pointing at the camera, "that didn't happen. Last night, it showed me things that—I swear on my mother's grave—were altered, my words, even your exact words, changed. And the business card-thing, okay, I admit it, that was all my idea."

"Why not just tell me that you were related to Powell?"

"I figured if I used my real name, then you wouldn't have done the interview."

"You don't know that."

"I don't, but what I do know is that these past couple of days, this entire interview, all of it has been tweaked to fit a completely different narrative."

"And what narrative is that, Wally—or Clay?" Blaine asked.

"That the puzzles were all a gimmick, smoke and mirrors to get the townspeople to buy the puzzles, all to profit Powell Printing Press, and that *you* were the one who killed both my grandfather *and* Thomas Bach."

"And you believe it?"

Wally paused for a moment to think about the question.

"No," he hesitated. "I mean, I don't know anymore."

"I didn't kill your grandfather," Blaine said convincingly. "As I stated in the police report, Bach, *not your grandfather*, died in the explosion."

"But why didn't you tell police that my grandfather was already dead? Or that you saw his body under Dark Hill?" asked Wally. "All they knew was that it was my grandfather who died in the explosion."

"*But it wasn't*," Blaine said. "And that's all that matters."

"But why lie?"

Blaine didn't answer the question. Instead, he brought himself back to the time he gave his statement in the hospital. *The lie*, he remembered, as well as the sacrifices he made in order to protect the truth from being unleashed into the world.

As Blaine shook the thought away, he stood up from his seat and walked Wally to that same locked door at the end of the hallway.

"Where you taking me?" asked Wally, as he tailed Blaine.

"There's something if I'd like to show you."

Blaine reached in his pocket and pulled out a key.

Before he unlocked the door, he turned to Wally and said, "What I'm about to show you doesn't leave this room, you hear?"

"How can I agree to something I don't even know what it is?" Wally said back.

"I'm asking you to trust me, Clay."

Wally took a moment. Then, he nodded his head.

"After you," he said.

Blaine unlocked the door, revealing the guest room, which had been converted to a puzzle gallery. On each wall were Chosen puzzles that had been framed and mounted. Each one showed the moment leading up to Blaine's death: Blaine sitting in a window-booth while eating lunch as an out-of-control vehicle was about to come barreling through the fast-food restaurant; another one of Blaine working on a lawnmower in the backyard while a rogue lightning bolt was about to strike him dead; then, another one of Blaine grabbing his chest in what appeared like a soon-to-be heart attack as he played with Damiere at Jezebel's house; another of Blaine walking through the parking lot of a shopping center, a round and incredibly bulky shadow looming next to him; then, another of Blaine strolling next to wobbly electric ladder perched against the side of a garden aisle inside a Depot. There were hundreds of these detailed puzzles of Blaine doing everyday activities, like Blaine running errands and whatnot, so many that he couldn't fit them all on the walls. Instead, whenever he received a new puzzle and put it together before that deadline—two minutes after midnight—he'd take one off the wall and stack in the closet, only to make room for yet another one.

"Every month," Blaine said to Wally, "*It* sends me a puzzle. And every month I complete it in time. For the past thirty years, I've been putting together puzzles. For the past thirty years, *It's* been trying to kill me."

Wally wandered over to the puzzles on the wall and stared at them in child-like wonder.

Blaine walked behind Wally to a more recent puzzle. The puzzle was a picture of Blaine sleeping in bed with a tall man dressed in a black hoody looming over him. The mysterious man had a knife glistening in his hand.

"The day I received that one I called the cops and told them about a suspicious man hanging around the house the night before," Blaine told Wally. "That night, after I finished the puzzle before the deadline, cops found a kid who was breaking into cars in the middle of the night. I still wonder if *It* has people out there, tirelessly working for *It*, people like Bach or Christenson or any of the other minions involved in all of those senseless killings."

Wally asked Blaine, "When did you start getting these puzzles?"

"Ever since I left Maven."

"But the printing press was destroyed."

"That's what I thought."

Blaine walked over to the latest puzzle he finished, which he recently framed. The puzzle showed Blaine pushing Damiere on a swing set—"The Swings," he called the puzzle.

Like "The Swings," he had names for each puzzle: "Playground;" "The Park;" "The Lightning Bolt;" "The Steak Knife;" "The Kid;" "The Vandal;" "The Drunk Driver;" "The Obsessed Fan;" "The Man in Black;" "The Nail;" "The Slip;" "Insurgence;" "Slaughter;" Wrong Pill;" "Angry White Man;" "Jezebel's Plight."

Blaine looked over every inch and detail of the latest puzzle; but, for the life of him, except for the suspicious-looking hawk flying overhead, he couldn't find any imminent danger in the puzzle.

He flipped over the box and read from the labels on the corner of the box.

"This one here was printed in New Jersey." Blaine showed Wally, then pulled out another box from the back of the closet. "This one was printed in Connecticut." Another. "South Carolina." He handed Wally the box in which the puzzle was shipped in. "Every now and then," Blaine said, "I'll call up the manufacturers and ask them about the puzzle and they'll have absolutely no recollection of the puzzle—*how* it was sent, *when* it was sent. The puzzle wasn't even in their systems. Yet, it was. It's like this evil moves from one place to another, like a virus, sort of like myself back in the day, always moving, never settling. It's almost like It's trying to throw me off or something. I did some research after my last puzzle and found out the press in New Jersey is one of those on-demand printing presses and that most of their orders come in through the Internet. So, I started to think: *It'd be the perfect place to disguise itself,* wouldn't it? *Of all places, the Internet.* On the upside, I don't mind putting together the puzzles. Hell! The puzzles help keep my mind sharp."

Wally asked, "But how in the hell can you live like that, Blaine, knowing that there's something out there trying to kill you? How do you do it, Blaine? Don't you think you should tell somebody about this? Someone who specializes in—"

"—In *what* exactly?"

"I don't know," Wally stuttered. "The supernatural. How about a priest?"

Blaine laughed to himself.

"A priest can't help me."

"Then, who can?"

Blaine shook his head.

"Nobody can," he said and faced Wally. "Let me ask you something, Clay, if you don't mind. Why now? You had years to confront me about what happened to your grandfather. Why now, Clay?"

Wally hung his head for a moment and thought long and hard about the question.

Then, he shrugged his shoulders and walked to the puzzle, Wrong Pill. Which showed Blaine standing in front of the bathroom mirror, about to pop a "tainted" pill into his mouth.

"My father died when I was just a kid," Wally said. "Overdose. My mother, my real one that is, died some years before. From what I heard, she had problems too. I didn't know much about either one of them. My father's sister was basically my mom. She raised me. Never spoke a word about my father or his father. For years, I felt as if there was a force guiding me along a path where the only end was behind a jail cell, like nature was trying to correct itself and wipe out a bad gene. After I dropped out of high school, I found myself following in my father's footsteps. But I realized the drinking was all a front, an immediate distraction that was pushing me farther away from the truth. One night I woke up covered in my own shit and vomit, not knowing how in the hell I wound up in this strange place. My clothes were drenched in blood. It was that moment when I realized the only way to overcome this problem was to peel back the layers of lies that my mom fed me for all those years whenever I brought up her brother's name and confront the truth. Most importantly, I had to confront myself."

"Now, you see, Clay."

Wally wandered around the room and once more, looked over each puzzle but this time more closely.

"*It's* keeping you here," Wally said with clarity. "*It's* punishing you."

"You see now, don't you, Clay? This is my prison." Blaine turned away and mumbled to himself, "My hell."

"Blaine," Wally said, closer, "*you're* only punishing yourself by carrying this *secret* around with you. You need to tell somebody. Unburden yourself. Set it free once and for all—"

"—But I'm telling you, *Clay*." Once more, Blaine faced Wally. "Forget about the videos. If there's one thing I've learned about this. . . *thing*. . . *It* can't touch what's in here." Blaine pointed to Wally's temple. "You may be able to fool you with what you *see* or what you *read*, but It can't fool the light inside you. Memories, the good and the bad. Every now and then, the light shines the brightest on the bad because it's the light, Clay, that's reminding us that the bad does *exist* beyond the good, dwelling in the darkest corners in each and every one of us. But you see that the good *cannot* be touched by the bad—or the evil or whatever—and vice versa. But it's what we do, Clay, with the bad that makes us who we are. We can either let the bad consume us, even destroy us—as it once did me—or we can learn how to live with it. Like a nuisance hanging in the corner of the room, you know It's there, nagging at you. And you do everything in your power to ignore It. Most of the time all It wants is attention. And sometimes we have to give It attention, talk to It, ask It what It wants," Blaine grinned, "set aside one day out of the month for It and put together a puzzle. Most importantly, we have to treat It with the utmost compassion and try to understand It and why It does the nasty things It does. And I guess. . . that's what I've been trying to do ever since my Mira was taken away from me: trying to decipher the Darkness by shining my light on the places those chose not to see."

⊞

A little over a month after Blaine last spoke to Wally, he received an unexpected knock on the front door.

He and Damiere were in the living room watching a VHS tape of The Jam taking on The Rex Brothers in a tag team match with Too Smooth, a longtime rival who agreed to partner up with The Jam only if The Jam's flamboyant, rambunctious manager, Chrome Daddy, would be Too Smooth's butler for a week.

Curious, Blaine checked the front door, only to find a UPS deliveryman scurrying through the lawn, which was covered in five inches of snow.

Blaine thanked the skittish driver before he got back into his truck and looked down at the package on the front step.

"You're late," Blaine said, worried about the timing of the arrival.

He carefully picked up the package and held it close to his body.

The address read: "Lexington, Kentucky."

"Kentucky, huh?"

Blaine walked back inside the house and while Damiere continued to watch the wrestling match on TV, he crept into the other room. He already had everything set up and laid out, the empty tumbler, the bottle of liquor, the freshly rolled cigarette. Everything was ready and in place. Blaine set the package on the table and opened it. . .

Inside was a new puzzle, as expected.

Blaine couldn't help but laugh at the absurdity of the puzzle. He was standing in a defensive stance on a familiar highway not too far from his house. From the whiteness of the road, Blaine could tell it had recently been salted. Parked not too far away was his car, which appeared all dented up, the windows cracked as well as shattered, the passenger seat caved in and covered in long slash marks. In the open trunk sat a couple of worn boxes of old wrestling memorabilia. Other cars were parked all around Blaine, the drivers inside watching intensely, as he stood in the middle of the highway with Damiere clinging to his leg. Circling around Blaine was a ravenous pride of lions, each one ready to tear into Blaine, as well as his grandson. One particular detail stood out the most and that was what Blaine had on. He was dressed like he was today, khakis, dark green cardigan, collared shirt, checked socks, wingtips. However, worn on top of the cardigan was his patent pink Jam vest. He also wore his old wrestling gloves, both as worn and crusty as chapped leather. Both his hands were curled into fists and he appeared as if he was ready to take on each lion in a battle to the death. Blaine smirked at the moment captured in the puzzle, the randomness of it. He placed the puzzle aside and walked back into the living room. For a moment, he stood behind the couch and watched Damiere and the way his head was cocked back, eyes glued to the screen. It had been a while since Blaine had felt any joy in what he used to do for a living; however, when Blaine saw Damiere's fascination in the wrestling match, he couldn't help but smile.

Damiere sensed his poppa's presence. He turned his head over his shoulder, saw his poppa, and then stood from his seated position on the carpet.

"Do we have to leave?" asked Damiere, pouting.

"No," Blaine said patiently. "Not if you don't want to."

Damiere shook his head.

"I wanna stay."

Blaine paused for a moment and turned to the front door.

"I have an idea," Blaine said. "Want to put together a puzzle or go outside and build us a snowman?"

Damiere thought about the question for a moment, the two options.

"Snowman."

Blaine turned to the other room behind him and closed the door.

"I guess the puzzle can wait," he said to himself.

As Blaine grabbed Damiere's coat from the kitchen, Damiere stopped the tape in the VHS player and switched the input back to cable where the news had just received a BREAKING NEWS report.

The anchor was talking about a bunch of lions that escaped from the zoo.

"Lions, huh?" Blaine said, as he strolled back into the living room and helped Damiere slip his arm into the coat.

Whatever you do, do not approach the lions. They are considered very dan—

Blaine turned off the TV before Damiere could get lost in the story.

"But what about the lions?" asked Damiere.

"The lions can wait," Blaine said. "We have a snowman to build."

He walked Damiere into the kitchen where he helped him put on his boots. On the way out, Blaine grabbed the car keys from the kitchen countertop.

Just in case he changed his mind.

THE frayed primrose yellow signs taped around two of the eight Doric columns, which guarded the entranceway of the historic *Bakerford Hall*, read:

THE DARK LECTURES:
MONSTER MYSTERIES REVEALED
GUEST SPEAKER:
AUTHOR, NEIL REDDY

Underneath the bold black caption of each flyer, which was "thrown together" at the eleventh hour by an art history major named Steve Windle on a trial version of Photoshop, was a disfigured silhouette of a horned beast hunching like an old, doddery man with crippling-arthritis over a secluded seaside town crookedly sitting on a hill overlooking the turbulent North Sea. The sea, vast in its own right, with whitecap waters raging against the sides of bluffs, the perfectly round hills, the quaint Scottish town, and then that frail-looking giant, were all monochrome and grainy from the poor scan of a photocopy machine but still visible enough to entice guests.

A sudden gust of wind tore one of the many promotional signs from the side of the building and sent it whimsically skipping across the front steps until it stuck to the back of Anissa's calf.

Standing alone in front of Bakerford Hall, the young sophomore reached down and peeled away the yellow flyer from her panty hose, which acted like Velcro.

Shivering from the chill, she gave the flyer a glance-over. Then, after a survey across the empty parking lot, she held the flyer above her head and released it into the wind, causing it to flap away like a paper bird into the night darkness.

She folded her arms across her chest as if, by hugging herself, they would make her feel warmer. The gesture gave her only temporary comfort.

"Where the hell are you, Kali?" Anissa said to herself.

To the right of her, she heard the metallic *clank* of what she might've thought was a sign of some sort banging against something. A building perhaps?

Without anything else to do but just wait here like easy prey, she turned to the noise and swore she spotted somebody—a shadow—darting around the other side of Bakerford Hall. Shadows, noises, the cold and the dark, being all-alone, were all triggers to negativity. She couldn't help but think about all of those "creepos" who had been busted with their pants down—both literally and figuratively—last week for the recent attacks against other students, particularly women students.

Anissa, whose father had been on The Force for over twenty-something years, once told her, "Expect for the worse and hope for the best."

Prepared for the absolute worst, Anissa, who considered herself "old school" for still rocking the purse, brandished a can of Mace from her nifty bag of goodies just in case some creepo decided to run up on her.

As she reaffirmed her grip around the Mace, the can suddenly slipped from her grip and went rolling toward the stairs.

With her body leaned forward like a hunchback, Anissa ran after the can and as the can was about to roll over the edge of the top step of the steep stairway, a brilliant white sneaker with a wiggly red swoosh lifted upright like a stern salut and with the sole, gently pressed against the can of Mace, prevented it from tumbling down the stairs.

Anissa's eyes trailed upward and landed on a shadowy-faced man kneeling down. She carefully followed him as he reached down and picked up the Mace underneath his sneaker and then handed to her while, at the same time, carrying a smile that lasted well after their encounter. During their handoff, the man's index finger grazed the side of Anissa's hand.

"I *believe* you dropped this, ma'am," he said, his voice silky smooth.

Anissa was left utterly speechless by the older man's charm; however, his outfit was another story. He wore a white suit with a red shirt underneath—the top two buttons unbuttoned, exposing several curlicues of chest hair. He had long white hair with hidden shades of deep-dark highlights that looked like a finely combed horse's mane draped over both his shoulders. He had eyes as green as emeralds and when the moon hit them, they gave off a bogus glass-eyed shine. Not to mention the scar on his face. Which should've creeped out Anissa. But strangely, she felt comfort in it. He was a man who had traveled many miles. A wise and compassionate man. She figured he had the scar ever since he was a mischievous little boy who had learned his lesson at a young age for playing too hard.

"Ah—thanks," Anissa drawled, as the white-haired man walked inside Bakerford Hall.

Anissa found herself holding back a laugh, not from the comic-book character look of the man, but from the complete randomness of their encounter. Not only just that! But the fact he appeared out of nowhere! She put aside his toothy smile—I mean, Anissa thought, *nobody smiles like that anymore, unless you're some nut job who just escaped from Cornerstone.*

In annoyance, Anissa checked her watch twice to make sure she was reading the time right. The "event" started around nine o'clock and it was already a quarter past nine.

She told herself *two more minutes* and she was going in without Kali.

Plus, she recently got over a nasty cold, which had lasted for a good two weeks and other than lugging around a headful of phlegm while dragging herself to class with a box of tissues, it was nice to get out of the apartment, phlegm-free.

After the two minutes were up, Kali was still a no-show.

"Screw it," Anissa said, as she checked her watch one last time.

As Anissa was about to head inside, she heard yet another *clanking* sound but this time much closer. The noise was so close that it rattled Anissa.

With the can of Mace held tight in her hand, she surveyed the night but didn't see anything suspicious. Which made her even more skittish.

As she turned back around, Kali was standing right in front of her. . .

She saw her face but only in a flash.

"*Surprise!*" she yelped.

On impulse, Anissa suddenly closed her eyes and sprayed Mace in Kali's face.

Kali grabbed her face and screamed out, "What the hell, Anissa!"

"Sorreee," she whined.

"Sorry?"

Kali started to claw at her face.

"Don't rub them," Anissa urged Kali, as she examined Kali's face. She could hardly open her eyes and when she did, her eyes were so bloodshot.

Kali cried out, "It burns! It burns!"

Anissa couldn't have been more sorry; in fact, every other word that shot out of her mouth was either *sorry* or another version of *sorry*.

She dug through all of the junk in her purse and finally pulled out a tissue. The tissue was balled up and possibly carried a dried-out snot rocket.

Despite the grossness, she steadied Kali's head and wiped as much of the Mace from her eyes as she could.

"I heard milk helps with the burning," Anissa said.

"Sure," Kali snapped. "Let me pull some milk out of my ass! You know me and how I always be carrying around milk with me everywhere I go—"

"—How about your nipples? I read somewhere that most women start lactating at the age of eighteen—"

"—Very funny, Anissa."

Anissa couldn't help but laugh at the comment.

Kali smacked Anissa on the arm.

"I'm trying to help, Kali. Chill."

"Chill?"

"Don't be so overdramatic."

"Overdramatic?"

"—Don't get mad at me, Kali."

"Nah. I ain't mad at you," she said politely. Then widened her red eyes. She snapped, "I'm going to blind cuz of you!"

"You're overacting, Kali. You're not going to be blind."

"Me? Overacting?" Kali took a pivot-like step away from Anissa. "Says the one who shot mace all up in my face."

"You're the one who about gave me a heart attack."

"Now, it's all my fault, huh?"

Kali started to cry and the tears made her eyes burn even worse.

Anissa had no other choice than to console her by hugging-it-out with Kali.

"I'm sorry, Ness," Kali said with her head down, "the way you were standing there, it was like you were begging for a scare."

Anissa let out a relieving sigh.

"You still wanna go inside?" asked Anissa, tilting her head to the side.

Kali sniffled and said finally, "I dunno."

"This is supposed to be fun. Remember?"

"Fun for you maybe—"

"—By the way, I saw a lot of hot guys going inside."

Kali lit up.

"Really?"

"Shit yeah."

"How long you been waiting here?" asked Kali, wincing as she cleared away leftover Mace from her cheeks.

"Long enough," Anissa said emotionlessly, as she shot a glance at the desolate parking lot.

※

INSIDE a half-full Bakerford Hall stood author, movie critic, and college professor, Neil Reddy, behind the podium. He was dressed in a corduroy jacket that looked as if it came from a time period when mustaches were not a trend but a bold statement of masculinity. Underneath the jacket, he wore a red polo shirt, which was a size too small.

Directly behind Neil was a projection of the *Headless Horseman*, who was—as Neil described—a fictional character in *The Legend of Sleepy Hollow*, which was a story written by New York native Washington Irving.

In the slide, the Headless Horseman was depicted without a head—hence the name "Headless"—riding on horseback and carrying a pumpkin in his hand while chasing down Ichabod Crane.

Neil changed the slide; the sudden flick of light in the dark auditorium caused a momentary dizzy spell.

On the projection behind Neil shone a gloomy picture of Victor Frankenstein and his twisted creation.

"I'm sure most—if not—all of you have heard of the legendary monster often depicted with two massive bolts projected from the sides of its neck. Some of you may have even dressed up as it for Halloween." Neil turned to the hazy audience and through the glare of the projector, said to them, "Anybody? Please raise your hand if you went trick-or-treating as Frankenstein when you were a child." Just a few students in the audience timidly raised their hands. Neil changed yet another slide to a more "commercialized," a more "Americanized" monster: a pea green-faced, square-headed, crinkle-lipped, cartoonish abomination with zigzag "stitch marks" uniformly running across its neck. "*So*," Neil emphasized to the audience, "for those of you who raised your hand, you *all* should know that I am, in fact, in the wrong when I referred to the monster as the name of its creator, Victor Frankenstein, even though popular American culture has widely referred to the monster simply as Frankenstein. So, wrong! But thanks for playing."

Several students awkwardly laughed from Neil's dry sense of humor; however, most of them weren't at all pleased by his remarks.

During the break of silence, he heard one of them in the front row saying sarcastically to the student next to him: "That's original."

The student hushed him.

Neil ignored the students and proceeded with the lecture.

"The monster was first introduced in the novel, *Frankenstein; or, The Modern Prometheus*, which was—get this—published anonymously in 1818; however, it wasn't until five years later that the author's name was known. Her name was Mary Shelley; and it's fair to say Shelley, who—believe it or not—was no older than most of you in this auditorium when she wrote the novel, introduced the world to one of the most erroneous characters to date." From the confused expressions on the students' faces, he could tell half of them didn't even know what the word *erroneous* meant. He witnessed a few of their faces light up from the glow of their smartphones. "In the novel," he continued, "*Frankenstein; or, The Modern Prometheus*, Frankenstein's monster is often identified as the 'monster,' or 'creature,' 'demon,' even the word 'it.' However, if there's anything Shelley's novel taught us—besides raising the ultimate questions such as 'Who is our maker?' and 'Why are we put here?' which is understandable, considering the age that the novel was written—it's the *undoing* left behind man's greatest adversary: himself. The resulted abomination of man simply going by his or her means to play god? Which brings us to our next monster in literature."

Neil changed the slide.

"Doctor Jekyll and Mister Hyde," he turned around and glanced at the image behind him. "In Robert Louis Stevenson's novel, *Strange Case of Dr Jekyll and Mr Hyde*, Doctor Jekyll creates a serum in order to help 'mask' the evil urges inside him, thus creating an 'alter ego.'"

Neil changed yet another the slide.

"*Dracula* is next on our list. You may know him as the vampire Dra-*coo*-la or Count Dracula or that white dude with fangs who sucks the blood from your neck, particularly from 'young' attractive women." Neil glanced down at the front row where a couple of young female students were sitting. "*Or*," Neil said over the pause, "that one guy who turns into a bat. But did you know," Neil changed the slide, which showed a werewolf, "Dracula and the werewolf have much more in common than you may think. In the controversial *Dracula's Guest*, a short story published posthumously seventeen years after *Dracula*, the popular vampire was considered to be depicted as a werewolf. Which instantly brings to mind the ability to shapeshift into creatures other than hu-man. No doubt Stoker's character inspired many interpretations of the classic vampire," Neil changed several slides showing various kinds of vampires, as well as werewolves, in movies and television. "Characters described and on many occasions, identified as 'creatures' of the night, 'demons,' 'devils,' 'things,' '*its*,' or 'manifestations,' most importantly, 'monsters,' the same ones we see in the movies we watch, all inspired by real-life humans." Neil changed the slide showing a gory still taken from filmmaker Francis Ford Coppola's 1992 adaptation of "*Dracula*" to a slide showing a painting of "Vlad the Impaler, who was believed to be the sole inspiration behind the fictional character."

Neil sped along changing slides.

"Now, what about the non-human monsters, more primitive ones that kill *not* based on 'evil' or some 'hidden force,' a 'superiority or 'vanity,' but merely as a means of survival?" Behind Neil was an image of a dark sea monster crushing a boat in two with its massive tentacles. "We begin with the kraken, which is often depicted as a 'giant squid.' You can also find other sea monsters in Herman Melville's *Moby-Dick* or Jules Verne's *Twenty Thousand Leagues Under the Sea: A Tour of the Underwater World.*" Neil continued to change slides. "Let's go further back to the Tanakh—which is also known as the Hebrew Bible. This particular sea monster, which, like the kraken, has also been depicted as various creatures. In this particular case, a crocodile, a hippopotamus, or even a whale. The *leviathan*," Neil stumbled with the word as soon as it reached his lips. He found himself drifting from thought once he spoke that one particular word *leviathan*.

A distant memory came to him, one so distant it nearly left him breathless. He witnessed his younger self—not young enough to be a boy but not old enough to be a man— falling through a sheet of ice on Bleu's Lake.

Then, the previous word, *kraken*, flooded his thoughts.

The feeling—or lack of—escaping from his body. The numbness, then a hand grabbing hold of his ankle in the black water below, as he violently kicked and thrashed through frigid water, every muscle in his body tightening, making it harder to squeeze his hands. He didn't exactly know whether or not it was his nerves screwing with him and squeezing certain parts of his body. This must've been the first time Neil experienced such pain, his great pain. Then, that cryptic sound jolted him like an electric shock. The sheets of ice *cracking* all around him as he desperately tried to climb from the frigid waters. Neil never knew water, a necessity for everyday survival, could cause so much pain. However, that noise, the awful *cracking*, deep and resonant yet, at times, as sharp as glass.

Neil canceled the sound of ice cracking and changed the next slide to another monster.

"Cerberus," Neil said with his throat tightening. "In ancient Greek mythology, Cerberus is often depicted as a three-headed dog guarding the gates of the underworld. Other depictions show Cerberus standing next to Hades, god of the underworld." He threw in a little dry humor: "God's best friend, right?"

The comment drew a couple of laughs from the audience.

Before Neil changed the slide, another image came to mind: Three black Labrador Retrievers barking at Neil as two of the neighborhood kids extended a broken tree branch toward Neil.

Why three dogs?

The neighborhood kid—*Paul*, he thought—went everywhere with the dogs and if it wasn't for them, Neil would've never made it out of Bleu's Lake alive. Neil remembered one of them clamping the sleeve of his coat with its teeth and pulling him from the water since the branch wasn't helping at all.

While Neil was on the subject of "Greek mythology," the next slide showed an image of the "Cyclops, the one-eyed giant."

That kid, Paul, he, too, had one eye. Well, not entirely. The year before Neil's near-drowning experience, Paul was hit in the eye with a hockey puck and he lost part of his vision and every time the kid slapped around the puck, he had to wear a patch over his "bad" eye because the doctor said he was one more hit away from losing his vision.

Following the Cyclops, Neil showed a slide of Leshy roaming through the forest, then another slide of the ape-like creature, "Sasquatch"—best known as Bigfoot.

When Neil was younger, he and the few neighborhood friends he had used to call Paul's dad "Sasquatch" because he was big and hairy like one.

Neil thought more about the slides and why they were arranged in that particular order with Cerberus following the sea monster and then the Cyclops following Leshy and Sasquatch. He didn't remember arranging slides like that. Maybe, before the lecture, a student had messed with the slides.

"*Monsters,*" Neil finally said, as if he was muscling through the word. He refocused his eyes on the upcoming slides. "Myths," Neil continued, "legends, inspired by the nature around us."

Neil cleared his throat and as he reached down to pick up the perspired glass of water, his hand nearly slipped. He regained control and took a sip of water. Even the way the water sloshed down his throat felt as if he was swallowing sludge. He tried not to think of words like *sludge* or *mud*—for some reason, these words reminded him of the word *vomit*, "trigger words," and the last thing he wanted to do was vomit all over the podium in front of hundreds of curious eyes—and cameras. He thought about the idea of becoming a trend or viral sensation: "Monster writer pukes all over the stage in front of audience." Talk about embarrassment! It'd be one thing to vomit all over the stage in front of an audience without the risk of being filmed. In today's age, with people's shortened attention spans, it'd all be forgotten, like Neil's own "incident" on the frozen lake, a distant memory left to surrender and fade. But once the video wound up on the Internet, it'd be there for eternity; and every time Neil wanted to rehash an embarrassing moment in his life, all he'd have to do was type in the word *author*, then his name, *Neil Reddy*, and the word, *vomit*, into the search engine and voila! The verbal diarrhea that spewed from the dankest, hairiest corners of the Internet: "Feast your eyeballs on The Tool of *all* Tools who hurled up his momma's spaghettiOs all over the micrOphone."

Powering through the lecture, Neil adjusted the mic and darkened out his audience by concentrating on the circular light before him.

"Take the legendary chupacabra," he said, "Spanish for goat-sucker. The chupacabra was a creature that didn't fail to live up to its name. It was also known to kill other livestock, including sheep and other farm animals, by sucking the blood from their bodies. Remind you of someone?"

Neil changed the slide, which was one that he showed earlier in the lecture, the one of Dracula.

"In this instance, you have a fictional character, like Dracula, inspiring—dare I say—fueling the imaginations of those who claim they have a legend right in their own backyard. When it comes to monsters, the door swings both ways."

91

Neil changed a slide to a gnarly-looking fox with sores covering its dead body.

"There have been many cases in the Americas of the legendary blood-sucking chupacabra; however, in this particular case, experts concluded that it was simply a fox with a parasite." Neil turned his shoulder and examined the picture of the dead fox. "As you can tell from the raw areas on the body, this particular creature was infected by a skin disease, *mange*; and for those who don't know what mange is, it's caused by parasitic mites—and although rare, *yes*, for those of you who are wondering, it can be transmitted to humans."

The comment received a more verbal rise out of several members of the audience.

"How about this one?" asked Neil, loosening up.

He changed the slide, which showed a CLOSE-UP of a dark figure with a long neck and giraffe-like head poking out of what looked like a body of water.

Neil asked the audience, "Can anybody guess the name of this particular monster?"

Right off the bat, several students yelled out in unison, "Loch Ness Monster."

"Loch Ness Monster," Neil repeated. Then, "Are you sure?"

He changed several slides repeatedly, one after another, which displayed the same exact image, however, each one had panned farther out until it reached the last slide, which showed the hairy back of a shirtless man and the supposed "Loch Ness Monster" happened to be an infected hair follicle.

"No," Neil said in a dry tone, "but, again, thanks for playing!"

Neil changed the slide, which showed the famous "Surgeon's photograph" that was taken in 1934.

"Here is the 'real' Loch Ness Monster—Nessie, as the Scots call the creature—*or*, is it simply a toy submarine? Elaborate hoaxes? Nothing more than campfire stories we tell those with innocent ears and imaginative minds? Or, is it just another one of those bizarre cases where a simple 'lie' or 'false' account or even a 'joke' becomes a legend in its own right?"

Neil changed several slides showing several different monsters.

"The Jersey Devil," Neil listed, "the Nandi Bear, Yeti— or what most of you know as the 'Abominable' Snowman— the giant Windigo; the manticore; or Basilisk, a mythical reptile known to kill those with its gaze. Sound familiar?"

Neil changed the slide to one of Medusa, a Greek mythological figure who had snakes for hair and the power to turn any mortal to stone with a single gaze.

Then, Neil kept changing slides.

"The mare—similar to the demon incubus—is said to haunt those while they slept, resulting in nightmares. Other stories involved the mare 'riding' the chest of people. As I mentioned before, the incubus that takes the form of a man, has a female counterpart, which is known as the suc- cubus. Like its male counterpart, the succubus appears during one's sleep and unlike the incubus, it seduces men."

Two male students in the front row started to tease, one saying during the silences between slide-changes that he had himself one helluva sexy *succubus* visit him last night in his dorm room and when he woke up the next morning, his boxers were all sticky-icky.

"*Banshees*," Neil said louder, trying to drown out the per- vert in the front row. "Sirens. Poltergeist, which is Ger- man for 'noisy ghost.' Or, the folklore of the flying head known as Penanggalan; the changeling or ogbanje; golems; the 'man-eating' Rakshasa; selkie; púca, even the 'combus- tible' gumberoo, which derived from lumberjack folklore— yes, just look it up, Google it, there is such a thing as 'lum- berjack folklore.' Then, if you turn toward movies, you have monsters inspired by animals or even animals depicted as monsters, such as the feeding machine that is the great white shark in Spielberg's classic, *Jaws*, or the dinosaurs in *Jurassic Park. Cujo, Planet of the Apes*, Brundlefly in the movie, *The Fly*: all treated or depicted as monsters. Then, you have devils in disguise: *The Witches of Eastwick*; *Rosemary's Baby*; *The Omen*; *The Exorcist*, all monsters. Then, aliens:

the Xenomorph in *Alien*; the Blob in the movie *The Blob*. *The Thing*. Now," he changed more slides at rapid speed, "let's look at plants: the pods in *Invasion of the Body Snatchers*; the giant venus fly trap in *Little Shop of Horrors*, the veins in *The Ruins*; the tomatoes in *Attack of the Killer Tomatoes*." More students laughed at the latest slide of *Killer Tomatoes*. Neil changed the slide. On the screen displayed a still from the movie, *Nightmare on Elm Street*. "How about a 'man' with burn marks on his face? Not so scary. But, otherwise, effective in its terror to haunt its prey while he or she sleeps." He changed more slides. "Then the iconic monsters such as vampires, werewolves, and mummies. Don't forget zombies—which seem to be one of the more 'popular' monsters today. Then you have *Godzilla*, *King Kong*, the Creature in *The Creature from the Black Lagoon*: these are considered monsters, for instance, a character like *King Kong*, meant to draw sympathy from the viewer, is considered probably one of the most controversial monsters to date, a monster worshipped yet feared by many, and *yet*, a monster whose heart was surprisingly captured by the most unlikely source, a beautiful blonde haired starlet. If such a terrorizing figure like *King Kong* can find love, then what does that say about man's interpretation of what a monster should be? Which ultimately begs questions: Are monsters reflections of our own selves, be it warped or exaggerated? Why do monsters exist at all? Are they used as devices in order to understand our own identities? Or, are they used simply for entertainment? To scare us? Like ghosts? *The Boogeyman*? A slasher? Creature? Archetypes specifically used to flesh out our greatest fears in order to overcome and inevitably, defeat them? With that said, are all monsters considered bad or evil? And why are 'we' the ones who get to determine who or who isn't a monster? Is it based on actions or behavior? Or, *looks*? Is a monster considered a 'monster' because it, he or she, doesn't look like us? Or, sound like us? Or, dress like us? Or, even act like us? Are unknown species—still unidentified by man—considered monsters? How about an animal that lives among the shadows? Or, do we label these unexplainable 'forces' as monsters in fear of the truth of reality? Is it our own coping mechanism to triumph over our own internal battles? Or, are the labeling, and 'shaming' of 'different' life forms as monsters, such as a fellow man, animal, or plant, man's self-righteous attempt to prove worthiness of others? A half-ass attempt to climb the ladder of social status or hierarchy? *Or,* is it in our DNA—our fabric—to paint with broad brushes and without any diagnosis, categorize 'things' that we do *not* understand as monsters?" Neil walked to the very edge of the stage and peered out into the dimly lit audience. "Most importantly," Neil said directly to the audience, "what is a monster?"

♦

AT the table, Neil was signing the first pages of his new novel, *The Monster Inside Us: The Oral History of the Monster,* for his Readers. Neil didn't put much stock into his signature; in fact, Neil signed his John Hancock like he signed for UPS packages, quick and painless, with a swooping archway of an N followed by a wavy line and then ending the first name with a rabbit ear of a loop, which was supposed to be a L, then the last name, sloppier than the first, starting with a letter R, which closely resembled a number 2, followed by scribble that could pass as a mountainous landscape with a sharp crag, which was supposed to be a Y.

During each encounter, he'd ask for the Reader's name, scribble his signature on their personalized copy of his book, then smile for a Reader and most importantly, *thank* the Reader. Neil wasn't much of a smiling man, but he'd force himself to smile for anybody who showed the least amount of interest in him. He did this over and over for each Reader, signing and smiling, smiling and signing, until his wrist and cheeks grew sore.

After the first wave of Readers passed, the crowd started to thin out.

Neil was approached by the same older man from earlier, the one in the striking white suit. The sight of the strange man sent a ripple of nausea through Neil's gut.

Neil didn't know whether or not it was the way the man smelled—his body odor reeking of rotten fruit—but the sight alone of the white-haired man caused him to pause for a moment while his mind raced to locate where exactly he had seen him before. Neil froze in thought: An image of the darkened audience initially came to mind, a horse-haired man in the back of the audience, grinning, and that white suit of his dancing like a floater in the corner of his eye.

As the strange man hunched over the signing table, Neil got a better look at his face.

Immediately what stood out was a dime-sized starfish-like scar right below his right eye. Immediately, Neil thought gunshot wound; the word *gun* ringing in his head. Before the man could utter a word, Neil had the man's entire story running through his mind. The word *felon* was used throughout; then *ex*, specifically the letter X; then two x's drawn over both his eyes representing the cartoon-like portrayal of death.

He reached into his white sports coat in the same position as a shoulder holster. All Neil could think about was *gun*—a popular one, like a Smith and Wesson—and for a moment, he imagined the *handle* of a gun tucked underneath the assassin's armpit.

Neil braced himself, everything in his body braced, including major organs.

Then, relief came over him as he pulled out a crinkled, partially torn paperback from inside. He then placed the old book on the table. Neil was more focused on the stranger's gnarly nails and the dirt underneath them than the book that was he placed before him.

Neil turned his focus on the book, *his* book. He picked it up as if he was picking up a wild animal. He held it close to his face.

The title of the book read: *The Dark One at The Landing*.

The faded cover showed a painting of a young, skinny, exhausted Indian boy at the end of his difficult westerly journey across America. He was slouched over a perfect rectangular cutout in the scorched desert landscape with a range of snowcapped mountains in the background. The opening in the hardpan appeared to be a secret door leading to a secret room—or dungeon-like "chamber"—with a staircase leading into the earth below. The boy's warped shadow stretched along the steep sides of the opening as if the darkness was tugging on an elastic shadow.

"Where did you find this?" asked Neil, more curious in the book than the man behind it.

"The one place where one can find anything he or she desires," he said charmingly.

"*The Internet*," they both said in classical jinx-style.

Neil wasn't even about to buy the man a coke, but he'd gladly give him a John Hancock.

"That's something," Neil said, shaking his head in disbelief. "This baby was published when I was—"

"—Twenty-two years old," the strange man finished Neil's sentence.

Neil paused.

"That long ago, huh?" he drawled.

"Funny how fast time flies when you're living the dream," he said.

Neil hesitated, was tempted to correct the man.

"Well, I'm glad there's someone out there who enjoyed it," Neil said, clearing his throat. "If Readers knew how hard it was for me to write this book," he said, as he carelessly flipped over the book, "then maybe it would've been more successful."

"But it was successful, *for you*, to be able to write in detail about something so personal. . . about American life, about your father."

Emotion ran from Neil's face, leaving it as austere as the hardpan on the cover.

"It's only fiction."

"Yes, of course, but where does one draw the line between fiction and nonfiction?"

"With facts," Neil said bluntly and then asked for the man's name before signing the book.

The strange man hesitated.

"Sergey Tavitian," he said with a grin creeping onto his face. "Just make it out to Serg."

"Just Serg?"

"Yes."

"Easy enough."

"S-e-r-g?"

"That's right," the man confirmed.

Neil signed the book and handed it back to the strange man, who called himself Serg but Neil was pretty sure that really wasn't his name.

During the handing of the book, both their hands touched, Serg's finger grazing the side of Neil's hand.

Neil didn't think anything of the touch, even though it appeared deliberate. He made sure to thank the man for taking him down memory lane and then, before he could make sense of the brief yet unexpected interaction, Serg had already vanished into the crowd.

"*Strange*," Neil mumbled to himself.

Another Reader came by the table, wanting her book signed.

Neil signed it.

And then smiled.

❦

IT was starting to rain when Neil left Bakerford—and not like a steady drizzle but a hard and pounding rain, which usually resulted in the Shill River flooding in a matter of hours. Most of the attendance had cleared out, making it easier for Neil to make an uninterrupted escape toward his car.

As soon as Neil stepped outside, he laid his eyes on a couple of groupies disguised as curious-eyed students who were all for picking Neil's brain about monsters; however, he had already seen the flick before: a once-respected professor at The CW gets busted for sleeping around with his students and loses his teaching job and is forever labeled by Internet Mobs as a "creepo" for the rest of his sorry existence.

From first glance, the two attractive, provocatively-dressed girls were of age, possibly post-grads who didn't want to deal with going back to a home where certain rules were regulated, so they ended up "sticking" around after graduation and finding part-time jobs outside of their business majors.

Neil smiled off the girls as he made a detour around the two; and without feeling the least guilty about his lack of sexual potency yet instead thinking about an alternative route on the way home, Neil headed straight toward his car, which he purposefully parked in the back of the parking lot.

Using the coat to shield his head with one hand and his car key brandished in the other, Neil sprinted to his car.

Once he reached his car, he stopped for a moment and looked back at Bakerford Hall and the spotlight shinning on the columns. He seemed more interested in the Greek architecture of the building than the two attractive girls wanting him, which brought into question his motives for the night.

He unlocked the door without a hitch and hopped inside; and from the rearview mirror, watched the girls scurrying away into the rainy night.

It wasn't until Neil pulled onto the main highway that his mother called him on the hands-free Bluetooth.

As soon as Neil answered the call with a hello and then a drawn out "mom," he realized that someone might be following him. The car tailing him looked like a sedan, dark paint-job, maybe a dark green or midnight blue; halogen lights for sure; however, he couldn't quite tell who was behind the wheel of the car for the cover of night. It could've been maybe one of the two girls from the lecture—"fans gone wild"—however, the more he thought about the notion about the avid "horror" fans wanting to do things to his body, and all of the freaky fetishes some of them were into, like playing "dress-up" and having sex in costumes, the more Neil realized how absurd it sounded in his head. Spending most of his adult career writing about monsters and the certain nocturnal creatures that went bumping in the dark had brought a certain type of "crazy" to slither out of the woodwork; however, Neil didn't have any "hardcore" stalkers—at least none that were worth the trouble or who'd commit bodily harm to Neil.

Keeping the unique halogen headlights in the corner of his eye, Neil mistakenly asked his mahm how she was doing, which was more like a glaring invitation for his mahm to tell him a "story" about how her day had gone.

"Fine," his mahm started out, then followed by telling Neil every little detail that she had done that day, including what she ate for breakfast, then a little "incident" she had at the grocery store, involving a racist checkout clerk trying to overcharge her—in his mahm's point of view, anybody who was ever "rude" to her or showed the least amount of attitude toward her was considered a racist—then her grip about the sudden spike in the cost of regular gasoline and how it nearly cost "twice" of what she normally paid to fill up her green economy-friendly spit of a car that looked as if it ran on batteries, then that lazy "dickweed" of a neighbor's no-good mutt doing a number two in the front yard that John recently sodded and when she got back home from the store, she stepped in a mound of it, like all the way in it, full-on sole to shit, and unknowingly, she ended up carrying the smelly business into the house and stinking up the entire house for a good hour and she and John had to open up the windows in order to air out the house; however, the smell didn't quite compare to the days when Ajay had bowel movements.

Usually, when his mahm got going like this, like, for instance, when she was all revved up from a recent disagreement with John, it was best that he let her tire out and get what she had inside her all the way out through whatever possible orifice she had at her disposal—in most cases, either her eyes—she was a crier—or her mouth. Eventually, the topic of Neil's brother came about, his condition, and how he was running a mild fever last night and they suspected it might've been a urinary tract infection due to the dark color of his urine.

She filled Neil in on a new aide that was starting her first day tomorrow.

A surprising frustration rose inside Neil, borderline anger.

"New aide?" he repeated, as if he didn't hear his mahm correctly the first time she spoke it.

"That's what I said, didn't I?"

"What about Janine?"

"Janine? I thought you knew," Mahm said. "She's moving to Colorado."

"Right," Neil corrected, as an overwhelmingly sense of glum washed over him like a cold, hurtful tide. "I knew that," he said, the end of his words trailing off into a tremble. "I thought she wasn't moving until later this year."

"No," his mahm said. "She's moving next month. Today was her last day."

"Next month, huh?" Then, a dim glint of hope flashed inside him. "Is she going to stop by tomorrow? I mean she has to go over everything with the new aide, right?"

"She doesn't have to. John and I will be here. We can show her what to do."

"What about a meet and greet?"

"We already had it," Mahm said. "Yesterday."

More anger rushed inside Neil, but this time not as violent.

"Why didn't you tell me?" asked Neil. "I'd like to know the person who's going to be looking after my brother when I'm not there."

"I didn't tell you because you were busy with the book tour," Mahm said. "Do not retort, Neil Reddy. I *know* you—don't think I don't. I know how you get before one of your lectures. You're as wound up as John on Sunday Fundays."

The sound of his mahm using "Sunday Funday" as a new word to her vocabulary was clear indication of how Americanized she had become.

"Yeah, but you could've at least filled me in."

"Well, I'm 'filling' you in right *now*, Neil Reddy."

"Okay," he said. "So, I'll stop by tomorrow after class. When does this 'new' aide start?"

"Her name is Kamaria Solarin and her shift starts at eleven o'clock."

Kamaria?

"I won't be able to make it by then," he said, "*but* I can be there at three o'clock."

"We'll be here."

Before Neil hung up with his mahm, he moved his eyes toward the rearview mirror and witnessed the same car following him as he made a right turn onto the highway.

BEFORE heading home, Neil decided to stop at a convenient store called Firsty's, which was located a few minutes away from his apartment.

More worried than curious, he checked the rearview as he pulled into the parking lot and didn't see that same car tailing him anymore.

Relieved, Neil stopped thinking about who might have been following him and listened to his belly, which was murmuring like a bitter, tongue-less old man.

As soon as he entered an empty Firsty's, he went straight to the candy bar section in the first aisle and spent a few minutes contemplating whether he wanted peanut butter or nuget. The first bar, *Polar Bear*, was filled with both peanut butter and peanuts and topped with white chocolate. One of man's greatest concoctions—as Neil referred to the bar—was known to give him a bit of energy, like a cup of coffee but without the jitters, which he could use right now; however, the other bar, a *Gauntlet* bar, was a five-pack flavor of bliss packed with finger-sized pretzels stuffed with chewy nuget and tiny crumbles of dark chocolate and cherries. After just one of these—or in Neil's case, five—he was destined for a hard crash.

As Neil stood in the middle of the aisle and glanced around the desolate store where not even the clerk remained in sight yet he was somewhere cowered behind a rack of ecigs, he thought about how unapologetically mundane his life had become. He had two crazy-eyed girls back at the university who were ready to ride him as if he was a mechanical bull and here he was, deciding which candy bar to take home and snuggle up with tonight. At this moment in time, these were complicated issues for Neil. He pushed aside any doubt and reconsidered his options. Instead of choosing one, he decided to go with both because he could.

After the decision was made, he grabbed himself a sixteen-ounce of Coolwater from the refrigerator and brought his snacks, as well as his drink to the cluttered checkout counter where the well-known small-talker, Todd, partially sat with one cheek on a bar stool behind the cash register.

Todd was a bearded, heavyset fellow who appeared as if he carried the physical attributes of a character plucked straight from a *Game of Thrones* episode, yet he dressed as if he was still in the third grade.

"If it ain't the Doctor of Horror in the flesh," Todd said, as he checked out the three items on the counter. "Looks like it's going to be quite a fun night tonight," he said, as he rang up Neil.

"Think of it as brain fuel."

Todd let out a booming laugh.

"Brain fuel, huh?" Todd repeated. "So, you cooking up a new book or what?"

"Maybe," Neil replied, as he handed Todd the money for the snacks and drink. "If the mood is right. . . "

"If the mood is right," Todd joked to himself, punching in a couple of numbers into the cash register with his chubby digits. Shaking his head, he said, "I don't know how you do it, my spooky little friend. Me," he said, more upbeat, "I can't get past thirty minutes of *Friday the 13th* before I start freaking out."

"Nah," Neil waved off the comment. "It's only a movie, Todd. There's nothing to be scared of. Plus," he leaned in closer as if there was someone else close by whom he didn't want to offend when, in reality, it was only he and Todd inside the store, "chicks dig horror movies—"

"—Yeah, but do horror movies give you nightmares and panic attacks?" Todd asked Neil but was really shedding a more personal light on himself.

Neil paid for the candy bars and drink.

"You know, Todd, you didn't peg me as a scaredy cat."

"Well, when the end of the world starts, guess who's going to show up at your door, ready to be your bunk buddy?"

"I don't know," Neil said mindfully, as he gathered his items. "Santa Claus?"

"No, dingbat. *Me.*"

Did he just call me dingbat? People still *use that word?*

Todd smiled widely and exposed his brown-stained teeth. In all these nights of small talk, which were mostly centered or revolved around Todd's minor critics, his "stating" of the obvious, his negative outlook on life, his social criticism, or—in this case—his fears, Neil had never seen Todd's teeth in their entirety. He had always picked up a glimpse of them, either catching them in the far corner of his eye or missing them as soon as Todd closed his mouth. Now that he had seen the teeth, he couldn't stop thinking about them and the next time Neil had another one of these unavoidable "run-ins," the thought of his teeth would be there in the back of his mind, as if they had become a distinct feature for Todd, a trademark, like the same way a satirical cartoon artist treated a character and found one feature on a character's body or his or her face and highlighted the feature until it was popping out of the page.

"Well," Neil said over a pause and made his way toward the door, "when that day comes, I'll be waiting on you."

Todd pointed at Neil.

"I'll be there, believe me," he said, as Neil awkwardly laughed off the remark.

As Neil was about to open the door, he saw Todd's deadpan face in the reflection of the front window. He was making a face at Neil, but he couldn't quite tell what kind of face it was until he took a second look. Todd was staring directly at Neil with these wide, bright, maddening eyes. The color in his face had changed dramatically as well; and Neil wasn't so sure if it was the greenish lighting above the checkout counter or a sudden illness that had come over the jovial clerk.

Whatever the case, a sudden chill crept up Neil's spine.

With his eyes pinned on Neil, Todd spoke to Neil as if he was finishing a sentence that Neil had caught off short with a manufactured laugh.

I'll be there, believe me. . .

"Bowing down to the great Drómos."

Neil peered closer at the reflection and soon realized it wasn't the lighting or a sickness inside Todd. His skin was much paler than normal, his lips purple in hue as if he was running out of oxygen. All of the Bic lighters and tiny gadgets, nudy magazines of the rack, as well as the plethora of cigarette boxes stacked like paperbacks in the shelves behind Todd, were no longer apart of the reflection. Yet, the background was much darker. Todd's clothes started to move and shift as if he was submerged in water. His once greasy hair appeared weightless as well, as it floated above his head like wavy Mexican feathergrass.

Feeling the skin stir over his shoulder, Neil slowly turned around, only to find Todd reading a cyberpunk issue of *Heavy Metal* behind the checkout counter.

"You say something?" asked Neil.

Todd removed his eyes from the magazine and looked up at Neil.

"Sup?"

Neil hesitated, wondering whether or not Todd had heard him the first time.

Over a pause, Todd asked, "Something wrong, dude?"

Neil shook his head, said goodnight, and proceeded outside.

As Neil stepped outside, he instantly smelled a pipe burning. The smell of the tobacco was pleasant and forced Neil to pinpoint the smoker.

In his survey, he spotted a black town car pulling up beside his car. It wasn't until Neil walked closer toward his car that he realized it could've been the very same car that was following him. He noticed the headlights on the car. It wasn't strange for a car to have halogens; however, it was rare to see them, especially the farther you drove from the city. The tinted backseat window was rolled halfway down and through the narrow crack of the window was a set of red eyes lit up in the darkness of the vehicle. The ember nestled inside the end of the pipe glowed in the dark and lit up the bottom half of a man's face in a warm orange light.

In Neil's study, he noticed another passenger sitting next to the smoker in the backseat.

The car crept underneath the overhead fluorescent light of the gas station, partially casting an artificial light on the smoker's face.

Before Neil could make sense as to why he was following him—or at least, it appeared that way—the strange man rolled up the window. The car drove off.

Neil's eyes remained on the car until its red taillights faded into night darkness. He got back inside his own car and immediately checked the backseat, first looking through the rearview mirror and then, second, facing the backseat and giving it a thorough inspection.

The black town car was gone, so was that strange man.

Yet, Neil had a feeling that he was still there.

Watching him.

✦

THE *Dream* began with Neil, only thirteen years old, mindlessly stomping through twelve inches of fresh snow behind his childhood home in New Brunswick.

Standing behind the kitchen window was his mahm who was stirring a pan of Campbell's tomato soup while tenderly rubbing her baby bump in circular motions as she shot warm glances at her son playing with his one-eyed pal, Paul, in the backyard.

From the woods behind the house, a cloud of smoke from a cigarette or cigar—Neil didn't quite know—floated from behind a tree.

Neil heard the sudden *crack* of a twig breaking.

While he honed in on another cloud of smoke, which appeared from the same spot behind the tree, his pal, Paul, ran off to grab the sled from the garage. Neil thought the smoke might've not been smoke at all but maybe a person's breath—someone maybe hiding behind the tree, watching Neil, visibly breathing.

As soon as Neil stepped closer to the woods, a body came into the picture, revealing one half of a man with long, silky dark hair that ran over his broad shoulders. He was wearing dark camo—possibly a hunter, Neil suspected. He was carrying a pipe in his hand, no rifle, though. Once more, the strange man puffed away on his pipe, which was as warped and gnarly as a tree root, then he turned his back to Neil and walked deeper into the snow-covered woods.

Curious of the stranger, Neil followed him but ended up losing him.

Unaware of the path which took him back home, he grew worried as a sense of panic crept in. He smelled something in the air. Neil became dizzy trying to pinpoint the origin of the smell. On the verge of fainting, he looked down and as his mahm had taught him, counted to ten. By the time Neil reached the number two, he found an eddy of smoke on the ground and then tracked the smoke to a glowing ember burning a hole through the snow. Neil looked back up and found that same strange man standing with his back turned to Neil a couple of feet away in front of him.

"Mister?" said Neil, as he approached the darkly dressed man.

Words—the dialogue between Neil and the stranger—though verbally spoken aloud, sounded muffled, almost muted, as if they were filtered through thick terry cloth.

The strange man finally rotated around and said "hello" to Neil. Neil couldn't make out his face for it was blurry and Neil struggled to make eye contact. Neil couldn't make out his voice either for it was as soft and delicate as freshly baked bread. He did, however, read the strange man's lips, which, Neil knew, mouthed the word *hello*.

Without questioning the strange man's actions, Neil was handed a dark tinted bottle that reminded him of a bottle of cough syrup.

Through the man's lips, he was given specific instructions to place "one drop" of medicine into his "mahm's cup of tea."

The man specifically told Neil that the medicine would "help" his mahm, who, as of lately, had been awfully sick with his unborn brother. He told Neil "not" to "speak" to his mahm about their conversation for the medicine "would not" work properly or to its fullest extent and that, whatever happened, their "conversation" was their own little "secret." Neil specifically remembered that one word *secret.*

After Neil pocketed the bottle, the man kneeled down to Neil's level.

He drew a strange symbol in the snow below and said to Neil, "*Fool thy foe as a friend for its rapport is all but a fool's errand.*"

Neil heard these words as clearly as the sounds of his deep inhale.

From the perplexed expression on his face, as well as the lack of response, it was evident that Neil had no idea what these old words meant.

The strange man clarified, "In other words," he said closely, "keep your friends close and your enemies closer."

Before Neil could recognize the man's face, a chill came over Neil.

♦

NEIL jolted from sleep, trying to piece together the design of the strange symbol before it crumbled and vanished from his thoughts.

The deeper Neil dug into his thoughts, shuffling, pulling, and casting aside one thought after another as if he was sifting through a spool of tangled wires, the further the thought of the symbol slipped away.

He *had* seen the symbol before, but he didn't know where.

Neil rolled out of bed, sipped faucet water from the bathroom sink, and paced around the dark bedroom as if, by doing so, the thought would come back to him. The quicker he paced and moved his legs as if they were the vital components of a steam locomotive, the sooner the thought would resurface in that engine upstairs.

Neil stopped in his tracks in front of the window and glanced down at the tiny scar just above his right foot.

The memory flooded both Neil's mind and body, bringing him back to the day he was wandering deep in the woods behind his childhood home in New Brunswick, after the last snowfall of winter when the ground started to clear and spring flourished in all its majestic colors. He remembered it was during that spring after a particularly harsh winter that he felt the most alone. Former sidekick, Paul, was nowhere around nor were any of his other neighborhood friends. He wasn't quite sure if it was he who abandoned his friends or his friends who abandoned him. But one fact was clear: *he felt alone*, even though he was anything but. Neil remembered that particular spring day wandering through the woods when, all of a sudden, Neil nicked the top of his foot—the exposed area right above the shoelaces hung like bunny ears underneath the tongue of the shoe—causing Neil to stumble hard upon a swollen tree root protruding from the earth. Then, next, feeling the radiate sensation course throughout his entire body as soon as his eyes met the light below. Not a pain—his great pain—but a sensation that left him growing several inches with confidence.

All of a sudden, the smell in his bedroom was different; and he could smell the scent of pine trees in the air. The sappy smell gave way to a hint of smoke. Ever since he was a boy, he knew there was a particular reason he found this particular light—*The Light*. Now, many years later, as an adult, Neil still felt the same way. He didn't exactly know why, but he knew there was a reason and somehow, after all of these years of suspicion, it was finally calling to him.

Neil concentrated on the sun hitting the metal in the snow, resulting in a blinding glare.

The light was so bright, Neil ended up shielding his eyes.

Neil *snapped* from the distant memory; however, the light was still there.

Blinding him.

The light softened, making it easier for Neil to see.

A beam of a headlight oscillated through his bedroom.

Neil checked the window, only to find a suspicious car pulling into the parking lot outside his building.

He waited for a moment, staring intensely. The car could've been the same car that was following him earlier that night.

The suspicion was short-lived.

Eventually, his neighbor stepped out of the car, the headlights switching off as soon as he exited the car.

More relieved yet still gripped by the childhood memory, Neil sauntered to his closet and searched inside, starting with the top shelf and working downward. He didn't find anything out of the ordinary; in fact, Neil didn't really know what he was looking for.

DREW waited for an answer from a still-faced Neil.

He asked the question once more.

"Neil, what are you going to do?"

Neil snapped from his trance. He turned to Drew with a foolish expression on his face. The brow bending into his forehead indicated confusion. Yet, the curl in his lip, gave off a sense of annoyance, as if Drew had not pulled but jerked him from a thought that he didn't want to desert.

"Huh?"

"Come back to me, Neil," Drew said, touching the side of Neil's arm.

"I'm here," Neil finally said, as he started to walk toward the Morrison Building.

"You sure?" Drew persisted. "You looked like you fell down the rabbit hole."

"I hear you, Andrew. To be honest, I really don't know what I'm going to do after the semester ends. The fact of the matter is I've been teaching this class now for four years and from what I've gathered, the students seemed to enjoy it. So, it doesn't make any sense to me as to why now, out of the blue, my class is considered 'offensive' to some. If you want my honest opinion, Andrew, I think it's the dean who doesn't want me here anymore because I made a harmless crack about him while I was teaching my class about the Hunchback of Notre Dame a couple of weeks ago. I'm thinking—"

"—You're thinking one of your students ratted you out?"

"Precisely."

"So, what was the joke?"

"All I did was compare Dean Merkel to the Hunchback of Notre Dame," Neil said. "I was out of line. *Clearly.*"

"Not really a joke," Drew said, lowering his voice around a couple of nearby students. "You're just stating the obvious." As Drew shouldered past a couple of students in the courtyard, he turned to Neil and said in a softened tone, "I didn't know Quasimodo was considered a 'monster.'"

Neil turned to the professor with the same expression from earlier, only without the confusion.

"Sorry," Drew said and held up his hands in surrender. "So, the board actually said your class was 'offensive' to students."

"That's the word they used, '*offensive.*' Apparently, they've been drinking the Kool-Aid, as well."

"Well," Drew said over a pause. As soon as he found himself away from students, he leaned closer to Neil and said, "Just think of it like this, Neil. The kids nowadays have become—how do I say in a diplomatic tone—more aware."

"More aware? You can't be that naive, Professor Carroll."

"How am I being naive?"

"I know what you're really trying to say—"

"—Is that so?"

Drew grinned, as he held open the door for Neil.

"Well, Professor Reddy, it's always good to think before you talk—or in your case, crack jokes about the very man in charge of the university where you teach."

"Bite me, Carroll."

Drew burst out laughing as he slapped Neil on the back.

"That's more like it, Professor Reddy."

They both stepped inside the Morrison Building.

A sudden thought came to Drew.

"By the way," he said, "how'd it go with the lecture last night?"

"It went well," Neil replied.

"You didn't puke all over the mic again, did you?"

This time, Drew held in a laugh.

"How many times do I have to tell you, Drew, it was 'food poisoning'?" Neil said defensively. "Besides, that was only one time. Good for me people caught it with their eyes and not their phones."

"Think again, buddy. There's a video on YouTube. It's already received three million views. They're calling you, 'The Amazing Vomit Man.'"

"Funny guy, you are."

"Hey," Drew said, nodding at Neil, "I get it from watching the best."

"So, I'm that bad of an influence on you, huh?"

"You know, according to a recent CSquare poll, I read that over eighty percent of all Americans are more terrified of 'public speaking' than they are of 'dying.'"

"What was number two?"

"Nuclear war, I think."

"Death wasn't even on the list?"

"I think it was like number five, I think. Amazing, huh?"

"Normally, I wouldn't believe a word that comes out of your mouth, but in this particular case, I think you may be correct. There's nothing that terrifies me more than standing on stage in front of an entire audience of people waiting to listen to me speak."

"Must be something then," Drew said, "conquering your worst fears everyday. You underestimate yourself, Neil, my friend."

"And you?" asked Neil. "What makes your skin crawl?"

"Me, uh," Drew hesitated. He stopped in his tracks for a moment, face blank and all, as Neil waited for an answer. "Crossing bridges," he finally said.

Neil was surprised by the answer.

"I hate bridges," Drew said.

So did Neil.

"I confess I hate them so much that they trigger panic attacks." Drew paused. "For the most part, I try to avoid them whenever I can and if he have absolutely no other way around one, driving over a bridge is ritually accompanied by *Enya*."

"Enya?"

"You know, the Celtic singer."

"Oh!" Neil lied, "I don't know her."

"Imagine me like a horse wearing a set of blinders while the stereo remains on full-blast," Drew said. "If that's not fear, then I don't know what is."

Neil didn't know exactly where the fear of bridges had begun for Drew, but he certainly knew where it had started for himself.

Drew interrupted Neil's train of thought: "Speaking of worst fears," Drew said, "how was that date with what's-her-name?"

"Kate?"

"Yes," he said, as they proceeded toward the offices. "That one."

"It went pretty well," Neil said. "Bre didn't approve, though."

"Didn't approve, huh? So, I see she's still calling the shots."

"Not calling the shots, just offering up a second opinion, one in which I highly regard when it comes to dating women."

"Why don't you two just get it over with and hook up?"

"No," Neil said louder. "Of course not. My relationship with Breanne is completely platonic."

Drew protested in disagreement.

"Neil, buddy, *pal*, don't you think it's rather odd for a grown man to be hanging out with a woman of the same age?"

"Not if you look at her as a sister."

"A sister?"

"Sure," he said. "People often confuse us for siblings whenever we're in public."

Drew paused and tried to envision Breanne in his head. He immediately shook away the thought before it could take hold.

"I don't see it."

"Well, unlike you, my friend, Breanne makes one hell of wingman."

"Hey!" In disbelief, Drew pointed at himself as he made it to his office. "I can make a good wingman."

"You're married."

"So?'

"So," Neil said. "Not the same. Not only is Breanne a single woman, but she is also a woman who knows exactly what kind of woman I prefer. Which, if you think more about it, gives me an advantage when it comes to determining whether or not a potential partner is interested in pursuing any long-term relationship with me."

"Nyeah," Drew drawled. "You're not missing out on much, Neil. Trust me."

"Please. . . "

"Whatever," Drew waved off Neil. "We're going out for drinks this weekend. *And* I'm going to be *your* wingman."

"We'll just see about that," he said and walked off. As Drew was about to enter his office, Neil stopped in midstride, turned to Drew in curiosity, and asked, "Are you serious about that video of me on YouTube?"

⁑

As Neil was teaching the history of the widely varied shapeshifter known as the Aswang in Filipino folklore to the class, he was struck by yet another momentary dizziness brought on by a loud *crunching* sound of one of his student's teeth digging into the hard flesh of an apple. The sound closely resembled that disturbing sound of the ice from the frozen lake *cracking* beneath his feet. Each bite, each *crunch*, brought Neil back to that very moment in time when he nearly lost his life. Neil was forced to take a moment of pause in order to control his own bearings. Pinching the bridge of his nose, he leaned against the podium until the dizzy spell passed. But, again, he heard that awful sound of *crunching* and *cracking*, as if the sound alone was bouncing off the acoustics of the arena-like classroom and corkscrewing inside Neil's head; however, the sound didn't seem to bother any of the other students in the classroom; more so, background noise to them, just one of their fellow classmates squeezing in a post-lunch snack. Yet, to Neil, the sound was amplified, concert-like; and the closer the student got to the core of the apple, the closer the sound twisted inside Neil's brain.

As Neil's jaw tightened with rage, he suddenly shouted, "For crying out loud, would you please stop making that goddamn noise!"

The student, who was seated in the second row, paused during mid-chew. One side of his mouth was ballooned outward, his eyes wide. The other students were turning toward both their professor and the student in the second row as if there was about to be an epic showdown between the two.

As the student slowly and cautiously finished the rest of the bite, Neil decided to power through the shapeshifter that was known as Aswang.

"In Filipino folklore, the Aswang has been known to shapeshift into a bat. . . "

As Neil looked back toward the students before him, one student in particular grabbed his attention.

The student's name was Nicole Preston, "Nicky," she liked to be called, a mediocre student who, at times, seemed as if she attended the class for other reasons. At first, it was the hair that grabbed Neil. He wondered why she chose that one color in particular. Of all the colors, why choose the color white? He specifically recalled her hair being the color orange last week and then fiery red a couple of weeks before that, as if she wore her hair to match the seasons. White was certainly not her natural color, her natural color being brunette; in fact, Neil thought she must've had it dyed over the weekend. From the way Nicky wore clothes to match her hair—a white blouse, red skirt—it looked as if she was making more of a fashion statement in front of the students than a desperate cry for attention. Unlike the loudmouth in the second row, Nicky was definitely *trying* to make an impression on the professor.

In one fluent yet exaggerated motion, Nicky secured the cap onto the end of a ballpoint pen; and with her pinkie and ring finger fanned outward, she inserted the other end of the pen into her mouth as if she was giving a "How To" demonstration for an audience—particularly, Neil being her most eye-worthy spectator.

With her plump cherry red lips puckered like a fish, she started to suck on the pen; and at times, she even licked the sides of the pen in a rather suggestive manner. Her intentions soon became evident to Neil as soon as she started to bob her head back and forth while beginning to deep throat the pen.

Neil quickly turned away once the blood started to move in other, swampier areas of his body. In a way, he felt as if it was morally wrong to be aroused by Nicky's blatant tease, Nicky being nearly half his age but still, legal. Neil strictly reminded himself that she would've been a baby around the time he first got his driver's license. His focus was thin, though, fragmented. He leaned closer to the podium in order to hide the growing bulge in his pants.

"*The Aswang*," Neil said, clearing his throat, "has also been known to shapeshift into a werewolf. . . "

Neil tried not to look at the flirtatious student; however, she made yet another sly move that caught Neil's eye.

She slid father down into her seat and spread her legs open.

For the slightest moment, Neil glanced below the desk and caught a glimpse of the red skirt pushing farther up her legs. Neil zeroed in on what she was wearing underneath—or wasn't wearing.

In that moment of great arousal, he thought about the Siamese hanging above the door of his apartment. Neil spent the entire morning over a cup of coffee and morning news trying to obliterate the notion from his mind—*What kind of individual would've done such a thing?*

Neil's heart started to race. He could hardly even finish the rest of his sentence while some of the other students—the more concerned ones—were shooting long-faced glances at one another as if they should say or even *do* something. Neil focused on the elusive Aswang. Then, his mind started to retrace the last few moments of the lesson, as if the images had become freeze frames inside his mind, still images, close-ups of what was causing Neil's blood to race: Nicky's piercing brown eyes; her wet tongue, moving and curling; those amble thighs opened wide underneath her desk like a sprung trapdoor; her lips; then, her other lips.

Tempted to turn toward Nicky for one last glance, he remained attached to the word *Aswang*. Somehow, during his brittle concentration, the word morphed into other words, words like *ass*—in particular, Nicky's ass, Nicky's round, incredibly firm ass—then *wang*—in particular, his wang, raging hot and throbbing against the seam of his pants.

Neil moved his eyes toward Nicky. The pen was no longer inside or anywhere near her mouth. Instead, she was inserting it into another part of her body. She closed her eyes as she penetrated herself and let out what sounded like a moan.

Two male hormone-driven students sitting not too far away started to smack and grab each other on the arms as if they couldn't believe what they were witnessing before their eyes. They displayed their restrained excitement by pointing and giggling to themselves like two closet-pervs watching what they'd later brag about as a real-life porno to brothers.

In his best acting, Neil looked down at the watch on his wrist and then shut his book on the *Ass-Wang* and said to the class, "I think we've listened to enough of me talking about the Aswang for one day. Why don't we call it a day?"

Before the students could gather the rest of their belongings, Neil was already out the door.

✦

NEIL pulled his car up to the beat-up beige Mazda parked on the curb in front of his mahm's two-story house in Mulberry.

As Neil made his way around the car and onto the pathway, a pile of books in the backseat of the strange car had caught the corner of his eye. He stopped for a second, retraced his steps without drawing too much suspicion, and peeked inside the back of the car. Scattered along the backseat were dozens of Bibles, different versions and editions, both Old and New Testament, King James. There was also the Islamic sacred book, the Qur'an—or Koran. He also spotted what looked like the Bhagavad-*Gita* underneath one of the Bibles. He could only make out part of the word *Gita*—*And* he was ninety-nine point nine percent certain it was the same Gita that he knew all about. But why would *she*—if it really was the new aide's car—be driving around with different religious books in the back of her car?

As Neil was about to pull himself away from the window, he gave the inside of the car one last survey. He spotted yet another item that caught his eye: a white pawn hanging from the rearview mirror by a string of red yarn. The end of the string was tied into what appeared to be a noose wrapped around the neck of the pawn. Neil was quite familiar with the game; however, why would *she*—if the vehicle belonged to this Kamaria woman—be carrying around a chess piece? Of all chess pieces, why a pawn? And why in that particular manner?

Pushing past the contradictions inside the car, Neil knocked on the front door. Nobody answered after the second knock. Neil decided to enter. The door happened to be unlocked, which was unusual. His mahm *religiously* locked the door.

Neil stepped foot inside the house.

"Mahm," he said but received no answer.

He called out for John, but like before, received no answer from him either.

Once Neil closed the door, he thought he heard people talking toward the back of the house. He listened closer and concluded that it was people not talking but whispering. Their voices were unrecognizable. Yet, they sounded shrill.

What?

A stir of panic crept inside Neil, causing his stomach to tighten.

The only thought that came to mind: somebody—possibly more than one person—was inside the house and he or she or even *they* were trying not to make any presence known. He quietly stepped inside the kitchen and saw a jar of trail mix overturned on the countertop. The jar was opened. Trail mix was scattered everywhere on the countertop, as well as the floor.

Keeping quiet, Neil grabbed a steak knife from the knife holder. He accidentally stepped on a pretzel, making that familiar *crunching* sound. He blocked out the memory before it could take hold of his thoughts and focused on more important issues, like the safety of not only his well-being, but also Ajay's.

Neil, too, tried not to make his presence known as he followed the whispering to Ajay's bedroom.

As soon as he stepped foot into his room, he saw his mahm holding Ajay while the new aide—or what he assumed to be the new aide—cleaned Ajay's backside. His mind raced, thoughts bleeding into other thoughts. A pungent stench of poop suddenly punched Neil directly in the face and left him reeling in his tracks, as if he ran into a wall of the foulest, most revolting smell on earth.

Neil took a step back, as if, by doing, the smell would be less intense; however, that wasn't the case at all. To Neil, it felt as if the smell was growing as if it was its own entity feeding off Neil's transparent distaste.

Covering his nose, Neil said, "What happened?"

His mahm poked her head over the aide's shoulder.

"Hi, Neil," she said shortly. "That bad, huh?" She noticed the disgust written all over her son's face. "Your brother just had himself a bowel movement, a real whopper." She turned to Ajay, "Didn't you, Ajay?"

Neil couldn't see his brother's face for he was rolled over on his right side, but Neil was pretty sure his brother was making a face.

"No," Neil pointed to the kitchen, "in the kitchen."

"Kitchen—"

"—There's a mess."

Her eyes lit up.

"Oh!" she said. "Right. I was trying to open the lid to the Trail Mix when, all of a sudden, the jar slipped from my hand. If it wasn't for your stepfather and his greasy hands, then it would've never happened."

"Where is John?" asked Neil.

"Guess," she returned.

"I don't know," Neil said. "Playing nine holes?"

"Yes," she said, her tone bitter. She said to the new aide, "I swear, the man is always playing golf. I tell him, with all the golf he plays, he should go out on tour and play with the pros and make some money. I figure if you're going to play a sport, you might as well make some money out of it."

Neil knew that really wasn't the only reason why she sounded upset. *She* was here on "cleaning duty" while *he* was outside soaking up the cleaner air with his drinking buddies and spending the afternoon smacking around a little white ball.

"Let me give you a hand," Neil insisted.

"It's okay," his mahm said. "We're almost done."

"You sure?"

"By the way," she said, as she finally addressed the strange woman standing on the other side of the hospital bed. "Neil, this is Ajay's new aide, Kamaria, from Vista Cove Home Health Care. Neil is Ajay's older brother."

Kamaria stopped cleaning Ajay's backside for a moment and turned her head over her shoulder. She reached out her gloved hand, which was covered in brown spots and tire track-like smears.

Neil hesitated.

Realizing what she was about to do, Kamaria looked down at her hand.

"My mistake," Kamaria said skittishly. "I'd shake your hand, but, as you can tell. . ."

"Yes," he said, the tone of his voice sounding as if he was backing away. "Of course."

Somehow, Neil got the impression that she didn't want to shake his hand in the first place.

"Pleasure to meet you," she said.

He could only see one half of her face for the curtains were partially closed and the light was rather dim inside Ajay's room. He guessed she was probably in her forties, maybe in her fifties. A black woman's age was hard to guess—the saying "black don't crack" wasn't just a rhyme or myth but gospel truth. Her teeth were what really grabbed his attention. Her teeth glistened around her dark skin, as if, somehow, the teeth looked as if they didn't belong to her, like they might've been dentures maybe. He didn't put too much thought in it because she was too young for dentures. Regardless of her age, he was amazed by the sheer bright- ness of her teeth; and for a moment, he started to wonder if the woman was an actress or TV personality and the "nurs- ing gig" was sort of her side-hustle. All of Neil's unspoken superficiality of minor body critics would plunge heavy from his thoughts as soon as she turned back around and pro- ceeded to clean his brother in a remarkably timely fashion.

Neil's eyes went straight to the strange marking on the back of her lower neck. He didn't see it before. Maybe the stiff collar of her nurse's shirt was covering it up while she was carefully applying Desitin cream to Ajay's backside in order to prevent him from diaper rash. Or, maybe it was simply because Neil was too preoccupied taking jabs at the woman—the "elephant" in the room—her background, her behavior, her certain movements, what she was doing to his brother, how she was treating him, if she was gentle or rough, careless or compassionate with Ajay; ultimately, Neil was mentally comparing "Kamaria" to Janine, a young, beautiful, blonde, blue-eyed twenty-something who Neil would go out of his way to talk to any chance the moment would allow or make excuses to his mahm to visit the house, as if he wanted to pick up extra grooming supplies that John hoarded away in the secret nook inside the closet or make a sudden pop-in with hot food and eat lunch with Janine during his break.

While Neil was putting aside the fond memories Janine had given him, he was searching for any tell-tell signs that Kamaria was going to be a "problem" farther down the road, traits, ticks, bad habits, unflattering mannerisms, anything to convince him that Kamaria was unworthy of her new role that she was about to bear and that Vista Cove Home Health Care desperately needed to pull an "eleventh-hour"-type patch up job and find someone more "qualified" like Janine.

Not only that, the initial smell of Ajay's shit had made for one ruthless distraction.

But now, with all of that nonsense put aside, the marking on her neck appeared as if it was glaring at Neil. Before the marking disappeared underneath the stiff collar of her shirt, he made note of it. The marking was no larger than the size of a fingernail, pale, slightly discolored, raised, and nearly popped through her dark skin as if it was an old scar or even a brand, like one from a fraternity. However, he thought about fraternities. She'd have to be in a sorority, being a woman and all. Neil had never heard of pledges getting brands in sororities for it was a rather masculine—barbaric—thing to do. But he certainly didn't rule it out. He guessed anything could happen these days.

As soon as the two finished cleaning Ajay, Neil, who was lost among his own thoughts while cleaning up the mess in the kitchen, heard the *thudding* sound of heel-heavy footsteps walking along the hardwood floors behind him.

He pushed aside the idea of the marking before the soon-to-be encounter.

Maybe it was a *burn mark she got as a child.*

His last thought brought him more ease, knowing that the person standing behind him was, in all respect, normal.

He stood up, turned around, and as predicted, found the aide standing right behind him. He got a better look at her face and body in a more artificial light. She was sporting a formal red suit. He assumed the white silk scarf lying on the purse on the recliner belonged to her as well.

At first, he didn't know what to think of her. Her taste in clothes was professional, unlike Janine, who used to wear the same burgundy nursing scrubs. Her face appeared like a vague dark blur, her eyes, however, startling. Neil looked at both of them, her eyes, as if he was unaware of which one to look at for one was slightly looking off into another direction while the other eye was pinned on him like a thumbtack.

They both stood at a standstill, an awkward silence filling the air around them.

Acknowledging that her hands were both bare and free of any gloves, Neil was tempted to shake her hand. As before, he felt as if it was forbidden.

"Excuse me," she said flatly to Neil and walked straight to the refrigerator to grab a white lunch box before Neil could offer up his hand.

By the time she reached the refrigerator, Neil was fishing for something to say to the woman. They both had already been introduced to one another, his mahm acting as universal mediator. During a tense silence, he briefly thought about asking about her background, where she came from, what was her last job, how long she had been an aide, or if she worked at the hospital; but, again, his mind circled back to the marking.

He had *seen* that marking before.

But where?

As he was about to ask Kamaria about her last job, she brought up the subject of Neil's writing.

Not aware of the possibility of his mahm mentioning his occupation to Kamaria, Neil said aggressively, "Excuse me?"

"Working on a new book?"

Neil paused, the tension mounting.

"Your mother told me you were a writer."

"Yes," Neil said, more relieved. "Of course. Unfortunately, at this moment—between promoting my latest novel and teaching at the university—I haven't been able to find much time to sit down and draft a new project. However," he pointed to his head, "I guess I can say I have a couple of ideas brewing upstairs."

Upstairs, Neil meant, as in his brain.

"You're a teacher?"

Professor.

"Correct," he said hesitantly.

"—Don't be so modest, Neil," his mahm said from the bedroom doorway, as she was drying both her hands with a paper towel. "He teaches over at Christopher Wensburg."

"Is that so?" Her face lit up with what Neil thought to be artificial astonishment—some kind of phony, to be blunt. "What subject do you teach?"

Again, he was tentative to respond to the question. Normally, his answer received varied responses or, in some instances, gestures. Usually, though, depending on the depth of the individual asking the question, his reply prompted a laugh but never. . .

Nothing.

Not a laugh, a giggle, a chortle, a chuckle, a curl of the brow, the widening of eyes, or even, almost *always* a follow-up.

Neil received nothing from Kamaria; in fact, she appeared as if she had history with the word.

"What Neil means to say," his mahm stepped in, "the study of monsters, both fictional and nonfiction."

"Nonfiction?"

"As in real-life monsters," his mahm said before Neil could explain, "as in serial killers and murderers. Who was that one you were recently talking about the other day?" She drifted into thought, as Neil remained silent, "Anyway, I particularly do not care for the nonfiction part of his studies."

The sound of his mahm speaking for him drove him into a barely controllable state of unease. Neil clenched his teeth so tight that he could not only hear, but also feel his top teeth grating against the fillings of his bottom teeth. He was a single man with an English major and a minor in art history who had spent the first two years of college taking classes to steer him toward a criminal justice major, only to realize he didn't have the stomach to have a career in law. He was also living on the wrong side of thirty while, at the same time, clinging onto what little hair remained on his head; and yet, on many occasions, his mahm acted—or worse—treated him as if he was still her little boy.

"*I see*," Kamaria finally said, her voice as well as expression as flat and blank as an empty canvas.

Neil examined the expression—or lack thereof—and witnessed a slight quiver in her lip, as if she had swallowed an ill remark, defensive in nature. Her eye timidly turned to Neil, then snapped back to his mahm; then she readjusted her grip around her lunchbox as if the sight of Neil and what he did for a living prompted a nervous reaction.

His mahm brought up yet another subject, one in which he did not want to talk about, especially in front of a woman whom he had just met. Being a successful professor herself who not only taught Creative Writing at Western, but also came from "literally" nothing, she was brazen enough to go on a selfish rant about today's "entitled kids" and how fluffy-soft they had gotten, as if everything should be handed to them on a silver platter, today's pocket-sized "dictators," only to become tomorrow's future "tyrants," who'd make former hippies, like herself, look like conformist pigs—these kids, his mahm carried on, nothing but spoiled rotten, ill to the core, with not an ounce of adversity in their bones. Her rant morphed, as did her tone, and she started talking about how much she constantly worried for her son, a bachelor, in the wake of the woman's movement that drew more rage—and "obvious" divisiveness—than it did resolve. He had to put an end to the rant before it turned ugly.

Despite what he mentioned to Drew, in all sincerity, he didn't exactly know the real reason as to why his class was being dropped after the semester, even though his mahm acted as if she had it all figured out.

She backed off as soon as she witnessed frustration building in her son's face.

Neil excused himself from the kitchen while his mahm, more civil, redirected the conversation back to Ajay and guided Kamaria to the DVD rack next to the television where she went through certain movies Ajay enjoyed to watch during the "slow" parts of the day.

While his mahm was going through movies, all ranging from action-adventure to science fiction—Pacino being an actor who, surprisingly, drew the most stimulation from Ajay—Neil visited with his younger brother.

The odor was less intense and most of it had dissipated over the heavy spraying of Lysol air-fresheners throughout Ajay's room, which was shared by both his mahm and John.

As Neil stood by Ajay's bedside, he asked his brother how he was doing; and as his brother often did, he responded by giving Neil a thumbs-up while his four fingers remained curled into the edge of his palm. Except for Ajay's eyes or the two to three facial expressions he had, his thumb was his only line of communication. A thumbs-up for Ajay meant it was a good day; and as the days powered by, Neil knew there were very few good days left for Ajay.

&

AFTER his visit with Ajay, Neil, more skeptical about the new aide and whether or not she could be trusted to care for his brother, called up his devout wingman—or, better yet, wing*woman*—Breanne. As he did nearly every time he shot her a text or if he had the time to call her, Neil happened to catch Breanne at the perfect time. She recently got off work at the IP Studio located downtown and was dying for a drink, primarily one with alcohol. They both decided to grab a "couple" of drinks at a part wine-part lounge bar called Cork Out, which was easily mispronounced as Corkin' Out or often used as "Corked Out," a verb to describe getting wasted, drunk, blitz, lubricated, tipsy, or buzzed after a late night out at Cork Out; however, according to Breanne, the place was one of her best and proven most successful go-to spots to hit on business-types during happy hour.

Over the first two drinks, Breanne did most of the talking while Neil mostly sat back and sipped from his lager and, every now and then, asked a question. Most of the conversation was centered on Breanne giving updates on a new app that she was currently developing. The smartphone app, a throwback to scroll games, was tentatively called "Roam's Quest." The game followed Roam, a boy who roamed across a deserted landscape collecting hidden artifacts from collapsed civilizations and using those artifacts to rebuild his own civilization.

By the time Neil was halfway through finishing his second drink, he started to catch a buzz. Breanne knew there was only so much of the game she could talk about before she completely lost Neil's attention.

The conversation shifted toward Neil, his book, his class, *his* life.

Sipping from a glass of Zinfandel, Breanne noticed the redness in Neil's eyes.

"How about one more?" Neil suggested, as he diverted the conversation before it turned more serious than he wanted it to be.

Breanne looked around the lounge area and didn't see any "potentials." As far as she was concerned, most of the men either had the flu or were taking the night off or had simply given up on meeting women the "old fashioned" way.

"You sure?" asked Breanne, glancing over her shoulder. "I think they may be understaffed tonight. Lately, though, I've noticed the service around here sucks." She pointed out a young waiter who was scrambling around from one table to the next while the two bartenders were busy scrolling through their smartphones behind the bar and not paying any attention whatsoever to serving guests. "I swear this place changed dramatically ever since they changed management. Remember how quickly we used to get our drinks?" Before Breanne gave Neil a chance to respond, she said with bitterness, "I should write a review."

"Nobody reads reviews anymore. Besides, ninety-nine percent of reviews are either paid-reviews or written by competitors. So basically it's all fabricated."

"Well," Breanne said, looking around once more, "it's kind of dead here anyway, don't you think? *And* no offense, Neil buddy. But you look like you've had enough to drink."

"Me?" he said, laidback. "*Nah*, Bre. I'm cool."

"You don't look so cool."

Neil lowered his head, his eyes pinned on Breanne, jaw slackened in what Neil demonstrated as his most exaggerated primitive male gaze.

"That's not a very nice thing to say, Breanne."

"Hey," she said, "I'm just being honest."

"Well, you should learn when to lie and when to tell the truth," Neil said, "and I think right about now is the most ideal moment to come up with your most decorated lie, such as, in a swift response to my comment about how cool of a guy I am: 'Well, Neil,'" Neil said to himself in his best impression of Breanne, "'you are one cool dude; in fact, you must be one of the coolest, sexiest dudes on planet Earth. *And*,'" he emphasized, "'I believe you should have another drink; in fact, I believe you should have as many drinks as your big heart desires.'"

Breanne returned with her own primitive look.

"Are you through?" she asked.

Neil waved off the dry humor and ordered yet another lager by waving down a bartender and motioning to the near-empty glass.

"It's just," Breanne started and thought over her next remark, "it's not the end of the world, you know? Eventually, you'll write yet another book. *Eventually*," she said, "you'll find a woman who adores you. It might not happen tomorrow or months from now, but you'll know when that time comes. And, trust me, it'll be worth the wait."

"Like you should know," Neil said. "You thought what's-his-name—Toby—was 'the one' but look how he turned out." Breanne didn't follow up with a reply. Instead, she sat back and waited for Neil to finish what was really on his mind. Neil finished the last bit of his lager and acknowledged a sudden quietness in Breanne. "Sorry," he said to her. "I didn't mean it like that, Bre."

"I know you didn't."

"What I mean is. . . do you ever feel like you're *not* in control?"

"No," Breanne said, thinking. "Not anymore. I used to, though. Absolutely."

"Ever since I put out the new book—I dunno—it just feels like someone's been playing a game with me."

"Really, Mr. *King* of Pranks? So, what? Now, the shoe is on the other foot—"

"—No," he said flatly. "It's not that. I think somebody was following me last night. There has been other instances in the past, but last night, it felt as if I was actually being—I dunno—watched. . . " Neil trailed off, ". . . Or something."

"You know what your problem is, Neil," Breanne said over Neil, "you think too much. You've been so wrapped up with your work these past few weeks that it's starting to affect your personal life. I think it's unhealthy for you to go on like this, Neil. Take a step back from work, go to Hawaii—"

"—Someone *was* following me, Bre."

"Then, who?" She leaned in. "A woman?"

"No," Neil said, shaking his head. "I mean, I dunno."

"A fan perhaps? Maybe an avid reader of yours? Maybe the FBI? Maybe the ghost of Lee Harvey Oswald?"

"I'm serious."

"I'm just trying to help."

"I don't think a 'reader' of mine would hang a dead cat above my front door."

"Serious?"

"This morning, I found one hanging upside down above my doorway. Its guts were hanging from its body."

"That's terrible," Breanne said, repulsed.

"A Siamese," he said in reflection. "Think it belonged to one of my neighbors. Not sure."

"Did you contact the authorities?" asked Breanne, more concerned.

"No," he said.

Breanne waved her hand, as if she was trying to play off a legitimate concern.

"It was probably just some kid screwing with you."

"Probably."

Breanne noticed Neil and how he wasn't his usual more "talkative" self.

"So," Breanne said, more caringly, "what's really bothering you?"

"I just feel like my time's running out, you know? Like I'm undeserving of another woman's affection, like I'm being. . . " Neil suddenly paused. His train of thought was distracted by the sound of a man obnoxiously chomping on ice next to him. He couldn't help but focus on the sound, that familiar *crunching* sound caused by teeth chewing through ice cubes. The man lifted up the glass to his lips and grabbed yet another ice cube from the bottom of the glass and started *crunching* away.

Without hesitation, Neil turned to the man and asked, but, from his harsh tone, was really demanding.

"Can you stop that please?"

Wide-eyed, the man turned to Neil.

"Excuse me?"

"Can you stop making that damn noise?"

In no mood for confrontation, the man shook his head, mumbled something to himself, and then found himself another seat at the other end of the bar.

"You okay?" asked Breanne.

"Yeah," Neil finally said. "Fine."

"Being what?"

"What?"

"You were saying like you were being. . . "

Neil paused.

"Punished."

Breanne leaned in closer.

"Punished for what?"

Neil's shrug of the shoulders came off as an inaudible "*I dunno.*" To Breanne, however, it appeared as if it was glaring "yes" to something.

"Neil," Breanne said, leaning in toward Neil, "we're the same age. I certainly don't feel as if *my time* is running out. You shouldn't be talking like that, especially at your age."

"What about, you know, starting a family? Raising a child? Being a mother? Don't you want any of that?"

"No," she said after a short pause. "Not really. Besides, I can't have children. I thought I told you."

"Right," Neil replied. "I mean, sorry."

"Don't be."

"But, eventually, you do want to start a family. You can always adopt a kid."

"Yes," Breanne said uncertainly. "Sure. I could. One day, maybe, I guess. I don't know. I'm not really thinking about that. The idea of starting a family isn't something that keeps me up at night, if that's where you're getting at."

"But don't you ever feel, you know, alone?" asked Neil.

Breanne shook her head.

"No," she said confidently. "Believe it or not, I enjoy my life. I have a dream job. I have my own place. I go to the movies whenever I feel like it. If I want to go out for drinks with a friend, like you, whenever the mood should strike me. . . I don't have anybody breathing down my neck or watching me all the time or telling me what to do. I can't complain."

Neil *thought* about Breanne's remarks. He thought more about her game and if she ever finished it, she'd have nobody, like a loved one, to share it with or even a son or daughter to hold it proudly in their hands and brag and flaunt to everybody they met in the world about the game that their mother had created.

Breanne recognized the pensive expression on Neil's face.

"You remember the first night we met?" Breanne asked.

Neil snapped from his trance.

"Ah," he said, thinking back. "Yeah. Sure. It was at that one club—what was it?" The name came to him before Breanne could answer. "Lure," he said. "The club that shut down last year. They had the best oysters in the city. Why do you ask?"

"I don't know," she said. "It's strange to think about, but if I didn't get away from the situation I was in with Toby, with all his manipulation and possessiveness, then I honestly don't think I would've made it out there alive."

"Did he ever hit you?" asked Neil.

Breanne lowered her head. She didn't even have to answer Neil. Her gestures were like full-page summaries of what Toby had done to Breanne.

"Sorry," Neil said quietly.

Breanne shook her head and finally raised her head.

"Don't be," she said, as if the moment of pause had given her strength. "Toby and I were opposites. That's probably the reason why I was so attracted to him—at first. He was valedictorian in high school. I was home-schooled. He was from the city. I was from a small town in Florida—"

"—I didn't know you were from Florida."

Breanne cleared her throat.

"I don't remember much," she said over a pause. "I got the hell out of there as soon as I found an opportunity."

"Where'd live at in Florida?"

Again, Breanne fell into a pause.

"Josey Town," she said shortly.

"Josey Town, huh?"

"*Anyway,*" Breanne said, as she pushed through the interruption, "He was 'Mr. Popular All American Stud Who Every Girl In His Class Wanted to Jump—'"

"—I know the type," Neil interrupted again.

"I had very little friends growing up," Breanne said over Neil. "I was basically a ghost throughout my entire childhood, whereas he was opposite of a ghost. He was a city-boy. I was just a small town girl, a nobody—"

"—You mean, he was alive," Neil said, leaning in. "So are you."

Breanne smiled off Neil's flimsy perceptivity.

"About a year after I moved in with Toby—which, we all know is like the precursor for marriage, that, then a dog named Spots—we turned into strangers living under the same roof. The night I met you was the night I finally killed that person who he had turned me into. For so long, I had been running from that weak person who would fall for about anyone who gave me the slightest attention. That night, I found my new self, the person who I always wanted to be but never had the chance to be. And for the first time in a very long time, I felt as if I could *live* again. When I was living in Chicago, I had a decent job that paid very well, had lots of friends, *but* I wasn't at all happy the way my life was going. I was stuck in some kind of vicious loop, waiting for something bad to happen."

"What motivated you to make a change?" Neil asked.

"One day, the idea came to me, as if it the idea was there, inside my head, all along, yet, for so many years, I ignored it. I guess I just couldn't take it anymore. So, I pulled out a map, skimmed through it, and after the first city that my finger landed on, I said to myself, 'That's where I'm going.' I didn't do any research. I didn't have any doubts or regrets about moving. I packed my bags and left; and not once did I ever look back. That easy."

"That easy, huh?"

"*That easy*," Breanne said directly to Neil.

"I wish I could make decisions like that, just 'go.'"

"What's holding you back?"

"I dunno," Neil said quietly. "Ever since I could remember I felt as if I've had this hand on my back."

"You can *feel* this hand?"

"Yes," he said, more seriously. "I know it sounds weird, but it's true. And at times, I can feel it pushing me in certain directions. It's like, no matter what, it's keeping me here. With Ajay. Even when an opportunity arises, one that may take me somewhere else, I can feel that hand, like a voice inside me, telling me *not* to go."

"If you're worried about Ajay, he has other people to look after him, like your parents and the aides. Don't you trust them?"

"No," Neil said, sighing. "I mean, I do. Well. . . "

"—By the way, how is your brother?"

Neil paused.

"He recently got a new aide."

Breanne's voice rose.

"Oh yeah," she said. "How is this new aide?"

Neil gave his most diplomatic response: "*She* is old fashioned."

"You mean, like the Ms. Ratchet type."

"Not really. More like she hadn't updated her look since the 1950's. And, not only that, there's a creep factor to her."

Breanne shrugged.

"Some people are just creepy by nature. *Like you*, for example."

Breanne smiled at the remark, Neil not so much.

"You're just full of wisecracks tonight, aren't you?"

Once more, Breanne shrugged.

"I guess your dry sense of humor is starting to rub off on me."

Breanne paused, creating a gap of silence. She cut through the silence before it turned uncomfortable: "So how's your family doing? They still living off what's-that-street—"

"—Meadow Springs," Neil answered.

"I know a guy who lives in Mulberry."

Neil perked up.

"Do you, now? Do tell. . ."

Breanne made a frown.

"It's not like that," she said, displeased.

Silence sat over the dwindling conversation.

In all seriousness, Breanne asked Neil, "What's really holding you back?"

Neil thought about the question but didn't answer.

"Neil," Breanne said over the silence, "it took me awhile to finally understand that there's no such thing as wishes. You only have two choices in life: you either *do* or you *don't*. I guess I was tired of thinking all of the time, thinking about my life, thinking whether or not he was going to hit me or talk down to me, thinking about how pathetic I was for still being with him. Now," Breanne said, as she too drifted in thought, "looking back, I only had one choice, really, and I guess I'd be lying to myself if I was doing everything in my power to convince myself that there were 'other' ways. There was only 'one' way, and that was to leave before he destroyed whatever good I still had inside me."

"Deep," Neil said without thinking much of his response.

Breanne widened her eyes, as if she was surprised by Neil's remark; and being the intellectual he was, she appeared as if she expected a more profound response. She downed the last two gulps of the Zinfandel and said, "If you will excuse me, I gotta use the little girl's room."

"I'm right behind you," Neil said.

Breanne smirked.

"Coming to join me, are you?" she asked.

"You know what I mean."

As Breanne stood up, she nudged Neil on the shoulder.

"Teasing," she said and walked off.

As Neil was about to stand up from his seat, he heard that same sound of an ice cube *crunching*, as if, somehow, he'd find the same man from before sitting in the same seat as before staring at Neil as he purposefully chomped ice cubes.

He turned to his left and didn't see anybody sitting beside him.

As panic started to creep in, Neil looked around the bar as if he was searching for that man. He tried to remember his face, but the only image that manifested in his mind was a vague white blur of a face, his eyes like two black dots and the right side of his flabby cheek swelled outward.

Neil heard the *crunching* sound yet again followed by shorter bursts of crunching. Which could only mean one thing: someone at the bar was chewing on ice. *But* he couldn't pinpoint the chewer.

As Neil tried to convince himself that it was only noise and soon it'd pass like any other noise, his thoughts started to drift.

Snow-covered images ran in his head until he was seeing pictures. He visualized kids, a group of them, his hockey friends, the same ones he used to hang with when he was old enough to play without a chaperone, flapping around in the water below, trying to doggy paddle toward safety, while he was looming above on uncracked ice, not attempting to help them. Instead, Neil was just standing there, as if he was watching these so-called friends drown.

He shook away the images before they could take hold and as he pushed in his seat, he witnessed a trembling man, not the chomper from earlier but a familiar man staring directly at him from across the bar. His curly hair was drenching wet, his clothes as well. His face was bluish pale and he appeared as if his entire body had been recently thawed from ice. He had dark circles around both eyes, so dark that he mistook them as empty eye sockets. His lips were a purplish color, which could pass as black. The extremities of each feature on his face, parts of his nose, including the tip, as well as his ears, were dark as well, and the color of his skin indicted the obvious signs of gangrene, which had been brought on by frostbite. Neil realized that the trembling man was his friend, Jean; however, he was much older and Neil could hardly recognize him. *But* it was him—Jean the Juggler.

Jean cracked open his mouth and water started to pour out. As water continued to stream from his mouth, more water started to pour from other orifices, his eyes, nose, and ears, drenching his clothes and splashing over the bar.

Neil heard a voice from behind: "Neil?"

He turned around and found Breanne standing behind him.

"Yeah," he said.

"What are you doing?" she asked.

He took one last glance at the frozen man across the bar; however, he was nowhere to be found.

Neil faced Breanne.

"I'm just going to the restroom," he finally said.

"Okay," she said, weirded out by Neil's skittish behavior.

As Neil rounded the corner of the hallway, which led toward the restrooms, he witnessed that same bluish face in the reflection of a rectangular mirror hanging at the end of the hallway. Neil noticed Jean was following him. He wasn't just a random manifestation in his mind. He was *real. . .*

Startled, he spun around, only to find a guy, one who looked nothing like Jean, walking toward the men's restroom. The guy acknowledged Neil and gave him a half-smile, not so much exaggerated or in Neil's face but, more or less, another way of saying "hello" to a fellow man.

Trying to make sense of what was going on, his thoughts were like a relentless barrage of unfounded speculations.

One of the most prevalent thoughts was that he had been poisoned, his beer spiked or tainted, possibly by one of the two bartenders—maybe both. They both looked as if they'd rather be somewhere else instead of pouring drinks to miserable saps like himself. Or, maybe someone, maybe that jerk, had walked past him and slipped something into his drink while he wasn't looking—a ruffy?

As Neil mindlessly ambled toward the restroom, a waiter carrying a tray of hot food shouldered through the swinging kitchen doors and bumped into Neil. Plates of a variety of cheeses and fruits and hot soups crashed to the floor in a deafening ring!

Neil stood still, his body flexing as if he was bracing himself. Once he saw the mess the waiter had caused, he held his arms out in utter disgust. He looked down at his pants partly stained with some kind of orange soup. Then, the knife erected upward on the floor. The knife had penetrated the wooden floor just an inch away from his foot, meaning if Neil had turned his foot an inch to the right then he'd be in agony city right about now and more than likely fuming over the inevitable trip to the emergency room.

The rattled waiter couldn't have been torn up enough from his sunken posture. At first, he just stood there as if he didn't know what to do. Then, as soon as the waiter acknowledged the soup on Neil's pants, he grabbed a towel from his apron and made his best attempt at cleaning up the spill. He pulled the knife from the floor and placed it back on the tray.

"My bad," he said casually to Neil.

A sudden rage came over Neil.

"You're damn right it's your bad," Neil seethed. "Now, how about forking out an apology? You could have hurt somebody!"

"I said, 'My bad, dude.'"

"Dude?" Neil repeated. "Do I look like a dude to you?"

As red clouds began to form in the waiter's cheeks, he held his head downward in what looked like shame.

Neil's apparent rage acted like a virus and spread to the young waiter, causing his teeth to clench in what Neil soon learned was a more deep-seated issue.

The disturbed waiter couldn't even hold up his head to look directly at Neil.

Realizing that any moment the waiter could snap, Neil backed away.

As the waiter started to angrily place plates and bowels back onto the tray, Neil washed up in the restroom. The whole time Neil checked his surroundings, mentally marking possible weapons to use if that waiter should happen to follow him into the restroom and commit bodily harm to Neil.

The door swung open!

Neil's heart started to race. He turned toward a trashcan and thought maybe if the waiter made a move, then he could possibly use the trashcan to his advantage. Turns out it was just an older gentleman who was about to piss his pants.

Neil left the restroom feeling more upset, not at the waiter but, more so, at himself for lashing out at the waiter, who was probably having a bad day.

When Neil passed the spot where the waiter bumped into him—or as he told himself, where "he" bumped into the waiter—the waiter was no longer cleaning up the accident; in fact, the accident looked the same as Neil first left it and it appeared as if, as soon as Neil entered the restroom, the waiter hadn't even made the effort to clean it up. Neil figured he was off grabbing a mop or even a roll of paper towels from the back.

Neil made it to his seat where Breanne was sipping from a full glass of wine.

Breanne asked, "Did you hear that noise?"

"I heard it all right," Neil said, less annoyed. "I accidentally ran into one of the waiters and caused him to spill a tray."

Neil extended his leg from the seat and showed Breanne the wet spot along the bottom of his pant leg.

"Was he not looking where he was going?" asked Breanne.

"No," Neil said. "It was my fault. I was distracted."

Breanne tried to hold in a laugh.

"I felt somebody brush by me a couple of minutes ago."

"Was it the waiter?"

"I think so," she said. "Whoever it was, he was pissed. He looked—how do I say—determined."

"What do you mean 'determined'?"

"Like he was on a mission."

"Where'd he go?"

"He stormed outside," she said. "He made quite an exit too."

"Really?"

"Yeah."

"Geez," Neil said. "I feel so bad."

"Why? You said it was an accident."

"Yes," Neil said. "It was."

"Then, don't worry about it. . . "

The door violently swung open, grabbing people's attention!

At the doorway stood the same waiter as before.

Neil asked Breanne if that was the same guy who brushed by her and she said it was.

Curious, Neil gave the waiter a second look and in doing so, noticed he was holding his arm behind his back. Both of his eyes appeared vacant. His once red face was pale and much whiter than his average tone. The slack expression on his face had also seized Neil's attention. He appeared as if he didn't have an ounce of life in him.

As the waiter pulled his concealed arm around the front of his body, a woman suddenly cried out in horror!

Following the scream the word *GUN* shrieked throughout the bar!

The first victims the waiter picked off happened to be a group of four business colleagues sitting at the front of the bar. He shot two of the four people directly in the head, killing them instantly; the other two were hit in the body as they both ducked under the table. He didn't bother finishing them off. Yet, the dead-faced waiter stalked from one table to the next shooting randomly at times, while, other times, aiming directly for the head.

Neil grabbed Breanne and yanked her from her seat. The two hid under the bar while a clamor of screams and gunfire roared all around them. A few people were scrambling to the front door, trying to flee to safety. The waiter shot anyone who darted past him, as if he was playing a shooter game and the more bodies he piled up, the more points.

During his rampage, he cracked what one of the survivors later described as a "sick-looking" smile on his face, as if, somehow, he was receiving pleasure out of shooting people. Neil didn't have the least amount of energy or the focus to survey his surroundings, search for possible weapons to use to take down the waiter or find openings or windows to pounce, and make his best heroic attempt to bring down the shooter. His only mission was to protect the one person who sat trembling inches away from him, cowering and crying as she squeezed Neil's hand.

In his flutter of thoughts, he remembered seeing an *exit* near the restrooms. He grabbed Breanne by the hand and told her to stay low and follow him.

They scurried as low as their bodies would let them toward the back of the bar while bullets hissed overhead and forced the two to take cover behind a wall.

The waiter reached the bar area. He picked off a couple of people who were hiding behind the bar, including the two bartenders who were furiously texting.

During the pause in the gunfire, Neil and Breanne made a dash toward the back of the bar. Again, keeping as low as they could, they scurried to a hallway. Two bullets pierced the wall next to Neil and came inches away from hitting him. Neil believed it wasn't random gunfire or the works of a victorious maniac aimlessly shooting the air and magnifying his own masculinity as if the "gun" itself was an extension of his male might.

Without even turning toward the direction of the waiter, he knew in his gut that he had been spotted. Luckily for Neil, the waiter wasn't a good long shot.

As Neil and Breanne made it to the back hallway, Neil frantically searched for that exit sign.

The *four* green letters suspended on the ceiling above a door caught Neil's eye.

"There," he whispered to Breanne.

The escape was a straight shot, from A to B; however, Neil felt as if he had a ways to go. Ducking into the kitchen had crossed his mind—*hiding*. Maybe finding safety in the freezer or a nook in a cabinet or recess until help arrived would suffice instead of running the risk of being shot in the back during their flee. The exit seemed so far away and besides the two restrooms and the kitchen, he had no more detours or barriers to hide behind.

It was that "slight" hesitation that kept both Neil and Breanne from fleeing the waiter.

As Neil made up his mind to make a run toward the exit, the waiter stepped in front of the exit door from another opening that Neil had missed.

Both Neil and Breanne were met by the lifeless waiter.

With Neil and Breanne in the waiter's sights, they backpedaled and attempted to flee back through the main lounge area.

Gunfire went off behind them!

A bullet struck a column right behind them, forcing the two to face the waiter.

"Please," Neil begged, as he held up his hands in surrender, "take me. Let her go."

The waiter remained without words as he stalked closer.

As the waiter approached Neil, his walk became unsteady, slower.

The gun started to weigh down his hand.

As the gun lowered completely by his side, the waiter's eyes filled with terror as if the sight alone of Neil had frightened him enough to cause the waiter to back away.

"Please," the waiter begged, "don't kill me. . . "

Neil turned to Breanne, who was equally confused.

All of a sudden, the waiter fired at Neil but the only noise that came from the gun was the sound of the trigger *clicking*.

Out of bullets, the waiter tossed the gun to the floor and hastily exited through the back exit door.

Relieved, Neil embraced Breanne and asked her if she was okay but, like those who had survived the shooting, was still shaken up and couldn't find the words to convey how she truly felt.

All of a sudden, a car *horn* blared from the front of the bar!

Following the horn was the screech of tires skidding along the asphalt.

Then, a loud *thud*!

Neil told Breanne to take cover under a table while he checked out the noise.

On the way to the front of the bar, he passed several people who had been shot dead. A distraught woman was tending to a man's gunshot wound in the shoulder. Neil grabbed the woman's hand and specifically told her to apply pressure to the wound until paramedics arrived.

Outside, Neil witnessed more commotion. A car was stopped in the middle of the road. A few people started to gather around on the street, forming a crowd.

As Neil cautiously made it outside, he witnessed the waiter awkwardly lying in the middle of the road. Strings of blood were streaming from his nose and mouth. A puddle of blood was forming underneath his contorted body.

Neil eavesdropped on a couple of nearby pedestrians who said the man had just run out in front of the car, screaming about some "monster."

Intrigued, Neil butted in between the pedestrians, "Did you say 'monster'?"

"I'm pretty sure that's what the boy said," one of the pedestrians said.

The driver of the car was slow to exit. He looked about as shocked as everybody else.

One man walked up to the motionless waiter, kneeled down over his body, and carefully checked for a pulse on his neck. Then, he turned to the pedestrians, who were standing by, and shook his head no as if he was informing onlookers that the man was no longer living.

"He's dead," the man finally said, as he stood up.

As Neil was about to go back inside the bar, he smelled a familiar smell in the air. He followed the smell to a smoldering ember of cherry tobacco lying on the edge of a curb next to an empty parking space.

He knew that smell.

And the person behind it.

⚲

NEIL hung around Cork Out until the police arrived and gave his statement about what happened inside the bar. Altogether, there were nine fatalities, despite what the competing news outlets had prematurely tallied as eighteen or even greater. Six people were badly injured, four stable, while the other two in critical condition with life-threatening gunshot wounds. Neil came to his own conclusion that what happened prior to the deadly shooting had no bearing in the outcome of the situation, considering the waiter had targeted "other" guests inside the bar and didn't initially go after Neil, at least that was what Neil had gathered; however, in the back of Neil's mind, he still held onto some notion that he may have been responsible, in a sense, partially to blame for the mass shooting. Maybe the minor accident before the shooting was the waiter's final straw, that little extra "nudge" to push him directly over the edge. Even though Neil wasn't the individual to, in a sense, pull the trigger, a part of Neil felt as if the words he used didn't help deescalate the situation but rather the opposite. In his statement, he left out the exchange he had with the waiter and called it exactly what it was, an accident.

When Neil made it back home, he was still jacked up from the leftover adrenaline and desperately needed to decompress with a stiff drink.

He grabbed the hourglass-shaped bottle of Hobbles whiskey that had been collecting dust in the back of the pantry and poured himself a shot.

Neil's phone suddenly rang as soon as he downed the shot of whiskey with an exaggerated grimace. The whiskey burned his esophagus, as well as his stomach.

He looked down at the name on the caller ID: *M.*

For Mahm.

As the phone continued to ring, Neil took yet another shot.

The more he drank, the less his insides burned.

Since he was in no mood to talk to his mahm, he let the call go to voicemail.

The second time she called, she left a message. Neil figured she'd been watching the nightly news and saw what happened at Cork Out, considering she knew it was a place that Neil had frequented with Breanne. She didn't mention anything about the shooting in the voicemail. Instead, she was calling about the razors that John had bought in bulk at a discount at Club Mart. He completely forgot to take them with him when he left the house. Since the call wasn't an emergency, Neil decided to put his phone on silent mode and call her back in the morning.

❧

SOMEWHERE between flipping from one news channel to another and researching ancient and controversial symbols throughout history, Neil dozed off.

He found himself drifting back into a similar dream as before, approximately two to three months after Ajay was born. Neil was thirteen and colorfully emotional. The days swayed from red to blue, angry to sad. It was late spring, going on summer. A blue day. The lakes were thawed and serene. He was hanging out alone on the shore of Bleu's Lake, which was located not too far away from the house, walking distance.

With a stick, young Neil was carving a strange symbol into the muddy shore when his mahm pulled her car up from behind Neil in the gravel parking lot. She stepped out of her car and walked down a small incline before reaching her son, who remained transfixed on the symbol in the mud below. He continuously went over the symbol with the tip of the stick, not knowing where he had seen the symbol or where it had come from. He made sure the lines were smooth and deep like trenches.

His mahm called out from behind.

Neil couldn't bring himself to look at his mahm; in fact, he pretended as if she wasn't even there and the words that came out of her mouth were no different than mouthed syllables.

Zoned out, Neil barely brought himself to look at his mahm. He didn't have to hear what his mahm had to say to him. After months of the two alternating shifts, devoting their time to Ajay, eating two of their three meals from the cafeteria, and basically, living in the hospital, he already knew exactly what she was telling him, that she was going to relieve John at the hospital and stay the night with Ajay and that Neil should be the older brother and see his baby brother for once, that it'd be good for Neil to visit with him, that his brother would love to see him, to hear his voice: the same ole-same ole.

As before, Neil responded with the shake of his head.

Then, like always, Neil could feel the disappointment pulling over his mahm's face like the black-netted veil of a black pillbox hat, the one worn at a funeral. In a way, Neil felt as if there had been a funeral, *not* for his baby brother, but for his relationship with both his mahm and John.

Neil's mahm walked up to him and placed her hand over his back.

Intrigued, she peeked over his shoulder and noticed the strange symbol that her son was carving into the shore.

As the curiosity soon melted from her face and left her without any expression at all, she backed away from Neil, got back into her car, and then drove away.

Neil didn't fully turn his shoulder until his mahm was finally gone.

Relieved and, at the same time, discouraged for not choosing to visit his baby brother, he went back to work on the symbol. He spent only a couple of seconds on the symbol before the frustration took hold. He snapped the stick in half and chucked it into the lake.

An object banging against the side of the dock caught his eye. . .

He decided to check it out.

When Neil arrived at the dock, another feeling came over him, similar to what he felt with his mahm and how he knew exactly what she was going to say before she even said it. A part of him knew exactly what was floating in the water, and it certainly wasn't an object, but something else.

As soon as he stepped onto the dock, he realized it was, as first predicted, a body. Immediately, he noticed the similarities in the body. He grabbed a paddle from a boat and used the broad end to poke at the body in the water. He first recognized the long scar slithering like a serpent along its side, similar to the scar on his side, if not a near carbon copy.

Frightened to turn over the body, he backed up and told himself that he refused to do it. *But* he had to know.

With sudden anger, Neil tried once more to turn over the body.

He drove the broad end of the paddle into the body's left shoulder, forcing it to sink slightly back into the water. In its slow float to the surface of the murky water, the body finally faced young Neil. Its face looked identical to Neil; however, its body was much frailer. Both of its eyes and mouth were opened wide and for a moment, Neil felt as if it was looking at himself.

Neil's eyes suddenly switched open.

146

As he rose from the damp bed, the dream—or memory, Neil couldn't quite tell if it was real or not—was still lingering inside his head.

The body.

Dazed, he looked around the foreign bedroom. At first, he didn't know where he was exactly. He had been here, in this room, at one point in time.

He rolled out of bed and once he set his feet on the shag carpet, he knew where he was. His old downtown loft. He used to live here before he landed a job at the university.

But *how did I get back here?*

Instead of thinking of an answer, his mind went straight to the very things that were attached to the loft, the memories and whatnot, the long days of drinking and writing and half-dressed women visiting him late in the night. He used to hit up a buffet at an Indian restaurant not too far from the loft. He remembered they made the best Red Curry Chicken.

Shivering from the chill in the air, Neil grabbed his clothes, which were spread out along the floor. He slipped into a pair of pants and checked the window. The sight of snow reminded him of Canada. From the light dusting on the sidewalks, it appeared as if the snow had just started.

As Neil watched the amber streetlights highlight the snowfall, he witnessed a young man hunched over on the street corner. The young man was thin, his hair long and scraggly. None of his features stood out to Neil. It was the fact that he wasn't wearing any clothes. Even though he looked incredibly familiar, Neil was more focused on the young man's lack of public health.

What kind of person walks around during a snowstorm without any clothes on?

Neil put on a shirt, slipped into a pair of tennis shoes, and walked outside. On second thought, he walked back into his loft and grabbed an extra pair of clothes for the young man and then walked back outside.

He tried to track down the young man on the street corner, but he had no luck.

After a thorough survey across the desolate street, he spotted him darting into an alleyway. One object stood out the most and it was what the young man was carrying. From where Neil was standing, it appeared as if it was a hockey stick.

Neil chased after him.

Once he reached the alleyway, he lost the young man.

"Hello," Neil said, his voice clearer.

Sounds were brought forth.

The first sounds to come forward were the loud *bangs* and *thuds* of what Neil assumed was the same hockey stick striking building walls, as well as street signs in a state of rebellion. Neil walked through the alleyway and followed the sounds to yet another alleyway where he came across the same young man standing in the middle of the alleyway. Neil soon realized the young man was himself, a younger version, not a young man but a boy, an old boy, a thirteen-year-old boy.

The boy grinned at Neil.

"I brought you some clothes," Neil said to his younger version.

The boy took off running.

As soon as the boy turned his body to Neil, Neil noticed that same long, jagged ugly scar along the side of his body.

Neil chased after the boy but ended up getting side-tracked by two rats gnawing on what looked like a body part, possibly an arm or part of a leg. He approached the rats and realized it was much too thinner to be an arm or, most certainly, a leg.

Neil placed the spare clothes on top of a closed dumpster and then tried to shoo away the rats.

The two ravenous rats didn't budge, though.

Instead, they continued to wrestle over the foot-long rope-like part.

Enraged, Neil shouted at the rats and then stomped the heel of his foot on the ground.

Eventually, the rats darted into the shadows.

Neil kneeled down and examined the bloody part.

Horror flashed over Neil, his eyes widening, his mouth opening wide in a gaping yawn. He couldn't believe what he was staring at. He didn't want to believe it was what he thought it to be and that, at any moment, he'd wake up from this horrible nightmare and by the rein of time, he'd soon forget such a graphic image had entered his head for other more pleasant images would come and go, pushing the horror back to the darkest places of his thoughts.

Neil followed the trail of blood to an opening behind a loading dock. The old warehouse appeared abandoned.

More curious than concerned of the source of the blood, Neil followed the trail into the dark warehouse. He started to wonder if that younger version of himself was even real but more so a doppelgänger luring him into danger, a possible ambush.

Eventually, Neil located the source of the blood coming from a massive puddle in a well-lit area of the warehouse.

Hazy light from amber-colored streetlights beamed through the openings of the ceiling and cast dark rectangular-shaped lines of each upper window frame along the dusty floors. Neil stepped from the shadows and leaned over the puddle.

The puddle was dark, brownish, but favored heavily to the resemblance of tar; and when Neil reached down, dipped his fingertip into the puddle, pulled away a drop, just a drop, and then held his finger to the light, he witnessed a tinge of red.

Carefully, he rubbed both the tip of his index finger and thumb together in a tight smear, revealing more of that photogenic red color along the edge of his finger.

"Blood," Neil whispered to himself.

He peered closer at the blood and for a second, he swore he saw it move on his finger—actually, move!

Suddenly, Neil stood up and backed away from the puddle of blood. He frantically looked around the warehouse, trying to find the source of the blood; however, except for the rat tracks dotting back toward the alleyway outside, he didn't see any other blood trails leaving the puddle.

He heard a few more of those *bangs* coming from the darkness surrounding the beams of hazy light. The sounds started to circle him—the ambush!

Neil asked, "Who's there?"

As the sounds started to dampen, Neil spun around, leaving his back turned to the puddle of blood.

Before the silence could settle in, a couple of hanging canned lights above him suddenly popped!

Sparks rained down on Neil and darkened the already dimly lit room.

Behind him, a red humanly figure started to rise from the puddle. The figure, man or woman—it was still unclear what sex it was for it had no genitalia—stood at Neil's height, its entire body soaked in thick, red blood.

In the stark silence, Neil heard a *dripping* sound behind him. Each drop sent a wave of terror through Neil, causing him to tremble.

With the same horrified expression on his face, Neil slowly turned his shoulder and found himself standing face-to-face with the bloody figure. Neil studied the figure's face and didn't see one feature that indicated it was human. No nose or mouth and even if it had eyes, they were covered in blood. Neil couldn't make out its skin either, for it was covered in all that blood. The figure's arms remained down by its side, closely resembling a stiff manikin.

More intrigued by the motionless figure, Neil took a step closer to it and carefully touched its face with that same finger. He couldn't feel any texture below, no skin, just that red liquid. Since he had gone as far as the first knuckle, he decided to keep reaching. Neil continued to move his finger farther into the figure's head until nearly his entire hand was inside its head. He kept reaching.

Now, wrist-deep, Neil reached until his bloody hand came out the other side of the figure's head.

Startled by the discovery, Neil slowly pulled his hand from the figure's head.

"What are you?" asked Neil.

In its liquidy voice, the blood figure spoke to Neil: "*Beseech thee O lord. Becometh who thou meant to be.*"

Neil didn't know where the voice was coming from since the figure didn't speak with a mouth. He didn't even have lips or a tongue for that matter.

Confused, Neil looked down at his hand, which was covered in red blood, and then turned his eyes back to the strange figure.

Neil finally asked, "Become? Become who?"

All of a sudden, Neil felt a tingly sensation on his hand. He looked back down at his hand and witnessed the blood moving up his wrist and forearm; however, with only his forearm rested in a declined position, the blood continued to move around his elbow and then *up* his bicep.

Neil suddenly freaked. He started to shake away the blood from his right arm. The blood continued to move father up his arm until it reached his shoulder.

With his other hand, he tried to wipe away the blood.

The blood continued to crawl; in fact, now his other hand was covered in blood and that blood started to move up his other arm.

As the blood crawled up Neil's neck, around his chin, and into his mouth, Neil started to claw at his face. He dropped to his knees and the last image he saw before everything went black was another dark figure with long white hair—a man, Neil could tell from the man's posture—standing in the doorway.

A door slammed shut!

⚓

SWEATING profusely, Neil bolted upright from the slam of a door!

His throat was tight, closing. He violently coughed, trying to open up his airways.

The lamp, which was still turned on above the couch, immediately gave away the impression that it was daylight, specifically around noon.

He rolled from the couch, so too the book which was left on his chest when he dozed off.

As he was about to scramble to the bathroom, he noticed a strange smell in the air. First, he smelled himself and realized the smell wasn't coming from him. He turned to the door and swore he saw a shadow moving underneath the doorway.

He checked the front door and opened it. Peeked outside but didn't see or hear anybody in the hallway.

He felt something strike the top of his hand. He looked down and saw a drop of blood on the back of his hand.

Again, he saw yet another drop of blood land on his hand.

A sudden terror gripped Neil, which left him trembling as he slowly turned his head above him. Neil was expecting to find something dead, maybe gutted like a cat, hanging above his doorway. He didn't see anything. He touched his face and realized the blood was coming from his nose.

He closed the door and went to the bathroom where he sipped from the faucet, which alleviated the tightness in his throat.

The water swirling through the sink changed colors.

Neil pulled his head from the sink.

More droplets of blood started to fall from his face. He looked up at the mirror and saw his nose gushing blood. He grabbed a couple of squares of toilet paper and plugged both of his nostrils. He remembered he used to get nosebleeds when he was much younger, usually brought on by allergies or the change in weather.

Neil stepped out of the bathroom and walked over to the window. He opened the curtains and saw the first soft bluish glow of dawn breaking through the night sky. The sky was clear, he realized, *not snowing*.

Unable to breath properly through his nose, Neil decided to remove one of the twirly wads of toilet paper from one of his nostrils. He held the wad of toilet paper before him and stared at the end of it, which was saturated with blood. For a moment, he drifted off into a daze and remembered a fragment from the previous dream: *the disturbing mental image of a severed umbilical cord, which had been gnawed through by rats.* He could see the incredibly vivid images as if they were right in front of his eyes: On the ground below laid an umbilical cord; snowflakes were falling all around him, not the light and powdery kind but the dense and wet kind; to the right of him, a white tabby mottled with dark continent-shaped spots scurried into an open window on the side of an abandoned building; on the ledge of the building perched a crow, which appeared as if it was waiting for Neil to leave before it could swoop down below for a quick nibble of tonight's main entrée. Then, finally, Neil saw himself kneeling down over the bloody umbilical cord, wondering where in the hell it came from since there wasn't any baby in the vicinity—at least none that he heard.

Neil wondered, *What did it mean?*

Never had such a tangled question seem so complex and impossible to unravel. Neil couldn't possibly come up with an answer to the question nor could he even come up with anything remotely plausible to justify as an answer. It was fair to say Neil was a highly intelligent individual, top of his class, bookworm, a future rock star among generations to come; however, when it came down to turning inward and attempting to solve the very riddles surrounding his adolescence, he was left with only chewed up and spat out images from a violent history of unspeakable acts.

⚲

NEIL piddled around the house for most of the morning, mostly digging up photo albums and old postcards from storage and giving his scout's best to grasp an understanding of his most recent dreams that could pass as repressed memories.

When his mahm called, Neil was relieved to say the least to take a break from all of the madness. He put aside torn boxes and answered before the call went to voicemail.

"Yes, Mahm," Neil said, as he tried to catch his breath.

"Is everything okay?" she asked.

"No," Neil started, "I mean, yeah. I was just going through some old things."

"Did you get my call last night?"

"Yeah," Neil said. "I was meaning to call you back, but I wasn't feeling well."

"I was worried for a moment."

"Worried?" said Neil, as he stepped over a couple of boxes on the floor. "Why would you be worried?"

"Did you not hear?"

"No," he said. "What happened?"

"There was a shooting at Cork Out," she said. "Didn't you tell me once that you used to frequent that establishment?"

Neil wasn't quite ready to tell his mahm about what happened last night.

But he felt as if he had no other choice.

"Yes," Neil said finally, his voice weak. "About that. . . "

⚲

KAMARIA'S Mazda was parked outside the house in the same spot as last time.

Neil parked behind her car and while, on his way to the front door, checked the inside of the car. He didn't see any religious books inside; in fact, the entire interior of the car was clean and appeared as if it was brand new.

Neil pulled his face from the backseat window and saw what looked like a pale face hanging in mid air over his shoulder in the reflection. The sight of the face caused Neil's insides to stir; however, he remained remarkably still.

Cautiously, Neil turned around and witnessed an older woman with frizzy gray hair standing behind the front living room window of the house across the street. She had a smile stretched out along her wrinkly face, which appeared as if it could have been made into a Halloween mask.

Neil thought she was maybe smiling at someone next to him, maybe his mahm who had come out of the house. Or, Neil wondered, maybe she wasn't even smiling at anybody. Instead, she had a son who was obsessed with Norman Bates and the fictional character had put some "ideas" in her son's head, ideas involving her son to become fixated on his mama, so much that, after she croaked, he ended up having a taxidermist stuff the poor ole woman. Then, daily, he'd place her at her favorite spot by the window.

As the hair started to rise over Neil's skin from the sight of the woman standing behind the window, Neil slowly turned around toward the house behind him. His mahm was nowhere around. He turned toward the neighbor's house, thinking maybe Mahm's chatty neighbor, Sue Ellen, was standing on the porch. As much as he dreaded talking to that yappy closed-minded bitch, for a moment he yearned to see her sitting in her squeaky rocker on the porch, ready to fill Neil in on the latest gossip and "trending" stories spewed from the decayed mouth of television, as if it was the TV that had a wicked spell on her and told her "what to say" or "how to think." Sue Ellen was not there. In fact, *nobody* was there, not on the street or on the sidewalk or on the porch, not anywhere. He realized that he was the only one in the woman's range of view.

He turned around and stared back at the old woman. He didn't know her story, didn't know her name. He couldn't recall his mahm mentioning anything about her, only that she had a daughter, he thought. Whoever the woman was, she continued to look directly at Neil and deliberately smile at him.

Neil gradually raised his hand in a wave.

The woman didn't wave back.

Instead, she just stood there, forever smiling.

🪶

AS soon as Neil stepped into the house, his mahm gave him a hug and expressed to him how glad she was that he wasn't injured. Only a couple of minutes of Neil being inside the house, his mahm delved straight into "lecture mode," instructing her son to stay away from bars, never to go there ever again, telling him that they there were nothing but trouble, despite his mahm not even stepping foot into one in the past thirty-plus years. His mahm had clearly been talking to Sue Ellen.

Neil took her sharp criticism and redundant advice on the chin and made his way toward Ajay's room. His body tensed up once he saw the empty hospital bed in the room. His mahm walked past Ajay's room, leaving Neil more confused as to what was going on.

Before he could ask her what they—as in her and Ajay—were doing outside in the garage, he noticed Kamaria sitting next to Ajay's wheelchair. Dozens of open boxes were scattered throughout the garage, half of them looked as if they had been picked through.

"What are you looking for?" Neil asked his mahm.

"We're just going through some of my old clothes," his mahm said to Neil, as she started to open boxes and remove stacks of folded sweaters and pants. "I was going to donate the clothes to Goodwill, but, since Kamaria and I are the same size, I was thinking about giving them to her."

"I see," Neil said, his voice trailing off.

Kamaria closed the hardback she was reading as Neil walked down the ramp. Once he reached Ajay, whose wheelchair was parked at the edge of the garage, he glanced over at the book resting in Kamaria's lap. He couldn't tell what book she was reading for both her hands were covering the cover, although he had an idea.

Neil said to Ajay, "Sup, Ajay."

Ajay responded with a thumbs up.

Neil's eyes traced his brother's arm. He found a squared piece of gauze taped on the inner part of his elbow. He couldn't help but notice several other red dots around the gauze from where he had been poked by a needle.

His mahm recognized Neil's devout interest in Ajay's arm and as he turned to his mahm wide-eyed and ready to ask the inevitable question, his mahm chimed in, "Ajay had his blood drawn this morning. I thought I told you."

"No," he said with surprise.

In return, she turned to Kamaria and talked about Neil as if he was standing in the same room as her.

"As you can tell," she said to Kamaria, "Neil is very protective of his brother. I remember when he was little he'd stand outside Ajay's room, watching him with intensity.

He'd stand there for the longest time, just watching Ajay—
"

"—Mahm, enough. . . "

He turned to his mahm and was no longer wearing another question on his face but the mask of humiliation.

"Doctor Singh wanted to check Ajay's liver function since he recently changed medication."

"Looks like the nurse had a time finding a vein," Neil said, as he examined his brother's forearm.

"Don't get me started on her," his mahm said, holding out her right hand like a preacher exercising demons out of gullible churchgoers. "That woman was nothing but incompetent."

"Your mother told me what happened last night," Kamaria said to Neil, as if she was trying to defuse the soon-to-be eruption from his mahm.

"It's terrible," his mahm said before Kamaria could finish a thought. "It's been all over the news. They're thinking that he might've been a terrorist."

Neil was ready to tell his mahm that "they" didn't know what "they" were talking about and that she shouldn't always take what "they" said word-for-word.

"You have good karma," she went on to say.

"I don't think karma had anything to do with it, Mahm," Neil said.

"Sure, it did," she said, as she turned to Kamaria and held up a red sweater for her. She asked her, "What do you think?"

All Neil could think about while looking at that sweater was the graphic images of last night's dream: that puddle of blood in the abandoned warehouse, that strange figure rising from the blood, and then, waking up to a nosebleed.

"It's lovely," Kamaria said, pulling Neil from his thoughts. She turned to Neil and said to him, "Red happens to be my favorite color."

"Well, you're in luck," his mahm said, digging through a box. "I have plenty of red."

Neil pushed aside his frustration and couldn't help but turn his eyes toward that strange marking on Kamaria's neck. From the better angle, Neil could get a better look at the marking underneath her collar—which, turns out, wasn't a marking at all but more so a brand, like a cattle brand. He could see the pink brand raised on the back of her neck. The symbol was more distinct.

"*What are these?*"

Neil turned to his frantic mahm, who was holding up an old and crinkled *Playboy* magazine, which looked as if it was as old as dirt.

His mahm tossed the magazine back inside the box, which was packed to the brim with other nudy magazines.

In great disgust, she closed the box.

As she was about to place the box in the trash pile at the end of the garage, she saw the bold letters "**JOHN'S THINGS**," which were written in a Sharpie on the outer fold of the box.

She curled her shoulders into her body and said innocently to Kamaria, "*Oops a daisy.*" She started to blush. "I completely forgot about John's 'secret stash.'"

She carried it to the trash pile anyway.

"Mahm," Neil said in a rare defense of his stepfather, "shouldn't you consult John before you throw away his *things*."

"Excuse me, Neil, but these don't belong in my household."

Neil couldn't help but look back at Kamaria, the marking—or brand—on her neck, then the smirk on her face. Before he could lose himself in the strange expression, she turned her head toward Neil, who, in return, immediately looked the other way as soon as he saw her eyes pinned on him.

Behind Neil, John walked up the side of the driveway and stopped at the front of the garage as if he wasn't allowed to enter. Neil nodded hello at John, who followed with a subtler nod. But it wasn't John's lack of enthusiasm in the informal greeting that caught Neil off guard. It was the tension that immediately followed as soon as John found himself in the vicinity of Kamaria. His mahm didn't notice—or maybe she did but wasn't saying anything—but it was clear to Neil that something was going on between the two. Kamaria directed her attention toward Ajay and started petting the side of his arm.

Neil wondered if it was the fact that John knew Mahm found his secret stash and he wasn't saying anything, not a word, as if John didn't want to bring up the subject or draw anymore unnecessary attention to the subject and end up making himself even more uncomfortable than he already was.

John asked Neil to grab the trowel, which was hanging on a hook on the wall.

While John and his mahm started arguing about the weeds in all of the flowerbeds and how John wasn't doing a good enough job at picking them—which Neil thought was his mahm's subtle way of retaliating for finding John's nudy magazines—Neil saw a golden opportunity and decided to take advantage.

Neil discreetly pulled the phone from his back pocket while reaching for the trowel on the wall. He carefully moved his arm underneath his other and held the phone by his waistside. Without anybody noticing, mainly Kamaria, he snapped a photo of the brand on Kamaria's neck.

After he grabbed the trowel, he slid the phone back in his pocket, walked over to John, and handed him the trowel. John thanked Neil. Then, as John went back toward his business in the garden, Neil caught his eyes moving toward Kamaria's direction. Neil felt as if John was watching Kamaria but not watching Kamaria, if that made any sense.

Feeling like one big elephant in a roomful of elephants, Neil said to his mahm, "Well, I'm going to take off."

"But you just got here," she replied, sounding disappointed.

"I gotta lot of things to do today," Neil said, feeling a headache tightening inside his head.

"Okay," his mahm said. "Well, I'll walk you out."

"You sure?"

"I don't mind," she said. "I need to stretch my legs."

As she was about to show Neil to the front door, John stopped in his tracks and turned around. "I almost forgot," John said directly to Neil. "You still want those razors?"

"I can get them some other time," he said to John.

"You might as well take them with you while you're here," John insisted.

"John's right," his mahm said flatly.

Neil never thought he'd ever hear his mahm speak those words about his stepfather.

As Neil made his way back up the ramp, John walked around the house and entered through the screened-in porch, which was connected to the garage.

Neil thought it was odd for John to walk around the house when he could've walked straight through the garage. Nevertheless, John grabbed the jumbo pack of Shtick razors from his bedroom closet and brought them into the kitchen where he handed them to Neil, as if it was his way of trying to buy Neil's attention. He thanked John for the new razors, which he'd most definitely put to good use; in fact, he had enough razors to last him well past the year.

With the razors in hand, Neil said his goodbyes to John, who, instead of walking Neil to the front door, turned around and made his way back outside.

As Neil was about to head toward the door with his mahm, he said, "I forgot to say goodbye to Ajay." He held out his hand, as if he was motioning for his mahm not to move.

As he stepped into the garage, he saw John and Kamaria arguing. He couldn't hear exactly what they were talking about, but he was sure that they were arguing from the redness in John's face.

As soon as John realized Neil was standing in the garage, he suddenly became all quiet and proceeded back to the flowerbeds, not even uttering another word to Kamaria.

Neil walked back down the ramp, said his goodbyes to Ajay, then, lastly, Kamaria, who could only shortly muster the word *bye* through her shaky voice.

During the brief exchange, her shyness was as plain as day to Neil. Neil didn't know whether or not she was shy

by nature. Where she projected professionalism and confidence in other areas, especially in the role of taking care of
his brother, Kamaria nearly clammed up whenever she was,
at times, in Neil's presence.

As Neil walked away, she cracked open her book and
buried herself between the pages, as if she found more comfort in a book opposed to a human.

For a moment, a sense of shame came over Neil, realizing he had taken a photo of Kamaria without her permission. But Neil started to wonder if Kamaria somehow knew
that he had taken the photo; yet, she didn't say anything
because maybe it wasn't her place.

Once Neil made it back to his mahm, who hadn't moved
a single inch from the last time he left her, he said bluntly
to her as if he was geared up for a fight, "Already two days
with this woman and you're already giving away your old
clothes to her?"

Thinking maybe Kamaria had super hearing, she told
Neil to lower his voice.

"She can't hear me," he said, glancing over his shoulder.

"I'm just being nice, Neil, and if you don't like it, then
that's just too bad. You don't have a say so in who I give my
clothes to."

"Being nice?" Neil said closer, "You don't know this
woman."

"She's been good so far, Neil," she said. "Besides, Ajay
seems to like her."

"Well, I don't like her."

His mahm's stern face melted with confusion.

"What don't you like about her?" she asked. "So far she's
done a splendid job. She has his routine down pat: which
meds he takes, what time we turn him. She reads to him.
All in all, she's good with him—as a matter of fact, great.
She's a quick learner and acts as if she's one step ahead of
me, whereas most of the aides in the past have acted as if
they were going through the motions and doing exactly
what they were told. She's very articulate—much better
than Janine. That's for sure—"

"—Mahm."

"What, Neil?"

"I just have a bad feeling about her."

"Lately, you've had a bad feeling about everything."

"I'm serious, Mahm," said Neil. "Something's 'off' about her."

"Give it a rest. Will you, Neil?"

Neil backed off.

His mahm's face went vacant.

All of a sudden, her face lit up with great joy. She moved her eyes to the front door and smiled widely.

Neil turned toward the door and saw that same woman from earlier, the older one with a Joker's smile, still wearing the same wide smile as she approached the house.

A car was passing by while she was crossing the street. She didn't stop, didn't react, didn't even look as she made her way to the house. From the front window, Neil saw the vexed driver of the car tempting to slam his fist into the horn but instead gave the old woman the "Are-you-nuts?" expression with his hands.

Walking beside the older woman was a much younger woman who appeared as if she was closer to Neil's age.

"It's Verona," his mahm said, as she mindlessly made her way to the front door.

Neil warily followed his mahm toward the front door.

As Neil made his way through the foyer, he caught a dark figure in the corner of his eye. He looked upward and saw a familiar young man—a boy, Neil realized—standing at the top of the landing. He looked closer. The boy was the same one from his dreams, a younger version of himself, looming above, looking down on Neil. In his right hand, he was holding a hockey stick, which from Neil's point of view appeared as if it was a scepter carried by someone of royal power.

He attempted to shake the hallucination. He looked yet again at the top of the landing and the boy was still there, looming above like a sovereign king. The boy emotionlessly turned to his right and walked straight into the guest room.

"Neil?" a voice said next to him.

Neil turned and saw his mahm standing at the doorway.

"Are you coming outside?" she asked, her face expressionless.

"I got to use the restroom real quick," he said and walked upstairs.

"But you can use the one down here," his mahm hollered out.

"Just give me a minute," he said, as he made his way up the staircase.

An overwhelming sense of tedious familiarity came over Neil once he reached the top of the landing. He turned his shoulder and looked back down at the foyer below and a wave of clarity washed through his body as if he had been here before, right here, as in he had lived through this *exact* moment, his mahm waiting on the porch outside while he went off upstairs. He didn't remember what exactly he was doing up here or what had prompted him to go upstairs. He remembered the boy walking into the guest room, as if to show Neil a part of him that was buried many years ago.

Neil stepped into the guest room. He didn't see the boy anywhere in the room; and for some strange reason, he knew he wouldn't find him in here.

But something was in here.

He looked around the room until his eyes landed on one particular oddity.

The bottom drawer of the dresser had been partially cracked open.

Neil decided to open the drawer. He had absolutely no idea what he was looking for or why he was looking for it. He kneeled down and opened the drawer. In the bottom of the drawer were stacks of old records and papers. Neil came across three baby books, each one called *A Baby's Days*. Neil opened the first book, his *Baby* book. He skimmed through notes, which were written in his mahm's handwriting, notes like where he was born, when he was born. Then, he cracked open the other *Baby* book, Ajay's. He flipped through photos of Ajay in the hospital, photos of Ajay in an incubator, photos of Ajay spending nearly his entire childhood in and out of a hospital, hooked up to wires and tubes as if he was a cyborg.

He respectfully put back his brother's *Baby* book in the drawer and opened the other one, the third one.

The book was empty.

He went back to his own baby book. Immediately, the name *McLloyd* jumped out at him, not the other. He skimmed through the details of his birth. "I was delivered by: *McLloyd, Harriet.*"

McLloyd.

Neil ripped out the page from the baby book and pocketed it.

As he made his way back downstairs, he noticed the front door was opened.

His mahm was outside standing with her neighbor Verona and whom Neil suspected was Verona's only daughter. They weren't talking, though. Which he found was odd since he had been upstairs snooping around for at least five minutes.

As soon as he stepped outside, Verona said to his mahm, "Why, hello there, Tanisha!"

His mahm returned by asking how she was doing. Which Neil found incredibly odd. He couldn't help but wonder what the women were doing all this time when he was upstairs.

Staring wide-eyed at Neil, Verona pointed her arthritic finger at Neil and said feverishly to his mahm, "This must be your son."

"Yes," she said, turning to Neil as he approached the three. "This is Neil."

"I know all about you," Verona said, as she pulled out one of Neil's books from behind her back. "In fact, I've read everything you've written."

"You never told me you were a fan, Verona."

"Not a fan," she corrected her, "actually, I tend to think of myself as more of a follower."

"Really?" Neil's mahm said, surprised by the recent revelation that her neighbor ended up being one of her son's Readers who after seven years of living next door to the Reddy's hadn't uttered a single word about Neil's writing.

Neil moved the pack of razors underneath his armpit and freed up his hand for Verona's hand. The handshake wasn't even of this millennium nor did it come close to resembling any handshake he had ever seen throughout his lifetime, but rather more of an unpleasant rubdown of his hand. She squeezed and at times, prodded at random areas of Neil's hand, as if she was making sure that the person standing in front of her was the same Neil Reddy who was on the back flap of her books.

"Nice to meet you, Verona," Neil said unsteadily, as he removed his hand from Verona's grip.

Verona gestured toward the quiet woman standing next to her who Neil assumed was her daughter, considering the two had a similar nose, mouth, and jawline.

The younger woman handed the book, *The Dark One at The Landing*, to Neil.

Verona asked Neil if he could sign her copy of the paperback.

Neil was glad to sign the book, but he didn't have a pen on him.

No problem.

Before the thought popped in his head, Verona was already holding out a pen for Neil.

"You always carry a pen with you?" asked Neil, as if he was making a joke.

Verona didn't laugh from the dry remark. Instead, she displayed a nervous smile for Neil and said under her toothy smile as if she was a ventriloquist's doll, "Only when I know I'm going to be in the company of a genius."

"Thank you," Neil said, as he, like before with Kamaria, furtively swallowed a pit of shame down his throat for passing judgment on the old lady without even talking to her. "That's really sweet," he said with a quiet charm.

Verona handed the pen to Neil, then the book.

"So," he said, "who do I make it out to?"

"Verona," she said, "Verona De Rose."

Neil signed the inside cover of the paperback:

"To Verona De Rose,
Thank you for all of your support
— Neil Reddy."

Neil handed the signed copy to Verona.

She read the message and then pressed the book against her chest like a mother nestling a baby.

"Thank you so very much," she said, her hands shaking.

"Your very welcome," Neil said.

She reached over to the other more skittish woman, grabbed her hand, and then yanked her closer.

"This here is my daughter, Lilith," Verona said to Neil.

Immediately, the younger woman's name jumped out at Neil.

Being an individual who always saw the symbolism in nature and looked at a person's name more as a symbolic reference of the physical embodiment of the individual who held the name—for instance, Neil himself, sharing the name, *Neil*, with the first person to walk on the moon, felt a sense of great pride knowing his name was among a hall of champions—Neil's mind went straight to the name, *Lilith*.

According to Jewish folklore, as well as described in a range of historical texts, Lilith—which in Hebrew-language text, appeared in Isaiah 34:14 in a list of "unclean" animals—had many descriptions, the most notable and common one being a female demon who stole and killed newborn babies in the middle of night—or "darkness." In the Bible, she was Cain's first wife. In other ancient texts, Lilith was Adam's first wife before she was dispossessed by Eve.

Even though the woman standing before him was not the "night creature" who was known as Lilith, Neil couldn't help but pay attention.

Over a tense pause, Neil eventually managed to barely nod his head in vacant acknowledgment.

"Hi," he uttered, as if the rest of the sentence had become lodged in his throat.

"It's a pleasure to finally meet you," Lilith said bashfully.

Neil didn't know what to say to the pallid-skinned woman. She had greasy red hair, which stopped right above her shoulders, her split ends like tiny pitchforks, her bangs brushed out in front of her forehead and had been crookedly trimmed an inch over her brow. She carried herself as a woman who looked as if her mother had cut her hair every other Tuesday. Her clothes looked like her grandmother's hand-me-downs saved from her days as a child of the flower power.

Hesitant, Neil said back, "Pleasure to meet you."

"So," Lilith started, as she struggled to look Neil in the eye, "what's it like being famous and all?"

"I don't consider myself famous—"

"—Don't be so modest, Neil Reddy."

Lilith let out a nervous giggle as she touched Neil on the arm.

Verona and Neil's mahm stepped aside and left Neil and Lilith to talk among themselves, as if the whole greeting was some kind of setup for a date or hookup.

Neil eavesdropped on his mahm, who was asking the neighbor about her roses and how she grew them so lustrous. Verona told his mahm that she used crushed eggshells to enrich the soil and combat diseases.

Once they saw Neil eavesdropping, Verona guided his mahm over to her lawn, leaving Lilith behind with Neil.

"*So,*" Neil said over the awkward silence, as if it was the only word to start off a seemingly unwanted conversation, "how long have you been living with your mother?"

Lilith ignored Neil's question and stepped closer to Neil, close enough to smell last night's alcohol on his skin.

"What do you say we go somewhere more quiet," she turned to Verona, who, in return, glanced over at her daughter, and then redirected his mahm's attention toward her bright red roses along her walkway, "you know," she said, facing Neil, "away from curious eyes."

Neil didn't know before it was too late. But Lilith's hand had already made it to his belt buckle and was making its way into his pants.

Once Neil felt Lilith's cold fingers rubbing against his lower abdomen, he suddenly recoiled and redirected her hand away from his body.

"Did I do something wrong?" asked Lilith.

Neil said to her, "I have to run. But it was nice to meet you, Lilith." As Neil made his way to the car, he called out to his mahm from across the street, "I'll catch you later."

Before his mahm had a chance to say goodbye, Neil had already taken off in his car.

⚲

ON the way to the university, Neil couldn't get the color red out of his head. Everywhere he turned, he saw the color as if he was looking for the color. He passed red cars on the road. Red signs. Spotted pedestrian dressed in red clothes, even dogs, one in particular, a cockapoo wearing a red sweater. On the patio outside a coffee shop called The Louvre located in the university plaza, students were wearing red. The coffee cups were red. Of all colors, red. Red was everywhere.

Distracted, Neil took his eyes off the road for a moment and once he faced the road, he saw red glaring at him. He slammed on the brakes and came inches away from driving into a busy intersection.

Right then and there, he knew he wasn't fit to go to class.

He had red on his mind.

⚲

ONCE Neil stepped into his apartment, he rushed into his office and plugged his phone into the computer. He pulled up the recent photo of Kamaria's marking—or brand—on the screen. As he was inspecting the photo, he noticed Ajay and the face he was making during the precise moment when the photo was taken.

He zoomed in on Ajay's face and made note of his facial expressions: his brow shaped into a crooked letter v; his nose crinkled; his teeth nearly barred. It was obvious to Neil that his brother appeared enraged by Kamaria—which, except for maybe every now and then when he was about to do his business, was incredibly odd because Neil had never seen his brother make such a distinct facial expression. Neil couldn't help but wonder if his younger brother was trying to tell him something that he couldn't tell him in front of Kamaria but only in a photo.

Neil printed out two photos, one being the original size and the other being a blown up photo of Kamaria's neck. He held the photos underneath the desk lamp and with a pen, began to trace the symbol onto a napkin that was leftover from a greasy bag of fast food.

Once the symbol was written down on the napkin, he removed all of the photos and notes on each monster he had researched and wrote about in his latest novel, including monsters from different folklores around the world, as well as fictional characters such as *Dracula, Frankenstein's* monster, *Wolfman*—or Lycanthrope—and every monster in between, from the walls in his office and placed the photos on his desk.

Now, with his walls bare of monsters, he tacked the photo of Kamaria's neck, as well as the napkin with the symbol on the blank wall.

Neil said to himself, "Where to start?"

As Neil did before he drafted a novel, he asked himself the one question: *Why?* Then, the simple question started to grow and take shape. What's the reason for writing a book? To inform? Neil immediately threw away the idea of writing for the need of public consummation. Right now, he didn't care about the public—or the public's perception.

All Neil had was suspicion. If he knew where the symbol had come from, then he knew it would lead him directly to the questions he needed to be asking, which would inevitably lead him to the answers as to *why* he felt so strongly about researching a symbol. Kamaria, whether purposefully or not, was giving him a sign that he couldn't ignore.

Before Neil started digging through the books in his library, he pulled out one particular book, his book, the very first edition of his debut novel, *The Dark One at The Land-ing*.

Three people have now approached me within a week, Neil thought to himself. One, an older woman who had never pegged as a fan, then, the guy from the book signing, then, the young woman, who mentioned to Neil about how the book had changed her, turned her life around, since she, too, had grown up medicated. She, too, had lost a father as well and spent the days after soul searching.

But why the sudden attention to this *particular* book?

Of all the books Neil had written, this one was, by far, the one he tried to put behind him. But, over these past couple of days, the book was revealing itself yet again and again, as if it was reminding Neil of what really happened on that lake, making him question himself whether or not if his childhood friends jumped into icy water, as if it was he was the one who "dared" them to jump in or convinced them or even pushed them in.

In the book, he wrote that he fell in; but deep down inside, he always felt as if it was he who had "jumped" in, not his friends, not anybody.

What he did know was the feeling he experienced after he wrote the book, the immediate relief, that instant grati-fication, which was followed by weeks of severe depression. In an uncomfortable interview with Diane Harwich of the magazine, *Reader's Circle*, Neil said that writing the novel felt like "giving birth."

Neil put the book aside for the time being and started going through the books in his library. He pulled out every book on folklore and mythology, searching for that particular symbol on Kamaria's neck. He had seen the symbol before; otherwise it wouldn't have grabbed his attention like it did when he first met Kamaria.

But *where*, Neil wondered, *where did I see it?*

He pulled out the hardback *Greek Mythology: The Stories, Myths, Legends* and skimmed through the book but couldn't find the symbol he was looking for.

Next, he tried various books on folklore that involved creatures or monsters—which was Neil's specialty—as well as ancient symbols; skimmed through books on Jewish and Germanic folklore, Old Norse, Medieval, The Dark Ages, then the Bible, both Old and New Testament. Old Hebrew text. Russian text.

Frustration mounted after he went through every *Book of* (fill in the blank). He pulled out a book called *Greek Geek*, which was a book on *All Things Greek*, and went through the Greek alphabet, starting from *alpha* and ending with *omega*. He compared the symbol on Kamaria's neck to each letter but only had luck on the letter *psi*, the twenty-third letter of the Greek alphabet. The shape of the symbol was similar in nature and partially resembled *psi*; however, the ends of the symbol curved outward like snakes, whereas *psi* looked more like a pitchfork.

He kept searching and moved onto books on the Mayans (*The Mayan Calendar: Is the End of the World Nigh?*), then the mighty Aztecs (*Place of the Gods* and *Autumn 1519*), Mysteries of the Ancient Americas. He didn't have any luck, so he moved onto Hieroglyphics, thinking maybe the Egyptians may throw him a bone. No luck. He moved onto Old Norse (*The Vikings*). Immediately, the runes grabbed his attention. He flipped through the pages like a madman. One letter in particular looked similar to the symbol; but, like the letter *psi* in the Greek alphabet, it looked more like a pitchfork—or one may even look at it as a stick figure with only two arms, which were both extended outward. Either way, it wasn't the symbol he was desperately trying to find.

During Neil's thorough search of flipping through one symbol after another in popular and religious culture, both controversial and historical, from the swastika to the shatkona to the sacred symbol of Om—or "Aum"—to Dhammachakka (*the wheel of Dhamma*) to the Hammer and Sickle to the Pentagram to the Caduceus to Ouroboros to the Eye of Horus to Yin Yang to the Labyrinth to the Christian fish, he received a text on his phone.

Even more frustrated by the sound of the phone *chirping* at him like a brat, he put the book aside and grabbed his phone.

A string of texts were coming from Breanne.
The first text read:

I was thinking about you. How are you holding up?

Neil didn't like the question and those two words *holding up*, like she had reason for being concerned. He read more texts.
The text read:

I can't get any work done. I need a drink.

The last text didn't sit right with Neil; in fact, it was made him angrier than the one before.
"Good for you," he said to himself. "Then, you do that. Why do you need me to hold your fucking hand all the time? You're a grown woman."
Neil didn't write that in the text, never would, but he actually thought about it. Even started out writing it, then quickly deleted it before he sent it.
Breanne sent yet another text, the inevitable text:

Do you want to meet up?

"Do you want to meet up?" Neil repeated, as he fumed at the phone. "Excuse me? What do I look like to you—"
All of a sudden, the phone responded back to Neil in mid-rant.
"*I have very few wants,*" the monotone voice of his phone spoke to him.
He looked at the wavelength of his phone's voice assistant moving on the bottom of his phone's screen.
"I wasn't talking to you, you fucking robot," Neil said to his phone.
The phone went silent.
Then, another *chirp*!
Neil received yet another text, his last text:

Are you okay?

172

"Am I okay?" he said. "Why wouldn't I be okay?"

Neil was tempted to text Breanne, but he figured, considering his current state, it was better to leave her alone.

He switched the phone's ringer to silent, including vibrate, which he switched off as well, and hid it in the bottom drawer of his desk.

As Neil was about to get back to his search, he closed the book and slammed it against the top of his desk.

He thought about the text, all the distractions while he was trying to get to the bottom of why he was so suspicious of Ajay's new aide, then the phone, and then Breanne, being his number one distraction.

She doesn't care—never did, Neil thought. *If she cared*, she *wouldn't be asking me to grab a drink* with her—wouldn't be *enabling me.*

In a state of uncontrollable rage, Neil grabbed the *Viking* book with both hands and flung it against the shelf, knocking over several other books to the floor. He didn't stop there. He grabbed other books that he had already skimmed through earlier and threw them around as well while, at the same time, screamed so hard and loud that the veins started to protrude on the top of his forehead.

Lastly, in one sweeping motion, he ran his arm across the shelf closest to him and dumped nearly an entire row of books onto the floor.

Once he tired himself out with all the screaming, he collapsed to the floor. At that moment in time, he couldn't even tell the difference between a "breakdown" and a "breath through." He was pretty sure that he was having one or the other. *But* did a person know—even recognize— that he or she was having a breakdown while he or she was going through a breakdown? *Or*, was this something else?

Neil closed his eyes while he rested on the floor for a minute and tried to catch his breath.

Once he was calm, he opened his eyes. He couldn't help but notice one particular book lying page-side down on the floor. He noticed a white smear on the side of the spine.

Intrigued, Neil sat up and crawled over to the book. He tilted his head in order to read the spine.

Neil read the title to himself, "*The Unspoken: A History in Indo-European Linguistics.*"

With his index finger, Neil touched the white gooey substance on the back of the book and rubbed it against his thumb.

At first, he thought maybe it was spit or phlegm, but, after thorough inspection, realized it was too thick to be either.

He pressed both the tip of his index finger and thumb tightly together and then felt the stickiness of the strange substance as he pulled his fingers apart.

"Glue," he said in fascination.

Neil flipped over the hardback and paused in thought. He couldn't recall going through the book; however, Neil couldn't recall much of anything during that red, violent haze. Also, he didn't have the faintest idea of where the glue came from. Did *I* even *own glue*?

After Neil cracked open the book, he skimmed through the pages and noticed a few pages were stuck together. The glue was soft, delicate, and incredibly weak, like the glue-stick kind, and strangely, still moist enough not to ruin the page.

But why?

Neil asked himself, Why these pages?

Was there *somebody* really *in my apartment*?

If somebody wanted to cover up these pages, then *why not just remove them? Why keep them in the book* for me to find?

Or did I glue them together in the past, when I was drunk or passed out? Neil wasn't known to sleepwalk, but he had heard stories of people doing the craziest things while sleepwalking.

Carefully, Neil unpeeled the sticky pages.

The symbol. . .

He immediately snatched the napkin from the wall and compared the symbol on the napkin to the symbol on the page.

They both matched!

He researched the symbol and after a quick read, learned that the symbol came from an ancient cult, a Proto-

Armenian tribe known as the *Patver*—or most commonly known as "Children of the Order." While serving as regent around 800 BC and ruler of the Neo-Assyrian Empire, Shamiram—or Semiramis—who was often depicted as a mythical figure in Persian mythology, waged war against the Patver in order to defeat her husband's elusive murderer named Derasanner—"Dera," a two-headed serpent monster who dwelled at the base of Mount Ararat. Members of the Patver worshipped Dera as a god, the supreme ruler, not Shamiram.

With the symbol fresh in his mind, he knew exactly what book he needed next in his research. He went straight to a book called *Armenian Folklore* and flipped to the chapter on "Derasanner, the monster whose arm had been chopped off during a violent battle against Shamiram, thus spawning an army of demon warriors through the spill of its blood." According to the folklore, Shamiram ended up retreating to the top of the mountain in defeat for Derasanner's army was too great of numbers. There, at the summit of Mount Ararat, the once valiant warrior wept for months. Shamiram wept so hard that the rivers had formed below the mountains; and the spirits of those who bathed in the ancient waters were cleansed of all evil and impurity. Neil was aware of the enigmatic monster, Dera, aware of the legend, aware of the many variations, one of them being Droki from India, then in the *Lamboroti*, which explained the creature *Druch*—or Dera— in detail and how it was able to move through blood, as well as infiltrate the body of another life form, including man or animal.

In *Buch der Mythen*, Druch was known to have acquired the ability to consume the human soul—"Geist"—from the Great Manipulator, Teufel—or the "Devil." Druch was known to feed off the soul, leaving its host without a soul, not dead but mindlessly going about life in the most primitive manner.

Neil found a picture of Druch, its "true form," which was a glutinous creature with arms like tentacles, its blubber consisting of mostly water-weight.

Another picture showed a depiction of a pagan ritual in Alemannia. The warrior of the Germanic tribe, who was dressed in a wolf-like costume, was "exploding" in blood; the blood was splashing onto the warrior's gathered around him—or what was left of him.

Neil considered writing about Dera and the many variations of its origins in his latest novel but chose not to. At the time, he was too hung up on movie monsters, resulting him to ignore the ones that inspired them. He was also aware that Dera, playing a crucial role in Armenia, was inspired by Dromes—or Dromopates—or best known as in Greek mythology as "Drómos."

In a dizzying speed, Neil grabbed another book, in fact, the first book that Neil picked up while researching the symbol.

Back to square one: *Greek Mythology: The Stories, Myths, Legends.*

He flipped to the chapter on Drómos, a tumorous-skinned troll who dwelled in a beehive type cave—or tomb—along Styx River. Drómos was well known for deceiving Charon with the promise of food and vast riches in order to lure souls into his hollow where it'd consume their souls before reaching the gates of Hades. He was known as one of the most deceptive gods, most notably known for being cast from Mount Olympus for his pranks and trickery against Zeus and company.

Neil flipped to one particular photo with droves of nude and bosomy women surrounding Drómos in a dome-like hall, beautiful women feeding and pleasuring Drómos. According to one myth in the *Ancient Welders*, Drómos had a child with Artemis named Styxis.

But, Neil wondered, *what does Drómos have to do with the symbol?*

Neil dug deeper.

One day, Drómos bit off more than he could chew when he attempted to prank one particular soul, a half-mortal half-god named Axlar. Through the power of manipulation and deceit, Drómos lured the vulnerable Axlar into his cave, which was filled with mounds of gold and emeralds, as well as a spread of the most succulent meat and fruit. With his head plagued by Drómos's trickery, Axlar took the bait; and as he was filling his belly full of swine, out of the shadows swooped Drómos for an attack. Out for retaliation against Drómos, the ferryman, Charon, who had been concealing not only himself, but also Axlar's blade underneath the invisible cloak of Nartucka, tossed Axlar the famous blade, *The Blade of Axlar,* which he had used to kill one of the sirens. Before Drómos could pounce on Axlar, Axlar severed Drómos's arm and sent it scurrying back to the shadows where it dwelled for hundreds of years. However, Axlar's historical victory was short-lived. Three days later, Drómos lured the half-god half-mortal into yet another one of his traps. Axlar was baffled, thinking maybe Drómos shared the traits of a lizard that could grow back its own tail—in this particular case, its arm—since the creature had the same exact arm that Axlar had severed. Axlar soon learned that the creature ready to destroy him was Drómos's great adversary, Drómia, a shapeshifter who had spawned from the very arm that he had severed with The Blade. Drómia ended up destroying the legendary warrior, Axlar. The blade would later be discovered by Charon, who then carried it back to the Land of the Living.

What made the blade unique—in fact, Neil struggled to remove his eyes from it!—was the symbol on its handle. The symbol was similar to the brand on Kamaria's neck but not the same. The upper half of the symbol had five squiggly lines squirming outward above a finely pointed arched doorway with a line down the middle, which looked close to the top of a blade. Maybe the symbol had been *altered over time,* Neil wondered.

While searching through the hardback, *Éllinas Theós,* Neil found a painting by Urbano, an Italian painter of High Renaissance. The painting was called *Schédio.* In the painting it showed "creode," an advisor to Drómia, standing next to Drómia who had taken the form of Hades, the god of the underworld.

As Neil continued to dig up more stories on the mythological creature, its story started to evolve and so too the creature itself. There were legends in the Pacific Northwest of an infamous troll that lived under bridges. Locals referred to it as "Droll." It was said that Droll used to lure innocent children under the bridge.

In one case in Seattle, a child had been abducted and one witness claimed the child was taken by the elusive Droll.

Other reports varied along the coast: "strange" and unexpected deaths, locals claiming friends or loved ones had become "possessed," "exorcised," even "demented." One school shooter who shot up a high school not too far from the adduction claimed, "a *'blood monster'* told him to kill his classmates;" then other reports of "blood gods" or "blood demons" "moving through the water" or these "parasitic creatures that latched themselves on hosts," appearing before in several victims' drawings and sketches. But as with the Loch Ness Monster, there wasn't enough substantial, as well as credible "evidence" to prove such claims.

Neil kept coming back to that blade, The Blade of Axlar.

The dream, he thought. *The memory. His* memory. He remembered a distant one, deep within the spaghetti-tangled thoughts, one where young Neil was sitting on the shore of Bleu's Lake, scribbling a strange symbol—possibly the very same one on the blade's handle—into the muddy shore.

In a state of awe, he searched for a piece of thin paper inside. All he could find in his office were old newspapers that he had saved in his bottom drawer. He collected the newspapers after tragic events, as well as significant dates throughout history. From presidential elections to riots to mass shootings and catastrophes, whatever made waves throughout the country or was noteworthy enough to land on the front page of a newspaper, Neil had a special drawer dedicated to current affairs. He even had newspapers dating all the way back to September 11, 2001, when two commercial airliners were flown into the World Trade Center in New York City. This particular newspaper happened to be from two months ago, when police apprehended a chic fashionista known as "The Snipper," the most sought-after serial killer since the Golden State Killer. He tore a piece of the newspaper off the back page of the paper and then tore that piece into two other pieces.

With a bold Sharpie, he then sketched the symbol on the blade's handle onto a blank space on one piece of newspaper, then sketched the other symbol, the one on Kamaria's neck, onto the other piece of newspaper. He made sure to press extra hard against the paper so the black ink would bleed through the paper and was legible enough to read if another piece of paper was placed on top of it.

After the two symbols were written down—hard and with multiple strokes—he placed one piece of newspaper over the other and vice versa.

The marking on Kamaria's neck matched the upper half of the symbol on The Blade of Axlar. . .

📌

SOMEWHERE between researching Drómos and his adversary, Drómia, as well as The Blade of Axlar, Neil dozed off. He wound up in the woods again; however, he wasn't younger, commonly thirteen. He was the same age as he was when he dozed off.

As the memory hinted, it was late winter, going on spring. Snow was melting. The floor of the woods was damp and covered with leftover patches of snow in the most shaded spots, whereas areas on the ground where the sun had shone was carpeted with bright colors of new vegetation, greens, browns, yellows, and reds.

In a trance, he wandered deeper into the lush woods as if he was tailing the distant memory, searching for resolve. The last sunrays of daylight cut through the openings in the trees and shone on an object wedged underneath a protruding tree root in the exact spot where he first discovered the strange light when he was thirteen years old, a few weeks after the incident on the ice. The object looked as if it didn't belong to nature; yet, it was either placed there deliberately or accidentally.

By the time Neil reached the fading light, he heard the sound of a *crack* coming from a cabin. The crack was sharp, higher in pitch, like a tiny crack spreading across a pane of glass. He checked out the noise, ignoring the moments before.

When he reached the cabin, the sky turned to twilight, the cover of trees making the atmosphere appear more like night. Dim candlelights flickered inside the cabin. The sight of beating light created more tension in an already tense atmosphere. He couldn't remember seeing this particular place before, not when he was thirteen, not ever. For a brief moment, he thought about turning back around or— worst-case scenario—grabbing a tree branch for his own protection.

As soon as the thoughts came to him, they left him; and he pushed forward.

He made it to a window on the side of the cabin. He peeked through the window.

Bowing before a shrine surrounded by candles were both his mahm's neighbor, Verona, and her daughter, Lilith. The two women were unclothed, their greasy, uncombed hair worn down. On the center of the shrine was a photograph of Neil framed with dead snake's skin. The photo appeared as if it was taken at a professional studio by a photographer and resembled one that normally would've been taken during high school. He was well dressed and groomed, the lighting smooth and even along his face. He was perched on top of a jagged boulder, his shoulders square, chin held tight and upright in superiority.

Verona lifted her head from her bowing position and pulled out a small knife.

Without any hesitation whatsoever, she stabbed the palm of her hand with the sharp end of the knife and held her bleeding hand over a wooden bowl. Next, she handed the knife to Lilith, who, in similar fashion, stabbed the palm of her hand with the knife and then, in similar fashion, squeezed every drop of blood from her wound into the wooden bowl.

Once the bowl was filled with their blood, Verona stood up and placed the bowl before the shrine.

All of a sudden, Neil heard the *snap* of a twig behind him!

He turned his shoulder and peered into the dark woods but didn't see anything out there. Neil shrugged off the noise and figured it was a deer or rabbit or maybe even branch had fallen from a tree.

As soon as he turned back around, Verona was hunched behind the window, her face inches away from Neil's. Her saggy breasts hung downward like water balloons that hadn't been properly fastened around the sphincter-like opening. Her bush was gray and hairy and looked as if it hadn't been manicured since that one experimental year during her freshman year at college. She was holding her left hand into a tightly balled-up fist. Strings of blood dripped from her curled white knuckles. She wasn't wearing that same creepy smile on her face either, the one Neil had imprinted on his mind. She had no expression at all on her face. She was wearing the face of a woman who was long past dead. . .

⚲

FUCK!

Neil suddenly woke up gasping for a breath.

The glob of drool settled on the corner of his mouth acted like adhesive to his skin.

All he could picture in his head was Verona, that creepy bitch staring at him. He could still feel her presence pressed up against his face, still staring. Somewhere in his black thoughts, a smile was growing on her pallid face.

Neil peeled away the right side of his face, which was adhered to the top of the desk, and tried to shake the image from his face.

For a moment, he didn't even recognize where he was. The entire office was a complete mess: books scattered everywhere, some books overturned while others flipped to certain pages and positioned strategically for Neil to find as quickly and precisely as possible, as if he was categorizing his own madness.

Neil decided to freshen up in the bathroom, first by hitting up the john and then washing his hands before rinsing out his mouth with mouthwash. He checked the time on the nightstand while leaning out the bathroom.

Where has the time gone?

As he returned to the sink, he removed his shirt and applied deodorant underneath his armpits. He couldn't help but stare at the scar on his side, which he had ever since he could remember. For years, he never questioned it. He obtained the scar after a complication during his mahm's pregnancy, which left her with no other choice than to have a caesarean section performed on her. So, in a way, the scar was his birthmark—at least that was how he had viewed it because, for years, that was how it was explained to him as a child being a receptacle of curiosity, not a scar but something that was solely him, wicked-looking but his and his alone, like a mole or freckle, only Neil's was way more pronounced, like a road map. Neil wished he only knew where his road began and where it ended.

Or, did it even have an end?

Was life a vicious cycle of reoccurrences?

Random and unexplainable flashes of former lives intertwined inside a dusty ball of cosmic yarn?

Neil curled his shoulder into his body in order to get a clearer look at the scar. He ran his finger along the scar, which stretched down the entire side of his ribcage and abdomen.

When Neil looked at the scar, all he could hear was the screaming. He didn't have an image or a thought when he looked at the scar. Screaming, as if it was a part of the scar, as if it somehow lived inside the scar, its irregular treble moving through his flesh like a dynamic wavelength.

As Neil normally did, he shrugged off the scar. He dragged himself back into the office and decided to remove the phone from the other bottom drawer.

Apparently, from the dozens of texts and emails, Breanne had been blowing up his phone.

Concerned for Breanne, Neil called Breanne.

She answered right before the call went to voicemail.

Neil immediately noticed that her voice was shaky.

"What's up?" Neil asked.

Breanne was hesitant to respond to Neil's question.

"Breanne," he said, "is everything okay?"

She said finally, "I think somebody was. . . was following me on the way home from work."

"How do you know?"

"I just had a feeling. That's all."

Neil fired off a series of questions: "What did he look like? What kind of car was he driving? Did you get a good look at his face?"

"Not he, Neil. A *she*."

"A woman? Really?"

Neil's tone suggested that the woman was following Breanne for other reasons.

"It wasn't like that, Neil."

"I didn't mean it like that."

"Sure, you did."

Neil did—in a way. From Neil's male perspective, the idea alone of a woman chasing after another woman all in the name of love sounded like a fantasy.

"Well," Neil said, as he rid the thought from his head, "who was it?"

"All I know is that she was a black woman."

Kamaria immediately came to mind.

Neil's manner changed. His face turned pale and softer.

"Black?" he said, visualizing Kamaria's face in his mind. "What did she look like? I mean, was she tall? Thin? Did she have high cheekbones?"

"Why does it matter?"

"It doesn't," Neil said. "*But* there has to be a reason as to why she was following you. Have you seen her before?"

"No," Breanne said. "I mean, I don't think so. I don't know. I know she was following me. And I know it wasn't what you think it was. I think she wanted to do harm to me. I mean, she could've been like a stalker."

"A stalker? Why would anybody want to stalk you, Breanne?"

"Thanks," she said, more displeased.

"I didn't mean it like that. I mean, do you have enemies?"

"I don't know."

"You want my advice, Breanne?" Neil asked but didn't expect an answer from Breanne. "Call the police. Lock your doors. Tell them exactly what you told me. There's absolutely nothing wrong with being over precautious. Listen to yourself. Listen to your gut. If your gut is telling you something is wrong, then, more than likely, it is."

"Or, I'm just being paranoid?"

Neil wanted to tell Breanne that she was probably being paranoid. But he had a gut feeling that she wasn't.

"I don't know," Breanne said over a gap of heavy silence. "So," Breanne said, making a noticeable sigh over the phone, "what are you doing?"

Neil looked around the messy office.

"You don't want to know," he said to Breanne.

"Forget I asked," Breanne said with a suppressed laugh trying to break through her tight voice.

As he did whenever he found himself relaxing, he reached into his pocket. He felt an obstruction inside.

Curious, he pulled out the piece of paper that he stole from his own baby book. His eyes moved down the page until he came across that one name, *McLloyd*.

He couldn't get that name out of his name.

McLloyd.

Worth a shot?

Neil heard Breanne chirping in his ear.

"Listen, Breanne," he said over Breanne's voice, "Can I call you back?"

¿

LEANING over the railing on the outside balcony while waiting for the receptionist to transfer his call to the nurse's station, Neil finally got hold of a hospital worker.

He asked the hospital worker if they had a "McLloyd" who still worked at the hospital. The person didn't know of any nurse or midwife of that name who currently worked at the hospital and ended up transferring the call yet again to maybe someone who would know, but turns out, after the third transfer, the hospital and its staff members weren't allowed to give out any information on the hospital's employees.

The call was a dead end.

Neil walked back inside his apartment and logged into his laptop. He googled the name *McLloyd* and *nurse* into the search bar.

The search results left Neil flabbergasted.

With his face slack, Neil scrolled through pages and pages of news articles on Aideen McLloyd, the "Killer Nurse" who made Doctor Death look like a frivolous tourist. She went by many names, such as the "Killer Nurse," the "Queen of Dope," "The Dripper," most notably known for administering her "Drip of Death" to her patients at the same hospital where Neil was born. During her killing spree, McLloyd killed forty-eight patients under her care. Neil wasn't at all interested in the awful crimes she had committed. He was more hung up on the fact that this woman—a convicted murderer—had delivered him into the world.

Neil came across yet another intriguing news article from the *Opecka Star* saying that Aideen McLloyd, the Killer Nurse, was involved in a twisted death cult and each one of the killings was, in a way, a sacrifice to her deity. Nobody could confirm *Opecka Star's* claims were remotely credible since no evidence had suggested that the nurse was involved in any death cult of any kind. Another article stated that she was helping put patients—some being terminal—out of their "misery." Whatever the case may be, McLloyd's story became a legend around New Brunswick.

While scrolling through an article from the *Mantaw Tribune*, Neil came across a black and white photograph of McLloyd being escorted from her home in handcuffs to the back of a squad car through a crowd of reporters after a brief standoff with Mounties. Neil read that Aideen McLloyd was accused of stabbing her husband, Stammy, to death and burying his body in a shallow grave, which was later discovered by cadaver dogs in the woods behind her house. The discovery of the body opened up a murder investigation, Aideen McLloyd being the main suspect. According to reports, Stammy died from multiple stab wounds by what they believed to be a sharp object of some sorts, possibly a blade or hunting knife. Investigators never found the weapon that was used to kill Stammy; however, while the investigators were searching Aideen's property, they found more shocking evidence, a special "cocktail" of drugs, as well as artifacts she collected from each of her victims, which would end up linking Aideen McLloyd to the deaths of forty-eight patients. Aideen never confessed to killing her husband; however, she was charged and convicted for the deaths of forty-eight people, thus branding her with the name "Killer Nurse" or the various names she had earned from her crimes.

Neil zoomed in on the photo and after a close inspection, saw a similar marking on the back of McLloyd's neck.

Part of a symbol—The Blade of Axlar?

Neil ripped off another piece of newspaper, traced the symbol onto the paper, and compared it with the symbol on the blade and then held it against Kamaria's neck. The marking fit exactly on the lower half of the symbol on the blade's handle and when held below Kamaria's marking, it ended up fitting like a piece of a puzzle, forming the same exact symbol on The Blade of Axlar. . .

The whole story, the symbols, the strange markings, were all like peeling back yet another layer of darkness surrounding Neil's childhood, making him question whether or not it was all those murders that eventually drove Neil, as well as his mahm, John, and Ajay out of Canada and not Ajay's illness or search for better house care or doctors. Yet, in a way, Neil's baby blues had seen the story before, when moments came in the form of shapes and colors.

NIGHT was upon Neil.

He spent the entire day scraping the bottom of the Internet bowl, digging and then printing out as much information as he could on McLloyd, as well as her current whereabouts. McLloyd was dead, had died a few months after her conviction around the time Neil was learning how to walk. Neil learned that she had died the same way as his father. The discovery alone drew a distant image from his memory, one he desperately wished to forget. The image of McLloyd lifelessly hanging from the bars of her prison cell by a noose that she had made from a blanket acted as a visual aide to the memory Neil had stashed away. He couldn't help but compare the two images, McLloyd's death and the one of his father hanging from the closet rack by a belt. Even though the details of the suicide were obscured, it was the shape that remained rooted in his mind, a shape that Neil realized would be the theme of tonight's dream.

Turns out McLloyd also had a sister named Eileen, who had changed her last name to Doyle due to all of the public scrutiny that she received in New Brunswick. Neil came across dozens of documentaries on Aideen McLloyd, her murders, as well as interviews with both the survivors and relatives of the victims. In one documentary, filmmakers tried to contact Eileen to give her side of the story but refused to show her face on camera.

As Neil continued to dig, clicking on one article after another, he found an article on Eileen Doyle, formerly known as Eileen McLloyd or "The Killer Nurse's Sister." Eileen died from a heroine overdose four years after her sister was convicted in a court of law. He searched for pictures of Eileen but couldn't find any. He read that Eileen was survived by her parents, "Ealga and Ronan McLloyd," who, like Eileen, had also moved to the States after their daughter's conviction.

According to the obituary, Ealga and Ronan McLloyd lived in Lupine, Florida. He found a Florida address. Then went on American Wings website and found a flight from Wensburg, Virginia to Orlando, Florida. Since the drive from Orlando to Lupine was about an hour away, he'd have to rent a car. He had everything set up, his planet ticket, his rental. His next move remained a click of a mouse away.

🖈

WITH the screech of his mahm's distant scream *ringing* through his ears, Neil suddenly woke in the middle of the night.

He rolled out of bed and walked over to the closet. He cautiously opened the closet and flipped on the light, only to find a rack of shirts.

After all these years of burying the memories that once haunted him, he was remembering again.

But why now?

🖈

NEIL spent the entire flight to Florida mapping out questions to ask Aideen's parents, which would act as "topic points" for the "new book" that he was "supposedly" drafting.

Since Neil didn't have enough time to eat before the flight, he made a pit stop at a McDonalds in Orlando and grabbed a quick bite before they stopped serving breakfast. On the way to Lupine, he ate in the car and rehearsed each question in his head.

When he arrived at the address, he parked in front of the one-story house. An older woman, who was probably a few years older than his mahm, answered the door.

Neil's first question, which he was counting on not screwing up but rather delivering in a smooth and confident manner: "Are you Ealga McLloyd?"

"Yes," the old woman snapped. "Can I help you?"

"Well, my name is Neil Reddy," he said, as he pulled out an ID from his wallet. "I'm a college professor at Christopher Wensburg University—"

"Is that supposed to mean anything to me?"

"Well, I was hoping—if you don't mind that is—if I can ask you a few question about your daughter, Aideen."

Ealga immediately rolled her eyes.

"So, what?" she said, her voice trembling with anger. "You come here to harass me, like all them others?"

"No, ma'am," Neil said. "I working on a novel, part fictional-part autobiographical, and with your help, I was hoping you could shed light on your daughter Aideen."

"You're not a reporter, are you?"

"No—"

"—Or, one of them podcasters or whatever the hell you call them?"

"I'm not a podcaster, Mrs. McLloyd."

"It's *Ms.* McLloyd," she said, as anger started to rise in her face. "Mister died three years and thirty-nine days to the day. While I'm on the subject, I should inform you that it was one of them 'podcasters' or whatever who killed my Ronan. Gave him a heart attack. That little narcissistic shitbag," Ealga said from the side of her mouth, as if she had Tourette's. "That *boy* wasn't even born the time Aidy was locked up. Yet, he comes over here on his white horse, acting like he was the one paying the goddamn bills. I even tried to sue his skinny ass for painting my Aidy as a monster and sensationalizing the facts in order to put more money in his pocket. That little shit," she snapped, "taking advantage of other people's misfortunes to make him feel better about his sorry self. Why shouldn't I come into his sorry life and start snooping around and digging up dirt on him? Exploit all of the shit he's done for the world to devour, huh? Wouldn't that be something? If the little shit didn't have a rich daddy who had himself a hotshot lawyer on speed dial, I probably wouldn't be living in this dump."

"I didn't mean to bring up any grievances you may have—"

"It's all in the past, right? Who needs pieces of shit like that? The world is filled with enough little assholes as it is." Ealga gulped a breath. "Like he's any better," Ealga said, leaning in. "You know what I like to call people like that?"

"No, ma'am."

"Ambidextrous," she said directly. "They're waving their little finger at you with one hand while, at the same time, they're whacking off with the other."

The term *whacking off* was a new one to Neil. He thought it might've been a term she picked up while in Florida.

"Even till this day I still don't know what in the hell a podcaster does," Ealga said. "My daughter made her mistakes and she paid for them dearly. Now, years later after her death I have to relive those *awful* years over again. Talk about hell! I tell you what it is." Her brow sharpened to a point; both of her eyes sharper on Neil. "It's goddamn social media; made these damn kids ornery, these little shitbags think they can walk all over you and exploit you all for 'likes' or to heighten their own self-proclaimed 'celebrity status.' Life's too goddamn short for people like that."

"I'm truly sorry for your loss, Ms. McLloyd, but the truth is," Neil paused for a moment, "your daughter, Aideen, was the first face I ever saw when I entered this world. It was your daughter's hands, which were the first hands that ever touched me. And to say that a 'monster' helped bring me into the world would be a fabrication of the truth."

Ealga smirked.

"You were born in New Brunswick?"

"Yes, ma'am."

"No offense, young man, but you're too tan to be from New Brunswick."

"Before I was born, my parents, who were originally from Kochi, moved from Rajasthan to a small town outside Moncton. From all the stories I gathered from my father— my *Baba*—was an engineer who worked on ships in Fisher's Bay. I don't know my Baba. I never did. He died when I was four years old." He paused and thought about the way his father died, the shape. "At the age of fourteen," Neil said, "my mahm and her second husband decided to move to America in search of the *American Dream* but during the first three years in the States or what my mahm often referred to as 'difficult times,' I soon realized you had to be asleep to even come close to touching this so-called 'Dream' Americans often spoke of. When I got older, I realized people have their own versions of this Dream and it wasn't all cut and dried as they originally made it out to be. I realized, Ealga, it doesn't matter how many 'likes' you have or 'followers.' I just wanted to write about the things people chose not to write about. I chose to be myself, and that, for me, is the American Dream. Ms. McLloyd, Ealga, I didn't come all the way from Virginia to paint your daughter in a negative light. Maybe she was a 'monster' as all of those shitbags described her as being." He pulled out his birth certificate, as well as the description page that was taken out of his mahm's *Baby* book. "Frankly," Neil said, as he handed the page to Ealga, "I don't give a damn about any of that crap. I'm more interested in the woman who helped deliver me into the world, *not* the supposed monster."

Ealga read her daughter's name on the page. Her eyes drifted in thought as she tried to put stock into Neil's proposal.

She didn't think for too long.

✦

EALGA escorted Neil into the living room where a bloodhound named "Droopy" sat next to the couch.

"Fitting name," Neil said, keeping his distance from the dog.

"Well, he keeps me company," Ealga said. "Droopy actually came from a dog that belonged to my daughter. She had a bloodhound that ended up having a litter. I ended up adopting Droopy here when he was just a pup."

Again, Neil kept his distance from the dog.

"She won't bite."

"Wanna hear a joke?" Neil asked.

"Not really," Ealga said flatly.

"What was the name of Dracula's dog?"

Ealga didn't put much thought into the question.

"I don't know," she pointed at Droopy. "A bloodhound?"

Neil's joke didn't get any reaction from Ealga.

"Forget it," he said, as Ealga went to the kitchen and fixed Neil a cup of tea.

From the kitchen, she asked, "So, what kind of stuff do you write about?"

Having lived in the state of Florida for over thirty-something years, her Canadian accent had softened and leaned more toward a Southern drawl; however, her "abouts" still sounded a bit like "a-boats."

Neil paused and thought about the genre.

"Historical fiction," Neil said instead.

Ealga said over her shoulder, "And is that where you think Aideen's story belongs? Historical fiction?"

"No, ma'am—"

"—I appreciate you being polite and all, but you can drop the 'ma'am' part already. I know I'm old. You don't have to rub it in my face."

"I apologize," Neil hesitated. "Wasn't my intention."

"I know."

Ealga placed a pot of water on the stove while Neil wandered around the living room. He stopped in front of a silver framed photograph of what looked like a much thicker and younger version of Aideen on the side table next to the couch. She was wearing blue jeans and a college hoody. Neil could only make out the letters CU on the front of the burgundy hoody. Her hair was trimmed short, like a crew cut. Her frame was masculine. Even though she shared the same facial features as Aideen, she looked nothing like Aideen, shape-wise.

"Was this Aideen when she was younger?" asked Neil.

Ealga poked her head out of the kitchen and looked at the photo in Neil's hand.

"No," she said. "That's Aideen's twin."

"Eileen?"

"You've done your research."

"I'm sorry," he said. "I didn't know she was a twin."

"Eileen passed a few years after her sister's conviction. I'd tell you how she died, but I'm sure you already know that."

Neil nodded.

"Right," he said under his voice.

Ealga nodded at the photo in Neil's hand.

"That was taken some years before she started using. Towards the end, Eileen had turned into a skeleton. I couldn't recognize her, my own daughter. She was a stranger."

She threw a hand towel over her shoulder and walked up to Neil. She grabbed the photo from Neil's hand and looked down at it.

"She would've made a fantastic mother," Ealga said in reflection. "She did, at least for those first couple of years. A year before she died she wasn't all there. It's like she was already gone. The dope had taken her spirit hostage, leaving me with this *stranger.*"

"How many kids did Eileen have?" Neil asked.

Ealga hesitated for a moment. She glanced over Neil, as if she was attempting to read him.

"Just the one," she said finally. "A boy named Ryan. He was adopted." Ealga paused once more. "Eileen, well, she was barren."

"I see."

"She must've picked it up from her poppa's side," she said candidly. "Ronan's sister couldn't squeeze one out either. I guess it's God's sick way of telling you 'up yours,' you're not meant to be a parent."

"What happened to her son, Ryan, after she passed away?"

Ealga paused yet again.

"Her lady friend," she said with rancor. Then her voice trailed off, "Partner or whatever the hell their little 'community' is calling themselves these days." Ealga let out a sigh as if the thought alone of her daughter's "lady friend" put a knot in her stomach. "*She* took off with the kid. Haven't heard from them since. For all I know, she turned that poor boy into a girl, with all of the dressing up and playing hooky all the damn time."

"When was the last time you saw Ryan?" Neil asked.

Ealga leaned closer.

"The day we buried our daughter," she said angrily. "That's when."

Ealga placed the photo on the table, walked back into the kitchen, and poured the pot of boiling water into two cups with teabags.

She handed Neil his cup of tea

Neil thanked Ealga for the tea.

"So," Ealga said, "what you want to know about Aidy?"

⚑

AFTER the visit with Ealga McLloyd, Neil made the difficult decision to stay the night in Lupine to digest all of the recent information before he flew back home in the morning. Most importantly, Neil just needed to clear his head. In a way, he felt Ealga was lying about *not* knowing anything about the symbol on her daughter's neck. Which made him more curious as to why she'd lie about the symbol. He decided to grab a late lunch at a fast-food joint that had the word *burger* in the name. As before, he ate inside his car, chewing and thinking, thinking and chewing.

Once his stomach was full, he brought himself back to reality and searched for a place to stay. Neil didn't have to look far. Lupine had only one, a hole-in-the-wall motel called—of all names—*The Inn*. The motel looked as if it was a meth lab during the day and a brothel at night. Neil had a feeling about the place, as in his gut was screaming at him to keep driving, go back to the airport, try to catch some z's inside a terminal if he had to but the thought alone of sleeping in a chair made his back ache. The closest Best Western was at least forty miles away, and he wasn't about to waste any more gas driving around Florida and risk getting lost in the swamps.

Not only that, the bottom of the sky opened up late afternoon, turning day into night.

Thinking maybe the rain shower would pass, Neil parked in front of the motel and waited in the rental.

Twenty minutes went by and still, the rain looked as if it wasn't letting up.

He decided to brave the rain, threw his jacket over his head, and darted to the main lobby where a slick-haired, greasy-faced man was waiting behind the check-in counter. He appeared subdued, medicated.

With his gut still screaming at him, Neil paid for a room anyway.

In return, the clerk handed Neil a key, which looked like a skeleton key to a dungeon, with a red chewed up fob around the key ring that read something completely different than the current name of the motel.

Neil braved the rain once more. He hurried inside the rental and read the fob.

"Comfort Lodge," it read.

With every force in his body trying to convince him to turn around and drive back to the airport, he drove to the other end of the motel and parked the rental in front of his room.

Room 36.

"Just one night," Neil told himself.

He grabbed his bag and hurried through the rain. The overhang had taken out most of the suspense of unlocking the door without getting drenched.

Once Neil stepped inside the room, which had a faint aroma of winter spice, he closed and then locked the door behind him. He flipped on the nearest lamp and looked around the room, inspecting it closely. The room still had shag carpet. Of all colors, the color red. Crimson red. The two beds were made, the floral comforter tucked so tightly into the mattress it looked as if it was painted on the bed. The first—or second thing—Neil did once he entered the room was check for any peepholes. He checked the bathroom first and then the closets. Checked the vents. Then items on the tables: a clock, which read the wrong time; a dusty Holy Bible inside the top drawer of the nightstand, the book looking as if it hadn't been cracked open since its first publication; a beige ice bucket that still had a dark ring of hardened grime around the bottom; a TV remote with dead batteries. Neil wasn't in any mood to call up the motel clerk on the phone and start complaining about amenities. He figured, since he paid for a forty-nine dollar-a-night room, he was going to get forty-nine dollar-a-night-amenities.

"Just get through it," Neil told himself once more.

As soon as he sat himself down on the edge of the bed, he received a text message from Professor Carroll.

Neil read the text out loud: "Dean told me what happened. Is there anything I can do for you?"

Neil texted back:

> **Thanks for your concern, Drew. But, no. I'm okay. Just a little under the weather.**

In a way, even though he wasn't sick, the text wasn't really a lie. All he had to do was replace "a" and "little" with "literally," like the kids do these days.

Professor Carroll immediately texted Neil back:

> **I'll let you go. Let me know if you need anything. I mean it. Anything.**

Neil responded:

> **Will do.**

Neil placed his phone on top of the nightstand and manually switched on the television.

⚲

NEIL dozed off while watching some dolled-up woman peddling golden bracelets on QVC. He was half-asleep and for some reason, his thoughts turned to the one time he and Breanne almost hooked up. Almost, as in breaths and inches. He replayed that one night in his head. Breanne had invited him out to a bar to meet a "friend" of hers. Over the phone, Breanne explained to Neil that she had this one friend—*interested* was the word she used to describe her. Her friend had recently gone through a contentious divorce and was now looking forward to dressing up to mingle with other lively males after spending the last eight years with one who made decent men look divine. He couldn't remember her name, but in the half-dream, half-memory, the name "Cassandra" was used several times. All three of them met at a Martini bar. Breanne was first to show, then Neil. By the time the two delved into their second drink, her friend finally arrived. She was quiet, Neil remembered—boring was another way of describing her. But he figured she was rusty to the point of being new to the game after being away for so long. Neil and Breanne's "friend" didn't hit it off. The only sparks came from her cheap cookie cutter lighter, which was running low on Butane. Neil considered himself a social smoker who, outside of drinking, hated smoking and normally, hated himself even more the next morning while washing the bitter smell out of his clothes or coughing up a lung or trying to sweat out the nicotine over the treadmill. The color on the woman's teeth suggested that she didn't only smoke when she found herself around a strange crowd. That night, Breanne drank more than she could handle and was in no condition to drive. She ended up crashing at Neil's, which was only a couple of blocks away from the Martini bar. Neil couldn't get the kiss out of his head. Everything after that remained suspended in his imagination. He remembered that he didn't catch a single wink that night. Instead, the entire night was spent lying next to Breanne in bed, his body just inches away from spooning with her's; however, their bodies never touched once. In lengthy gaps of Breanne slurring his words, she confessed to Neil that kids used to make fun of her when she was younger. They used to tease her, call her bad names. When he asked her why, Breanne told Neil that she used to be a tomboy.

🙴

NEIL woke up to the stark images of Breanne lying in the bed with him. She was wearing an *Ocean Pacific* tank top, as well as the baggy mesh gym shorts he had loaned her. He was tracing his fingertip down the side of Breanne's broad shoulder blade. The last image that came to mind was the pale jagged line that closely resembled a scar on her back.

He shook away the image before it started to take shape and sat upright in bed. He glanced around the empty motel room. The channel was still set to QVC. He couldn't help but notice the watches, which were being sold for dirt-cheap on TV. He heard a familiar sound to the left of him. At first, the noise startled him. He turned to the sound and realized it was his phone making the noise. He heard that noise again, that chirping sound. Somebody was texting him.

While wide-awake, Neil rolled over and picked up the phone.

On the screen read the text: *"I've been thinking about you."*

Neil unlocked the phone and went through the new texts.

They were all from Breanne.

"That's strange," Neil mumbled.

She wanted to know if Neil wanted to hang out tonight. Since Neil was still in Florida and Breanne was in Virginia, the answer was a definite "no."

She *has other friends*, Neil thought to himself.

Why does she keep bugging me?

His attitude from earlier in the afternoon was still lingering around like an unwanted guest craving attention.

He ignored the texts and placed the phone back on the nightstand, thinking that Breanne would get the message from his lack of response.

Since Neil was awake, he decided to do some research on Eileen McLloyd.

He googled her name and then listed off words like *baby, death, adopted child, adoption, son, twin, murder, murdered, Moncton, New Brunswick, Canada, Lupine, Florida, relocated, overdose, custody, divorce,* or *separation,* and hoped that the words would help tickle the database for answers as to why Ealga's adoptive grandson was kept so secret from her.

Nothing credible appeared in the search engine.

As he continued to search, his laptop suddenly died. He went through his bag and searched for the charger but couldn't find one. He must've been so caught up on catching a flight that he completely forgot to bring one.

Frustrated, Neil tossed the laptop across the room.

He checked the time on his phone.

It was only a quarter past nine o' clock.

He told himself that he still had time to grab a drink.

ON the way, Neil bumped into a young couple who looked like runaways walking to their room.

He asked one of them where he could grab a drink around here. The guy mentioned to Neil about a place called "The Foxhole," which was within walking distance. Neil remembered passing on rundown place on the way into Lupine. The kind of place you could miss if you blinked.

Neil decided to walk.

NEIL could see the orange bar sign from his motel.

When the street was clear, he crossed the other side and walked facing traffic. Along the way, Neil heard a familiar sound from a distance. He listened in closer, making sure it wasn't the traffic ambience that was deceiving him. He heard the sound again, a *cluu-claa-cluu-clk*.

The blood suddenly rushed from his face.

He contemplated turning around, going back to the motel, take a hot shower, hit the hay, and sleep off the notion of having a drink.

As he was about to turn around, he heard the sound much closer; in fact, to his immediate right, away from the highway. He turned to the sound where he spotted the shadow of a kid darting across a dimly lit alleyway between two rundown buildings, one, which looked like an old garage that had been shutdown years ago, and the other being boarded up with slabs of warped plywood.

All of a sudden, Neil heard the stinging *slab* of a stick smacking the ground.

Somehow, Neil knew what kind of stick it was. He had been here before, *not* here, as in Lupine, but in a dream where similar events played out.

As Neil continued to push forward, he passed a group of young kids, whom he assumed were probably no older than twelve years old, on a weed-infested blacktop next to the building. They were slapping around what looked like a smashed soda can into the cutout of a cardboard box as if it was ghetto hockey.

Neil stopped and stared at the kids.

One of them pulled himself from the game and turned to Neil with a scowl on his face.

He couldn't help but wonder what these kids were doing out here at this hour.

Where are their—

"Hey," one of the kids shouted out. "What the fuck you looking at, bitch?" the kid snapped. "You got an eye problem or something?"

Neil didn't respond to the kid. Instead, he kept walking when everything in his body was telling him to turn around and walk back to the motel.

✦

FROM the look of the crowd, Neil was clearly the "out-of-towner" who looked as if he happened to stumble into the wrong place. Some of the loyal patrons sitting at the bar turned to Neil and stared at him funny, as if he was some kind of exotic bird.

Neil found an empty stool at the end of the bar. He looked over the massive American flag draped over the beer selection. In the beer department, he had only two choices: regular beer or lite beer. Behind the bar stood at duo, both staring at Neil but not approaching.

When finally approached by the smirking bartender, the male who had a cowboy-like aura with a queer cowboy-look in his eye, Neil ordered a beer.

One beer turned into two beers.

On the third beer, Neil finally had someone to small talk to other than the other sassy bartender, who made it her mission to find out what Neil did for a living.

The burly man, a local of Lupine, ordered Neil a shot of whiskey.

Then one shot turned into two shots.

Before Neil could even check the time, he was seeing double.

*

NEIL woke to a *tapping* sound at the door.

The side of his face felt warm to the point of feeling feverish.

The sun poured through the narrow opening in the curtains and shone over his face, causing the insides of his eyelids to glow. He slowly cracked open one eye as if he was opening a window tinted pink.

Confusion swept over him.

As he did with his eyes, Neil sat upright, slow and gentle, as if he was trying to keep the heavy throb in his head restrained with easy movements.

Another *tap* at the door.

By the third tap, Neil realized he was back in his room. *But how?*

Most importantly, *when?*

Another tap.

Neil heard the sound of keys jiggling behind the room.

"Just a sec," he shouted out, his voice dry and cracking.

As Neil peeled away the comforter from his body, he immediately noticed that he wasn't wearing any pants or underwear. He was bare down below but not entirely. He peered closer. The only thing he was wearing was a used condom that looked as if it was carrying a load. He attempted to pull off the shriveled-up condom, but it was on there good and tight like a disposable latex glove on a sweaty hand. During the second and last attempt, Neil ended up putting too much muscle into it and resorted to yanking off the condom. The removal felt as if he was peeling off an old Band-Aid. He was sore and red down below, sorer and redder than usual. He examined the rest of his body.

The shirt, he realized, was the same one that he was wearing last night—or so he thought. The last thing Neil remembered was drinking a beer with some local, who was missing half his teeth. He pinched the collar of his shirt and held it underneath his nose for a whiff. The shirt reeked like an ashtray. The smell alone of his shirt made him more nauseous than he already was.

In a frantic survey, he finally located a pair of pants draped over the TV; however, the pants didn't appear as if they belonged to him. They had holes in them, which were deliberately cut out in a repugnant taste of ragged fashion, which one could easily find the inspiration behind them while browsing through the cheese aisle in a grocery store. He spotted his boxer-briefs hiding underneath a woman's blouse at the base of bed.

More confusion swept over him.

The blouse?

Then. . .

Neil felt a sudden stir next to him.

A hand touched Neil on the shoulder.

Startled, Neil rotated around, only to find Breanne lying in bed with him.

"Breanne?" he uttered.

"Breanne?" the young woman let out a grunt, as she started to come to. "What you say? Breanne? Who the hell is Breanne?"

She brushed the brown hair from her face and mouth. She had a similar profile as Breanne, but Neil realized after another study that the young woman lying in bed with him was not Breanne; in fact, she was much younger than Breanne. Her eyebrows had been finely plucked and trimmed into perfectly symmetrical lines. She had piercing greenish-blue eyes. Her tits were disproportionate to her frame and appeared like implants. She was attractive enough to be on a magazine cover.

He started to question whether or not she was even eighteen. She had an older face, but a young, tight body.

The thought alone of hooking up with someone nearly half his age caused his insides to churn with exaggerated paranoia. In his head, Neil immediately tried to justify her age. If I met her at that bar—he forgot the name for a moment, then it came to him—The *Foxhole*, she had to be at least twenty-one. At least.

Dumbfounded as to how the young woman ended up in bed with him, he carefully backed away, covering his dick with the bottom of his shirt.

The young woman sat up on her elbow and scanned Neil from head to toe and then her eyes landed back down on his other concealed head.

"Wouldn't be the first time I've seen one," she teased.

Neil heard a racket outside.

"Will you excuse me," he said, not asked, as he grabbed his boxer-briefs from the bed and slipped them on.

He went to answer the door. Sure enough, a maid was standing outside, ready to clean the room.

Neil said to the maid, "Come back another time, will you?"

She didn't say a word in return. She stared at Neil blankly and then pushed the cart of cleaning supplies to the other room.

Neil closed to the door behind him.

The young woman was still in bed, as if she was waiting on Neil to return back to bed.

From where Neil was standing, he had a better look at her. She certainly didn't look like a woman he'd pick up at a bar. Which made him think about how much he drank last night. I must've *upped my game last night*, he thought, looking her over.

"You got some moves for a sand nigga," she said, her voice sounding unclear.

Neil couldn't believe the words that came out of her mouth.

"Excuse me?"

She readjusted herself in bed and stuffed Neil's pillow underneath hers in order to prop herself upright.

"I was just saying you got moves for a brown fella."

He moseyed around the room. He completely forgot what he was looking for.

My pants, he remembered.

"Yeah, well," Neil said, as the woman found his pants lying on the ground next to the bed. "It was us 'brownies' who wrote the Kama Sutra."

She handed Neil his pants.

"Thanks," he said, taking the pants with him to the bathroom.

"Is that that book with all them different sexual positions?"

"That's the one," he said from the bathroom. He contemplated what to do with the wadded condom in his hand.

He decided to flush it down toilet.

"You know, for a moment," the woman said, her voice raised over the whooshing sound of the toilet flushing, "it felt like I was being fucked by an *animal*."

All Neil could make out was the word *animal*.

He stepped from the bathroom.

"Guess the alcohol does that to me sometimes," he said from around the corner.

When Neil returned back into the room, she was sitting on the edge of the bed.

She looked over Neil with a hint of disgust.

"Whatever." She grinned and brushed her hair back and wrapped it in a ponytail with a red band she was wearing around her wrist. "I ain't complaining. So, got any *big* plans today—"

"—I actually got to hit the road." Neil said, "I'm going to miss my flight."

Everything about her dropped, the expression on her face, then her shoulders.

"You said you weren't leaving till Sunday."

"I said that?"

"Think so."

"Again, probably the alcohol."

The woman let out another grunt, this time deep and demonic.

"I know when I'm not wanted," she said sharply.

"It's not like that," Neil said, trying to keep the peace. "I have to go."

"Then, go," she snapped. "Why you still standing there talkin' to me?"

"I'm sorry," Neil said. "I had a good time, though. I mean, I haven't done this in long time. I mean what can I do? How about you give me your phone number, that way I can call you the next time I'm in town?"

She thought it over.

Neil tried to make it easy for her to decide.

"I was actually thinking about coming back here next week."

"Really?"

"Yeah," he lied. "I have to follow up on a new lead."

Neil couldn't help but think of how he sounded like a detective.

The woman ended up tearing out a page from the Holy Bible from the nightstand. She used the motel pen to write down her number on the back of Genesis.

Neil thanked her as she handed him the number.

"I hope I don't go to hell for this," he said, joking.

"I thought you 'brownies' don't believe in heaven or hell."

"Right," he said, looking down at the name below the phone number. "Odin," he read, mistaking the cursive capitalized A for an O.

"Adora," she said with attitude. "It's Adora."

"Right," Neil said again. "Of course. I knew that. I'm basically blind without my glasses."

"You weren't wearing glasses last night."

"Right," Neil stuttered. "I mean, reading glasses."

The woman, Adora, let out an airy sigh loud enough for Neil to sense the frustration in her voice. She got out of bed and gathered the rest of her clothes, which were scattered throughout the room.

Before she could dress herself, Neil was already heading out the door.

✦

WHILE driving to the airport, Neil felt as if he was fleeing from a crime scene. He wasn't entirely spewing lies about having to leave town in such a hurry, although he could only imagine what he told Adora last night in order to get into bed with her. A part of Neil felt as if he was in a hurry to leave, to go back home, and forget he ever came here. A part of him wished he knew what he was running from.

✦

AS soon as Neil got off the ramp, which would take him to the airport, he pulled over on the side of the road to vomit.

Since he hadn't eaten breakfast yet, he had nothing in his stomach to throw up. He mostly dry heaved, like it was his stomach's way of telling him to feed it so it had something to throw up. The dilemma of a brutal hangover, especially involving a man who already had a weak stomach.

The day had just begun, and he already wished it to end.

✦

NEIL vomited once more after he grabbed a few bites of a turkey flatbread that he bought from a Hot Java inside the airport. He ended up sticking with plain ole water to get him through the hangover. But really, all Neil needed was rest. He figured he was riding on at least two or three hours of sleep. The fact was that he didn't know exactly when he came back to the motel room last night or how long he was with Adora. What made it even more irritating for Neil was that he knew all the answers. They were right there, lost and lonely in that noggin of his, beyond the drunken blackout.

After Neil left the restroom, he found a seat away from passengers near a window overlooking the tarmac. He managed to catch at least thirty minutes of uninterrupted sleep, which had given him enough energy to get through the morning.

He woke to a vivid image of a white boy's face covered in red and blue lights. He couldn't remember where he had seen the face before, but he had seen the face before. Somewhere.

As Neil found a well-needed solace in watching planes take off next to him, he received a phone call from his mahm. She was probably worried about him, Neil guessed before he even answered the phone. For a moment, he was hesitant to answer. Neil knew that, with Lupine out of the way and in his rearview, he had lots of work to do, in essence, it was game time, especially with the recent discovery of Aideen's twin sister, Eileen McLloyd.

Neil answered the phone.

She asked how he was doing.

He told her—more so lied about his condition. Neil wasn't interested in small talk. Except for trying to unearth the mysteries of last night's fiasco, he had more important issues on his mind.

Neil thought about bringing up the scar—or "birthmark," as she described it—but he had no easy way of slipping it into the conversation.

"I'd rather not talk to you over the phone about this, but there's been something that's been weighing heavily on my mind these past couple of days."

"What is it, Neil? Is something wrong?"

Neil said the words that were at the front of his mind.

"Did I have a brother that I wasn't aware of?"

His mahm paused.

"Neil," she said, more concerned, "where are you?"

"I'm waiting on a flight."

"Flight? Where are you?"

"In an airport—"

"—What airport?"

"A Florida airport."

"Florida? What are you doing in Florida?"

"I can't explain right now, Mahm. Did I have a brother?"

"Why are you asking me this?"

"Well, did I?"

"No," his mahm said. "Of course not. Where would you get such an idea?"

"My *birthmark*."

His mahm went silent on the other end of the phone.

"Mahm?"

"Why are you so interested in the past, Neil?"

Neil stood up from his seat and stood in front of the window.

"I need to know."

Neil could hear his mahm sighing.

"You were no more than nine months old when it happened," she said. "It was an accident for crying out loud. Is that what you want to hear from me? That I was a bad parent? That I turned my eyes from you for one minute?"

Neil asked, "What happened?"

"I was in the kitchen when you slipped outside. I looked all over the house for you but couldn't find you anywhere. When I came back into the kitchen, I heard a baby crying outside. I went outside, fearing the worst." She told the story in pauses and heavy sighs, as if it was the first time she had told the story ever since it happened and the words nearly stole her breath away. "Somehow, you managed to crawl through the doggy door. You fell off the side of the deck, scrapping your side along a protruding nail on the way down. I'm so sorry, Neil. I can't tell you how many times I wanted to tell you the truth. . . "

Neil remembered having a labradoodle named "Doodle," but he didn't remember anything about it, playing with it or going on any adventures with it; nor did he remember a doggy door, as his mahm described. He only knew it for like a year or two; then his mahm had it "put to sleep."

Over his thoughts, Neil heard a sniffle. He never heard his mahm actually crying, but he could tell from the tremble in her voice that she was upset.

Then, he heard other noises over the phone, sharper and metallic.

"What's that noise in the background?" he asked his mahm.

"It's just Kamaria doing the dishes."

"Can she hear you?" Neil asked, wondering in the back of his mind if Kamaria was close enough to hear his mahm share a personal story with him.

The thought alone of the aide—that stranger!—eavesdropping on the conversation sent a ripple of anger through his body.

"Why does it matter?" she asked.

Neil could hear more dishes *clanking* against one another in the background.

"Mahm, why is she doing the dishes and not taking care of Ajay?"

"We just had lunch, Neil. Relax."

"Lunch? Now, you're making lunch for this woman."

"I don't see what's the big deal."

His mahm kept the same tone throughout the conversation as if she had no issue with Kamaria listening in on the conversation.

Neil tried to contain himself and not make a scene in front of the other passengers, which were beginning to fill the once-empty seats.

He started to pace through the terminal as he struggled to keep his voice down: "Don't you think you should've left the room before speaking to me? This conversation does *not* involve her, Mahm. What else are you telling this woman about me? How about the neighbor, Verona? What have you been telling her about me?"

"Verona?" Clear confusion in his mahm's voice. "Verona doesn't know you?"

"Doesn't know me? Don't you remember the other day?"

"What other day, Neil?"

"You don't remember introducing me to her the other day?"

His mahm didn't miss a beat.

"No," she said. "Neil, are you okay? Tell me what's really bothering you."

He heard an intriguing NEWS REPORT on TV above him. He rubbed his bloodshot eyes, looked up at the TV, and saw a news crew at a crime scene along the highway. He remembered seeing a couple of cruisers on the way to the airport—in fact, he saw a lot of cruisers—but he was so out of it at the time that he really didn't think too much about it.

Neil?

"Listen," he said to her. "I can't do this right now. I have to go."

Neil ended the call with his mahm without saying good-bye.

The reporter at the scene was talking about a deadly hit and run last night.

A young boy was run over by a car.

One of the boy's friends described the car as being a dark sedan.

A thought came to Neil—or what he realized was a memory. . .

He saw himself standing outside a crime scene. Red and blue lights from the police and fire truck sirens were flashing everywhere. Maybe a dozen or so pedestrians were gathered outside the yellow crime scene tape. Neil shouldered his way through the sparse crowd until he found himself at the front. He witnessed a young boy lying in the puddle of blood on the side of the street. The boy's body was contorted, his limbs broken and twisted. He peered closer at the boy's face as if he was stretching deep inside his mind.

Neil pulled himself from his thoughts. He turned his attention back to the TV and saw a picture that the mother had provided for the station. He saw the boy's face, the same one that matched the one from his memory.

Anther memory came to Neil, a deeper one, and it came with words too.

"What the fuck you looking at, bitch?" the kid snapped at Neil. *"You got an eye problem or something?"*

Neil didn't want to believe it was true.

But a part of him knew the truth.

✦

SLEEP was all Neil could think about once he left Wensburg International.

As soon as he stepped foot into his apartment and dropped his bag on the floor, not bothering to unpack, an overwhelming sense of relief washed over him.

He headed straight to the living room and plopped himself down on the couch. He rested his eyes for only a few minutes, which somewhat caused his headache to mellow. He couldn't get what Breanne once told him out of his head. He tried to ignore her, her words, but they were burrowing deeper into his head. He specifically recalled what she said about being followed by a "black woman"—or as Breanne put it, being "stalked."

He rolled off the couch, stormed to his office, and pulled out notes while his laptop was charging. He pulled out the photo of the brand he took of Kamaria's neck—the Patver. He then compared another photo he had printed off, the one of Aideen McLloyd's neck during the time of her arrest. Both the symbols were the same and both were staring directly at Neil.

But *why?*

Were these true-crime conspiracy theorists right about Aideen?

Was she involved in a cult?

He decided to do one thing that he swore he wouldn't. He waited till his laptop had enough battery-life to get him through a quick search. Then, he googled Kamaria Solarin. He found a match to the name on a link to a local newspaper in Gaspin, Georgia called *The Gaspin Runner*. He clicked on the link and was taken to the local newspaper's website where he came across an article of a "MISSING" woman with the same name; however, she went by the name, "Adede." She went "missing" three years ago after her house was broken into. According to the investigators, there had been a struggle inside the house. Traces of Adede's blood were discovered throughout areas of the house; however, a body never turned up and the case, like several other similar cases in and around the Gaspin area, had gone unsolved. Investigators never found a suspect either, not one, which made it even harder to track down Adede.

Neil scrolled halfway through the page and found a photograph of "Adede Solarin," which was taken from a family photograph with her husband and six year old son, who had both died the year before Adede's disappearance in an "automobile accident" on October 30, the night before Halloween. The photograph looked identical to Kamaria; however, her hair was much longer and straighter, shoulder length, and both her eyes were straight, not wall-eyed.

More questions came to Neil, more thoughts.

All Neil wanted was at least a solid eight hours of sleep, but his mind wouldn't grant him such privileges.

⚓

NEIL arrived at his mahm's house ready to fill her in on the aide who was looking after her son.

His plans took a sudden detour as he made his way toward the house. He spotted Kamaria's car parked in the driveway behind the house.

Being the non-confrontational person that he was, he decided to sneak around the house. He heard a strange humming sound coming from Ajay's bedroom. He found Ajay's window. The curtains were closed; however, he found a narrow gap wide enough to peek through. The bedroom was dark. The only light came from candles, which were scattered throughout the room. He spotted two figures standing over Ajay's hospital bed; one of them was clearly Kamaria who was speaking in what Neil thought sounded like tongues. Neil couldn't make the other shadowy person in the room for it was too dark. He tried the other window, which was curtained off as well; however, like the other window, he had a sliver of a view.

Vigilantly, he pressed his cupped against the window and used it as a visor to look through the window.

As soon as the other person stepped forward into the candlelight, the neighbor cranked on the lawnmower behind Neil!

Startled from the sudden roar of the engine, Neil turned around and found himself glaring down his neighbor, Sue Ellen's husband, Howard.

In abrupt awareness, Howard shut off the engine as soon as he saw Neil standing outside Ajay's window.

"Hey there, Neil," he said cheerfully. "I didn't see you. . . "

Neil remained frozen.

"Say," Howard continued, "your mother was telling me about your new book. I'm really interested in reading it sometime. . . "

In the corner of his eye, Neil witnessed a stirring of the curtain. He told Howard that he had to run and then he did exactly that, he ran back to his car.

↟

NEIL drove to a coffee shop not too far from his mahm's house and tried to make sense as to what he witnessed back in Ajay's bedroom.

By the time Neil finished his second cup of coffee, he decided to drive back to his mahm's house where he camped outside until Kamaria's shift was over.

Eventually, Kamaria left the house well past the end of her normal shift, got in her car, and drove away.

More attentive, Neil followed.

↟

KAMARIA ended up taking Neil outside the city in a run-down industrial park. He thought that maybe she was onto him or leading him into a trap or trying to lose her tail. He thought the area looked more like a place where one went to make illegal drug transactions or, even worse, get killed.

As soon as Kamaria parked the car in front of an old textile factory, Neil knew right away that something was off. Not only that, it was getting dark outside and he had no weapon and except for his car, had nothing to protect himself for that matter.

Neil made sure to keep his distance. He parked behind a building and watched Kamaria. She stepped out of her car and looked around before walking into the old factory.

Not too long after Kamaria stepped inside the factory, Neil heard another car coming. The familiar car pulled up next to Kamaria's.

Neil immediately knew the car but was skeptical about the person inside.

As Neil held his breath, John stepped out of the car.

He did exactly what Kamaria had done and looked around, as if he was making sure nobody was in sight before walking into the factory. He met Kamaria at the opening. She reached her arms out from the shadows inside and pulled John into the factory. He couldn't quite see what was going on, but somewhere during their make out session, a nipple had made its appearance.

Both Kamaria and John disappeared for a couple of minutes.

A dim light turned on at the top floor of the factory, revealing what looked like a furnished loft.

He witnessed both Kamaria and John both stumbling inside. The two of them couldn't remove each article of their clothing quick enough.

❦

BY the time Neil reached the rooftop of the building next to the factory, it turned dark outside and he had a clearer view of the action.

He witnessed Kamaria's naked body sprawled out on the mattress inside. The blood was everywhere, covering Kamaria, as well as splattered over the mattress and forming into a puddle on the floor below. He didn't see John anywhere in sight. Thinking John fled the scene, Neil rushed to the ledge and peered over. His car was still parked below.

All of a sudden, he heard the muffled sound of a *cackle* coming from inside the loft.

He redirected his attention back to the loft and witnessed John straddling Kamaria's body. Kamaria wasn't dead, as Neil first suspected, nor did she bear any cut or wound on her body. Kamaria was far from dead. Yet, she was alive, very much alive, and far from the God-fearing woman she let on to be.

John was holding a wooden bowl in his hands and carefully pouring blood all over Kamaria's body, starting with her mouth. From where Neil was standing, he couldn't quite tell if Kamaria was drinking the blood; however, her mouth was wide open when John starting to pour blood over her mouth and chin. He moved straight to her bare neck and chest, inched his way down Kamaria's body, pouring and then smearing blood over the most erogenous zones of her body.

Mortified by the cultish sex act, Neil hurried back to his car.

Once he drove off, he pulled out his phone and contemplated calling his mahm and telling her about John—that *low life*, that *cheating piece of filth*, that *human waste!*—How could that slimeball do this to her, especially after everything she had been through with her first husband? Neil wondered how long the affair had been going on—if that's want you wanted to call it. Thinking of scum of the earth, Neil shifted his thoughts to Kamaria. There was no way in hell I'm going to let that *sick bitch* anywhere near Ajay. When he thought more about Kamaria, he thought about his mahm and the lie she had hid from him for all of those years. Was she any different? It was only a scar, *but why, Mahm?* Why would you lie about a scar? Bad parenting, he wondered, was a poor excuse but deemed acceptable at face value. He was about as sure as Sunday that his mahm was telling the truth about her faults as a parent. But it was only a mistake. People—especially parents—made them all the time. Why lie about them? Why not own up to them and move on with life?

Torn up about his next move, he tossed the phone aside and found himself in the middle of rush hour traffic in one of the most congested parts of the city.

The traffic moved at a crawl.

While Neil was waiting at a red light, he found himself slipping into a trance.

In the blink of an eye, he had teleported himself to not only another place, but also to another time. One blink, he was in his car waiting at a red light, traffic all around him, pedestrians—businessmen and women—walking on sidewalks, faces behind windows. Then, the next blink, he was back in New Brunswick. The entire scenery outside his idled car was no longer skyscrapers but lush snow-covered pine trees. The streets, streetlights, and road signs were no longer there, either. Instead, Neil found himself on a dirt road at the end of a gravel driveway where a mailbox leaned over the road like a crooked tooth. Human life was replaced with animal life. Elk scurried into woods, which surrounded the desolate road. *And* it was snowing, too.

Cautiously, Neil stepped out of his car and looked around in bafflement. From a distance, he spotted his childhood home at the end of the driveway.

It can't be, he thought.

He walked up the driveway until he reached the old house. He heard a familiar noise coming from behind the house. He checked out the noise. In the backyard, he saw his younger self walking into the woods behind the house. He decided to follow his younger self.

By the time he reached the kid, the strange man, who was hiding behind a tree, had already handed his younger self the bottle of poison.

"Hey," Neil called out to the strange man, "get away from him!"

The man turned to Neil and revealed his face.

The man from the lecture, at the book signing—Serg?

"You?" Neil said with confusion. "What do you want?"

As Neil approached the strange man, the kid ran off back the way he came.

"You still don't get it, do you Neil?" he said, squaring his body to Neil. "All these years, it's the flesh that has been holding you back, preventing you from becoming who you were meant to be."

Already having a suspicion of what the answer to the question might be, Neil asked anyway: "Become who goddamn it?"

"You already know who, Neil," he said. "*Search* within yourself."

Neil searched.

The first thought that came to mind was Ajay sitting in a wheelchair inside the garage with a piece of white gauze tapped over his forearm where his blood had been drawn. The second was the blood demon rising from a blood puddle.

"Why do you keep coming back to this one memory?" the strange man asked.

Neil snapped from his sudden trance. He was still there, in the snowy woods.

"Think about it, Neil," he said. "Why did you try to kill your unborn brother?"

Neil searched and went deeper into his thoughts.

Serg made it clearer for Neil: "Only the one who shares the same blood of the Great Half can destroy the Great Half. One will thrive. *One* will perish. It's your choice whether or not you decide to continue to go on in that temporary vessel of yours, rotting away just like your other Half, lying dormant inside that broken body. But it doesn't have to end that way. With a swift stroke of a blade, you can finally become who you were meant to be. . . "

In his trance, he specifically recalled one time when Ajay had been admitted to the hospital due to an infection that had spread throughout his body. He remembered the way he was treated, dozens of incredibly attractive nurses surrounding his hospital bed, smitten by Ajay's presence as they rubbed on him, bathed him, combed his hair, and dolled him up as if he was a messiah. Then, he retraced his steps back to a recent image, one of the great Drómos lying in a domed hall with gorgeous mortals basking in his presence.

"Become who you were meant to be," the strange man to Neil.

"I can't—I won't!" Neil said, shaking his head.

Everything around Neil started to shake, the ground, the trees, even the air itself felt as if it had a sort of tangible vibration as it beat against his skin.

He peered closer at the strange man standing before him and immediately recognized a change in his face. Both of his eyes were a different color than the man whom he saw at the book signing. Dark bags, so dark that they looked as if they were painted on, appeared below his dark brown eyes. Even his frame appeared different, thinner. His hips were wider, his stature more upright. Neil thought he appeared feminine. In the final and most violent shake, he witnessed the strange man's face start to slip from another face hidden below. . .

Neil suddenly heard the blaring honk of a car *horn* next to him!

He blinked...

One blink, Neil was standing in the snow-covered woods, staring at the strange man who may—or may not—have been the same white-haired man from the book signing. Then, the next blink, Neil was standing on a congested street in the heart of downtown.

Neil turned to the commotion. A driver was standing outside his car, shouting at Neil to get back in his car. Neil glanced around the street and saw other crazy-eyed, red-faced drivers hanging out their windows, yelling as well as motioning at Neil to get the bleep back into his car. Eventually, he located his car a few paces away. Neil walked back to his car, got in, and drove away before the light turned red.

✦

DURING the drive home, Neil couldn't shake the memory—
or whatever—from his head.

Once he stepped inside his apartment, he went straight
to the cabinet above the sink and grabbed the bottle of
Hobbles. There was still enough alcohol left in the bottle
from the other night to get him pretty wasted—or, according to Neil's current mindset, to temporarily erase his memory.

Neil took a swig without a chaser. He pushed past the
burn and as soon as the whiskey settled in his stomach, he
took yet another swig. Then, another. He finished nearly
half of what he had left from the other night in a matter of
minutes.

Feeling the buzz creep in, Neil staggered toward the
bathroom, switched on the light switch to the vanity, and
ran his face under the cool water.

As he pulled his face from the sink, he looked into the
mirror. He could hardly even recognize himself, let alone
look directly at himself without feeling a sense of loathing
bubbling up inside him. He hated himself, hated what he
had become or hadn't become. His hair was disheveled.
His eyes were cloudy and red with extreme fatigue. He
hadn't shaved in a couple of days. His skin was as coarse as
sand. He leaned closer to the mirror, met his eye with the
demon inside him, and willed the mirror to shatter into a
million pieces.

A floater appeared in the corner of his vision. He leaned
back and saw yet another floater crossing his range of sight.
He refocused and witnessed snowflakes falling in the reflection of the mirror. He turned and faced the bedroom window.

He ignored the faucet and mindlessly kept the water
running.

Curious, he walked to the window. Each step felt heavy
like a dream.

Neil soon realized he was back in it—whatever *it* was, a
dream or memory, a whatever.

One blink, he was in one place.

Another blink, another place.

Another *another*.

He slid upon the door to the balcony outside, which was covered with at least a few inches of snow. He thought maybe he had accidentally left the balcony light on. The atmosphere was much softer and paler than what any eighty-watt could illuminate. He looked up at the low clouds above. The sky was dark, but it was day, not night. He started to question himself, as well as his reality—had he been drinking for so long that the time completely slipped his mind? Was it an hallucination brought on by alcohol?

Neil debunked his own suspicions as soon as he stepped on the balcony, only to find himself not on a balcony, but, of course, back in New Brunswick.

A flash of panic came over him but only for a moment. He rotated around and what would've been the door to his apartment was a stretch of snow-covered land met by the dense woods. He spotted Bleu's Lake at a distance. He walked across an alleyway of land with trees and forests surrounding him.

Before he reached the frozen lake, he spotted more strangeness, pivotal characters which had recently been a part of his life either it be through family members, friends, or occasion run-ins with everyday people, standing at the entrance of the woods.

On one side of the pathway stood Aideen's mother, Ealga, his mahm's neighbors, Verona and her daughter, Lilith, the woman who Neil supposedly hooked up with in Lupine, Florida—Neil thought her name was Odin for some reason but he knew that wasn't really her real name. Standing next to her was the Shooter who went all psycho at Corkin' Out; then standing next to the Shooter was the clerk at Firsty's, Todd; then, next to him, Professor Carroll. Then, next in the line, he saw a rough-looking man in a chocolate brown leather jacket. He had a strange tattoo on his neck. He also appeared a few years older than Neil. Neil had never seen the man before in his lifetime; however, he had a look about him, as if he wanted to harm Neil; and then, a couple of feet ahead of the others stood a man dressed in all white, looked like an orderly. Neil had never seen this man before either, but a part of him knew he would. Lastly, he saw his father.

On the other side stood his mahm, then the white-haired student from his class, the flirty one, Nicky, then his mahm's other neighbor Sue Ellen, who appeared to be standing farther out and closer to Neil than the other ones who remained at the edge of the forest, all of Neil's child-hood friends, not grown up but still the same age he last saw them, which was around the age of fourteen, before Neil moved to the States; nonetheless, each one of these people was standing tall and upright, appearing exactly the way Neil last remembered them. He couldn't help but look to the other side of the pathway, at his father, who was na-ked, his face purple, and he had a leather belt tied around his neck, worn like a tie. He saw others standing in the for-est; however, their bodies were shrouded by the darkness of the forest, their faces pale and ghostly.

During the long walk, Neil came across more strange-ness. A silicon mask was sitting on the snowy ground be-low. He kneeled down and picked up the mask and exam-ined it more closely. He couldn't quite tell whom or what the face belonged to. The empty holes around the eye sockets had made it nearly impossible to confirm his deep-est suspicions; however, the long white wig lying on the ground not too far away helped dissolve his skepticism.

Neil placed aside the mask and the wig, as well as the thought of being fooled by some con artist, and proceeded toward the lake. At the edge of the dock stood a familiar young woman. He had seen her before, possibly at one of his lectures or book signings. She was a Neil Reddy fan, maybe even a groupie. She was shivering badly—which appeared even stranger. To Neil, the weather didn't feel too cold outside; in fact, he was only wearing a light jacket and he was fine. Neil peered closer. She appeared more in a state of shock than anything. In her vacant stare, she looked up at Neil. He recognized her face from Bakerford

Hall, the one with starry eyes and a lustful smile. Her movements were seemingly mechanical as she turned to a hole in the middle of the frozen lake. Then, as before, she held her head back down and continued to stare at the ground.

Carefully, Neil walked out onto the ice.

Every now and then, he'd hear the sound of ice cracking before his foot, forcing him to slow his walk to a creep.

A gust of wind forced Neil to remain still on the ice. The strong gust managed to blow apart a blanket of fresh powdery snow covering the thick ice, revealing hundreds of dead bodies frozen underneath.

He pulled his palms from his face.

Neil thought about turning around, walking back to land, and not facing whatever it was that he was about to face inside that hole. The ice, however, started to crack below the heel of his foot, veining out specifically toward the path leading back to land.

Determined, Neil continued to walk toward the hole, despite the feeling of impending doom overwhelming his thoughts.

He walked toward his closet.

Once he reached the edge of the hole in the ice, he peered down into the water and caught a glint in the corner of his eye. He looked closer at the strange object glinting and twinkling like a tiny star within the darkness below.

On the count of three, he dove into the water on two. The feeling alone of diving headfirst into the frigid water felt like thousands of pinpricks against his skin. He swam deeper into the lake, toward the glint of light.

He grabbed the box from the top shelf of the closet.

A beam of daylight opened up from the sky above and made his path more clear.

Once Neil reached the bottom of the lake, he pulled the blade wedged between two rocks.

Neil found himself back in his office, kneeling over an open box with a blade resting inside a cushioned cutout on the floor. His hair was drenching hair; water droplets were dropping onto the blade; the upper part of his shirt was completely soaked as well.

As he held the blade in his hand, he felt as if, for a moment, he was both discovering and rediscovering the strange weapon. He rubbed his fingertip along the raised symbol inscribed into the handle of the blade.

He gently picked up the blade and held it in his hands as if it was a living creature.

"The Blade of Axlar," Neil said in awe.

Not once did he ever question as to how such an ancient blade wound up in his closet.

Neil had no more questions.

Not even one.

⚲

WITH The Blade of Axlar in hand, Neil left his apartment. He didn't even bother to bring his phone with him. He didn't need it, not where he was going.

⚲

NEIL drove about a mile down the road before he realized his tank was on E. He stopped at the first gas station that he saw, which happened to be Firsty's.

As Neil was filling up the car, he noticed Todd staring at him through the convenient store window. The clerk was grinning from ear-to-ear at Neil. His teeth were warped like wet woodchips protruding from his mouth, both his eyes black and empty, his facial features exaggerated.

Neil only put enough gas in his tank to reach his mahm's house.

He couldn't get out of there soon enough.

⚲

AS soon as he pulled in front of his mahm's house, he knew there was something terribly wrong. He parked the car, shut off the engine, and cautiously stepped out with The Blade of Axlar in his hand.

He noticed a delicate ember of cherry tobacco still smoking on the sidewalk in front of the house.

As he made his way up the pathway, Neil stepped on the ember, smothering it with the sole of his shoe.

Every single light was turned off inside the house, except for one light in particular, which was coming from the living room in the middle of the house.

Neil realized the light was coming from the fireplace once he made his way up the steps on the porch.

Once he reached the landing, he saw that the front door was cracked open. The floodlight on the neighboring house shone just enough light to showcase a handprint of blood smeared but clearly visible on the side of the door. He followed the blood on the porch, squinting his eyes in sharp focus. A couple of droplets were covering the steps of the porch and trailing into the front lawn.

Careful not to touch the blood, he cautiously stepped inside the house and was immediately hit by the sour stench of something burning inside the kitchen.

Neil immediately recognized the severity of the situation. A much clearer trail of blood was trailing farther into the house. The droplets were closer together and not as far apart as the ones outside. He flipped on the light switch to the foyer but no light came on. He tried several times but soon realized the power was out, which immediately raised a red flag since there weren't any storms in the forecast.

The only source of light came from the beating firelight inside the living room.

With the no other choice, he walked toward the light.

Once he reached the open living room, which was connected to the kitchen, he witnessed the crime scene.

Streaks of blood were covering the walls and floors like an action painting.

A thick cloud of smoke was covering the ceiling. At first, Neil thought it was coming from the fireplace and that maybe the damper directly above the firebox was closed, resulting in the living room and kitchen to fill with smoke.

He rushed into the dark living room where furniture had been overturned and came across a body lying facedown in front of the fireplace.

"John?" Neil called out.

The body was male; however, he was much larger than John. The rug next to the body was all scrunched up into overlapping folds. The tools from the fireplace set were scattered about. One of the tools, the poker, was missing.

Neil carefully stepped over the overturned coffee table and walked to the body. He didn't know it until he looked down, but he ended up stepping in a puddle of blood.

Fearful of the strange man's current condition, he gently turned over the body. The man was dead, clearly. He had a stab mark in the neck, where he lost most of his blood—or bled out. Neil had never seen the man before, not in person that is; however, he *had* seen him before. He retraced his thoughts and found the man's unshaved face in his mind. Surrounding the face was the snow and trees. He was the same man from his head. The next thing that ran through Neil's head was intruder, a possible vandal or robber, a premonition. He ruled out vandal since the man looked exactly like he did from his previous encounter, leather jacket, rough, approximately in his early forties.

From the disorderly look of the living room, there had been an obvious scuffle. Neil thought about John. Maybe he had battled with the intruder. But he immediately ruled him out because he was off cheating on his mahm with Kamaria.

He took note of the strange man's knuckles, which were incredibly misshapen and covered in blood. Tiny pieces of bone were sticking out.

The smoke alarm suddenly went off!

Startled from the blaring sound, Neil turned toward the kitchen where he pinpointed the source of the strong odor.

Once he turned to the kitchen, he first saw another body lying on the floor and then the pot smoking on the stovetop.

Mahm?

Neil rushed into the kitchen where his mahm was lying on her side in front of the stovetop. The entire backside of her head was caved in, exposing parts of her cracked skull and brain, which appeared smashed. He placed The Blade of Axlar on the countertop and checked a pulse even though she was already dead and had been dead for some time.

He rushed into the living room, grabbed a pillow from the floor, and placed it behind her head as he gently rolled over her lifeless body. He couldn't even recognize her face due to the severe burns on both her face and neck.

The stew pot, which was bone-dry, was yet another indication of time.

He immediately put the two and two together: the severe burns on his mahm's face and neck as well as the empty pot, which was, in all likelihood, once filled to the brim with boiling hot water.

Overcome with emotion, Neil asked himself, "Who would do such a thing?"

He turned off the knob controlling the heat on the stovetop.

With the bottom of his shirt, Neil grabbed the piping hot pot from the stovetop and placed it inside the sink, burning his hand while doing so. He ran cold water over the pot, causing a burst of hot steam to shoot up to the ceiling above.

Next, since the blaring alarm was making matters worse, he removed the batteries from the smoke alarm.

Being able to think much more clearly, Neil inspected his mahm and the scene around her body. He located a bloody knife next to the kitchen table, which appeared as if it had been dropped hard to the floor due to the outward projection of blood on the floors and walls. Then, he went back to his mahm and examined her body. He didn't see any evident stab wounds on her body. He kept coming back to the back of her head, the massive hole inside it. Then, the dead man's hand, his knuckles broken and bloody. *No man could do that* to another person, he thought.

Then, the moments leading up to her death became clear. He couldn't find any marks around the top of his mahm's head. He examined her hands, then both her palms, which were bloody. Then, moved his way to the

stovetop, saw white rings along the stainless steel from
where the water had boiled over; however, he found no indication that she was trying to prevent herself from being
burned by the boiling water. He saw no bloody handprints
along the counter.

No struggle, as if she did it to herself.

The first—and only—detail that popped out was the
phone resting inches away from her hand. Neil picked up
the flipped phone and noticed several of the digits on the
keypad were covered in bloody fingerprints, his mahm's
prints.

As the panic sloshed around his body and caused his
hands to tremble uncontrollably, he checked his mahm's
call log. Went through recent phone calls. He found the
last call phone she made, which was roughly an hour ago.
Immediately, the number leaped right at him—Breanne?

Where did she get Breanne's number?

Neil thought about all the ways his mahm could've obtained Breanne's number. Phone book, possibly snooped
around his phone when he left it out for curious eyes to
see—however, that would've been impossible because you
needed a four-digit passcode to unlock the phone and she
didn't know it. He stopped thinking about the number and
shifted his thoughts to the name behind the number. He
put a face to the name.

Then, he went further, beyond the face.

A stream of memories flooded Neil's thoughts. He found
himself remembering a conversation he had with Professor
Carroll, about Breanne being like a sister to him and then
another conversation he had with Breanne, about coming
into her fullest potential after she decided to leave her boy-
friend, soon-to-be fiancé, Toby. He remembered a woman
staring at Breanne, *not* Neil, across the bar, deeply attracted to her. Then, he remembered the reason as to why,
for the life of him, he could *not* hook up with Breanne that
one night; remembered what Ealga had said about the boy
her daughter's partner raised, that boy, Ryan, about how
she always wanted a daughter, how she'd dress that poor
boy up like he was a girl sometimes and mess with his head,

confuse him. He remembered another specific conversation with Breanne, about him being a "prankster." She used that specific word, *prankster*, while referring to Neil. Then, lastly, Neil remembered the scar on Breanne's side when the two were in bed together. When he asked her where she got the scar, she told him a touching story about falling off the side of the deck when she was a baby. . .

Neil's chest tightened from the sudden revelation. His breath shortened.

With sharp focus, he turned to The Blade of Axlar on the countertop.

"Ajay," he uttered.

Neil rushed into Ajay's bedroom and checked on his condition. He was still in bed. He wasn't moving, which wasn't out of the ordinary. He checked his pulse. He was alive; in fact, he appeared untouched.

"We have to get out of here," Neil said to Ajay.

Since Neil had very little light to work with, Neil rushed back into the kitchen and grabbed a flashlight from the utility drawer. He switched on the light, placed it on the dresser, and aimed it at the bed.

"Okay, Ajay," he said to his brother, "I'm going to get you in your wheelchair. You're going to have to work with me here, okay?"

Neil hurried into the master bathroom where the wheelchair was parked, then wheeled the chair into the bedroom. Normally getting his brother out of bed and into his wheelchair was a two-man job without a lift; however, the power was out. Even the breaker box inside the garage had been destroyed with a blunt object.

After nearly breaking his back, Neil barely managed to hoist his brother into the wheelchair. He wheeled Ajay into the handicap van used to transport Ajay to and from the hospital and doctor's appointments.

Before taking off, he rushed back into the house and grabbed The Blade of Axlar, as well as his mahm's phone.

He rushed back to the van and made sure Ajay's seatbelt was fastened and secured around his body.

He reassured Ajay that everything was going to be okay and that he was going to finally set things straight once and for all. Neil kissed his brother on the forehead and told him that he loved him. Then, he got into the driver's seat, started up the van, and drove off.

AFTER serious contemplation, Neil decided to call Breanne.

She didn't pick up the first time. So, he tried her again.

"Pick up, Breanne," he whispered to himself.

She picked up right before the call went to voicemail.

"Hello," she said, her voice gravelly.

Neil asked, "Where are you?"

"Neil?"

"Who else would it be?"

"I've been trying to get a hold of you, but you're not answering your phone."

"I don't have my phone."

He gave Breanne a chance to fill in the blank as to whose number the phone belonged to. She didn't even ask him whose phone he was using. She gave him nothing.

"Where are you?" he asked again.

"I don't know," Breanne said more unsteadily, as if the words were starting to get clogged in the back of her throat. "Driving," she finally said. "You?"

"What happened?"

"Neil, I was going to tell you all about it—"

"—What happened?"

"I can explain, Neil—"

"—I found your number in my mother's phone," Neil said. "Tell me, Breanne. Why was my mother calling you?"

Neil could hear Breanne sniffling on the other end.

When she finally spoke, he could hear the emotion in her choppy voice.

"She told me that she 'needed me to come over.'"

"To the house?"

The pause was met by another sharp sniffle.

"Breanne?"

229

"Yes."

In his mind, the pieces started to come together.

She was there, he thought, putting Breanne at the crime scene. He kept coming back to the phone, his mahm's phone, bloody fingerprints on the keypad. How could his mahm talk to Breanne if she was already dead? He thought about how his mahm went out so violently, the horror.

Then, he immediately thought about the strange dead man lying on the floor in the living room. He couldn't help but imagine that dead son of a bitch standing his mahm upright and then punching a hole into the back of her head and using her mouth like a sock puppet.

Neil shook away the graphic image, even though a part of him knew the image to be true.

"Why did she want you to come over to the house?" he asked clear enough to demand a detailed answer.

"She said she was worried about you—"

"—Me? Why would she say that?"

"I don't know," Breanne said. "She said she thought you were having a mental breakdown."

"Well," he suddenly snapped, as if he was finally addressing the elephant over the phone, "did you go?"

"Go where?"

"Don't lie to me," Neil seethed.

Breanne confessed, "*She* was like that when I arrived."

"And how about the man by the fireplace? Did you know him?"

He retracted the words in his mind soon after he spoke them. Yet he should've been asking Breanne if she was hurt.

"*Did I know him?*" she fired the question back at Neil. "What is that supposed to mean, Neil? You think I had something to do with your mother's death?"

"I don't know what to believe anymore, Breanne," Neil said, his voice trailing.

He took his eyes off the road for a moment and peered through the rearview mirror where Ajay was staring directly at him, his head occasionally rocking back and forth along the headrest from each bump in the road. Neil moved his eyes to the driver's side view mirror where he found two headlights coming into focus. He looked back through the rearview. Ajay's head was obstructing the view. So, Neil kept the suspicious car in his side view.

"You didn't answer my question, Breanne," Neil said, his eyes sharpening over the road. "Did you *know* him?"

Breanne hesitated.

"No," she said. "I didn't know him. Do you?"

Then, *why'd you leave, Breanne?*

Neil wanted to ask but couldn't.

"Neil? Do you know him?"

"No," Neil said quietly, giving way to an awkward pause.

"What do you think he wanted?"

"I don't know," he said, clearing his throat.

Then, he started to go through a list of other questions in his head: *Why not call the police? Why run away from an active crime scene?* Most importantly, *what are you hiding from me?* Then, the most obvious: *Was that man dead before you arrived at the house?*

Breanne said over the pause, "I know what you're thinking, Neil. Why didn't I call the police?"

Neil kept the black car in his side view. The car was keeping its distance from Neil, even when Neil eased his foot from the gas pedal and slowed the van down to the legal speed limit. *If it was a cop* tailing him, he or she *would've already pulled him over* for speeding.

"Well," Neil said, "why didn't you?"

She said defensively, "I freaked all right. I was scared."

"What were you scared of?"

"Your mother," she said, "finding her with her head. . ." Breanne paused once more. She couldn't even utter the words from her mouth. "Then," she said, "that guy. . . I freaked. What should I have done, Neil?"

"Well," he said, taming back his anger, "what's important is that you're okay."

"Where are you?" Breanne asked.

Neil checked the side view mirror. The car was still behind him.

"Driving," Neil said, listening in closer.

During the gap of silence, Neil heard another sound coming from Breanne, *not* a sniffle but close to one, which sounded more like a hiss, as if Breanne was hissing from a hot pain and not great sorrow from the recent loss of Neil's mother but actual physical pain. What made it even more evident for Neil was the word—or better yet, sound—she used after that initial hissing noise, a word which could've easily been mistaken or even a concealed take of the words *ow* or *ouch*.

Neil finally asked, "Are you hurt, Breanne?"

"It's just a cut," she said accidentally.

More intrigued, Neil asked, "How did you cut yourself?"

"I must've cut my arm on a piece of broken glass," she said.

The first thought that came to Neil's mind was the over-turned coffee table and the shattered glass scattered all over the living room floor. It'd make sense if she cut her foot or toe on a shard of glass—that is, if she was wearing sandals or more plainly, no shoes at all.

Right away, Neil's face slackened with shock.

He asked Breanne, "Was he already dead when you arrived at the house?"

"Was who dead?"

Neil said loudly, "The man in the living room! Who do you think?"

"Yes," she said, not missing a beat. "You think I killed him?"

"Well, did you?"

"No,' she said. "I just told you. What's gotten into you?"

"What's gotten into me?" The anger rose in Neil, squeezing him. "Considering the recent events, Breanne— if that's even your real name—don't you think I have every right to be suspicious of you, especially with the lies you've been constantly feeding me?"

Breanne stuttered, "Lies? What lies? I've been nothing but honest with you, Neil."

"Bullshit!"

"Tell me one thing that I've lied to you about, Neil? Tell me!"

"For starters, the scar on your back," he said.

"Wha—what scar?"

"The scar on your back, Breanne," he said again. "How did you get it?"

"Neil," she said and paused, "I ah. . . I don't have a scar on my back."

"Yes, you do," Neil said, his eyes drifting from the glare in the road.

"Well, I'm glad you know more about my own body than I do—"

Neil heard the *screech* of tires skidding against asphalt in front of him.

As soon as he directed his attention upward, his eyes crossed the dark rear of a vehicle fishtailing in front of the van. Before he could even react by turning the steering wheel, Neil was violently flung through the windshield. All he could see was time and space jetting around him at a hundred miles an hour. Stars, as well as streetlights, acted like scanner beams running across his vision as his body flipped in a dizzying, uncontrollable state.

When Neil finally came back to earth, he did so with a heavy thud, causing the blood to rush through his entire body.

Neil blacked out for a moment and then came to, then blacked out once more.

With the side of his bloody face pressed against the street, he cracked open one of his eyes one last time, the other one being completely swollen shut. There, in the gray blur, Neil witnessed Kamaria—or someone who looked identical to Kamaria—park a car next to the violent car wreck in the middle of the intersection. She casually stepped out of the car, ignoring Neil, Ajay, or the other driver's condition. His eye caught more carnage on the site: the other driver, a young woman with blonde hair, was hanging from a hole in the bloody windshield. Then, back to the van where he saw Ajay suspended upside, the seat belt was wrapped around his neck, cutting off his air supply.

Neil tried to stand up but he couldn't move his legs; in fact, he couldn't move any part of his body, except for his eyelids.

Kamaria—or the woman who looked like Kamaria—walked to the totaled van, which had been flipped over on its roof, kneeled down next to the passenger side, and reached inside. She grabbed a glinting object from the passenger seat.

Then, she walked away.

And that was the very last image Neil set his eyes to before the blackness swallowed him, a tall dark figure walking away into the light.

🖈

NEIL cracked open his eyes.

The pain swelled over him, covering his entire body like sand. He tried to talk but couldn't. He tried to move but couldn't.

A nurse stepped into the hospital room and spoke words to him but he couldn't make out her words.

Neil drifted back into the blackness, where it was cool and inviting.

🖈

THE next time he swam back into the light was when a doctor was shining a flashlight into his eyes.

He blinked from the sound of her voice.

"Do you know what day it is?" she asked him.

Innately, Neil blinked his eyes twice.

"How about the year?" she asked. "Do you know what year it is?"

Neil didn't blink.

"Is it 2019?"

Eventually, he blinked his eyes once.

Then, blackness.

MORE light.

More people.

Two faces stood out among the other bodies in the background.

One man was black with a pencil-thin mustache, squared jaw, green eyes—the eyes were what stood out the most for Neil. Those eyes, brilliant and mesmeric, engaging, while everything surrounding them was etched with mileage. His stern exterior was carried like a shield. A strong, empathetic man who kept his struggle on the inside.

The other man was about the average size of a basketball player, his skin was off-white, sickly-looking, as if the man spent most of his days in the shade or indoors; he had writer's hunch and a five o'clock shadow, which he wore like designer shave; his hair was long and greasy, the ends curled like onion rings.

Their frames came into focus. The black man was standing with a notepad and pen in hand on one side of the hospital bed; while, on the other side of the bed, the slouched man held a manila folder tucked underneath his armpit. The black man was sporting over a black trench coat; whereas the other man, the white man, was dressed in a beige sports coat over a lime green dress shirt with the top two buttons unbuttoned, formal yet tasteful.

They showed Neil their badges. Neil tried to read the words but couldn't. The men standing on both sides of his bedside stated that they were detectives. They spoke their names to Neil; however, Neil only caught the last few syllables of one of their names, *tou* and *er*. He caught a "hi" somewhere in the gibberish.

Hightower?

More feeling came back to Neil, senses.

Along his wrist he felt a cold sensation pressed tight against his bones.

He moved his eyes downward and noticed his wrist was handcuffed to the bed railing.

"Are you aware that you were involved in a serious automobile accident, Mr. Reddy?" the black detective asked.

Neil blinked his eyes once.

The detective turned to his partner and whispered something in his ear. In return, his partner nodded his head.

He pulled out a several photographs from a manila folder and showed them to Neil.

The photograph was of his stepfather, John, lying on the street in an abandoned industrial park. The detectives said he jumped—or was pushed—from a building the night of Neil's automobile accident.

They showed Neil more photographs, two of them, a still taken from not only surveillance footage outside an electronic store, but also a still taken from a traffic cam. Each still showed Neil standing in the middle of the street a block away from the industrial park, yelling at drivers.

The detectives asked Neil why he was in the vicinity at the time before John's "alleged" suicide—or murder. But Neil didn't have a response for them.

They reworded the questions to yes or no, one blink or two blinks. Neil wasn't much help when it came to answering questions about John.

They went back to the manila folder and pulled out more photographs to look over. One was a still frame, which was taken from a camera above the convenient store, Firsty's. The detective informed Neil that they managed to salvage the surveillance footage from "whatever was left of the convenient store."

In the photo, Neil's vehicle was clearly visible and driving—or "speeding"— away from the gas station next to Firsty's several minutes before the "explosion." Which brought the detective to the next photograph in his hand.

The detective showed Neil a photograph of a charred gas station that had been completely flattened and reduced to rumble. He informed Neil that they had footage showing an expressionless man named Todd Rooks, a clerk who worked the night shifts at Firsty's—and an "acquaintance" of Neil—exiting the convenient store moments after Neil sped away. The footage showed Mr. Rooks using one of the gas pumps to pour gasoline over his body and then using a lighter to set himself on fire. The blaze spread to one of the pumps. Then, *boom*! However, Neil appeared as if he had no knowledge of the incident.

With both John and Todd's death out of the way, they moved on to why they were really here, the main entrée.

The detective pulled out two more photographs, one of a close-up of the dead man, which was taken at the crime scene at his mahm's house and the other, a mug shot of a younger man, the same man, only not dead.

He told Neil that the man was "Talib Dusant, younger brother of Kobe Dusant. Talib was recently released from Steely Pines Correctional Facility after doing a five-year stretch for assault and battery. The apple didn't fall too far from the tree. His brother, Kobe, was a former juvie who had his run-ins with the law. He spent his adolescence in and out of the JDC. Juvenile Hall. Last year, Kobe was found dead with a screwdriver lodged in his neck just out-side Josey Town. Investigators never linked any suspects to the crime. Eventually, the case went cold."

The reason as to why detectives were talking about Kobe Dusant, *not* because his brother was found dead inside his mother's home, but because forensic investigators "matched Neil's DNA to the same exact weapon," a screwdriver, that was "used to murder Kobe Dusant."

"To make things more interesting," the detective said to Neil as if he was reading him a bedtime story, "the neighbor, Sue Ellen, claimed she spotted you entering your mother's house with Talib Dusant on the night of his death." Which helped support the narrative, considering the investigators didn't find one shred of evidence indicating a forced entry.

The detectives came back to Neil's DNA, *his blood*, and how it was painted all over the crime scene.

Since the wreck had left Neil with multiple injuries, mostly internal and external, it was hard for investigators to distinguish what injuries had come from the accident and what had come from the crime scene at his mahm's house.

Finally, before their grand departure, the detectives shared a curiosity about the two phone calls which were made prior to Neil's arrival at the house, the one his mahm "mysteriously" made before her untimely death, then the one following his "fleeing" of the crime scene. Each call was made to the same number, Breanne's number.

The detective asked Neil about a woman named "Breanne Conway," and what his relationship was with Ms. Conway, a "friend," which received two blinks, and then, the obvious, "lover," which received a hard two blinks.

"According to your mother's phone records," the detective read from his notes, "Ms. Conway's phone was the last number dialed on your mother's cellular phone before her death. What was the relationship between Ms. Conway and your mother?"

The same questions were asked, however, worded differently.

Neil gestured "no" to all of them.

Clearly, from the detective's frustration, they were unable to track down Breanne.

They asked Neil about his phone, all of the calls Breanne made to it before the accident. Neil had absolutely blinking recollection of the calls; and from the detectives' standpoint, it was starting to look as if Neil was blinking involuntary, as if the blinking wasn't even an indication of an accurate "yes" or "no" answer, but, more or less, an internal reaction to words.

With their frustration in check, the detectives thanked Neil for his time—or, in Neil's case, what little time he had left.

They stepped out of the room to talk among themselves.

"You think it was self-defense?" the black detective asked his partner.

"Honestly," his partner replied, "I don't know what to think of it all. But what I do know," he said directly to his partner, "we need to find this Breanne Conway."

WHILE Neil was being transferred by ambulance to a "specialized" hospital called Greene Acres Mental Health and Wellness Center, which handled inpatients with all ranges of mental health disorders, Breanne walked into an interview for a new job as a dealer at the Knight's Bay casino in Las Paraíso. She looked sharp. Underneath a blue sports coat, which had matched the contacts in her eyes, she wore a black v-neck shirt and a pair of blue jeans that both looked painted on. Her lips were painted bright red. Her hair was tightly tied behind her head in a knot. Her look had somewhat of an Eighties-flare.

Displaying the utmost confidence, she handed her résumé to the man in charge of human resources, *firmly* shook his hand, and sat down in the seat on the other side of the desk.

"So," the human resources manager said, skimming through Breanne's résumé, "I see you have a lot of experience working in casinos. Silver Castle, the de Rio, Grigio. Impressive. However," he said, placing the résumé aside, "none of these jobs were as a dealer. So," he said, looking over the fresh scars at the edge of her collar and sleeves, "tell me, Ms. Kapoor, what makes you qualified for the job?"

Breanne thought carefully about her response.

Then, she confidently delivered.

⚲

SERG carefully moved the A'dorak piece, which was the tallest piece on the foldable wooden board and closely resembled a King on a chessboard but more decorated with an arch-shaped crown and five tentacle-like arms suspended overtop its scaly body, to the empty square along the far side of the board, forcing his opponent, Kamaria, to make her next attack.

✿

AFTER a morning spent in the recreational room with the other patients, Rick escorted Neil back to his room and sat him down in his chair in front of a window where he had a pleasant view of the courtyard. The sun crept over the corner of the rooftop and shone its light through the window. The beam of light was like a sword cutting through Neil's room.

The days at Greene Acres moved by the passing of the sunbeams along the room's walls and floor.

Sounds were stories left open for their own adaptation.

For weeks, Neil had mentally remained in a frozen state.

Throughout the brightest parts of his day, orderlies—one in particular named Rick—routinely checked on him and his status, and at times, kept him company by talking about the life that thrived outside these very walls.

The world outside Greene Acres had moved on without Neil.

It was relentless like that.

✿

IN the middle of the surveillance room, Serg and Kamaria, who were both dressed as security guards, were continuing a game of *deyja* on the back of a dead security guard's back. The guard had been stripped of his clothes and was lying lifelessly over a stool. The other one was dead as well and lying in a puddle of blood in the corner of the room, his clothes stripped off his body.

Kamaria pushed the white madeli'a forward into the black square in front of the white square where Serg's piece, the A'dorak, stood.

The madeli'a, with similar traits as a pawn, appeared like a warrior-like sculpture with wings.

"I'm almost forgot," Kamaria said in sudden revelation and peeled off the rubbery marking from the back of her neck, as if it was a sticker, and displayed it to Serg before flicking it aside.

"Nice touch," he said, surprised.

"It's all about the *subtleties*, D."

"You got that right," Serg mumbled.

Kamaria sat back and looked at the chess-like board from a wider angle.

She smiled, almost victoriously, as Serg looked over his options.

"Game's not over just yet," he said, eyeing the look on her face.

With a smirk growing on his face, Serg turned to the wall of monitors to the right of him and as he was about to make his next move, the orderly, Rick, came back into view.

꘎

FROM inside his room, Neil heard *footsteps* growing louder outside.

Each step echoed off the massive walls.

꘎

BOTH Serg and Kamaria watched intensely as the orderly made his way toward Neil's room.

He was carrying a book in his hand.

꘎

BACK to the room where Neil heard the door *squeaking* open behind him.

Without showing any emotion, Rick stepped into the room, placed the book on the desk next to Neil's bed, and then left the room.

Neil mechanically turned to the desk and the crinkled paperback resting on the very edge of the desk. He stood up from his chair, walked over to the book, and stared at the white madeli'a resting on top of the book for a moment before finally picking them both up. He placed the piece on the desk and then held the book up to his face. The book was his debut novel, *The Dark One at The Landing*.

Inside the front cover was Neil's signature. He immediately recognized his writing, his signature. He had signed the book for a man named Serg.

"*Just Serg*," Neil uttered, as thoughts started to come back to him.

Images.

Neil cracked open the book to a page that had been dog-eared. About halfway down the page a paragraph was underlined with a pen.

He read the excerpt to himself:

> "*. . . Gleaming lights left me in a raw state of wonder, blissfully hopeless yet unearthed like a fossil fuel. Piercing city lights clashed with one another in brutal harmony, highlighting the beautiful monsters surrounding me like dusty, animated antiques moving to and fro through the artificial life, remotely humming from the perpetual buzz of energy promoting a rot inside me, pseudo-voyeurism and idled hands, dilated pupils and twitchy eyes, glamour and greed, order and tamed chaos, and the thrill of living vicariously through God's creation's creation, the unbounded Holy Loot, and the ingenuous power granted its unholiest of adversaries. Tonight, I pawned away a piece of my heart in Las Paraíso, a city which I fantasized to one day call my own.*"

After reading the excerpt, Neil pulled the book away from his face in deep reflection.

The words.

His words.

It was there, in that mental flood, when he recited the words back to himself as if it was he who was his most perceptive audience: "Until my return, I long to feel what I felt during those strange, soulless days in the 'City of the Wicked,' to visit *her* once again and rightfully reclaim what was stolen from me."

Neil placed aside the book and picked up the chess-like piece on the desk.

The longer Neil stared at the madeli'a, the closer he came to remembering the life before the car crash. He was torn by two sides, pushing and pulling at him.

A part of him was being called upon by a higher force, the Great Manipulator tweaking his thoughts and paving Neil's destiny. Another part of him yearned for a time when memories did exactly what they were intended to do.

He leaned toward the latter.

.

GAME *over. . .*
   . . . Game over. . .
   . . . Game over. . .
   . . . Game over. . .
   . . . Game over. . .

Underneath the decayed modulation of a pipe organ, neon pink words GAME OVER flashed over the screen of the hand-held gaming console in a thinly repetitive eight-bit cheeping noise.

The hands of a child tightened around the console; however the sudden break wasn't caused by the physical exertion of a firm grip. The tiny *crack* veined outward like a lightning bolt across the middle of the glass screen and revealed over dozens of ghostly pale eyes in the warped reflection of electronic blackness.

THURSDAY APRIL 8, 1999 1:23 PM

"AFTER months of gaining worldwide attention, the infamous group known as 'The Trio' *is indeed at it once again,"* stated the

upbeat reporter, who was occasionally swatting at a bug in the air during her report. Behind the reporter, yellow caution tape marked off a violent scene consisting of overturned vehicles, a leveled overpass, destroyed buildings, which had been reduced to piles of rubble, and a massive cargo ship on its side with hundreds of steel containers scattered like giant Lego blocks on what was left of the street. *"Directly behind where I'm standing lies the aftermath of the Trio. Clearly, by the devastation, their work is being felt all around the world."* She paused through mid-sentence as a housefly landed on the side of her neck. In a natural reflex, she squashed the fly with her hand and continued her report, *"The three children's identities, as well as age, still remain a mystery and have not yet been confirmed by any relatives or loved ones. Many questions continue to linger: Who are these mysterious children? Where did they come from? One thing we do know is that these three children possess extraordinary abilities one would only see in the movies."*

MAURINE found a cool pair of brown-tinted Aviators hanging from the rearview mirror of a movie-blood red Corvette parked next to Darlene's Roadside Diner. The driver's side window was rolled halfway down. The sucker was even trusting enough to leave his Powerbook on the passenger seat, as if it was demanding to be stolen.

That has to be worth over at least a thousand dollars, Maurine thought to herself as she started to run down a list of things she could buy from the pawnshop with all of that money. She'd be able to squeeze at least five hundred, maybe more with Azure's help. Maybe Azure could turn herself into one of them ruffian-type psychos who'd embody enough testosterone to cause a grown man to involuntary pee. Maurine told herself that we already had heat as it was and that, despite all of the enticements the laptop provided, we didn't need anymore.

With her trucker hat worn low and sporting a new pair of Aviators, Maurine stepped inside the diner and remained pedestrian as she went straight to the register to pick up her order. The time was well past the normal lunchtime, and yet the place was hopping. Which made Maurine more uncomfortable.

Maurine gave the local cashier with a local smile the same name that she had given her over the payphone.

"Pamela," she said.

Behind the cashier was a row of to-go bags, five of them, and each one was full to the brim.

"You must have quite an army to feed," the cashier teased.

"Yes," Maurine said, keeping her head down. "Family reunion."

"Don't you hate those," the cashier said, trying to start small talk. "I swear, they're almost like choirs. . . "

Maurine moved her eyes upward for a moment and witnessed a smaller version of herself, a grainy black and white image of her walking through a convenient store, plastered all over the TV above the diner's bar.

On the TV displayed an elaborate shootout with both police officers and militarized FBI agents. The environment around both officers and agents was changing dramatically and at times, "folding" and "blocking," revealing yet another environment. In one particular shot, the once bustling highway folded into a stretch of overgrown countryside.

At their limited disposal, news outlets had several camera angles from surveillance cameras to up-close shots by video journalists and future "stringers," as they liked to call themselves—to a pedestrian who happened to be caught in the middle of the action with a handy camcorder on hand. The quick-draw with shaky hands happened to record the rare video from behind the rear of his vehicle. The video showed a young girl—who was no older than eight years old—shapeshifting into an adult police officer and shooting at the other officers and agents along a stretch of highway. Before the officers could return fire, the other child, a boy of the same age, opened up the space behind the shapeshifting girl in a similar fashion as a Rubik's Cube turned and twisted, revealing a square void-like gateway which displayed an entirely different environment. The space behind the hole wasn't anything like the highway, yet it was hilly and rugged like the countryside miles outside the city.

In the video, the girl stepped through the hole and then, once he was through, the hole closed—or "folded" back to its normal atmosphere.

The reporter was brought back in the exclusive coverage. She was talking to one of the shaken up survivors, a middle-aged man who was trying to describe the chaotic scene with child-like sound effects, which were supposed to be the sounds of gunshots, as well as those *whaaf-whumpf*ing sounds of the boy using his power to cause a fifty-plus car pileup.

One of the patrons sitting at the bar next to the cash register joked about the children on TV: "Amazing how time changes everything. Our phones are getting smaller. Our TVs. Computers. Memories. Hell, even our monsters."

Over the untimely laughter, the word *monsters* sent a ripple of disgust through Maurine's body.

Maurine forced herself to tune out both the cashier and that mouthy redneck at the bar with one ear and then, with the other, listened to the reporter reporting on TV: "*As of now, we're still unclear as to whether or not these children are acting alone or if there is a parental guardian involved. Police have released an image of an African American woman, who is wanted for questioning. If you have seen this woman, the police want you to contact authorities immediately.*"

The cashier placed the bags of food on the countertop next to the register.

"Your total comes to eighty-seven seventeen," she said.

Maurine handed her a fifty, a twenty, and a ten-dollar bill, and told the cashier to keep the change.

Before taking off, Maurine spotted an enticing Key lime pie in the casing next to the bar. The sight of the pie caused her to stop and rethink the order.

She walked back to the checkout counter and asked the cashier, "Can I have your Key lime pie please?"

"A slice?"

"No," Maurine said seriously. "The whole pie."

MAURINE exited the diner more paranoid than before she entered.

Suspecting the heat lurking around every corner, she scanned the parking lot. She didn't see anything out of the ordinary, no agents posing as civilians or touching the concealed earpieces in their ears or anything of that nature.

With the paranoid put aside, she pulled out the small yellow fob, which was once attached to a keychain. She rubbed her sweaty thumb along the sleek plastic fob and then, without anyone looking, dropped the fob onto the ground.

IN a sudden rage, the young boy tossed the broken gaming console.

As soon as the console left his hand, it stopped in midair and then gracefully floated back into the boy's flexed hands and remained in the same exact position he was holding just moments ago. The once veiny crack cut down the center of the screen reversed its slow spread and retreated back to its original, unbroken state.

Once more, the words *Game Over* reappeared, flashing on the screen.

"*Try again*, Austin," the sarcastic voice of a girl said next to the boy, "*but this time, without the temper-tantrum.*"

Exercising utmost caution of her surroundings, Maurine finally arrived at the beat up burgundy van, which was parked in the back of the parking lot. She opened up the driver's side door and placed the armful of to-go bags on the passenger seat.

She turned to the three children sitting quietly inside.

"Who's hungry?" asked Maurine.

INSIDE a remote base camp located twenty miles outside East

Polke, a field agent named Ben Upshaw hung up the telephone with the local officer and rushed to the acting Director of "Operation Roundup."

Agent Upshaw said to Director Gaddy, "A waitress from Ragland claims she spotted the woman on TV picking up food from her restaurant."

"What location?"

"A diner called Darlene's, just off I-40," the agent said. "She also said she was driving a brown van."

"Did she get a plate number?"

"No, sir."

"How about the tweakers?"

"She just saw the woman and the van," he said. "That's all."

Director Gaddy took a moment to digest Upshaw's recent intel. Then, over a tense moment, he made a speedy response based on the information given to him.

"Activate the Scout," Director Gaddy demanded.

⁂

"DID you drop the—"

The girl was suddenly cut off by Maurine as she divvied out the food.

"Yes," she said. "I did exactly what you told me to do."

Maurine pulled out Austin's order.

"Remember, Austin," she said, as she handed the boy, Austin, the Styrofoam box of food. "Don't eat so fast. Remember slow, like ice cream."

In the back of the van sat "The Trio," as the media had branded them.

There was Austin, the first underling. Then, his other two underlings, Azure, the shapeshifter who was seen shapeshifting into a police officer on the TV, then Angela, who possessed the rare ability to control time. All three of the underlings could pass as triplets. As with the two other girls, who appeared the same age as Austin, Austin's skin was ghostly pale, sickly. Maurine dressed each one of them like any other

252

child and tried not to make them stand out, the clothes coming from a thrift shop somewhere along the outskirts of El Delanco. Austin was wearing a navy blue New York Yankees sweatshirt with a pair of blue jeans. Azure, seated behind Austin, was wearing a black and white striped sweater with red pants and a black hat worn boyishly low on her head. Next to Azure, Angela was dressed in an oversized pink sweatshirt with black leggings.

Austin finally brought himself to a nod of his head; and before Maurine could hand him the box of food, he pinched his face with concentration.

All of a sudden, he opened up the space right next to Maurine's hand.

Before the boy could snatch the food from Maurine's hand through the void-like square, Maurine pulled back the box of food.

"What did I tell you about using your powers with me?" Maurine snapped, her brow arched in clear anger.

"Sorry," Austin said, deflated.

The space folded back to its normal atmosphere.

Maurine handed Austin the box.

Acting as if he was starved to death, he hurriedly opened the box. His face immediately cringed in repulsion as soon as he saw what waited for him inside the box. All that green and earthly stuff—*yuck!*

Disappointed, Austin turned to Maurine, who quickly replied, "Don't give me that look, boy."

Austin pointed at the stack of pies in the other bag.

"But. . . " he murmured.

"*No buts*, Austin. Eat your greens, then you can have dessert."

"It's not fair," Austin said, his voice growing louder.

"Don't you raise your voice with me, boy," Maurine snapped.

Austin's face went dark and blank, his glowing eyes sharp underneath the top of his lowered forehead.

"Azure," Maurine said, "get control of your brother, will you?"

Azure stepped forward and inched toward the seat next to Austin; however, she was no longer Azure but a six foot-five, two hundred and thirty pounder man hunching underneath the roof of the van. The man happened to be Julius Dupree, All-Star center fielder for the New York Yankees. He was wearing his baseball cap and outfit and everything. Even signed a baseball card for young Austin.

Austin's anger eventually melted from his keen-looking face.

"Julius Dupree!" Austin exclaimed, as Mr. Dupree sat down in the seat next to Austin.

Julius leaned closer to Austin and told him how much he loved greens and how his momma always got on him for not eating them. So, one day, he decided to do what his momma had told him. It turned out Momma was right. He grew up big and strong and then, one day, that once frail boy ended up becoming a Major League slugger who won the World Series for his team in game seven.

Austin forced himself to eat his greens.

Maurine couldn't help but smile, not at Austin, but at the bond the three underlings shared.

For a moment, she actually thought they were, dare she day, human.

MONDAY JUNE 10, 2019 8:01 AM

MAURINE violently woke up from her unconscious state.

She frantically looked around but all she could see was the hazy darkness surrounding her and a spotlight shining directly down on her head. She made an attempt to move her arms but soon realized they were tied behind her back by what felt like a metal wire.

More lights switched on, revealing a room of stark reflections.

The walls were mirrors, like the ones found in an interrogation room inside a police station; however, all four walls were covered in mirrors. Even the floor, as well as the ceiling above Maurine, was made up of mirrors.

In awe, Maurine first looked up and saw her own reflection staring down at her in a chair. The image alone forced her to look back down and examine herself, then the chair, then over her shoulder where she saw her restrained fingers dangling behind her back. Her wrists were fastened to an aluminum chair, which was bolted to the glass floor. She even tried to shake the chair, but it didn't budge an inch. She examined her body next, her outfit. She was still wearing the same clothes as she was before she was taken, powder blue collared shirt, which was damp and spotted with perspiration, blue jeans, damp as well, and a partially worn beige cardigan.

A door suddenly opened up before her.

Two men, one with a crew cut, the other bald, both wearing cargo pants and dark shirts, stepped inside the glass box. At first glance, she determined which one was the good cop, the compassionate one, and which one was the bad cop based on his stony exterior. Regardless, both men were military, probably ex-military.

They first introduced themselves to Maurine. The man whom Maurine first suspected as the "good cop" was Rashid Shatt al-Euphratt—"Shakespeare" was what everybody called him. Then, the one who looked as if he hadn't gotten laid in this decade: Clayton-Antonio Poole. He went by "Poole."

Shakespeare rudely tossed a dark green folder on the metal table in front of Maurine, which made Maurine question whether or not he was good at all or just simply an asshole trying to rattle Maurine.

"Where am I?" asked Maurine, her voice sharp, despite her constant trembling.

Shakespeare arrogantly rolled up his sleeves and told Maurine, "You're in a secured underground location outside Rip Valley."

"And Detective Reagan?"

"I'm afraid the detective, as loyal as he was to you in his quest for justice, is no longer part of the picture."

Maurine attempted to pounce at Shakespeare, who, in her mind, was starting to look more and more like "bad cop"; however, she was completely restrained in the chair.

"What'd you do to him?" asked Maurine.

"Enough questions," he said and sat down at the corner of the table, "we'll be the ones asking the questions now."

The other man, Poole, who was hanging out in the corner of the room like a stealthy shadow, asked Maurine, "Do you know why you are here, Ms. Hatcher?"

Don't answer the question, Maurine thought. *He's testing you.*

Maurine didn't answer.

"If you're not going to talk, then we'll do the talking for you." Poole used the glass wall to bounce forward from his relaxed post. He unfolded his arms and paced around Maurine. "You are here, Ms. Hatcher, because for the past twenty years you have eluded police and eventually climbed your way to the FBI's Most Wanted List—"

"—You don't look like FBI."

"Whoever said we were?"

The man sitting on the table smirked at the other man, "I didn't know the FBI had a *look*."

"Listen, Ms. Hatcher, we know you have important information regarding the whereabouts of the shapers—"

"—Is that what you're calling them these days?"

"Just tell us where the underlings are and you will be released."

"Released?"

Maurine nearly laughed.

Keep pushing his buttons.

He's got them. They all do.

Poole said superiorly, "This conversation, Ms. Hatcher— because that's all it is, a conversation—can go two ways. You cooperate and tell us what you know about the underlings and you can go back to that miserable life of yours working at Food Way, struggling to stay afloat, or—the other way—if you don't cooperate, I'm afraid you're going to force our hand. We'll have to take extreme measures in order to protect national security. Now," he said, still pacing, "I don't want to break you, Ms. Hatcher, but I have a job and my job is to find out what you know. I want to know *why* you tracked down

Detective Reagan and provided him details of ongoing cases. I want to know *why*, after all these years, you resurfaced from the shadows. Most importantly, I want to know *what* you're thinking right now?"

"Just tell us, Maurine," Shakespeare said closely. "Where are you hiding the children?"

"You want to know what I'm thinking, huh?" she said with her head down. She smiled, looked up, and turned to the man pacing beside her. "I'm thinking: which one of you will be the first to die. Originally, I had my money on this fella right here," she pointed at the fair skinned man sitting next to her, "but the more you open your mouth, I'm leaning toward you."

"So, that's how we're going to play?"

Maurine tilted her head.

"Then, why are you here, Ms. Hatcher? Why are you wasting our time?"

"I came here to kill you."

The two men laughed.

"Kill us? And how exactly are you going to do that?"

"If I told you, then that would certainly ruin the surprise. Now, wouldn't it?"

"Enough of this bitch," Poole said grimly and nodded at the other man next to Maurine. "Bring in the Interrogator."

The door suddenly opened once more.

Never had a doorway looked so dark to Maurine.

TIME UNKNOWN

THE screen, which acted as both shutter and barrier along the massive stretch of wall, automatically slid open and revealed the hazy orange cityscape of Babylon City. Marked with hundreds of both old and modern skyscrapers, which appeared like warped silhouettes from the positioning of the obscured sun, the city birthed with artificial life from the constant flow of battery-operated, automatically GPS controlled hover cars zooming along virtual skyrise lanes of Al-dastia to swarms of cubical drones buzzing a smog-heavy skyline to the inaudible speedrail weaving throughout the entire city like a serpent.

Standing proudly at the balcony of R O A M, a branch of Orion Industries, was the great King Orion himself. He was dressed in a red silk robe with a stiff collar erected over his head, imperial-like; his ripped bare chest was exposed. He had the body of a twenty year old, and yet he had the face of a man well past middle age.

The door automatically opened at the far end of the massive hall of the spacious Egyptian-style room with golden-speckled columns.

Out stepped Jesseme, an attractive yet stern woman who could pass as a stick figure.

Not missing a beat, Jesseme walked directly to the King as if she was strutting down a catwalk. The reverberation of her stilettos brought out the deepness of the massive stadium-like hall.

"There's been another killing, King Orion," Jesseme said from behind. She paused and thought carefully about the delivery of her next statement. "It appears to be similar to the others."

"You don't sound too sure of yourself, Jesseme," the King said resonantly, as he peered out at the lively cityscape before him.

"It's just," Jesseme paused once more, "Babylonians want answers."

"Who do you think is behind it all?" asked King Orion.

"I don't know, Sir—"

King Orion faced Jesseme. His eyes honed in on the vampiric woman whose confidence was shrinking by the second.

"You don't know? What you mean to say is that you don't have an opinion. Am I correct?"

"No, Sir," Jesseme stuttered. "I mean. . . Whoever they are, they're making a statement—or overstatement. That's for sure."

"An overstatement? Which is?"

"Permission to be honest, Sir?"

"Honesty is the reason why I hired you, Jesseme. Please.

Indulge me."

"Well, Sir, I think they're trying to play god."

"So, you think it's a human who is responsible for these crimes?"

"Not a human, Sir," she replied. "A monster."

The king didn't respond from Jesseme's comment.

Instead, he turned back around toward the vast, jagged skyline and pondered over who—or what—might have been killing his people.

⌗

CIRCLED around the victim in the heart of Mesatopia Square stood an elite group of steely-eyed detectives wearing outdated tracers.

One of the detectives examined the victim's body parts scattered around the plaza.

Another detective was examining the victim's head, which had been placed on top of a stake protruding from the street.

The body appeared to be torn apart.

Above, the drones—particularly the daily data "collecting" and "archiving" drones—were capturing the detectives hard at work.

One detective shooed away the pesky drone.

"Scram, *cubey*," he shouted out, as he flashed a green light beam into its sensor, which caused the cubed drone to sputter and spin away. During its overcorrection, the drone diverted back to its designated lane, thus causing the drone to crash into another drone, which, in return, crashed into yet another drone and created an inevitable domino effect. The sight alone of watching the drones hit and bounce into one another like bumper drones in the air stirred a couple of laughs from the detectives. This would be the detective's only amusement for the day.

Everything else was cold and calculated, like a machine.

THURSDAY APRIL 8, 1999 3:18 PM

A tall Frenchman with black greasy hair walked into Darlene's Roadside Diner.

As soon as he stepped foot inside, he unbuttoned his black trench coat and followed Maurine's scent to the front cash register.

Due to the renegade-type aura that the strange man had given off, he gathered most—if not, all—of the patrons' attention. Some were even so inclined to snap their heads toward the loner in cartoon fashion, as if he demanded people's attention or even gave off an odor that reeked of something foreign, not in a homeless kind of way but more of an "out of town" kind of way, a way that raised one red flag after another, especially in such a small town as Ragland, which had a population roughly the size of a crowd at any run-in-the-mill bluegrass concert.

What stood out were the scars on his face; first, the most obvious one on the right side of his face called a Glasgow smile. Then, once he removed his John Lennon-inspired sunglasses, the Frenchman displayed the other less-obvious one, a lightning bolt-looking scar along the corner of his eye.

The Frenchman followed in Maurine's footsteps and walked straight to the cashier behind the cash register, pulled out a piece of paper, and showed her the same still image of Maurine on the surveillance camera.

"Excuse me, ma'am," he said in his best English, "my name is Jean Luere. I was wondering, by any chance, if you have you seen this young woman before."

The Frenchman, Jean, held the photo to the cashier's face. She looked it over twice. Then, shook her head.

"No, sir," she said, both smitten and yet, at the same time, terrified from the Frenchman's presence.

He carefully studied her face during her answer and immediately recognized the uncertainty both in her eyes and in her facial gestures.

"Are you sure. . . " he said more patiently, as he looked down at the name on her nametag, ". . . Charlie?"

"Yes," she said, her voice starting to shake. "I'm pretty sure. If you want, I can ask somebody else if they've seen the woman you're looking for."

"No," the Frenchman said abruptly. "You've been a great help to me, Charlie. Thank you."

"Ah—you're welcome," the cashier said, her voice trailing off.

As the strange man walked back outside, he noticed an object on the ground. He reached down and picked up the same yellow fob that Maurine had dropped after she left the diner. He held the fob underneath his nose and started to sniff it.

ONCE the Frenchman made it back to his brown Fifth generation Pontiac GTO, he stepped inside and pulled out an oblong football-shaped device made out of copper from a metal suitcase in the backseat. He placed the pointy device over his head, as well as his nose, and wore the device similar to a VR headset. The main difference in its design was the front of the mask, which curved and extended outward like the beak of a toucan. He then carefully placed the yellow fob underneath the device by locking it into a secured holder. Before he pressed the button on the side of the mask, he injected himself with a serum in the side of his neck.

He turned on the device, causing the mask let out a loud *hissing* noise.

The Frenchman braced himself.

The device locked in on the fob. It hummed at first and then made yet another sound, which resembled the sound of a computer rebooting.

After the combination of sounds, he jerked back into the driver's seat as if his body was trying to go right through it. There was yet another one of those *hissing* sounds, but this time from the man, who was embracing a deep inhale through his nose, with both his shoulders and chest puffed out. Following the deep breath, his body started to convulse in a seizure-like pace. He was bouncing all over the car, grabbing the steering wheel and center console and doing everything he could to keep whatever was inside him from escaping his body.

Before the Frenchman could pass out, he removed the device from his head. His body eventually calmed. Everything about the strange man had calmed, as if he had just taken a hit of a psychotropic drug.

⊥

THROUGH the rear view mirror, Maurine noticed Azure squirming in her seat.

"Azure, do you have to go?" asked Maurine.

Without saying a word, she bobbed her head.

Maurine ended up stopping at a crummy-looking gas station between towns.

As she parked the van along the side of the gas station, she asked the others if they had to go, but it was only Azure.

Maurine specifically told Azure to wait in the van until she got the key to the restroom, which was located on the side of the convenient store.

In the convenient store, Maurine made the mistake of asking for the men's key. She corrected herself and asked for the ladies. On any normal day, Maurine's untimely mistake would've drawn suspicion; however, the shaggy-looking clerk appeared to be in a world of his own.

With key in hand, Maurine walked around the side of the building.

Azure stepped out of the van. She handed Azure the key and told her that she would be waiting outside for her, but Azure begged Maurine to go in with her.

She didn't want to leave the other two underlings out of her sight; however, she knew how uncomfortable Azure got and didn't like to go while she was alone.

262

⌗

HOURS passed.

Miles conquered.

After a day of driving, Maurine ended up driving down a deserted dirt road in the middle of the woods on a piece of property that looked abandoned.

Once they reached the end of the road, the woods opened up to a vast stretch of grassland.

"How's this, Austin?" she said through the rearview mirror as she parked the van.

Austin didn't respond. Yet, he kept playing a fighting game on the portable handheld gaming console.

"Austin," Maurine snapped, her temper flaring.

Austin paused the game and moved his eyes toward Maurine, then the landscape outside.

"Will this work?" asked Maurine.

"Why doesn't Azure do it this time?" said Austin.

"Well," Maurine said, "I asked you, Austin."

"Why?"

Azure remained quiet, as she had been doing for the entire ride.

"Azure has had a rough day, Austin."

"Rough day? I moved an entire ocean. You know how hard it is to move an ocean. Well, it's pretty hard—"

"Austin, I'm not in the mood." She paused. "I'll tell you this. If you help, I'll let you have some dessert. How does that sound?"

Austin took one glance outside before he bobbed his head.

"Okay."

"Is that a *yes*?"

"Yes," Austin mumbled and got back to his game.

"Yes what?"

"Yes, ma'am."

⌗

THE three underlings waited outside while Maurine parked

263

the van behind a large beech tree. She covered up the van with bigleaf magnolia branches, as well as foliage from nearby shrubbery.

As soon as she concealed the van with nature around her, she grabbed the rest of her things, including the bag of pies and pastries and a gym bag with the butt end of a shotgun sticking out through the zipper, and walked back to the three underlings. She grabbed the gaming console from Austin's hands and told him to work his magic—she specifically pointed to an area in the grassland, which would be the most ideal spot for an altercation.

Austin acted as if he didn't want to alter the environment, but the only thing driving him was the Key lime pie.

Annoyed, he kneeled down to the ground and pulled out a few blades of grass from the soil below. He grabbed a handful of dirt and crumbled it in his hands to help release its aroma. He raised the handful of dirt to his face and smelled it.

He turned to Maurine and said, "The energy is weak here."

"Well," she replied, keeping her distance, "we can go somewhere else if you like—"

"—No," he said abruptly and turned to Azure, who was standing behind him with her arms crossed and giving him a 'What-are-you-waiting-for' kind of glare. "It's fine. *I'm* fine."

Maurine kneeled down and pulled out a pump-action shotgun, which was already loaded, and a gas mask from the gym bag.

For her own safety.

Not the underling's.

Ready to proceed, Austin took in several deep breaths, arched his body toward the ground, and started to cough, slowly at first, and then the coughs turning strangely violent and aggressive.

Angela glanced up at the sky and watched the clouds hovering closer to the sun directly above.

"Hurry up, Austin," she urged Austin.

"I'm trying," Austin said, coughing.

He resorted to the one thing he hated doing and that was sticking his finger down his throat.

Austin gagged.

Moments later, he ended up vomiting up most of his lunch on the ground below.

Once everything was out, the vomit started to. . . move!

Gradually, the vomit glowed and smoked, acid-like. The pale bluish glow of the vomit itself was nearly as bright as the sun above. The glowing vomit chewed and ate the soil and burned a perfect hole through the earth.

More focused than sick, he lowered his head with a menacing scowl, his skin dimming like a light bulb, as if he was turning off a light switch inside his body. Once he reached full on recharge mode, his skin was gray in color, his eyes glossy and dead-like.

In a mechanical state, his head slowly rolled backward. His body stirred and twitched slightly, as if there was something moving around inside the confines of that small frame of a body.

Once Austin's head settled between his shoulders with his face aimed directly at the sky above, his mouth stretched open in a slack yet gaping yawn, as if he was calling upon something deep inside him.

The last bit of sunlight shone down upon Austin's face. His throat gradually expanded and bulged outward and appeared as if he had major goiters protruding from both sides of his neck.

Right before the sun blotted out the clouds, two bluish marbled eyes appeared in the back of Austin's throat. He gagged once more, the sudden reflux forcing his entire body to drive forward.

Bracing himself on both his hands, as well as his knees, Austin closed his eyes and grimaced in great agony.

The sight alone of the boy regurgitating up something awful caused Maurine to pump the shotgun and ready herself.

As Austin's mouth stretched farther open, a scaly hand with talons the size of switchblades extended from Austin's throat. The hand kept reaching outward and grabbing at air until an arm nearly the size of Austin's own arm revealed itself. Once one arm was free, another one reached outward to free itself. The creature used the ground below to claw its way from Austin's body.

As the dark parasitic-like creature slowly emerged from Austin's frail body, Maurine steadied her aim.

The creature's entire body slithered from Austin and fell to the ground below. Altogether, it was slightly smaller than Austin. Instead of legs, however, it had a long scorpion-like stinger, which was attached to its muscular torso with arms similar to Austin in shape and size. Its head was oval-shaped with sharp quills on the back of its head running down its spine and back.

Exhausted and terribly weakened from the massive disgorge, Austin crawled away from the creature, which, in the wake of its release, turned to the sudden movement and sniffed Austin. Then, after it sniffed Austin, it then sniffed out Maurine, who, in return, readjusted her grip around the shotgun; her index finger rested on the trigger.

The creature looked over Maurine with its beady, darkening eyes; however, it was more interested in the hole forming in the earth.

As Maurine was about to squeeze the trigger, the creature darted into the hole below, bringing great relief, not only to Maurine, but also Austin as well. It didn't take long for his skin to return to its normal pale hue.

"I hate this part," he groaned.

Maurine asked, "How you doing, Austin? Would you like some water?"

"Fine."

Maurine kneeled down and reached in her bag for a bottle of water.

"No," Austin exclaimed, more annoyed. "I'm fine."

"Something's wrong," Angela said from behind as she remained still and listened closely to the creature below. "It's been down there for way too long."

"I told you," Austin said. "The energy is weaker here—"

"—Wait a sec. I hear it. It's on the move again. Get ready Austin." Angela took a step back, which caused Azure and Maurine to take a step back as well.

Austin crawled his way toward the hole in the earth. He peered down into the tunnel, which looked as if it had stretched miles deep into the center of the Earth. *Miles.*

He witnessed a glint of light deep inside the hole, a light that, in a matter of seconds, grew brighter and brighter. . .

Maurine wasted no time in putting on her gas mask.

More timid than determined, Austin backed away from the hole; and as he braced himself for impact, he cautiously reached out his shaky right hand directly over the hole.

"Remember to breath," Angela told Austin.

Caught off guard by Angela's comment, Austin turned to Angela as if her words didn't help lessen the already tense situation.

"Thanks for the ad—"

The sharp end of Austin's voice was suddenly cut off by the sudden burst of light beaming through the hole.

With his body curled inward as if he was about to be struck, Austin jolted backward.

The flash of a lightning bolt struck the center of Austin's palm. The force was so great that it lifted him off his feet and sent his body twirling in the air. The light was so bright that it momentarily blinded Maurine, Angela, and Azure. Following the sudden burst of light was a deafening blast, but not from Maurine's shotgun, even though the sound itself sounded familiar to the boom of a buckshot.

Once Austin fell back to earth, his entire body was smoking as if he was releasing steam from his pores.

Eventually, after the smoke started to clear, Austin stood to his feet, staggering at first.

Standing upright, he looked down at his glowing right hand and watched that bluish light travel through the web of his nervous system.

Maurine remained in a state of awe.

"Looks like he was given a full dose," Angela said casually.

Once the noxious gases dissipated into the air and young Austin returned to his normal child-like state, Maurine removed the gas mask from her face.

She pointed at the area next to a lone maple tree and told

Austin, "Go ahead. Magic time."

With his eyes sharpened in concentration, Austin stared at the maple tree. He completely recreated the area around the tree. The atmosphere folded outward, revealing a fancy resort in the middle of the open field.

"Something a little less obvious," Maurine said to Austin. "Something more modest."

Austin clenched his teeth together in anger and altered the environment once more.

The resort suddenly collapsed and folded inward as if the structure was made out of perfectly shaped blocks. He scaled down the size of the resort and by the time he reached the first level, the resort had transformed into a one-story home with white siding and black shutters.

Surprised, Maurine turned to Austin.

"Better?" he said.

Surprisingly enough, the house wasn't like any other house even though the house looked like any other house, a cookie-cutter house built in the late 1970's. Unlike the resort, the house didn't stand out or appear out of the ordinary. Surprisingly enough, the house looked as if it belonged in this grass-land surrounded by woods. Austin had even altered the land between the house and the dirt road, blocking together a gravel driveway that lead from the edge of the garage to the dirt road in order to sell the effect.

Surprised by the sight of the house, Maurine asked, "Where have you seen this image before, Austin?"

"In a photograph of yours," he said flatly.

Maurine had no words or thoughts.

"So," Austin said, his tone sharper, "will this do?"

Maurine cleared her throat.

"Yeah," she said. "I guess so."

Maurine gathered her things from the ground and with the three underlings by her side, walked up the driveway and made her way into a place that she had once called home.

As soon as Maurine stepped foot into the house, the smell alone of the inside brought back a wave of memories, some pleasant, while others not so pleasant. Nonetheless, she was overwhelmed with nostalgia.

She placed the bags on a wooden bench in the foyer and told the underlings to go into the living room and make themselves at home.

While the underlings were watching TV, Maurine moseyed around the upstairs of the house.

Still left in awe by every detail, Maurine found her Wabby, an old and weathered stuffed animal. When she was just a girl, she had named the bunny Wabby because, at the time, she couldn't quite pronounce her *r's* and whenever she spoke her *r's*, they sounded like *w's* instead. She picked up the stuffed animal from the bench along the bay window and stared outside.

Her days as a young girl flooded her memory. In her mind, she imagined her backyard, not the grassland, but her own backyard, the place where you could do anything or if you wanted, be whoever you desired, a place where she commonly chased Aimee around the backyard with the hose, splashing her with water.

The memory of her sister was so strong that she could no longer look out the window.

On the way downstairs, she crossed her parents' bedroom. She stood at the one place where she felt more comfortable. At the doorway, she peered into the empty bedroom and imagined both her parents sitting on the edge of the bed, going through photo albums, flipping through photos of Aimee; and then, every now and then, her momma would hold up a photo of Aimee and show it to Maurine's daddy and he'd start weeping like a boy.

Like the room before, the memories were too strong for Maurine to handle. Which made her wonder why Austin chose this one particular house. He could've made them a campsite, a hut, or even a small structure that had a roof and enough room to make it through the night without drawing too much attention.

More composed, Maurine checked on the underlings in the living room. Everybody was there, except for one.

"Where's Azure?" asked Maurine.

Austin shrugged his shoulders.

"Angela?"

Angela turned to Maurine and told her that she thought she was outside.

Maurine walked to the window and saw Azure sitting on a tire hanging from a tree branch.

With her Wabby in hand, Maurine walked outside where Azure was swinging from the tire. She could hardly even bring herself to lift her head up at Maurine.

Maurine let out a sigh before sitting down against the tree trunk next to Azure. She looked over her Wabby and then placed it on the ground.

As the two remained in silence, Maurine looked up at the birds in the tree above.

"When I was your age, I used to come out here all the time. I remember I used to give all of the birds names based on their traits or personalities. I'd create a whole background for each one of the birds and make up their own story. In a way, I guess I was closer to the birds than I was to people. So, clearly, as you can imagine, I didn't have what you'd call friends when I was younger. Strangely enough, I never saw that as a negative, yet, rather the opposite. By the time I finally reached college—"

Azure looked up from the ground and uttered, "*College?*"

"It's a place where older kids go to get an education before they enter the real world. Think of it as a school."

Azure lowered her head once more and stared at the ground below.

"In college, other girls were doing what other girls were doing, like they were pulled straight from an assembly line. They'd all dress the same, talk the same."

"What about you?" asked Azure.

"Me? I was just being," Maurine shrugged, "me." She paused. "After college, when I found a job in the real world, I ended up turning into a person whom I never envisioned of being when I was a little girl."

"How come?"

"Well," she sighed. "I dunno. Life, I guess." Maurine

said in reflection, "I wanted to fly airplanes. Then, one day, eventually, fly into the stars."

"Like an astronaut?"

"Just like an astronaut. Castles in the air, right?"

"Castles? What's that?"

Maurine waved off the comment.

"Forget about it."

Azure asked, "Why didn't you become an astronaut?"

"Well, you have to have money to live in the real world. Before I even knew it, those dreams I once had were gone, as if, over time, the real world had stolen them from me. When I first met you three, I finally decided who I wanted to be; and, in a strange way, I felt as if every road that I had taken throughout my life always led me here. To you. To *Angela* and Austin. I might be just a small part in your story. But being a small part beats not being a part of your life at all." Maurine leaned in closer to Azure. "You can tell me what's going on."

"It's Angela," Azure finally said.

"What about Angela?"

"She says I don't make it at the end."

"What do you mean?"

"She says I'm going to die. She says that she's tried to alter the timeline in ways that I wouldn't die. But, she says that in all of the scenarios, I die—"

"—You're not going to die, Azure, as long as I'm here."

"But you can't protect us forever. One day, you're going to die. Then, who's going to look after us?"

"By the time I die, you'll be a grown woman. You won't need anybody to look after you." The comment caused Azure to hang her head in what Maurine distinguished as a sign that she had already given up. "I know of a place, this safe place where they won't be able to touch the three of you. It's a place where you won't need your powers."

Maurine's words immediately caught Azure's attention.

"When I was younger—around the time I got my driver's license—me and a friend used to take these road trips to a lake called Devil's Throat."

"Devil's Throat?"

"Trust me." Maurine smiled. "It doesn't sound as ominous as the name suggests; in fact, it was like a hidden gem, untouched by the outside world. A place where *no one* can find you. My friend had a friend who had a relative who owned a cabin there. After this is all over, maybe the four of us can go there and lay low, for a while that is, until things settle down."

Again, Azure hung her head and acted as if she wasn't the least interested in Maurine's proposal.

Maurine leaned forward into Azure's narrow range of vision. She struggled to make any sort of eye contact with Maurine for both her eyes were pinned like thumbtacks to the ground below.

"Can you keep a secret, Azure?" Maurine asked over a moment of silence.

Pouting, Azure moved her eyes upward at Maurine. She barely brought herself to nod.

"Of the three of you," Maurine said, "*you*, Azure, you are, by far, the strongest. And it will be you who leads the others to where they need to be, *not* me, *not* anyone else. *Only you.*"

"But I don't want to," Azure whined.

"When the time comes, it won't be a matter of what you 'want to' but rather what you 'will do.' You won't even know when it happens. It'll just happen and you'll know exactly what to do and where to go."

Azure sniffled.

Acknowledging how broken up Azure was about taking the role as leader, she leaned forward and hugged Azure.

Azure started to cry into Maurine's shoulder.

Trying to hold back the emotion, Maurine said to Azure, "Nothing bad is going to happen to you, you hear? *Nothing.*"

"You promise?"

Maurine promised Azure, crossed her heart and swore to die, but it wouldn't be the first time she had broken her word.

Over Azure's shoulder, Maurine witnessed Angela standing behind the living room window.

The sight of Angela caused Maurine to pull herself away

from Azure.

In another silence, this time more comforting, Azure turned toward Maurine, wiped away the tears from her face, and asked her if she wanted to see something cool. Maurine didn't know what Azure meant by "something cool." Maurine's face was still, her eyes widening in suspense.

Azure held out her hand and puckered her lips together. She made a series of trills, tweets, and *purr-chkk-oh-rwee* notes at the birds flying and swooping down and landing all around them. The notes, *purr-chkk-oh-rwee*, sounded oddly similar, if not the same as the birds singing in the trees. Maurine was baffled as to how Azure was able to sound as if she was a bird herself.

In a whooshing flutter of air, an American Goldfinch landed on Azure's finger.

A breeding male as its brilliant yellow color and black cap suggested.

Maurine's mouth fell in disbelief.

"*Yellow Bird*," Azure said naively. "I'm going to call this one Yellow Bird."

"And where did you come up with that name?" asked Maurine with a smile gradually spreading across her face.

Azure carefully raised the Goldfinch to the side of her ear as if she was listening to the bird speak to her.

She pulled the Goldfinch away from her ear and she was no longer holding a Goldfinch on her finger, rather a cell phone in the palm of her hand.

"It's for you," Azure said and handed Maurine the cell phone.

Still amazed by Azure's sorcery, Maurine asked skittishly, "What did you do with the poor bird?"

In an empty stare back, Azure kept her hand extended outward as if she was waiting for Maurine to grab the cell phone and she wasn't going to respond to her question until Maurine played along.

Eventually, through her cautious stare, Maurine grabbed the cell phone from Azure's hand and held it up to her ear.

She heard the piercing *tweet* of a bird!

Both startled and disgusted by Azure's little magic act, Maurine jerked her head back and noticed the same Goldfinch in her hand. She quickly set the bird free. The bird flew away, so too did Maurine's amazement.

With slight discomfort from Azure's presence, Maurine faced the young girl who was laughing to herself; however, Maurine remained awestruck by witnessing such a rare wonder.

MONDAY JUNE 10, 2019 10:35 AM

AFTER the beating, the left side of Maurine's face started to swell.

In the blurry reflection along the mirrored wall, she witnessed herself as Angela sitting in the exact same seat where she was sitting, as if her body had been replaced with Angela's tiny body. She hadn't aged a day; and she looked identical to the last time Maurine saw her. However, her face was covered in a discolored patch of fresh bruises and blood. The sight alone of Angela brought back a memory, which she had, over the years, so desperately tried to forget. That night in New Mexico. When everything began and ended. The start of a series of unearthly nightmares.

Angela said to herself when actually she was speaking directly to Maurine: "You're *almost* there."

Maurine blinked the drop of blood from her eyes and once more, looked in the mirror, only to witness herself in the reflection, not Angela. Before she turned away, her eyes caught a scaly tail moving back and forth below the chair.

She flinched at the same time the door swung opened!

Maurine pulled her attention from the mirror, from that tail—which Maurine figured was all but a hallucination—and faced the same two men stepping into the interrogation room. They walked with a little more pep in their step as if they had just got done eating a light snack.

They went to their same exact positions: one man sat on the corner of the table while the other one paced around Maurine.

"Are you ready to talk?" Shakespeare asked Maurine.

"Let me think." For a moment, Maurine drifted in thought. "No," she said sarcastically. "As a matter of fact, I've been a bad girl who needs to be punished. So, why don't you go ahead and bring back that muscle of yours? He's more of a man than the two of you combined."

Unlike Shakespeare, Poole remained firm in his grilling: "The fun and games are over, Ms. Hatcher. Where are the underlings?"

"By the way," she said, sniffling up a string of nose, which was leaking from the corner of her nostril, "who in the hell gave them that name? Underlings? You guys have some sort of PR team working back there?" Before the two could answer Maurine's question, she filled in the blanks, "Let me guess. You took under and youngling and then married the two together like some cute 'It' couple, like Bennifer or Bradica! Or wait! How about this one? You numbskulls are what all those miserable saps on social media call 'closet ascenders.' Cult enthusiasts preparing yourselves for your great 'Ascension' into the 'Land of the Woke.' All for what? Your own personal awakening? Why don't you two yahoos and your ridiculous cult get on with it, like all your wannabe ascender buddies? Drink your fucking spiked punch already and save me the trouble in killing you myself."

"Your guess is as good as mine, Ms. Hatcher," Poole said humbly and ignored Maurine's loose spout. He stepped closer to Maurine. Dangerously close. In a gentlemen-like manner, he combed a band of hair from her bloodshot eyes and curled it over her ear. "Let's start simple, shall we? Where were you during the Spectacle of '98?"

"The Spectacle, huh? You mean the one which resulted in millions of people running to the church the next day? That Spectacle?"

"Yes," Poole said. "That one."

"I was at home, watching the *Price is Right* in my underwear while my cat, Theodore, licked the milk from my toes. What were you doing during that time? Oh, that's right. You were just some rotten teenager who spent your slow afternoons secretly stroking that little pecker of yours to the women's lingerie section in your momma's Spring Edition catalog."

"Tell me the whereabouts of the boy, Austin," Poole asked, his tone firmer. "Where have you been hiding him all these years?"

Maurine jerked her head away from the man's soft touch.

"So be it," Poole said, his jawline forming on the corner of his face in evident rage.

He nodded at his partner, who, in return, turned to the mirror behind him.

The door swung open yet again!

TIME UNKNOWN

SURROUNDED by an entourage of heavily armed bodyguards, King Orion entered the New Haven morgue, which was the size of an auditorium.

Shocked by the king's presence, the team of coroners stopped what they were doing and paid full attention to King Orion.

"Who's in charge here?" King Orion asked the group.

One fidgety coroner stepped forward and said, "I am, Sir."

"Show me the body. . . "

"Mory," he said. "The name's Mory Givets."

"Okay, Mr. *Givets*. The body. Now."

"Absolutely."

A fidgety Mory walked the king to the body—or what was left of it—on the metal slab in the center of the morgue. Several interns were gathered around not too far away, giggling among themselves.

Once they arrived at their destination, Mory pulled the plastic sheet from the remains, which had been pieced together like a jigsaw puzzle.

"Who was he?" the king asked.

"His name was Jacob Parsons. He ran a bakery in Section Seven."

"He was a baker?"

The king peered closer at his head. Both his eyes squinted in suspicion, as if he recognized or even knew the face; however, the king didn't want to bring up his relationship with the baker in front of the detectives.

Mory said finally, "Correct, Sir."

"Little far from home." The king turned to one of the detectives. "You said you found him in Section Twenty-One, correct?"

The detective stepped forward.

"That's correct, Sir."

King Orion asked, "What do you think he was doing all the way out in Section Twenty-One?"

"We found some paraphernalia on him—hypos to be exact. We think he was juicing."

"According to his blood analysis, he had extremely high levels of betatrait in his system."

"Betatrait has been outlawed for years."

"Maybe you need to get out more, King. It's everywhere on the streets. For the past few months, Blue Units have been swamped with cases of violent aggression toward—"

The King turned to the mouthy detective.

Before the detective could finish his sentence, King Orion flicked his index finger. In a simple flick of a finger, the environment behind the detective opened up into a dark cave and swallowed the detective whole like a mouth appearing out of thin air. The atmosphere returned to normal, masking the sudden shriek.

Everybody in the room remained in a state of shock from the detective's sudden departure.

"King Orion," another detective stepped forward, more nervously, "Detective O' Haire was one of our finest detectives on the case."

"Not anymore, he's not." The king turned to Mory, who was trembling and remained at a loss of words.

"So, did Mr. Parsons have any children?" asked the king.

Mory didn't respond.

Waiting for a response, the king said, "Mr. Givets, I asked you a question."

"Two," Mory blurted out, his confidence deteriorating before the eyes of his interns. "A three year old boy and five year old girl."

"I see."

"There's. . . there's one more thing that immediately stood out." He cleared his throat and pulled out an evidence container holding a piece of the stake used to spear Parsons' head. "We, ah, found an unknown black substance oozing from the edge of the spear."

The king asked, "What kind of unknown substance?"

"We don't know yet, Sir, *but* if we can locate where exactly this substance came from, then we might be able to track down our killer."

King Orion knew Mory wasn't going to be at all helpful. There was only one way to track down the substance. And the king knew that meant digging up the past.

⌗

ALONE, King Orion dipped out of his tower and hit the streets well after the curfew. Concealing himself as a member of The Geist, a leftover cult that have, over the years, gone underground and become like a myth around Babylon City, despite the king frequently using their black-cloaked disguise as a means to secretly slink around the city, King Orion headed directly to Section Twenty-One.

When he arrived at the crime scene, he turned back the day until it was moments leading up to the murder. Life zoomed past him. Lights and scanners. He stopped at Mr. Parsons. Right before his body was about to be torn apart, the entire city suddenly went pitch black. The king was left in the dark, as if time itself was preventing him from witnessing the murder. He meticulously moved forward through the timeline, shifting points of view in order to find the best angle; however, a hole, an obvious gap, rendered the king's powers useless.

FRIDAY APRIL 9, 1999 9:07 AM

THE Frenchman arrived at the same dirt road. He picked up Maurine's scent coming from two miles down the road on a raggedy stuffed animal in the middle of a grassy field; however, the last altercation had left a visible fingerprint for the device, which he had been using to track Maurine and the three underlings.

Through the tinted lens of the mask, the Frenchman witnessed the hazy blueprint of Maurine's childhood home and the warm positive light radiating from the life that once thrived inside the house.

⬚

"HOW much farther, Angela?" asked Maurine.

"We should be there by nightfall," she said.

Maurine turned to Angela, who was sitting next to her in the passenger seat, and couldn't help but notice her Monk-like composure. Despite being wanted by one of the most dangerous organizations in the world, Angela retained her innocence. The sight of Angela put a smile on Maurine's face.

As soon as she wore the smile, the smile melted. Her eyes flooded.

Angela couldn't help but look at Maurine and her miserable state.

"What's wrong?" she asked.

"Strange," Maurine uttered.

"Huh?"

Maurine shook the thought away and concentrated on driving.

"It's just. . . " she trailed off, ". . . it just feels like I've been here before. In this moment. Like, I dunno, Déjà vu or something."

"That's because you have been here. Not the 'you' now. But the 'future' you."

Angela's words went straight over Maurine's head.

"I call them *shadows*."

"Shadows?"

"Yeah," Angela said casually. "When you relive your future moment in your present timeline."

"So I. . . I mean, 'we've' been here? In this precise moment?"

Angela innocently bobbed her head.

"How many times?" asked Maurine.

"Hmm," Angela paused in thought. "About twenty-something times. I lost count after ten."

Maurine shook the thought from her head.

"What is it?" asked Angela.

"It's weird."

"What's weird?"

"The other day, I saw a slogan for Richard Peoples. I swore Linda Branson was president."

"She was," Angela said flatly. "In another timeline. So was a peanut farmer from Arkansas. Remember, Maurine. There are consequences each time we use our abilities. Like, for instance, when you throw a pebble into a pond, the pebble creates a ripple effect in the water. Think of the pebble as us and the water as time."

Maurine still remained at a loss of words.

"Don't worry," Angela reassured Maurine. "I have a good feeling about this time."

"You do?"

Angela bobbed her head once more.

"Mmmhmm."

Maurine turned her attention back to the highway before her and spotted the road sign that read "Albuquerque" "332" miles away.

She ignored the mileage, ignored the dull soreness on her bottom brought on by days of driving, ignored that tedious yet thoughtful road before her. Maurine felt painfully old after chatting with Angela.

Old and confused.

But more so confused.

MONDAY JUNE 10, 2019 1:56 PM

STAY with me, Maurine.

Maurine barely lifted up her head. Ropes of blood streamed down the corner of her face. She moved her swollen eyes forward and witnessed a young woman crouched over before her. The young woman was Angela, Maurine soon realized; however, she was older. Twenty-years older. Maurine's right eye lit up with surprise. The left one was black and puffy and nearly swollen shut.

Is that you, Angela?

It's me.

How' you get here? Is this really you 'you'? Or is this what I imagined what you'd look like when you're all grown up?

Maurine struggled to sit upright.

You're using this image of me because you believe it will give you strength.

Your hair, Maurine said, grimacing, *it's darker. You must've grown out of that blonde hair.* She held a band of the hair and rubbed it between her fingertips. *It's beautiful. You've always been beautiful.*

Listen, Maurine, they're going to ask you once more about what happened to Austin and if you don't tell them, then it's going to ruin the rest of the plan.

What happens if I don't tell them?

Angela said, *They're going to kill you.*

TIME UNKNOWN

KING Orion assembled a team of excavators and headed outside Babylon City into a vast desert, which was widely known as the Wastelands. Not much of anything survived in the Wastelands. The great, deadly storms had ripped through the desert landscape, bringing crippling snowstorms to the north, in the mountains, and furious sandstorms to the barren deserts, burying past civilizations in sand.

The team made their daring trip into the barren Wastelands.

⬚

AFTER miles of traveling, King Orion demanded the team stop and take a break. He came across the top of the sign that read GUNS and AMMO. The letters M and O in the word *ammo* were missing and all that remained were the outlines of M and O. The rest of the sign was buried in sand.

"We're close," the king said to his team.

FRIDAY APRIL 9, 1999 10:29 PM

MAURINE drove past the guns and ammunition shop on the corner of Alamanso and Hillock Drive.

"Take a right here," Angela directed Maurine, as she looked up at the flashing *AMMO* sign above.

Maurine did as Angela directed and took a right onto Alamanso.

They made yet another turn and drove about a quarter of a mile down the two-lane road until they reached an abandoned church at the end of Sanctuary. The church was called The Holy Trinity.

"This is it," Maurine said to Angela.

"You remember what happens?"

"No," Maurine said in reflection. "But I think I remember seeing this place in a dream."

"It wasn't a dream," Angela corrected Maurine.

Maurine pulled the van behind the rundown church, which looked as if it had slowly decayed into a shelter for the junkies and the homeless. Maurine had what Angela called a "shadow." Maurine's shadow came in the form of an image inside her head. One of her kneeling next to an altar as she cradled a lifeless Austin in her arms. The image was sudden, like a blinding flash, yet as soon as it entered Maurine's thoughts in the most vivid detail, the image was gone.

The more Maurine tried to mentally bring back the stark image, the farther it drifted into the deep, electric avenues of her thoughts, leaving her stuck in her own mental maze.

Ignoring the shadow, Maurine cut the headlights. She

turned to the other two in the back and asked them if they were ready.

They didn't say a word in return.

Yet, they both anxiously nodded their heads.

MONDAY JUNE 10, 2019 2:12 PM

"KNOWING the life you could've avoided, a life filled with paranoia, a life dictated by obscurity, a life filled with looking over your shoulder, you chose this path," Shakespeare said and leaned closer to a bloody, shaky Maurine. "This miserable existence you call life. A thorn in my side. Maurine, you can make all of this end right here, *right now.*"

"Those children were the best thing to ever happen to me," Maurine uttered, as strings of blood poured from her nose and mouth and dangled on her chin like red shoelaces.

"Best thing? How can you sit there and feed me that bull-shit? These children gave you cervical cancer, Maurine. Look at the facts, Maurine." He listed off these so-called "facts" with his fingers. "Healthy young woman; has no relatives who had cancer; good genes; doesn't smoke; not a heavy drinker—at least back then you weren't. So, tell me, how does a perfectly normal woman get cancer? These children," Shakespeare said closely. "They're a disease, Maurine. A parasite that doesn't belong to our race—"

"—Then, why are you so interested in finding them? I'll tell you why. Cuz' you and your company believe they're the answer to the world's problems. Face it. We! We are the disease! We are the parasites. It is 'we' who are responsible, *not* them!"

"After everything they did to you, you still pity them as if it was yourself who was to blame for their misfortunes." Shake-speare suddenly brandished a gun and held it to Maurine's head. Maurine turned away and in the corner of her eye, wit-nessed the reflection of herself in the mirror. She saw herself as Angela, who, like before, was in her late twenties. "Where is Austin?" He pressed the barrel of the gun against the side of her temple. "Where is he?"

"He's dead," Maurine confessed. "Because of me."

"You're lying!"

"I'm telling you the truth goddamn it!" Maurine cried out. "It's my fault. Mine!" The sudden burst of energy wore down Maurine's spirits. Struggling to hold up her head, she whimpered, "I let him out of my sight. One second Austin was standing right by my side. . ."

Her head budged to the left. The memory was so strong as she visualized young Austin by her side when the two cowered by a column inside Holy Trinity. The memory went black. She retraced the memory once more. She couldn't find Austin anywhere in it.

". . . Then the next second, he wasn't there anymore. When I found him, he was already gone."

The memory was back, the violence. Maurine cradled Austin's lifeless body in her arms. She ran her hand over the gunshot wound in the middle of his chest and tried to stop the bleeding.

Maurine said faintly, "I kept telling myself that he made a sacrifice. He sacrificed his own life to save Azure's. It's *my* fault. His death is mine to bear. So, if there's anyone to blame for Austin's death, it's me. *All* me."

TIME UNKNOWN

AFTER spending days in the Wastelands, unearthing old civilizations that had been buried decades ago, the team of excavators made a sudden discovery while digging through mounds of dirt and rumble.

One of the diggers shouted out to the king, who was shading inside a shelter that had been set up outside the dig site.

One of many advisors rushed into King Orion's quarters and told him in one breath, "Come quick! There's been a discovery!"

King Orion grabbed his golden staff and rushed to the dig site. Other diggers were gathered around in a circle. They soon made a hole for King Orion.

Once the king laid his eyes on a partial crucifix that was

protruding from the sand, he told his team that he had arrived at his destination.

"We're here," the king reinforced.

He went on to tell them to keep digging, but while doing so, exercise caution.

The other team members left their posts and all together focused on the area surrounding the crucifix.

FRIDAY APRIL 9, 1999 11:03 PM

THROUGH the cracked opening, which was about the size of a rock, in the corner of the stained glass window of Mary and Joseph, Maurine stared at a massive crucifix perched outside.

"Are you scared?" asked Angela from behind.

Pulled from her deep trance by a soft voice, Maurine faced Angela, who was standing both expressionlessly and motionlessly behind her. From her demeanor alone, Angela didn't look the least bit afraid of the looming confrontation. After all, she had already lived through the moment before.

"A little," Maurine confessed, clearing her throat.

"Don't be," Angela said confidently. "Everything will go according to plan."

"I hope so."

"Don't hope," Angela said flatly. "Know."

Maurine stepped away from the window and walked Angela down the nave of the church.

By the chancel, Azure was experimenting with many different characters by shapeshifting through potential players, from a police officer to a bodybuilder to a professional wrestler to a crafty marksman to a skilled swordsman to a Navy Seal, each one skilled in a particular combat.

While Azure was prepping for the unexpected, Austin was hanging out by the altar where he was testing out the trap.

Maurine nodded at the necklace with the heart-shaped pendant lying on the altar table.

"Why the necklace?" Maurine asked Angela.

"The necklace belonged to the Scout's daughter."

"What happened to her?"

"Her name was Juliette," Angela told Maurine. "She died from acute lymphocyctic leukemia at the age of six after the Scout flew her over to the States to try out an experimental treatment since they were having no luck in France. By that time, they had tried everything. They were desperate." Angela nodded at the necklace in Austin's hand. "He gave her that necklace just two months before she died."

"You think it'll work?"

"Austin is only using it as a distraction."

"Like bait?"

"Yes," she said. "You can look at it that way."

"But, if this man is as good of a hunter as you say he is, then won't he know he's walking into a trap?"

"He's not a man, not anymore."

"What is he?"

"He's been engineered by the Company, part man, part something else."

"What 'something' else?"

"He's been enhanced. I've heard that he's neither living nor dead, but somewhere in between. He's good at what he does, but he's not *that* good. I mean," Angela looked around, "we're still alive. Aren't we?"

"Do you have a backup plan, if it doesn't work—"

"—It *will* work." Angela looked at Austin and then looked back at Maurine with a sharp look on her face. She said to Maurine, "Trust me."

Maurine wanted to trust Angela, but a part of her knew Angela wasn't being completely honest with her.

MONDAY JUNE 10, 2019 2:29 PM

MAURINE remained in deep reflection.

She pulled herself from thought and readjusted herself in the chair. The subtle move caused her to grimace. She had at least one broken rib. Her other injuries were pending.

She refocused on the man's question.

"The plan backfired on us," Maurine said over the hot pain. "After the Scout grabbed the necklace, the trap was sprung. The Scout vanished before my eyes."

She took a moment to catch her breath and in doing so, thought about where Austin had really sent the Scout. He didn't vanish, as she told the two men. He didn't travel to another dimension or wherever. As soon as Austin opened up the floor below the Scout, he fell below into the undercroft.

"What happened next?" asked Shakespeare.

Maurine said, "We were ambushed."

TIME UNKNOWN

AFTER King Orion's team chiseled and brushed away years and years of dirt that had consumed the entire church, leaving only an outer foundation of the structure, one of the diggers suddenly fell through a weak spot along the crossing of what used to be the nave.

Other diggers rushed to the hole.

"Revon, are you injured?"

"I'm all right!" the digger finally called out from the dusty darkness below. The other diggers breathed sighs of great relief after listening to the exuberance in the digger's voice. "I think I'm stuck in some kind of chamber!"

The king didn't waste anytime, despite what his many advisors had told him. He secured a harness around his body. Other diggers urged King Orion not to go down because they weren't entirely certain of the stability of the archaic structure—possibly, at any moment, it could collapse—and the king might risk getting injured.

King Orion disregarded what each digger said and scaled down into the hole.

As the digger, still shaken up, held back, King Orion ventured deeper into the room. He manifested a flashlight into his hand and shone the light into what was left of an undercroft. A beam of light crossed a skeleton inside a steel cage. Between the spaces of the cage and protruding from the ribcage of the skeleton was a sword-like rod perched in the ground below. Next to the skeleton was the same tracking mask that he had been searching for.

The king inched closer for a better look.

Next to the cage was yet another skeleton; however, there was something unusual about the skeleton.

King Orion inched closer.

Inside the chest cavity was yet another, smaller skeleton; however, the skeleton wasn't at all human. The upper part of the skeleton was shaped very similar to a human, only it's skull was elongated and its teeth serrated like a piranha; whereas, the bottom half of its body was like one of a scorpion. Its bony tail was curled around the top of its skull, fetal-style.

Another oddity was what surrounded the pair of skeletons, one being human while the other being a creature.

Scattered around the human skeleton were these tiny worm-like parasites that looked like brown fingernail clippings in the sand.

The king leaned back after further inspection and observed the human skeleton from a broader point of view. It was much different than the skeleton inside the cage, not that it had a strange skeletal creature inside its chest, but that it was one of a child.

Possibly a boy.

MONDAY JUNE 10, 2019 2:44 PM

"I later found out that name, The Scout, was used as some kind of code name or whatever. He was using this other person, a clone possibly, as a decoy. The real Scout, the real Jean Luere, knew everything—I mean everything—that was going to happen, like he was one step ahead of us. . . "

"The Scout was a great asset of ours, the Company's own pet ferret—that is, before he went missing. Thinking maybe the ferret man caught himself in a jam with one of the shapers, the Company sent the dogs after him. But they found no trace of him. It was like he just disappeared off the face of the earth."

Maurine shrugged.

"I wouldn't know anything about that."

"So, you're telling us that the shapers didn't have anything to do with his disappearance?"

Maurine didn't answer.

"Maurine?"

Again, Maurine remained unresponsive. She drifted back into deep thought. She put herself back in that time, when Austin left her side, when she took her eyes off him for a moment. One moment he was there, by her side, then the next, he was nowhere to be found.

Moments after the cage had fallen onto the decoy Scout, sending him into the undercroft below the church, Maurine surfaced from the concrete pillar that she was hiding behind. She found Azure standing by the altar. She was using the same body as the decoy to fight the Scout to make the fight equal; however, the Scout was using the darkness to his advantage.

As Maurine was about to call out to Azure, the Scout crept up behind Azure with a gun.

Austin suddenly jumped in front of the bullet's path and ended up taking a bullet for Azure.

Austin stumbled backward and fell into the undercroft below.

Maurine ran to the hole in front of the altar and climbed down.

FRIDAY APRIL 9, 1999 2:11 AM

AS Maurine cradled Austin in her arms, she grabbed both of Austin's hands and placed them over the gunshot wound. While doing so, she witnessed the skin, a new skin, moving underneath the hole in Austin's chest. The skin was as scaly as a reptile. Maurine's skin went cold just from the sight of being inches away from the creature inside Austin. Its movement was slow, though, and getting slower by the second.

More determined, Maurine placed both of Austin's hands over the wound and specifically told him to press down on the wound to stop the bleeding.

"Press hard," she emphasized.

As Maurine placed her hand over Austin's hands and

pressed down hard as well, she told him that everything was going to be okay; but, in the back of her mind, she knew it wasn't.

She felt the pulse on his neck with her other hand. She felt two pulses, one slow and thready, and then, another one, a tingly one, which felt like the rattle of a maraca, a thinly piercing shake eventually fading over that thready beat.

Eventually, Austin started to fade.

As he took his final breaths, Maurine looked up for a moment and screamed out at Angela, who was waiting above, and told her to pull them out of the undercroft and do so quickly.

Angela said she wasn't as good as Austin at altering environments and that she hadn't done it in a while.

During Angela's complaining, Maurine felt a tug on her arm.

She drew her attention back to Austin.

The last words he told Maurine were *leave me*. Two words that Maurine tried to make sense of for the next twenty years. A constant debate about whether or not Austin said "leave me" or "believe me."

As Azure chased after the Scout, Angela attempted to alter the environment. At first, she struggled to create a staircase for Maurine to exit the undercroft. It was clear in her attempts that she wasn't, in fact, nearly as skilled as Austin; however, after Austin was gone, her power seemed as if it had been depleted, as if, without Austin, Angela had become strangely weaker. She kept at it. The more she concentrated, the quicker she started to pick up on the skill.

More poised, Angela honed in on the skill as if it was her very own.

After the fourth attempt, she manifested a staircase for Maurine.

Outside, a commotion was buzzing in the air, as well as humming along the distant highway. A swarm of helicopters, squads of cruisers and SWAT vans followed by the rumble of the National Guard, all were closing in—and fast!

"Leave him," Angela said, as she towered above the landing.

"I can't—"

"—You have to!"

"But you can use your power to take us back to the time before he dies! This time, I can save him! I'll save Austin!"

"You can't save him, Maurine," she said more seriously. "You *never* could."

"What are you saying?"

"I'm saying that he always dies. In every scenario, it's always Austin who dies. Even if we go farther in time, he eventually dies."

"But you said—"

"—I know what I said."

"Then, why would you lie to me, Angela? Tell me!"

"We're stuck in a loop," Angela said, as the noise outside grew louder and louder. "The only way to get through the loop is by moving forward in time. Into the unknown."

Maurine looked down at Austin, who had already died. She combed his hair over his head, willing a glint of life to shine inside his glazed eyes.

"I can't leave him like this," Maurine cried, willing for light.

"You have to, Maurine."

"Why?"

"Because you just do."

Maurine looked up at Angela and right then and there, she knew there was something else that Angela wasn't telling her, something that Angela had already known, as if it was already foretold; however, if she mentioned what it was or even uttered a word of it, then it would change the course of time.

The noise intensified outside, forcing Maurine to make a snap decision. She let go of Austin; and before she was about to walk up the staircase, the decoy, who was still trapped inside the cage, called out from behind.

"I'm sorry about the boy," he said. "It was never our intention to kill him."

Maurine grabbed a rod with a sharp end perched against the side of the stone wall; and without wasting any time, she drove the sharp end directly through the man's body.

"Fuck your sorry," she said to him.

⊹

ONCE Maurine made it to the top of the landing, Angela removed the staircase behind her and then closed the hole in the floor before the altar.

The task alone drained Angela completely and caused her to stagger and use the remaining strength to stand upright. Suddenly depleted of all strength, Angela braced herself along the front pew before the right transept.

"Come on, Angela," Maurine said, as she tried to carry Angela from Holy Trinity. Angela anchored herself to the floor and didn't budge an inch for she weighed at least triple Maurine's normal weight. "Don't do this to me now, Angela," Maurine snapped. "Let's move!"

"I can't," she said. "I have to hide myself inside you."

"You have to what?"

"The only way I make it out of here alive is inside you."

"Inside me?"

"It's me they're after, *not* you, Maurine."

"What about Azure?"

"Azure will be fine."

The chaos was directly outside the church.

"We can still make it. . . "

"No," Angela said weakly. "This is the only way."

As Maurine stared into Angela's wandering eyes, her face lit up with clarity.

"This has already happened, hasn't it?"

Angela nodded her head *yes*.

"The loop, remember? We have to keep moving forward. Into the—"

"—Into the unknown, right."

Maurine thought over Angela's proposal.

"We're running out of time, Maurine—"

"—Okay," Maurine said. "What do I have to do?"

"Nothing," Angela said. "You do nothing."

Angela reached out her hand.

"*People will die*," she said, looking into Maurine's eyes.

Having a pretty good idea as to what was about to go down, Maurine grabbed Angela's hand anyway and held it firmly.

Both of their hands combined suddenly started to glow with a warm reddish orange light, which soon changed over into a pale bluish color. The bluish light spread through Maurine's veins, so blinding it caused her to shield her eyes with her other hand.

After the cool light spread throughout her body, the light went out, leaving the spot where Angela once sat as cold and black as the night.

Maurine looked around and Angela's body was nowhere to be found.

She shouted out, "Angela?"

All of a sudden, the two doors at the front of the church burst opened. A platoon of armed soldiers came flooding in.

The sudden interruption caused Maurine to recoil and flinch. Her body was curled inward. Her eyes closed.

As soon as the tightness receded back into her body and she relaxed, she noticed the sudden change in noise.

There was *no* noise, *no* sound. Only a radiating silence.

Maurine carefully opened her eyes and looked around the church.

Soldiers remained completely frozen in their action poses.

Curious, she walked up to the soldiers and it looked as if time had stopped. Actually stopped.

As Maurine made her way to the front of Holy Trinity, she saw over dozens of cruisers outside. The sirens were not flashing. Yet, the red and blue lights remained in a still glare. Officers remained still as well, as they aimed their assault rifles and shotguns at the front entrance of the church.

As Maurine passed one solider in particular—a young slack-faced man who had sweat beads the size of bullets running down the sides of his head—she witnessed the first signs of movement. She pinpointed the quiver, which was coming from both of his hands. The sight alone of the soldier's hands was the first indicator that time was, in fact, thawing. Then, the next indicator, the police sirens were starting to slowly change from red to blue. Other sirens, blue to red.

Above, the helicopter's rotary blades started to move as well.

Before things returned back to normal, Maurine made a dash toward a strip mall not too far away. She managed to hide behind a nail salon before the chaos unfolded at Holy Trinity.

From a distance, she watched soldiers stumble into the church.

Above, the helicopter suddenly lost power and started to spin out of control. The pilot never regained control of the helicopter as it ended up crashing beyond the cityscape. From a distance, she heard the sudden blare of horns, as well as the crushing *boom* of cars crashing on the highway.

In a way, she knew that this was going to happen.

People were going to die based on her drastic measures in order to set things right.

Whatever Angela had done, there was, indeed, a ripple effect.

MONDAY JUNE 10, 2019 3:10 PM

"MAURINE?"

Poole waited for a response from Maurine.

"We buried Austin's body in the desert," she finally answered.

"We?" Shakespeare stood from the table. "You said Angela died during the shootout. And as for Azure, according to your story, she was off chasing after the Scout. To me, it sounds like you're either full of shit or you have some serious holes in your story. So, which is it?"

Maurine dropped her head and stared at the glass floor below.

"I'm talking to you, Ms. Hat. . . "

Maurine snapped her head back up and pointed her eyes at the rather abrasive man towering over her. Her irises were no longer brown in color. Instead, they were emerald green, brilliant. Even her dark skin looked younger and smoother, as if she had shed decades of aging from her body. Her crow's feet gone, smoothed out like an iron.

The sight of Maurine's abrupt change caused Shakespeare to backpedal.

"You didn't come here because you had information on the three underlings. You *were* serious. You came here to kill us, didn't you?"

Maurine responded, "It wouldn't be the first time, now would it?"

The two men were at a loss for words. All they had were shadows; however, neither one of them had any chance to stop and think.

"You are just two pawns part of a greater game," she said. "I could kill you, but your death has no effect on the outcome. I admit the last time I was here I got a little—how do you say—a little. . . Overboard. Carried away. Suffice to say, I ended up letting my emotions get the best of me. I destroyed your self-interested Company, which, in return, created a more ruthless, more *aggressive* organization to rise from the ashes of time. An organization constructed by a bottomless desire for power and dominance."

"*Angela,*" Poole said with clarity.

Shakespeare asked over Poole, "So if you're not here to kill us, then why did you come here, Maurine?"

"I came here to close the loop once and for all."

"What loop?"

Once more, Maurine lowered her head and strictly concentrated on the lives that she had lived, all of the pain that she had endured, the burden of every man, woman, and child. She collected it all, formed it, shaped, and balled it up into her chest. That altered, sleepless beast.

With her mouth closed, Maurine clenched her teeth. The corners of her face flexed with anger.

Clnnnk!

All of a sudden, the mirrored wall cracked.

The tiny crack suddenly spread throughout the entire mirror. The crack violently veined outward, spreading to the other mirrors on the walls and ceiling.

In a deafening roar, Maurine broke free from her restraints behind the chair and shattered the glass all around in a violent burst of rage. Thousands of jagged shards of glass hurled and showered through the air, forcing the two men to react.

Before getting struck, the two men ducked underneath the table. A shard of glass sliced the side of Shakespeare's face, nearly cutting off his jaw. The other members of the Company were revealed beyond what remained of the shattered glass in an amphitheater-like setting, which surrounded the interrogation room, as if, this whole time, Maurine had an audience.

Other guards rushed forward and aimed their weapons at Maurine, who had used up all of her energy in the release, slid from the chair and fell onto the floor.

One of the interrogators surfaced from underneath the table and ordered the guards to lower their weapons.

"Send her in," Poole said to one security guard.

Without the guards looking, Maurine furtively picked up the knife-like shard of glass from the floor and concealed it behind her wrist.

The other members who were gathered around the room stepped aside and made a hole for a young graceful woman.

Intrigued by her presence, Maurine used what little strength she had left and perched herself up onto her elbow. Her eyes, no longer green. Yet, they returned to their normal hazel brown color.

As the young woman, who appeared to be in her late twenties—specifically around the same age of Angela—made her presence known, a stunned Maurine couldn't help but look closer.

The young woman approached Maurine. She was stern yet confident in her manner. A young woman who demanded attention and, in return, received silent stares, at times, gawks and muffled whispers. She was sporting this custom designed silky black duster with a stiff collar. The end of the duster ran all the way down to the floor like an evening dress, very masculine. Her dark hair was gelled back and worn in a sharp ponytail. She wore very little makeup too.

"Azure," Maurine said, dumbfounded. "It's you, isn't it?"

"Hello, Maurine," Azure replied, as she kneeled down to Maurine's level.

Maurine skipped the awkward greeting and hugged Azure. Which made guards uncomfortable.

"Look at you," Maurine said, studying Azure, "you're all grown up."

"Been a long time."

"Twenty years," Maurine said, grimacing.

Azure looked over Maurine's injuries.

Maurine noticed that the guards weren't aiming their weapons at Azure, only her.

"You're with them, aren't you? What have they done to you?"

"You could've avoided this, Maurine."

Azure's cold lack of response to Maurine's question wasn't quite the answer she was looking for, but it was a clear answer as to what side Azure was on.

"I know I could," she said disappointedly. "But what in the hell does that say about these people? *Your* people?"

"They're not my people."

"But you are working for them, aren't you?"

Azure turned away for a moment and then looked back at Maurine. Her eyes keener.

"Yes," she said. "I'm afraid so."

Maurine hung her head in despair.

"Why?"

Azure paused and thought carefully about her next response.

"Do you remember the night at the church?"

"Do I remember?" Maurine returned. "I've spent the last twenty years of my life trying to forget it."

"A couple of days after you left me, the Company found me—"

"—Left you? I looked for you for days, weeks, months! I've spent the last twenty years trying to find you, Azure!"

"I don't go by that name anymore, Maurine," Azure said. "I haven't gone by that name since I was a little girl. Since," she paused once more, "since we went our separate ways. Face it, Maurine. This is my home now. This is where I belong."

Maurine's eyes lit up with hope.

"Well," she said, "are they at least taking good care of you?"

"Yes," Azure said. "They are. In fact, we're creating something truly special. Something that will change the world."

"Don't you see?" Maurine begged, her voice growing louder, "they're using you! All these people care about is what you can do for them and their own interests. They don't care about you, not like I do—"

"—If you cared about me, then where were you the past twenty years?"

"Please," she pleaded to Azure, *her* Azure, not the woman formerly known as Azure but her Azure, "come back with me. Please. I can give you a home. I can take care of you."

"You?" A faint smirk crept onto the side of her face. "You can't even take care of yourself, Maurine. How are you going to take care of me? You think you can just show up here, thinking I can just rewrite history? Maybe we had a good run, you and I." She pinned her shoulders back, her posture more stiff and masculine. "*But* that time is gone now," she said in a more austere manner. "It's time to move on. It's time to power forward, to the future and the great wonders it has in store for mankind. They're teaching me how to further develop my abilities; and in time, they believe I'll become a true artist, a visionary, a master, a legend."

Maurine's spirits fell, her face slackened.

"The planet is dying, Maurine; and with my power, I can save Earth."

Maurine laughed, and it hurt to laugh. Seeing the young woman whom she had known as Azure, the young woman kneeling before her eyes had brought her great joy, a joy only brought on by a proud mother embracing a daughter; but the words, Azure's words, her innocence yet her arrogance, had sent an awful wave of agony throughout every inch of her body and soul.

"You've been brainwashed," Maurine said despairingly. "Listen to yourself, *Azure*. You sound like a goddamn TV commercial."

"I tell you what, Maurine," Azure said, leaning closer. "Let me bring you in. Inside. I want to show you want we've been working on for all these years."

Maurine drifted in thought, as if Angela was once more surfacing inside her, showing her the very world she was speaking of, an untouched world filled with great wonder and mystery, yet a world marred by a stain so deep and intricate that it had eventually corrupted everything it touched.

As Maurine weighed her options, she longed to go back once more, back to the church, to Holy Trinity, correct the course, save Austin, save Azure, save herself, hoping by doing so, she'd set things right; however, Angela brought her back to the plan, the original plan.

She was, in a way, calling to Maurine, showing her the way.

In her deep trance, Maurine witnessed the life that Angela lived when she left Maurine behind in the undercroft and escaped all on her own and lived in a majestic place called Babylon City. She witnessed Angela age into an old lady roaming through Babylon City, spending her final years searching for the answer until one day she found it, the secret room behind a bird shop, that *answer*, which the king had stashed away deep within the city and guarded from the Company, as if it was a part of the city's design.

Angela took Maurine back to the time when Maurine and Azure were talking near the tire swing outside Maurine's childhood home. Angela was watching the two from the living room window. Somehow, she rummaged through Maurine's thoughts and found the same one where Maurine was having a meaningful conversation with Azure. Angela guided Maurine to that one memory where a Goldfinch landed on Azure's finger. Both Maurine and Angela wit-

nessed the smile on Azure's face but only for a split second—
that second forever stilled in time. For Angela, it was the first
time she had even seen her sister's smile.

Maurine was still not entirely convinced.

So, Angela convinced her.

Still tempted to travel back in time, Maurine remembered
what Angela had told her before she vanished, about going
"*into the unknown.*"

The unknown.

Death.

Her eyes suddenly changed color, not brown but green
again. She moved her eyes toward Azure, who was left in a
state of surprise from the change in her eye color.

"I'm sorry, Azure," Maurine said.

Before Azure could react, Maurine suddenly thrust the
edge of the shard into her flesh and opened up one of her major arteries along her neck.

Maurine fell backward.

Azure tended to Maurine, looking over Maurine with
great panic. She fought against Maurine and removed the
shard of glass, causing more blood to pour from Maurine's
neck. She tried to stop the bleeding with her hand.

"What have you done, Maurine?" she said, tightly pressing
her palm against the wound.

"It's the. . . only way. . . "

The blood streamed from Maurine's nostrils and mouth.
Each word flooded with blood.

"You could've chosen anyone to help you. . . " she said, as
blood choked her every word and trailed down the corners of
her mouth. "You. . . you didn't need to choose anyone. . . *But*. . . you chose me."

"No, Maurine," Azure said. "You chose us, Maurine."

Before Maurine bled out, she leaned in close to Azure's ear
with a final burst of life and whispered something in her ear.

With his weapon drawn, one of the guards stepped forward as Maurine let out her final gasp before the big sleep.

"What did she tell you?" asked the guard.

The young woman, formerly known as Azure, shook her

head.

"I don't know," she said coldly and backed away as a team of men started to work on Maurine.

But she was already dead.

To Maurine, she was dead the moment she chose to come here.

TIME UNKNOWN

WITH the tracking mask gripped securely in his hand, King Orion made his way to the highest point, Aphelion Capital, which was the tallest building in Babylon City.

Before stepping out onto the platform, which was five stories above the observation deck—or what was called "The Eye of God,"—the king switched on the device and placed the shrapnel from the weapon that was used to kill Jacob Parsons into the rotary sensor.

Once the device detected the scent, he stepped outside into the wispy clouds and peered down into the city below.

The device scanned the entire city, which gave the king an internal blueprint of Babylon City.

What King Orion witnessed after the scan was complete left him speechless.

The source of the substance traced back to the city.

Through the device, the substance was lit up with red light. The parts of the city, skyscrapers and building structures that had been marred by the storms, lit up the brightest. The storms weren't causing the internal rot and decay of the integrity of the damaged buildings, as first suspected by the engineers of the Company. The structural damage was coming from deep within the foundation. Each building, each business, each home, every single structure that made up Babylon City was infested with this unknown substance. The city was crawling with it, as if it had taken over the entire city. The strange substance even moved throughout the very platform that King Orion was standing on as if it was an entity that had been created over time. A corruption masked by years of an unquestioned, unadulterated creation.

⚏

ONCE King Orion made it back to his tower, two visitors were waiting on him.

They were both from the Company. Two old suits. One who had a scar running along the side of his face. The other had major artificial enhancements, including augmentation. They said they just stopped by to ask the king how the unsolved cases were going, if he had any leads on any suspects.

At that particular moment in time, the king did the only thing that he could do in order to protect himself.

He told the two board members of the Company that detectives had narrowed down their search to two suspects. He gave them a couple of names.

In other words, he had no other choice than to lie.

⚏

AFTER realizing that it was his own creations that had become monstrous with the city itself killing its citizens, the king ignored Jesseme's orders and took a speedrail down to Slum Park and paid a visit to Yellow Bird Emporium, a quaint bird shop outside Chinatown.

The king was greeted by the owner of the shop.

As soon as the owner recognized King Orion, he escorted the king to a secret room in the back of the shop.

The room was an exact duplicate of Maurine's childhood bedroom.

King Orion walked to the vanity where he found dozens of photographs held securely in wooden frames. A montage of the life Maurine had lived before she met the three underlings and then the life she lived after she met the three underlings. In each photo, the king witnessed pain, tragedy, and a life suddenly altered, going from mundane to perilous.

As the king went through each frame, the photographs started to change. The once dark photographs turned to ones displaying a life well lived. Photographs of Maurine's husband. Then, in the next, a photograph of a girl, Maurine's daughter, Azure. The photographs continued to change. The king witnessed the young girl, Azure, grow up into a strong, graceful woman who had a heart of gold. After college, Azure pursued a career in the arts. By the age of thirty, Azure ran a gallery in Manhattan. Then, later in life, she became an art teacher who ran a successful non-profit organization where she taught art to war veterans struggling with post-traumatic stress disorder.

King Orion drifted into a trance from staring at the photographs. He remembered exactly what Maurine had told him before she died, about finding her cornerstone in the back of Yellowbird, where all of the answers would be revealed. He remembered yet another memory, one where he was talking with Maurine on a tire swing. But he wasn't a boy at the time. He was a girl. Maurine told her that, even though she might be just "a small part" in Azure's "story," being a small part beats not being a part of Azure's life.

At that moment in time, he knew exactly what needed to be done in order to save Maurine.

SUNDAY OCTOBER 18, 1998 3:37 PM

As Maurine was waiting in the checkout line, she watched the cashier scan each grocery item along the scanner from the assembly line and slide them down to the bag boy. Each day passed with each scan. Everyday was the same, except it was raining outside. Somehow, Maurine felt as if she was responsible for the rain.

The upbeat cashier, who was chomping on a piece of bubblegum, scanned the last item, a can of Chicken Noodle soup, and read the total price of the groceries.

Maurine snapped from her trance and turned to the cashier, who was waiting for Maurine to respond.

"Huh?"

"Your total is eighteen-fifty."

"Excuse me."

"Eighteen dollars and fifty cents."

"Oh," Maurine blurted out, "of course." She dug in her

purse and pulled out a twenty and handed it to the cashier. "There you go."

The cashier punched in the money given to her. The register opened and she gave Maurine her change.

"Have a nice day," she said.

Even though the comment caused her insides to tighten with anger, Maurine smiled off the comment.

Maurine gathered her groceries.

As she left Food Way, Maurine stood underneath the overhang in the front of the store and thought about her umbrella and how she left it in the car. She didn't want to make a dash for the car either—since she had a carton of eggs in her bag.

As soon as Maurine decided to brave the rain, the rain stopped and strangely enough, the sun started to break through the ominous-looking clouds.

Halfway toward her car, her cell phone rang inside her pocket book.

She stopped in her walk and pulled out the cell phone.

The name of the caller ID read "Sasha."

Maurine hesitated to answer the call.

"What does she want?" she asked herself.

As Maurine contemplated answering the cell phone, a young voice suddenly called out beside her: "Excuse me, miss."

Maurine turned to the young girl standing in between two parked cars in the parking lot.

The young girl standing before Maurine was Azure, and she looked as if she was lost.

"Can you help me?" asked Azure.

"Sure," Maurine said. "What's the matter? Are you lost?"

All of a sudden, the horn of a car blared out behind Maurine and startled her.

Maurine turned to the car behind her. The man behind the steering wheel had his arms in the air and was giving Maurine an ill-tempered look. Maurine didn't budge from her tracks, causing the road-rager to speed around Maurine.

"Jerk," Maurine uttered and turned back around.

The girl was no longer standing there. She was gone.

Annoyed by both the angry driver and the cell phone constantly ringing in her hand, Maurine decided to answer the call.

First off, Sasha immediately apologized for what she had said to Maurine earlier on. However, the real reason she was calling was that she had good news—great news! She was pregnant, and she wanted Maurine to be the godmother of her child. Maurine didn't think for a second about her answer. More enthused, Maurine told Sasha that she'd be honored to be a godmother. Not only that, while Sasha was waiting to get her oil changed, she met a "cute guy" who seemed incredibly interested in getting to know Maurine.

"Me?" Maurine said. "What did you say to him?"

"I showed him a picture of you and said you were single. He happens to be single too."

"Why would you do that, Sasha?"

"Why not?"

"Sasha—"

"—You got to take them where you can find them. Think of it as me returning the favor for you getting me out of that jam yesterday."

"But Sasha, you didn't have to do that—"

"—It's already done," she said shortly. "You can thank me later."

Maurine found herself looking through the parking lot.

"Listen, Sasha, can I call you back?"

"I actually got to run myself. Dion's running around the house, looking for his brother's old crib. I just wanted to fill you in on the news."

"Yes," Maurine said. "Congratulations, Sasha. I'll talk to you soon."

Maurine hung up with Sasha and searched for the young girl. A sudden yet surprising sense of panic crept over her as she shouldered her way through the maze of parked cars in the parking lot. By the time she reached the middle of the parking lot, she completely forgot where she had parked her car.

During Maurine's frantic wander, she suddenly stopped and fell into a trance. Her eyes flooded with tears. She realized that she had been here before, in this very moment, in the parking lot of Food Way, searching. For some odd reason, though, Maurine knew that she didn't have to look for her anymore. She knew, in her gut, Azure was going to be okay.